Joseph Kirkland, Richard H. Wilmer

The Captain of Company K

Joseph Kirkland, Richard H. Wilmer

The Captain of Company K

ISBN/EAN: 9783337090517

Printed in Europe, USA, Canada, Australia, Japan

Cover: Foto ©Andreas Hilbeck / pixelio.de

More available books at **www.hansebooks.com**

Joseph Kirkland

"Detroit Free-Press" Competition, First-Prize Story.

THE

CAPTAIN OF COMPANY K

BY

JOSEPH KIRKLAND,

Late Major and A.-D.-C., U.-S. Volunteers.

PROFUSELY ILLUSTRATED FROM DRAWINGS BY HUGH CAPPER.

CHICAGO:

DIBBLE PUBLISHING COMPANY,

260 Clark Street.

1891.

To the

SURVIVING MEN OF THE FIRING LINE,

the Men who could See the Enemy in Front of Them

with the Naked Eye while they would have needed

a Field-Glass to see the History-Makers

Behind Them, this Story is Humbly

and Affectionately Dedicated.

FULL-PAGE ILLUSTRATIONS.

CONTENTS.

THE CAPTAIN OF COMPANY K.

CHAPTER I.

HOW THE CAPTAIN CAME TO BE CAPTAIN.

OH, Mr. Fargeon! why are men so foolish?"

Her voice suggested weariness of some old subject, perhaps a suit long urged by him and denied by her. Her slender hand lay more heavily on his arm; and (as he saw by the gaslight they were passing) her upturned face was brightened by a smile that shone through its habitual seriousness like a star through rifted clouds. The face looked sweet and grave and perfect—almost saintly, surrounded as it was by a halo of snowy knitted woolen fabric worn to keep out the evening air.

"*Why* are men so foolish?"

"Because women are so fair, I suppose, Miss Penrose."

"I'd be willing to stop being—fair, if you choose to call me so—if it would persuade you to stop being foolish about me."

"Perhaps I might never have begun being foolish—if

you choose to call me so—if you had never begun being fair; but now it would make no difference even if you were suddenly to begin looking like other women, instead of like a new-born angel, as you do this minute."

"Some day, if I live, my hair will be gray—"

"That will be becoming."

"And my face pale and thin and wrinkled; my shoulders bent, my hearing dull, and my steps tottering. Will all that be becoming, too?"

"Yes; lovely, if it is still *you*."

"I can already see where the lines will run in my face. Now—when we come to that gaslight—look!" [She raised her beautiful level brows and wrinkled her pretty forehead.] "And my hands—see." [She slipped off the mitten that covered her left hand and compressed the back with her right until it took on a little of the corrugation of age.]

"How about the dimple?" [Dimple, on hearing its name called, promptly made its appearance in its accustomed haunt, Sara's left cheek.]

"Oh, the dimple will turn into a wrinkle then."

"What sacrilege! But I don't believe old Time himself could dim the light of those eyes!"

"Then I will put on green goggles, for I just *long* for the time when looks will be off my mind! Now, let's change the tiresome old subject. Isn't the lake air exhilarating?"

They were walking briskly northward on the "long plank walk" which in those days (1861) separated the eastern front of Chicago from Lake Michigan. The ice was breaking up, but not gone, and they could hear the sullen moan of floe-burthened waves beating on the breakwater, while all was blackness out there and overhead, except where some low-lying spring snow-clouds were silvered on their under side by the reflection of the city lights.

"Yes, it is bracing. I hope it will brace up the boys to enlist."

"How goes on the good work?" she asked.

"Oh, it seems as if the first regiments that went off had taken all the available men. Now we're trying to raise this one in our own line of trade. To-day I got almost a hundred firms to sign a paper promising to continue the wages of any of their employés sufficiently to make army pay as good as their present pay."

"You are certainly doing your full duty."

"I do my level best. But what do you think! To-day Uncle Thorburn asked me why I didn't go myself!"

Both laughed at this suggestion. William Fargeon, merchant, philanthropist, Sunday-school superintendent, temperance orator—with hands white, linen spotless, and well-brushed hair growing thin in front—a soldier!

"What did you answer?"

"Oh, I told him my forefathers were non-resistant New Testament Christians, and I had been so long taught to turn the other cheek I didn't believe I could fight a flock of new-hatched wiggle-tail snipe."

"Of course you can do more good to your country than *that* would amount to! This meeting at the Wigwam to-night is of your getting up, isn't it?"

"Your father's and mine; but your father's speech will be the great card. Won't it, Mr. Penrose?"

He said the last words looking over his shoulder, but the quick-pulsed younger folks had outwalked the minister and his wife, and the latter were out of hearing.

"Never mind," said Sara, "we all have places on the platform. But who could imagine you a soldier!'

"There's not a soldierly hair in my head—and not too many of any kind."

———

The vast plain auditorium of the Wigwam (where Lincoln had been nominated for the presidency less than a year before) was cloudy with dust and echoing with noise.

And such a throng! Lydia Penrose (Sara's younger sister) afterward averred that she was so crowded that she hadn't room to stick her tongue out; but this was perhaps hyperbole. Her youthful brother expressed the view that it must be a pretty all-fired crowd that could make Bunny hold her tongue, whereupon she obtruded that member at him in a manner indicating scorn.

Flags, music, speeches, thunders of applause—it seemed as if the Union must be almost saved already. Fargeon made the best speech of the evening. Wit, humor, invective, patriotism, poetry—all were at his command, and at every pause a fresh cloud of dust arose from the stamping and was blown abroad by the waving of hats and handkerchiefs.

On long tables in front of the platform were offered eleven subscription papers; ten for signatures of volunteers for companies A, B, C, D, E, F, G, H, I, and K, and one pledging money for expenses, care of soldiers' families, etc.

How the latter filled up sheet after sheet, and how the other ten—did not! When the meeting adjourned, one company, K, had only eleven names on its paper. A committee was appointed to keep the Wigwam open and the papers accessible through the week.

On joining the Penroses, as usual, Fargeon found Mr. Thorburn—"Uncle Colin"—with them. He was a canny

Scot—shrewd, blunt, outspoken ; a merry twinkle in his eyes and a sharp tongue in his mouth. He was a favorite with them all, and he walked home with the party. All spoke well of Fargeon's efforts, Sally being especially ready with approving words—all, that is to say, except old Thorburn. He preserved an ominous silence until he and Fargeon were alone together.

"Willum, ma lad," said he in his rich Scottish burr, which, by the way, he intensified purposely or suppressed entirely, according to circumstances, "I mak na doot ye will be cockerin' up yersel' wi' the thought ye're puttin' in yer vera best stroaks for this gre't cause."

"Can you tell me how to do better, Uncle Colin?"

"Aweel, if all did as weel as ye, dinna ye think Sumter'd be takken back in a wee bit?"

"Oh, I don't complain of what others are doing or not doing."

"Noo, Willum, listen to me whilst I tell ye what'd be th' upshot if th' entire north wad rise oop and folly in your footsteps."

"Oh, don't give me too much credit—"

"Bide a wee, bide a wee, ma lad, until ye hear what kind o' creedit I'm a-gettin' at. Mayhap it'll no mak ye ower prood. Here it's. If a' were like William Fargeon, Esquire, evera last Yankee of ye all wad be seekin' aboot to find some ither mon t' gang doon Sooth an' do his fightin' for him."

They walked on in silence. When their ways parted Thorburn said:

"Aweel, ma laddie; all I've got to say til ye is just —good-night !"

Will had one of his old wakeful nights. For the first time he began to appreciate what was the

kind of feast to which he was inviting his fellow-citizens
—what a wrench of heart and soul and body and mind it
is for an ordinary man to say, "I will go to war. I will
bid good-bye to all that I love, all my dear hopes of fortune, my ease, my comfort, my safety of life and limb,
and go forth to stand up before the armed enemy in battle."

Next morning he walked abroad, breasted the sweet
spring sunlight—lovely, familiar, natural, unwarlike—
and, with face pale and set, went straight to the Wigwam. The twelfth name on the list of Company K was:

[So used he was to signing the firm name that he did
it unconsciously, and had to erase the closing part.]

What a buzz went up and down Lake street as the news
spread! Company K had its 100 names before noon, and
the regiment its 1,000 before night. The meeting which
had been adjourned for a week had to be called for that
very evening. The body of the hall was reserved for the
enlisted men, the place of each company being designated
by a little guidon. The ball was started and was gathering strength. The great building could not hold the
spectators, and the welkin could scarce contain the
cheers as those solid ranks of the ten companies showed
themselves in their respective places. After the band had
played the "Star Spangled Banner," Mr. Penrose opened
the meeting with prayer, as usual, and followed with a
speech of high and fervid eloquence. He held his audi-

ence spell-bound while he spoke, and even for a minute of silence after he closed, and then came a storm of cheers, with waving of hats and handkerchiefs, that only ceased when he again arose and asked a hearing.

"This platform is short one man—its best man—the man but for whom we should not be here to-night. May I ask Mr. William Fargeon to—"

But what he wanted Will to do could only be guessed. The cheers were wilder and more persistent than ever, and cries of "Fargeon!" rent the air. At last Will arose and the tumult died down, only to break out again and again until it ceased from sheer exhaustion.

"Mr. Chairman, I am in the ranks, where I belong. I shall have to leave to some one else the work to be done outside of them."

As he resumed his seat he knew, by inward conscious-ness as well as by public demonstrations, that he had made the best speech of his life. Already it sounded terse and soldierly. Already he was a man of deeds, not words. Yet his heart was troubled.

The meeting adjourned, and again he found the Pen-roses awaiting him. He only got to them after his arm was stiff with hand-shaking; but they were very patient. All had hearty words for him—Sally not quite so fluent and clear-spoken as usual; but then her eyes had taken on what seemed a new and different shape and expres-sion from that he had been accustomed to in the years he had known and loved her in vain. They looked at his a little longer, and wistfully, as if studying something they had never found in his face before. Her mobile lips. too, seemed slightly changed and quivering, and her sweet face was paler than its wont.

"You'll walk with us, Mr. Fargeon, won't you?" asked Mrs. Penrose.

"Sorry I can't. Not my own master any more, you know. An enlisted man now! Company K meets in a few minutes to ballot for company officers."

"Oh, indeed! So late? Well, if you must, you must. Good-night, then. Come and see us soon."

"Good-night—and good-bye!"

"WHAT!" cried Sally.

"We shall take the cars for Cairo to-morrow night, and I have not hours enough to do justice to my company and my creditors—not a minute for myself."

Sara placed herself directly in front of him.

"You can't go—like that."

"That is what war means."

"I wish to see you before you go."

"I have but twenty-four hours in which to do a thousand things."

"One hour for me leaves twenty-three for the rest."

He tried to smile, and gently, slowly shook his head. With a stubbornness in keeping with his new part he resolved not to see Sally again. Away from her spell he could trust himself; but suppose he should see her and —break down!

"I wish to see you before you go."

The young beauty spoke with assurance, as to a subject to whom her "wish" had long been law. But at this moment a voice called loudly:

"William Fargeon's ballot for captain of Company K is called for."

So he tore himself away and plunged into the work. Already he had missed his chance to do what he had intended—work with might and main for the election to

the captaincy of one McClintock, a man who had learned
real soldiering by good service in the Mexican war. But
the ballot was complete when he polled his vote—Fargeon, 99; McClintock, 1! In vain did he protest against
such action—decline the place—insist on another ballot;
his voice was drowned in a storm of "ayes" to a motion
to proceed to ballot for first lieutenant. McClintock was
elected, and the roster of the company was soon complete.

He thought, as he got up next morning—it could hardly be called waking, so broken had been his slumber—
that he was going to have hard work to keep his resolution to see his lady-love no more; but he was so over-
whelmed with work of all kinds that there came no moment when he had deliberately to deny himself the tempt-
ing joy.

Some far-seeing authority had requested that all officers should provide themselves with uniforms before
starting, so that at least a semblance of order and discipline might be maintained during the journey and on the
arrival at Cairo. Fargeon was, of course, one of those
whose energy and resources made it possible to comply
with the instruction.

Poor Sally! She could not at all believe that, even
after all her coldness, her bitter-sweet sisterliness, he
would have the heart to leave her so. While he was
working, she was waiting, waiting, starting at every sound
that seemed to indicate the approach of her dear and
splendid friend—her faithful lover through such long
discouragement—now her soldier hero!

"Going to war! Going to be killed in battle! I am
afraid he never would run away—even if great big cannons should be pointed directly at him and fired off—all

2

covered with blood—nobody to take care of him—in all the noise and under the feet of the horses."

Then she cried in pity of him and of herself.

After the early parsonage breakfast came the hours of waiting, waiting, that seemed an age to her disordered fancy. At last she burst into her father's study.

"Father, what are you thinking of?"

"Of my discourse for the Sabbath, of course; what do you suppose, at this time, Thursday?" Then, after a glance at her face: "Why, Sara! What is the matter?"

"Oh, father!" She burst into tears and kneeled down with her hands on his knee. "How *can* you—at such a time as this?"

"How can I write my sermon? Is the girl mad? What do you mean, my daughter?"

"I mean just that! How *can* you sit writing *sermons* when our friends are going to *war?*"

"But, my dear, is not such a moment the very time when our thoughts should turn to the God of battles?"

"Oh, father! don't *write* and *talk!* Do, *do* something!"

"Well, well, my love. There, there now—don't cry so. Stop, I say; stop at once—and tell me what you would have me do."

"Oh, put on your hat and go out like other men. Oh, I wish I were a man; I wouldn't be writing, writ·ing on such a day as this."

"Sara, my poor Sally, I forgive you, and I hope God will forgive you for putting other interests before His, even in these days. Will you pray to Him to do so?"

"Oh, father, I can't stop to pray now—or to argue. Was that a ring at our door-bell? No, it's only the milk! Oh, he is never coming! Dear father, do one thing for your poor Sally now, won't you?"

"What is it, daughter?"

"Just go to wherever Mr. Fargeon is and offer to do whatever he is doing, so he can come and see me—just for a few minutes. *Make* him come!—just for a few minutes."

"There, there; get up, my daughter; I will do as you desire. My sermon I can—"

"Now it's twelve o'clock. Do you think he'll be here by half-past?"

"How can I tell, dear?"

"Well, then, one o'clock. He must dine somewhere, why not here? If he can't come before one o'clock you'll come back and tell me just when he can come, won't you, father? Promise me, now! You'll have to come home to dinner, you know."

The dear old parson was a man whose careful walk, listening look, benevolent smile behind gold-rimmed glasses, cordial recognition even of persons he couldn't *quite* remember, proclaimed him one of those saints on earth, more careful of the rights and feelings of others than of their own. He gave his beloved first-born daughter—apple of his eye—the required promise and walked forth, as it seemed to poor Sally, with slower steps than ever. She told herself at once that half-past twelve was impossible, but she watched the clock as that hour went by. Then she tried to school herself into expecting her father instead of her soldier at dinner; but neither appeared at one, at two, or at three—it is five o'clock, and the pastor's dinner has been kept warm for him until it is almost dried up, when she hears a quick, firm young step on the plank sidewalk. It stops at the gate, it ascends the porch and echoes through the hall; the parlor door opens and her father enters, alone.

CHAPTER II.

WHERE is Mr. Fargeon?"

"I'm just going to tell you, Sally. Is my dinner saved? Let me have it at once, for I find myself famishing."

All bustled about to do their service to the reverend head of the house.

"Father, now tell me—"

"Yes, yes, my daughter. Oh, how good this tea tastes! But to resume" (talking with his eyes full of fire, his mouth of food, and his voice of excitement); "I found Capt. Fargeon at headquarters, where it had just been decided what the men were to take along. He was very glad to see me and said I was the very man he needed; said I must go out at once and buy 20 camp kettles, 200 tin coffee-cups, 200 tin plates, 100 sets of knives, forks, and iron spoons, 10 axes with helves, 10 balls of strong twine, 100 double blankets—dear me, what did I do with my list?"

"Then what did he say about coming here?"

"Please wait, Sally, until I have finished," he proceeded, dividing his time with much impartiality be-

tween eating, drinking, and talking. Poor Sara clasped
and unclasped her hands with trembling eagerness. One
might observe that she was a right-hander—that the right
thumb was always clasped over the left—so she was born
to be ruler in her household; but who can rule the
loquacity of excited self-satisfaction? As one of his congregation once remarked, "Brother Penrose is a very
fluid speaker."

"Well, I started out, list in hand. Oh, what could I
have done with that list?" [He paused to probe a
myriad of pockets in vain.] "Never mind; I went first to
Brother Bangs. Said I, 'Brother Bangs, I want 20 camp
kettles, 200 tin coffee-cups, 200 tin plates—'"

"Yes, yes, father, we know what you wanted."

"'—100 sets of forks, knives, and spoons, 10 axes with
helves, 10 balls of strong twine'—where can that list be?
I believe that was all in Brother Bangs' line."

"Then did you—"

"One moment. Said Brother Bangs, 'Brother Penrose,
are those articles for Company K?' 'They are Brother
Bangs,' said I; 'how much will they come to at wholesale prices?' Said he, 'That is none of your business,
Brother Penrose.' Said I, 'Brother Bangs, I never departed from you empty-handed, and I do not intend to
do so now, though I know you are a Democrat.' Said he,
'Brother Penrose, I shall demand full value for each of
those articles.'"

"What! Bangs, who goes to our church?" cried Mrs.
Penrose. "Did he speak so, knowing it was for Mr. Fargeon's company?"

"He did, indeed, wife, greatly to my surprise. But
mark what followed: He gave the order to one of his
clerks, saying, 'Send those things up to headquarters of

Company K at once.' Then turning to me he added, 'Now, Brother Penrose, you are going to give me full value for those things, as I said, and that's just one penful of ink, and I'll furnish the pen and ink. You sign William Fargeon's name to that receipt, per Penrose, and the account is square.'"

A silence fell upon the group, and some eyes filled with grateful tears. Just as Sara was thinking she might safely recur to the matter nearest her heart, her father began detailing his further experiences.

"I wonder what I did with that list." [Further frantic self-searching, as for some ubiquitous but evasive insect.] "But to resume; everywhere was the same thing. 'Is it for the volunteers? Then tell us what they want—that's all we ask.' And I walked those streets until I had provided every single thing that was needed." He beamed through his glasses on all about him (still refreshing exhausted nature), as if to say, "I am a humble instrument in the hands of a wise Providence for the maintenance of our Union—but I wonder what I could have done with my list!"

"Father! Tell me this minute what Will Fargeon said about coming to see me!"

"Why, daughter—in good sooth—I don't think I said a word to him on the subject."

———

All adjourned to the sitting-room except the mother and elder daughter, who cleared the table and prepared it for tea and, as usual, friends dropped in and additional places had to be set at the hospitably elastic parsonage board. At each new arrival Sara glanced anxiously into the hall, but no sign of Will Fargeon gladdened her eyes. She could hear his name mentioned in the animated conversation that came from the sitting-room, mingled with "100 double blankets" and "can't imagine what I have done with my list."

Once she appeared at the door and called to her sis-ter, a glowing and pretty miss, as breezy as her elder was calm and masterful.

"Lydia, see here a moment, please."

"Oh, Sally, you needn't make any mystery about it. What dish am I not to take any of to-night?"

"The cold tongue, dear," she replied without even a smile, though all the rest laughed so heartily. How could they laugh in the presence of battle, and murder, and sudden death?

But at tea it came out that Mr. Seward had said there would be no fighting to speak of. The whole thing would be over in ninety days. Then her spirits took a sudden rebound, Mr. Seward was such a great man, and was right there in Washington, too.

Yet Fargeon did not come!

The soldier train was to start at eleven, and now the wretched time approached when there was nothing left to do but to go down to the Central station and mingle with the noisy, tumultuous crowd, bidding good-bye to the departing regiment. Thither they went—Sara and her father.

"See, daughter! Each man in Company K has one of my blue blankets rolled up and tied with my strong twine, passed over his right shoulder and under his left arm, and hanging to the strong twine are my plates and coffee-cups. The camp kettles are in the baggage car, I suppose—and the—other things—that were on the list."

Sara saw it all, but did not see what she came to see. There was the interminable line of cars, stretching the whole length of the long gas-lit station and out into the darkness beyond—more than a thousand feet in all. At the cars marked "K" she saw some faces she recognized, for many of Fargeon's old employés had enlisted in his company. Little family groups formed about some of the men; women trying to be brave, and volunteers trying at least to appear so. No one could tell her where Captain Fargeon was. "Probably at headquarters," said they. "Perhaps at our house," thought she.

The happiest fellows were the young, the unattached, the adventurers, the laborers, to whom this meant food, clothing, pay, excitement, a sight of the world; the less happy, those who were better off, who just now began to realize how sweet home life had been, and what a blessed state is that of peace and privacy. The least happy were those who had to "bear up" and tear themselves away from clinging arms, tears, kisses—sobs not the less agonizing because they were suppressed.

How they wished that the parting were over and they speeding along the track!

Eleven o'clock approached and anguish was Sara's portion. She would have liked to go out and stand in front of the engine; for surely they would not run over a poor forlorn girl! But after all no such desperate expedient was called for. Just as the station clock marked eleven she (having forgotten all about the uniform) was startled to see a slender figure approach, tall, erect, glittering with sword, sash, shoulder-straps, and brass buttons; the face that looked out from under the smart kepi —Fargeon's!

"Oh, where *have* you been?" she asked, smiling and crying at once. "And why don't you shake hands?"

"Getting the stuff into the baggage-cars," he answered,

showing his gloveless hands begrimed with toil. "That kept me from looking for you and prevents me now from shaking hands."

"Nonsense! Give them to me! I am proud to shake them!"

He turned aside and tried to beat off the dust while he said: "I was hurrying fearfully—and as it turns out needlessly—for we shan't get off for some time. Seven men of Company C haven't got here from Aurora yet. Excuse me a moment; I will go and wash my hands, so that I may clasp yours once more."

He darted off; and while he was gone she overheard Superintendent Clark, whom she knew, talking with some one—probably the captain of Company C.

"You see," said the superintendent, "this is a big train —can't begin to make time—our regular passenger in the morning will pass it before it gets to Cairo. So we will start this now and let your men overtake you by the regular." And they passed on.

"Splendid!" thought Sara. "Now Will can do the same—stay till morning!" And when Fargeon appeared she was radiant at the thought and greeted him gayly. "Oh, Will! Superintendent Clark says the regular passenger train in the morning will catch this before it gets to Cairo. So you can go home with us and start tomorrow!"

As the captain's face broke slowly into a smile, and slowly but decidedly he shook his head in regretful negation, the color faded from her cheeks and the light from her eyes. Said he:

"What! start out among the laggards? Let my men go without me? Not if I know myself!"

Now, pretty Miss Mischief, what plot is working in

your small, imperious head, that brings the color to your face and the light to your eyes?   You surely are not contriving a plan to make your lover lose his train, just to give him a chance to repeat all the sweet things he has ever said to you, and you a chance to take back all the rebuffs you have given him!   Can one so young, so fair, be so deceiving?

Alas that such duplicity should exist where we least look for anything but transparent candor!   Let us watch. The first test point is: Will she tell him that Mr. Clark said the train should start at once?   She says nothing about it.   What next?

She places herself leaning against a barrier, her face turned toward the train, so that he must have his back to it in talking to her. Then her guns are unmasked.   She knows that he thinks her the prettiest when her hair is pushed back from her temples and tucked behind her ears, so back it goes.   The lips part smilingly; the teeth gleam, the dimple establishes itself *en permanence*, the eyes—but words fail to describe their fringed splendor, their effulgence, their transparent frankness, just when they are engaged in the most heinous deceit—and then the artful tongue opens fire, with a fusilade of nervous, laughing, fluttering, flattering words.

"Oh, woman! Only once deceived, and evermore deceiving."

Poor captain! Ambushed, surrounded and made prisoner, even before he is mustered into service!

She sees the train slowly start—victory must be hers —but at this crowning moment her unaccustomed role of deceit becomes hateful to her. She cannot keep it up. Fargeon sees her face once more paling suddenly, her eyes filled with tears, and the corners of her lips drawn downward like those of a repentant child. She seizes his hand, points toward the vacant track and cries:

"Look!"

He is off like a flash, running to catch the lumbering train, tearing through the obstructing crowd and disappearing as it closes behind him. Does she hope he will succeed? Or that he will fail and return to her yearning eyes?

CHAPTER III

FATHER AND SALLY VISIT CAMP.

H, how sorry I shall be if he misses his train! What will he think of me? And how sorry I shall be if he doesn't miss it!—goes away and doesn't think of me at all!"

Sally and her father stemmed the tide of humanity which slowly came down the platform. Fathers, mothers, sisters, brothers, wives, sweethearts, slowly dispersed to their homes; each home now, and perhaps forever, showing one vacant place at the fireside; each heart holding one image which can never grow old or change, except to fade slowly from memory if the soldier comes back no more.

When the crowd had gone, the station grown empty, and no Fargeon appeared, the minister and his daughter walked slowly homeward. They were silent; or if the good dominie talked, Sara took no part, not even that of listener. She gradually concluded that it was infinitely better that Will was not with them. "Better away wishing he were here than here wishing he were away." She had a revulsion of feeling. Her spirits had been low for twenty-four hours, and that is about the limit of sadness at her age. Her thoughts wandered from Will and caught what her father was saying—the close of some long monologue.

"Of the two horns of the dilemma, we will choose the least."

She burst out laughing.

"Why, daughter—what is there to laugh at in my view of the case?"

"Oh, father—I don't know.—I've been so wrought up that I laugh at nothing, I suppose. It just struck me— the funny idea—a dilemma—with one horn larger than the other—we taking the little one—leaving him a poor, lop-sided—kind of unicorn."

Her laughter, bubbling up and over, interrupting her speech, was so catching that her father was fain to forgive her and join in the fun—such as it was.

This untimely, undignified, unnatural hilarity lasted until after she got home, and did not pass without some mild disapproval—the only kind Sara had ever to meet.

Her mother (addressing nobody in particular) remarked that some persons would feel differently on the departure of such a man on such an errand. But some *other* persons had always seemed to think that they knew best which side their bread was buttered on regarding Mr. Fargeon. This gave poor Sara a new attack—her bread buttered on one side regarding Will Fargeon and the other side regarding somebody else! So she could only take refuge in her own room and let joyless cachinnation have its way, followed by a few tears after her face was buried in her pillow.

Letters between Cairo and "home" were many and pleasant during the early weeks and months of camp-life. Photographs sped to and fro and made those acquainted who had never met face to face. Fargeon told his friends about the absurd though natural blunders into which the greenhorns fell, and how in all trouble Lieut. McClintock was the never-failing resource. Mac supplied every deficiency and remedied every defect; Mac made rough places smooth; Mac was the captain's right hand, his guide, philosopher, and friend. Mac's steady devotion to duty edified the many who were eager and willing to do well. Mac's hand fell like iron on a few who were disposed to break rules.

Listen to Mr. Penrose, reading out one of Captain Fargeon's letters:

"Friends, I cannot tell you what it is to me to see Mac's face, at early morning, at high noon, by evening camp-fire. No countenance my eyes ever rested upon has given me so much delight except one." Mr. Penrose paused in his reading and smiled on his hearers.

"You see, my dears, Brother Fargeon excepts *one*. I am gratified to note that he does not forget the years through which he and I have fought in the Lord's war side by side."

Sally did not laugh. She only reddened a little; but Lydia, the irrepressible, was not so discreet. She burst out:

"Ho—ho! The idea of its being *your* face he meant, father!"

"Oh, Bunny!" protested Sally (Lydia had always been called "Bunny" and "Rabbity" because of two pearly teeth that showed below her short upper lip). "Dear Bunny, now please, *please* don't!"

"No, Sally; I will not 'don't' nor think of 'don'ting!' Father must be told whose face is dearest to Capt'n. Fargeon. It's mine!" All laughed at this unexpected turn, and Lydia went on:

"But mercy my! Who cares for *him?* If it were Lieutenant McClintoch! Mmmm! Why, Captain Fargeon himself says that the lieutenant is the finest man that ever lived. I guess he knows."

Mac was the subject of bitter rivalry between Lydia and her younger brother, and this dragging his name into the discussion prevented the question of "whose face" from being settled, for those two branched off into other matters—whether Bunny was so mighty old as she thought for, and whether it had been "fair" for Bunny to shut her mouth when she had her photograph taken to send to camp, seeing that she never kept it shut at any other time—and so forth, until Mr. Penrose put an end to the digression by going on with the letter.

These letters were all very well, in their way, but far as possible from satisfying to the soul of the repentant Sara. Oh, if Will could only "read between the lines" of her letters as she could between the lines of his! Then he would know how sorry she was for—everything. Then a sigh, and a hope it would come out all right before long.

———

In camp reigned toil and drill and study and heat and impatience at what the volunteers thought was an unreasonable delay in setting them at work; and permeating all, the ever-present homesickness. Fargeon would have been really an unhappy man if it were not for his instinctive effort to keep up the spirits of the rank and file. This, and the comfortable presence of Mac, kept him cheerful at his task.

Suddenly, one day, after the usual sun-beaten drill, he

found as he took off his sword that it persisted in rattling as he hung it up; his teeth chattered in spite of himself; his hands grew blue and wrinkled with cold, notwithstanding the fierce heat; and his rude bed (a row of cracker-boxes), when he lay on it covered with blankets, shook as if it would go to pieces. He wished he could get hold of a huge anchor to hold things still, himself and everything about him. Ague, of course! He had seen it in others; now he could study it to the very best advantage, for, in spite of the external fierceness of both chill and fever, his mind was strong and well as ever, and even his body was slow to succumb.

Small use in studying it, however. He could not see through its mysterious, inscrutable why and wherefore. It did not last many days, and when he could call it "broken up," he yielded to the persuasions of the regimental surgeon and his brother officers, took leave of absence and carried his gripsack into the town of Cairo.

He found a room at the St. Charles Hotel, on the levee —it was only a six-by-nine sky-parlor, but how palatial it seemed! A locked door, a glazed window, plastered walls, a half-carpeted floor, a furnished wash-stand, and, luxury of luxuries, a mattress bed, with a pillow and bedclothes; and (for the first time in so many weeks) a chance to undress himself and get between the sheets like a Christian.

He fairly reveled in the simple, plain little couch; luxuriated in it; explored all its corners with his long-hampered limbs, and rolled his face in the pillow like a strayed child restored to its mother's breast. After hours of sleep he heard the dinner gong sound, and was glad to hear it and disregard it in the greater enjoyment of the blessed mattress, pillow, and sheets.

His rest and recuperation went on for some days. The noisy, smoky bar and billiard room, full of soldiers drinking, smoking, talking, playing—officers and privates together—had no attractions for him, but he did much letter-writing, and there was always the blessed bed wherein he found refreshment even in lying awake. (His letters suppressed the fact of his illness.)

One morning he heard the usual tap at his door, and his second lieutenant, Barney Morphy, called out to ask how he was. He sprang up and began to dress.

"Oh, Barney, is that you? I'm all right now, thank you, and will go to camp with you shortly."

"By the way, Captain, here's a letter for you that came this morning."

The captain opened the door and seized the missive, and as he read it Morphy saw a smile steal over his face, and a flush of pleasure over so much of it as the kepi had preserved from a general brown tan too deep to show blushes.

"Oh, Barney, I beg pardon. We've got company coming. Our old friend Parson Penrose will be down to preach to the boys on Sunday."

"Ahem! Anybody coming with him, Captain?"

"Well—yes. Part of his family may be along."

"Well, now, hadn't you better just keep your place here? Not come back to camp to stay until they go away— the minister and the—part of the family?"

Fargeon's heart leaped at the suggestion. Everything seemed to favor it. Officers from every regiment in the brigade had taken leave of absence in order to disport themselves at the hotel, some of them in a manner scarcely creditable to the service. But good sense—or shall

3

we call it lover's instinct?—prevailed, and he put aside the temptation.

"What!" he thought; "let Sara find me once more a civilian, staying at a hotel, idle and unsoldierly, wearing a uniform as a cow might wear a saddle, while a better man is commanding my company? Well—hardly."

So he got back to his quarters in fine spirits, and even entered his tent with something like a home-coming feeling.

Was he walking on earth or on air? Within twelve hours he should see her! He pushed his eyelids to see if he was awake or only having another of those dreams. He was awake.

And the lovely Sara on her way to the meeting from which she hoped so much! How her eyes shone as she looked out of the car window on the great, grassy, sun-lit, blue-gentian-spangled Grand Prairie! How the lids dropped when she recalled her gaze and found her face the cynosure of masculine eyes all unused to such visions! How she beamed with innocent triumph and with the happy anticipation of meeting—all her friends of the Sixth! Yes; decidedly, she had never been so happy in all her life.

"Why, father, these men all have '39' on their caps! Is it possible that thirty-eight other train-loads like this have gone out before?"

"Yes, daughter, thirty-nine with this, from Illinois alone."

"I wonder where all the men come from!"

"So do I. I've been wondering at it for a long time. But I fancy that the men of fighting age must be about all gone now."

What would the good dominie have thought if he had known that the stream would flow on until 175 such regiments should have been furnished by this young state alone?

One man in the car, though so placed that he could have looked at her without rudeness, never did glance in her direction in all the long, long day's ride. On the contrary, he seemed to avoid her eyes, and once, at least, she fancied that he held his cap beside his averted face on purpose to escape being seen by her. As he so held it, she saw above the visor the magic figure 6.

So here, among the thousand and forty-five of the Thirty-ninth, was a man of her "own" regiment! Her interest was piqued, and she called her father's attention to the presence of a soldier who knew their friends and whom she would like to talk with.

The minister, with the simple directness of his kind, went to the stranger and introduced himself; and the man obediently, though reluctantly, came forward.

His was a repulsive countenance, marred with a dreadful facial deformity which, because of the lowness of the sphere wherein he was born, had never been treated to remove or mitigate its ugliness.

Sally gave one startled glance and then looked away, unable to disguise her instinctive repugnance.

The man spoke in a broad Irish brogue, and his peculiarity interfered with his speech.

"Yes, lehdy, I know the caftain. Me nchm's Marrk Looney, and I'm the caftain's ordherly. He's the foinest gintleman in the sarvice. He is—oah he is, he is." [This in a kind of hopeless monotone, the closing words nearly inaudible, a tone that would have been appropriate to announce something the speaker knew to be true but despaired of making the world believe.]

"When did you see Capt'n. Fargeon?''

"A Winsday, lehdy. I got three days' lave an' wint uf to Chicagy huntin' things for the caftain's mess. Mebbe the caftain was expectin' your lehdyshif."

"Was he quite well?"

"Fehth he was not, lehdy; no moar was he bad. Jest a bit av a chill, wid the harrd livin' an' the harrd worrk. Ye may be sure the caftain'll be well to resave your lehdyshif. He will, oah he will, he will."

At this Sally's heart softened a little toward the uncouth specimen of humanity, and she managed to look in his face, where (never losing sight of the blemish) she could see a pair of sharp, observant eyes that might have been almost attractive but for an expression of habitual suspicion or shamefacedness. The birth blemish gave his whole face a sinister look, and even his smile was a leer.

They got to talking about the other officers.

"What makes Mr. McClintock better than the rest?"

"Well, lehdy, he was wid us in Mexico.•

"Oh; you were in the Mexican war, were you?"

"I was, lehdy, I was, oah I was. I knew the liftin'nt there—he was ortherly sargint of my company. If it hadn't been for the liftin'nt I doubt wud they have left me into K company at-all at-all."

"Why—why not?"

"Well, lehdy—" he passed his hand lightly across his eyes) "fer raysons best known to thimsilves."

They had some further chat, and at parting she gave him her fair little hand and a dimpled smile that belied

the mixed feeling in her heart—that it would be a relief
to have him gone from her sight and hearing, and that
she hoped he did not suspect it.   [But he did.]

Once more Fargeon finds himself in his familiar place
at evening dress-parade.   The interregnum had made
him half forget how childish it was, viewed in the light
of common sense.

"ATTENTION — BATTALION! Shoulder —ARMS !
Rear rank open order — MARCH ! — HALT!   Right —
DRESS !   FRONT !   Guides — POSTS!   Present —
ARMS!   Sir, the parade is formed."

While one is learning it he is buoyed up with the notion that there is some mighty hidden power and meaning in it, to come out later.   Then when it becomes a
matter of dull, mechanical routine, behold! there is nothing in it, except a reminder to each of those 3,000 men
that he is no longer a human being, but is turned into a
mere cog in a machine.

Before the ceremony was half over Fargeon saw and
recognized among the citizen on-lookers the face and
figure of his dear Lady Disdain; that beloved vision that
had been his daily thought and nightly dream for so
many sweet, hopeless years.

As soon as possible he turned Company K over to Mac,
joined the new-comers, gave his friends his greeting with
enforced calmness, and explained to them the mysterious
doings before them.   Then he guided them to the camp,
Sally's wonder and delight growing with every word and
every step.

"Is this really your tent?   Do you really sleep on that
long, low, rocky mountain?   Oh, what craggy ridges and

chasms! Why, there is one precipitous cliff right in the middle! What is that ledge for?"

"Oh, that's where one under-lying cracker-box sticks up higher than its neighbor. It just fits the small of my back. I shouldn't know how to enjoy my night's rest without that—shouldn't know I was asleep."

"And there's where you hang up your sword. Oh, why did you take it off? It was so becoming!"

"It was becoming—tiresome. We don't care to lug them around any more than we have to."

"I should think you'd never go without them. And here's your Bible, I see—no, it's army regulations. Well, that is a kind of Bible in these days. And this is the corresponding hymn-book—yes, Hardee's Tactics. 'Shoulder arms! One time and two motions!' What does that mean? How can there be two motions of one gun at one time? Perhaps the man has two guns, one in each hand. What a splendid idea! Every soldier ready to kill two of the enemy!"

The gay beauty was rattling on, all excitement and curiosity, when a message came from Colonel Puller, hoping the minister and his daughter would favor headquarters with a call.

"Oh, father!" she expostulated, "must we go? I don't believe they want to see *me* any more than I want to see them."

"What do you think, Brother Fargeon?"

Moved by a beseeching glance from Sally, Will answered:

"Well, I don't doubt but that they wish to see Sara; but we can't have all we want in this world."

"True enough!" cried Sally. "And besides, in Chicago it is customary for the gentleman to call on the lady be-

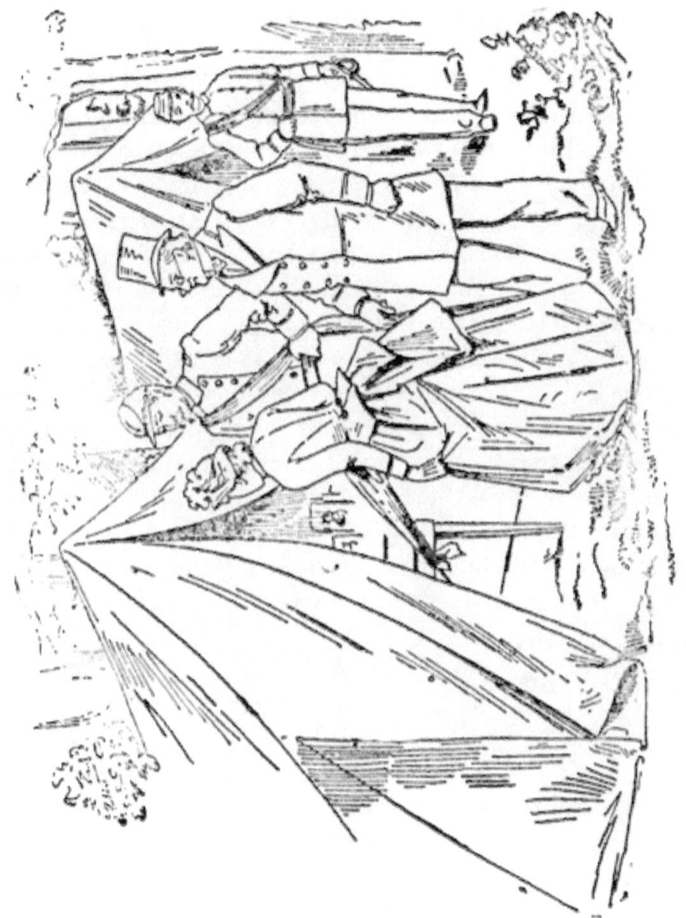

"Is this really your tent?"—Page 37.

fore he asks her to call on him. You go, father, and say that I am sick—headache—sunstroke—frost-bite—old age —gout—anything; only that I can't come."

Everybody might as well agree with Sara's views first as last. Her will was strong, her won't stronger.

When she and Will were left alone together my lady's mood changed; she laughed less and less, and became more disposed to listen than to talk.

"Oh, yes; mamma and all of us are very well, and everything goes on as prosperously as can be expected when our thoughts are far away. Now why do you stand up there leaning against that pole? Come, bring the camp-stool and sit by me—there, between me and the door, so the light won't shine in my eyes—the sunlight I mean." [If Fargeon had been very clear-sighted he would have seen that sunshine was not the only light her eyes loved.]

    *   *   *   *   *   *   *

"Oh, yes; I am—as happy as I deserve, I suppose."

    *   *   *   *   *   *   *

"Yes; the old interests are still there, but—somehow —they haven't the old charm."

    *   *   *   *   *   *   *

"To be sure. We are anxious, and we are a little lonesome—at least some of us."

    *   *   *   *   *   *   *

"Certainly. The soldiers' sacrifices are greater than ours. That's one thing that weighs on us."

    *   *   *   *   *   *   *

"Oh, there's no danger of our forgetting you! If we tried we never could—for an hour!"

And so on, little speeches and long silences. At last she broke down.

"Oh, Will! Can it be true—that you are a soldier and going to battle?"

Then she laid her hand on his arm and bowed her head on it and cried, not even caring whether her hat was on straight or crooked! Her father returned and looked in unobserved, but discreetly walked on. [Even middle-aged clergymen have some sense!]

Her heart sank lower and lower, and she felt more and more desolate as the minutes passed. Will soothed her as well as he could, patted her hand and begged her not to distress herself. Then observing that instead of growing calmer she was beginning to sob a little, he asked her if he should not get her some water—or call her father. She recovered herself with an effort and answered, petulantly, "No! Of course not!" withdrew her hand suddenly, arose, rearranged her hat before the little glass hanging on the tent pole, smoothed her hair, dropped her veil and went out. She took her father's arm and walked away, Fargeon following awkwardly, wondering to himself, "What have I done now?"

CHAPTER IV.

ALLY suggested that they visit the lieutenants' tent, the luckless captain following in silence, still asking himself, "What have I done now?"

At the approach of the visitors the soldierly Mac and handsome Barney Morphy hurried into their coats, laid aside their pipes, and greeted the minister and his lovely daughter with awkward cordiality, Sally responding with all the cordiality and none of the awkwardness. For some mysterious reason dear Lady Disdain seemed bent on ignoring her older friend and captivating these new ones.

"No, don't stop smoking! It looks so comfortable! I am perfectly enchanted with everything! I used to wish I were a boy, so I could play base-ball. Now I wish I were a man, so I could be a soldier! It is so dreadful to be afraid, as I am always, and as you never are!"

"We are as much afraid as you are, only we are more afraid to show it," said the gallant Morphy.

"If you were as much afraid as I should be, you wouldn't have to show it; it would show itself in spite of you. You'd tumble down dead and save the enemy all the trouble—unless he happened to be as much frightened as you, and tumbled down dead at the same time."

Everybody laughed at the picture of two armies all unanimously dead with fear of each other.

Then Sara spoke of home.

"There isn't a heart left in Chicago; you soldiers brought them all away in your haversacks. Every girl I know wants me to bring word what she can do for you. What can they do? Don't say *nothing.*"

"Ask them to follow your example, Miss Penrose—come down and see us."

"Oh, that would never do! The St. Charles would look like a bee-hive in swarming-time. But really, one girl did give me something to give *you*, Mr. McClintock, if I thought, after I got here, that you wouldn't laugh at it. Now would you?"

"Perhaps I should," answered the silent Mac. "We like to laugh once in a while."

"Well, you may if you like. Here it is."

She produced a little rolled-up thread-and-needle-case. It had a phrase embroidered on it, part visible and the rest concealed in the rolling, in a tantalizing fashion. Mac took it and read aloud in his strong voice, that seemed to make the little token more delicate by contrast: "'When this you see, remember'—may I open it and see the name?"

"Tell me first whose name you would like to find there—barring mine?"

"Your sister's, of course."

"Oh, you bold man, to take such a risk! Suppose it should turn out to be somebody else's name! Well, you may open it."

He did so, and read out: "When this you see, remember to put it back in your pocket."

They laughed again. "No one could complain of lack

of laughter while Miss Penrose is to the fore," as Barney expressed it.   Said she:

"After all, it *was* my sister who sent it."

"Did she—make it?"

"Of course."

"With her own hands?

"Yes; how else could she make it?   With her feet?"

Mac gazed at it long and curiously, his hard, soldierly face softening as he did so.

"You are not joking with me?"

"No, indeed!"

"Well—will you thank her for me?"

"No. She wouldn't thank me for second-hand thanks. You'll have to write."

"I haven't written a letter to a lady since I wrote from Mexico to my mother, who died before I got back."

"You can't begin that part of your education any too soon.   You will write, and she will answer, and—"

"Suffer is ready, Captain."

There was no mistaking Mark Looney's broken Irish. Sara recoiled from looking toward him, overcame the repugnance and forced a recognizing smile and a cordial word; and, after all, saw, by the dark, downcast look in his eyes, that he perceived the repugnance and the effort. She was afraid of Mark, and would tell Will so sometime —when they should be on speaking terms again. And she tossed her pretty head and went on devoting herself to the younger men, poor Will falling deeper and deeper into his puzzled gloom.

"Why, I have been *extremely* careful!   I haven't even hinted love to her since she came—never, since that walk to the Wigwam!"

They all had supper together around the camp-fire.

Milkless coffee was hard, and butterless crackers still harder; but then the coffee softened the crackers and the crackers took the edge off the coffee; and the cold ham was excellent—if it had only been all lean—and the wood smoke was interesting—in moderation. Why did it persist in following Sally's face, no matter where she sat? Well, in so doing it was only keeping in the fashion, for that was what the eyes of all the on-lookers couldn't help doing. The officers, from colonel to second lieutenant, the attendant orderlies (except Mark Looney), the more distant but observant rank and file, all had but one aim in life—to gaze at the lovely creature whenever they could do so without offense.

Would Miss Penrose like to see the manual of arms?

Miss Penrose thanks Mr. McClintock, and would like, of all things, to see the manual of arms. Mac whistles for a sergeant and whispers a few words, and in a short time eight men, the models of dexterity in handling the musket, stand in the firelight and go through the time-honored drill at the word of command. Next they do the whole thing in perfect time and perfect silence, no word of command being given.

"Let me look at that musket a minute," said Mac to one of the drillers. He took the piece, and seemed to be examining it awkwardly, as if he had never seen one before, while he moved about enough to clear a space beside the fire. Then suddenly he started into an exhibition of lightning gymnastic tricks with the heavy piece, bayonet, strap and all. Here, there, and everywhere it flew—above, below, in front, behind, whirling like a catherine-wheel, first in his left hand, then in his right, then in both so that it formed a circling halo in front of him—until, finally, he tossed it high in air, caught it as it fell, and came suddenly to "shoulder arms"* as still and rigid as a statue—a quietly breathing one.

This striking performance was greeted with a round of applause, in which Sally's hands had more share than could have been expected from their size and consistency. But louder than the hand-clapping and hearty words came a chorus of "heigh! he-igh!" from a throng of excited observers who had swarmed up from their tents as soon as the news went out that the veteran was showing his accomplishment. They had before heard rumors of it, but had never been favored with an exhibition. Even now Mac seemed ashamed of the business and said:

"Please don't tell—anybody—you saw me doing such monkey-shines."

———

Slowly and reluctantly the fair stranger left the camp-ground, with many a backward look; spell-bound by the romance of the gleaming fires, the white tents, the deep shadows, the lines of silent, slow-marching sentinels, and the sound—that monotonous yet varied hum—that comes from the presence of many men in orderly liberty and busy leisure.

They walked through the shadowy, balsam-scented pine woods. She hung on her father's arm, her heart softening toward poor, silent Will, and her gentle soul pondering how she could best make some advances toward renewed cordiality.

"Oh, father—I am so warm! Could you conveniently carry my shawl for me?"

'Yes, dear—I can manage it somehow, though I have

———

* "Shoulder arms" in those days was equivalent to "Carry arms" in the present manual.

my cane in my other hand."　　[As if she had not calcu-
lated on that!]

"Well—perhapsCaptain Fargeon willoblige me with *his*
arm."

Will tremblingly obeyed her behest, and she laid her
hand lightly on his coat-sleeve. She took off her hat
and hung it on her arm, so that the evening air could
cool her brow.

"You don't smoke, Will?"

"No!" (stoutly). "I never could see why a man should
fall into a vice merely because he is away from home."

"What comfort the lieutenants seem to take in their
pipes!"

"Don't they! It's quite absurd. The instant they get
through eating, or come off drill, or parade, or guard-
mounting, out come the pipes."

They neared the hotel. It was

"Blazing with light and breathing with perfume."

But the light was glaring gas, and the perfume was *not*
the incense which breathed in King Robert's banquet-
room.

"Father, dear, shall I go in and write a letter for
mother, to go by the morning train, or will you?"

"Well, love, suppose we both go. It is getting late,
and Capt. Fargeon no doubt is longing to get back to
his canvas home."

She looked up in Fargeon's eyes, a pretty, bashful,
smiling question in her own; to which he only answered
by pressing her hand to his side.

"Well, father, Captain Fargeon must sacrifice himself
for once, for my mind is not quite prepared for the change
from the quiet of camp to the splendor of the St.
Charles."

The dominie left them, and the matched but unmated pair walked on along the high levee to the place overlooking the junction of the mighty Ohio with the mightier Mississippi. There, outside the point where the embankment turns sharply northward, was a small bastion, built to hold a huge cannon, which pointed, sullen and silent like a couchant lion, down the Mississippi. Its traverse overlay the platform and its muzzle was depressed toward the water.

The gun squad occupied a tent a little inland, but a sentry paced back and forth between the bastion and the walk on the levee.

"Halt! Who goes there?"

"Friends," answered the captain.

"Advance one friend and give the countersign."

Will dropped Sally's hand, stepped forward and whispered the word for the day, "Cherubusco," and then Sally came up and they passed the sentry and walked out beside the big gun. It was soft moonlight; it was deep silence; it was sweet solitude; her hand was no longer on his arm; he could not help seeing that her

waist was within reach, unguarded even by a shawl.

He thought to himself: "What disaster might come to me here, now, in a second or two, if I had not had so many lessons, so many warnings." She laid a little white hand on the great, grim iron tube. To shut himself out of the way of temptation and catastrophe he stepped around the gun's muzzle, and so put between them the safe barrier of its mighty mass.

As he passed in front of the piece he drew out the great wooden stopper and lifted it so that she could see it. He told her it was called a tompion.

"Oh, that's a tompion, is it? I've often wondered what a tompion was; now I see it's what keeps a soldier's mouth shut—a cannon's I mean."

"Yes. You see, it fits tight over the muzzle."

"And do all soldiers have them?"

"All cannons? Yes; if it weren't for that, the rain and snow would beat in."

"Naturally! And that would be dreadful! But of course they wear them all the time."

"Always except when they are made ready to load. If it weren't for that, the moisture would rust the muzzle and extend down the throat—why, what are you laughing at?"

"Oh, nothing." [Struggling with her laughter.] "I always laugh when my feelings have been overwrought."

"And have they been to-day?"

She nodded; he thought of Mac, the great, irresistible lieutenant, and sighed deeply.

"That night after you left Chicago I got laughing on my way home and laughed after I got in the house, so that I had to go to bed in disgrace—charged with utter heartlessness."

"Was the charge just?"

She shook her head gently, in silence. Her arms rested on the gun and her clasped hands gleamed in the moonlight. [They had nothing else to do.]

"Do you know, Will—Captain Fargeon, I have an awful

4

confession to make?" He shivered at what was coming—would have turned pale if his sunburn had permitted. "I was tempted into a horrid thing that night. I made a plot—you'll forgive me, won't you?" [He smiled in deprecation of the thought of blaming her. Rhadamanthus himself could have done no less, placed as he was.] "Well, my plot was to keep you from catching your train! I knew it was to start at once, and I did not tell you—tried to engage your attention till the train should be out of reach—only my naughty resolution failed me at the last moment, and I sent you away!"

She covered her face with her hands.

"Did you care enough for me to do that, Sally?"

She replied with a nod almost imperceptible. Over the cannon he tried to take her hands from her eyes, but she gently resisted, whispering between her wrists:

"Have you forgiven me?"

"Yes—if there were anything to forgive." Then she yielded her hands.

He felt as if on the brink of a precipice where a thoughtless step must bring ruin. "I will not! I will not! I will not!" His heart-beats grew so fast and furious that she could feel them in his hands. He is surely going to speak—he does speak. He says:

"Do you think your father will be anxious about us?"

Her face blazed. Should she let her words blaze, too? No; one more effort of impatient endurance. She only shook her head and murmured: "Not yet; oh, not yet!" Their eyes are fixed on each other's, and she can only think *two* words—those two little meaningless monosyllables, "Not yet!"

CHAPTER V.

"NOT yet."

Did Will hear other words in her heart, or read them on her quivering lips, or feel them through her hands?

The latter, probably; just as the blind may learn what the dumb would say, by reading with the fingers words expressed in the manual alphabet. What makes it probable that this was the medium through which a bright inspiration came to his darkened soul is this; it was through Sally's fingers that he responded. Having her hands clasped in his, just as he had drawn them from her face, he dared—with fear and trembling—to lift the pink finger-tips to his lips.

The thin, frail barrier was breaking, was melting, was gone. Their faces inclined slowly toward each other, till his lips touched her forehead, just where the silky hair was parted. A little life-time seemed compressed into that moment—then he murmured:

"Dear Sara!"

"Dear Will!"

She let him separate her hands and lift them to his shoulders; and then—

Why, then, his kepi fell off and rolled under the gun so that they could recover themselves with a hearty laugh, and so that he could make his stooping to pick it up an excuse to come round to her side.

"Sally—my only love—is it true?"

"True, Will—true for life and death."

The next words he spoke were another whispered question:

"Since when, dear?"

"Since the Wigwam—where you snubbed me, and left me to go home alone, and cry myself to sleep, and long all day to see you—and you never came!" [A few hurt tears *would* start.]

"How much precious time I have lost!"

"Yes!" (with a reproachful little returning simile). "And I began to think you *never* would—would—do what you have just mustered up courage to venture upon!"

"I am properly punished for cowardice! Court-martialed and sentenced to be—promoted to the seventh heaven!"

Then a few minutes later:

"But sweetest, you must not forget that I had weeks, months, and years of defeat and disaster to recover from!"

"Don't—*don't* crush me with the memory of my folly!"

"Folly? No; true woman's wit! It is better as it is, dear. Nothing could be better than this."

"Well, if you are contented, I surely cannot repine; though I have been a little rebellious, since you wouldn't come to me before you left home that dreadful day,

when I waited and hoped for you—and you never came—
and you wouldn't even stay in Chicago till next day,
when I wanted you to so much—and you looked so
beautiful in your uniform—and to-day, the moment we
were alone there in the tent, you wanted to call in
father!"

———

"Halt! Who goes there?"

The words came clear and startling from the sentry's
beat, and Will, crying. "There's your father, I'm half
certain!" dashed suddenly from her side, nearly carrying
away her hat, and flew to the rescue of the preacher,
who he knew might be in bodily peril from the sentry's
bayonet. Sally followed at leisure, and found the three
men in conclave.

"Is that you, father?"

"Yes, my love. This gentleman with the gun objected
to my following you, although I explained fully our re-
lations and my peaceful purpose. He desired me to in-
form him of some word or other which I should have been
only too glad to do if he could have intimated to me
what the word was."

"Well," laughed Fargeon, "we need not quarrel with
the sentry, who, I am glad to observe, knows his duty
and does it." He saluted the man and they walked
away.

———

After some wakeful hours and several "cat-naps" Sara
got up, slipped her dainty feet into her slippers and
wrapped the bedspread about her night-dress. She
went to her wide-open window and stood there a
long, long time, drinking in the semi-tropical night, the
starry sky (the moon having set), and the distant for-

ests outlined against it—all making a peaceful contrast to her tumultuous feelings.

Even as she looked, she saw the first gray of dawn appear away off up the dark, broad-rolling Ohio. As it grew lighter she could make out the shadowy, misty foliage of the Kentucky shore opposite, and the black masses of the gun-boats anchored in mid-stream. All was dim, silent, mysterious, and thrilling. The horizon grew slowly lighter and more clearly visible above the funnels of the steamers lying at the levee.

There is a dash of red in the water. The sun is at hand. Now his glowing face peeps out, and the red in the waves changes to a long line of diamond-white sparkles. Just as his lower limb with a final kick clears the horizon, a flash of flame bursts from the port-hole of a gun-boat—the sunrise-gun. The sharp report follows, and after its noise has quite ceased, the echo comes back from the Kentucky woods, a long, sullen roar; and when this in its turn has sunk to a low murmur, the Missouri shore, off to the westward, tardily responds with a new growl of distant thunder. Again and again, some far-away point taking up the burden, the great sound reasserts itself, and rolls and rebounds back and forth, luxuriating in the vast silence. It seems as if the last mutterings would never cease.

It was wonderful! Oh, if Will could only be with her (if she had more on), to help her enjoy the sublimity of the scene! She stood spell-bound until the advancing morn brought again the sordid, prosaic beginnings of human daily life; then, like a sensible girl, she tripped back to bed and (the calm majesty of the outer world having dulled the turbulence of the inner) slept for hours, only joining her father when he was impatient for his breakfast. She too was ready to enjoy the meal, though rather startled to find herself the only woman present. When she got over her shyness and looked about her, she could not help noticing that, at each of the little tables, the farther side was the one the men preferred—so that they should not have their backs to her. Soldiers are *so* polite! [Dimple.]

Oh, if people *only* knew—all that she was thinking of! But no one knew. No one ever could have dreamed of such things, because nothing ever happened quite so thrilling!

Fargeon soon appeared, smiling and handsome, glittering in his best uniform and happiest glow. He became the envy of all beholders as he tucked Sally's hand under his arm and they started forth; she in exuberant spirits, escaping the awkwardness of either talking about last night or being silent, by a picturesque description of the wonders of the scene at dawn. They descended to the very meeting-point of the giant streams, and dipped their fingers in each. Then they looked up at the great gun, and secretly clasped hands in ecstatic recollection of all that had happened in its unconscious presence.

They climbed the levee again, stopped a few moments at the hotel, and then with Mr. Penrose strolled up the Mississippi side toward camp. The sun rose higher and hotter; and higher, hotter, and louder rose the saw-filing rhapsodies of the cicadas, till they seemed to grow frantic in a fierce rivalry, away up on the tall, pale, ghostly cottonwood trees.

At eleven o'clock, the Sixth, in holiday attire, paraded in a shady grove for divine service. The adjutant had spent sleepless hours in studying how to form a hollow square (Art. xiv. Tactics, p. 229, Sec. 999), a formation very important—for purposes of parade. For fighting service it was probably never once used during the war. One line (straight or crooked) two men deep, wherein every musket can be pointed at the foe, is good for all fighting purposes.

The square formed and then brought to "parade rest," Mr. Penrose preached them one of his most eloquent sermons.   How lovely the preacher's daughter looked in

her shade hat and her neat fitting jacket! There being no other woman present, no one but herself knew that her own deft hands had made that dress originally, and had re-made it, with toil and care (needless) in preparation for this very occasion. She was accustomed to such labors, and felt paid for many an hour of cutting, turning, piecing, trimming, when (after service) her lover remarked on the exquisite taste of her costume.   Glancing down he said fondly:

"That is the prettiest outfit I ever saw in my life."

"What?"   [Dimple.]

"Why, your dress and things."

"Glad you like it!"   [Smile.]

"Why, it's wonderful! Who in the world ever got it up —invented it—designed it—contrived it, or whatever you call it? What dressmaker has the honor of your patronage?"

"Oh—it was May Dover, as usual." She looked up to see if he saw her little joke.

"Miss May Dover? Never heard of her."

"No, not mis-made over; *well*-made over, by me."

Then he did see it, and they laughed as if something very witty indeed had been said.

At camp they found awaiting them Mark Looney, with a Sunday dinner prepared in the highest style of camp luxury. Fresh meat! Canned fruit!! Condensed milk!!! Sutler's pies!!!! It is fortunate Mark had not "made off" any more delicacies, or where could enough exclamation-points have been found? There was positively no drawback to their enjoyment of the feast—for who minds flies on an occasion like that?

The visit is done. She is gone. The sunshine has lost its gayety, the shade its calm repose, the breeze its refreshing sweetness, nature her charm, and duty its satisfaction.

"I say, Mac, the tender passion must be a big thing. Why don't you go in for the 'tender pash?'"

"Too old, Barney. You are just the age for the 'tender pash,' as you call it? There's the younger Miss Penrose—"

"Well, I don't know but I will—if I can get you killed off first. No chance whilst you are to the fore; but just wait till our first battle! If I have any kind of luck, you'll go dead and I'll be left—First Left., I mane—and have a clear field for Miss L. P."

"Oh, you cannibal! Want to get me killed, wounded, and missing right off, do you?"

"Killed, Mac, and killed dead, too. Nothing short o' that'll do me any good. You might lose all your arms and legs, and then your head and then your body, and still a woman—Miss L. P., for instance—might be mad in love with you."

"Why, Barney, how do you happen to know so much about the 'tender pash?'"

"Oh—I'm an Irishman."

"That settles it. Well, go in, Paddy. I give you leave."

"That's aisy said—you knowing I've not the ghost of a show."

Mac laughed, and for a long time his face wore that same gentle expression his fellow-soldier had never seen there before that day.

———

"Mac, why do you keep your tent all shut up these hot nights?"

"Well, Captain, because I prefer it, on the whole, to the hospital tent up at Mound City, or the grave-yard close by it."

"Why, isn't fresh air wholesome?"

"Worst thing a man can have."

"The beasts of the field and the fowls of the air take their air raw."

"So they do their rations, but we can't. We need to have 'em cooked, both food and air."

"The boys seem to take theirs raw for choice. Every tent-wall is rolled up to the pole. When I go the grand rounds I think I am making a field-survey of so many acres of naked flesh. Why don't they all die?"

"Well, sir, a good many of them do. And some that don't die have the ague." [This was a sly hit that told.] "And then, perhaps it's true that the mosquito-bites cure malaria—or perhaps there's so much flesh that there isn't enough malaria to go round."

"Fresh air and exercise—a cold bath and a brisk run

before breakfast—that's what I was brought up to think we all needed in our business."

"Ya-as," drawled the lieutenant. "Maybe—in the range of Chicago and Boston, not Richmond and Cairo. In this infernal river-bottom you want to lie still, and breathe through a sponge."

"What's a good fighting weight, Mac?"

"All the flesh I can get and all I can keep."

"Well, some of our brother officers don't look at things your way. Capt'n. Chafferty thinks Company C's men are soft and over-weight—thinks 175 pounds is right for a six-footer, and so on down—and he's going to try to train them down to his scale. Colonel Puller agrees with his theory and approves his proposed experiment."

"I know all about that business, Capt'n. Fargeon. A good deal more than you do, I guess."

"What do you know?"

"Chaff is going to have trouble with his men."

"Where and when?"

"Right here in camp, to-morrow."

"To-morrow? Why, good heavens! I'm officer of the day to-morrow."

"Then he'll shoulder off his trouble on you."

"What's he going to do?"

"Order out his company with arms and accoutrements, overcoats, knapsacks and blankets, for a two-mile stretch on the levee at double-quick; then a halt on the river bank, so they can go in swimming."

"What will the boys do?"

"As much as they have a mind to, and no more."

"Company C are good men, Mac."

"Yes; country farmers and farmers' boys most of them."

"Maybe they'll obey orders, live or die," said Fargeon, with a gleam of hope.

"But they won't," coolly answered the lieutenant.

"Then what?"

"Then Chaff will call on you, and you'll call out the guard to disarm the mutineers."

"Guard? Company C is as big as the guard, and armed the same."

"All right; you can call out the rest of the regiment, or any part of it. Call out your own Company K, if you like, with me at the head of it."

"Will you have our boys load with blank cartridges?"

"Not a bit of it."

"Won't you even have them fire high if they have to fire?"

"I'll fire ball cartridges right at their belt-buckles."

"Mac! what do you mean, when, after all, the poor boys are in the right of it!"

"I mean business. To-morrow is very likely a test day—a deciding point for the whole future of the Sixth Illinois. If any man refuses to lay down his arms when ordered, and succeeds in his disobedience, then good-bye Sixth."

Will groaned aloud.

"Great Scott! I wish heaven would kindly remove Chafferty to some brighter sphere, or that somebody else had the job of backing up his foolishness with powder and ball—anybody except me!"

"Why, Captain, this is the best luck you could have! A serious crisis—an armed mutiny to be put down, by tact or by force, and you outranking for the day every officer in the field; commanding the brigade and every man in it. Why, it's better than a battle for you!"

"All the same, I wish you had it to do instead of me!"

"It's all right as it is. Less likelihood of bloodshed that if I had all the responsibility. You've got the tact

which I haven't got. You'll use it to-morrow, and I'll
stand close by you with the force—you'll wear the glove
of velvet, knowing that the hand of iron is right under
it."

"Mac, you're a trump!"

"Captain, you're the joker!"

A sleepless night is much the same everywhere. A
monarch tossing on a bed of down—a fever-stricken patient facing the phantoms of delirium—a mother longing
for her sick child's final release from pain—a condemned
wretch trying to forget the waiting gallows—a sentinel
on post, in darkness, cold, and wet, and in deadly peril
from unseen foes—a Chinese prisoner sentenced to die
of wakefulness—what is there to choose between them? .

These are some of the thoughts that hovered about the
pillow (so-called; in reality a pair of blanket-wrapped
boots) of the captain of Company K, in the weary hours
preceding the day wherein he expected to have the bitter,
bloody task of subduing, by musketry, a mutiny in his
own regiment—to shoot down good fellows, brothers
in arms, who thought themselves in the right, and
whom he considered to be more sinned against than sin-
ning!

He heard, in succession, all the guard reliefs in that
long night. Indeed, the only knowledge he had of sleeping at all came from the fact that he had to be wakened
to make himself ready for the task. Sadly he donned
his uniform, bringing his sash not round his waist as
usual, but over his shoulder, to indicate his temporary
rank and responsibility—detestable distinction!

Grim was his effort at cool indifference as he joined
the mess at breakfast. He could not even command a
natural smile when Mark laid beside his plate an oddly-

shaped and corded express package bearing his name; nor did he respond in the proper spirit to the curiosity-inspired hints of the others.

"Don't hold back from opening your bale of goods on our account, captain."

"No, captain; we'll excuse you! And, if you're short of time, I'll eat for you while you unpack the parcel."

"Thank you, gentlemen; but (examining the string) it seems to be tied in a remarkably hard knot."

"Now, captain, I am a great hand at untying knots."

Fargeon shook his head.

"The fact is, Morphy," said McClintock, "I guess the captain sees an entanglement in that string that nobody except him can straighten out."

Then the captain changed the subject and began to talk about the trouble in Company C, which they discussed long and seriously, the captain and the first lieutenant taking divergent views, and Mac being much more severe on the men than Will thought just.

Fargeon was dreadfully startled when, after a pause, Mac rose and said with a very grave look:

"I have finally decided on the step I ought to take, and take at once. Orderly, go to my tent and fetch my sword."

"What is it, Mac?"

Mac shook his head in silence, and when Mark brought the sword he drew it from its scabbard and sternly presented the hilt toward his captain.

"What's the matter, Mac? You resign? I decline to accept your resignation! Put up your sword until we talk it over."

"Capt'n Fargeon, I tender you my sword, and respectfully but firmly insist on your accepting it."

"And I as firmly decline! I would rather leave the service myself! The company—the army can *not* spare *you!*"

The lieutenant stood like a statue, the sword still extended.

"Come, come, Mac! this is not like you! You are not going to desert me in this pinch! What did you promise me yesterday? And how can I maintain good order and military discipline if my own officers won't stand by me?"

No answer. Morphy laid his hand anxiously on Mac's arm, but the latter shook him off.

"Besides, Mac," added Fargeon, "I still hope that with a proper display of force we can bring Company C to reason without bloodshed."

Here a twitching that had been noticeable in Mac's face broke into a full-fledged laugh.

"Resign nobody! Bloodshed nothing! I only meant for you to use the sword to cut the strings of that infernal machine!"

When the laughter had died away Fargeon said:

"I'll forgive you, Mac, if you promise me one thing; that is, that next time you attack me with your sword you come on with it point-foremost. It wouldn't scare me half as much."

Before they had done breakfast there was a loud call for the officer of the day; and Fargeon, merely stopping to toss the package on to the cot in his tent, hurried off to hold a consultation with the colonel and the captain (Chafferty) of Company C regarding the threatened trouble. It was decided not to interfere until there should be an overt act of disobedience—in that case to disarm the mutineers with such force as might be needed (Company K to be called upon if needed)—then to punish them by an extra turn of "police duty," if no more severe measures should be called for. ("Police duty" means the servile tasks of ditching, draining, and cleaning camp.)

After morning parade, Capt'n. Chafferty (instead of the usual drill) had his men don their overcoats, knapsacks, and blankets, and start out for a "training-down", run all according to programme. They obeyed his orders in sullen silence; made the double-quick march along the levee, the sun pouring down volumes of heat on their heads, and the dust rising in a sand-storm from their feet. They threw themselves down on the river bank, declining, to a man, the proffered plunge. Then they marched home to dinner.

Fargeon, through his-glass, watched with compassion the moving cloud that marked their run; but he was immensely relieved by their apparent submission. He arrived at mess late for dinner, in high spirits. There he observed, with a laugh, that some one had taken the trouble to bring the mysterious package from his tent and put it beside his plate.

"All our troubles being now over, gentlemen, we will proceed to refresh the inner man, and then—"

He picked up the package with a meaning smile and replaced it in easy reach.

Yet the dinner was far from gay; for Mac ate in grim silence that seemed to say, "Over, are they? Wait and see." He evidently had heard something that lay heavily on his mind. And, to be sure, before they left the table a written message was brought to Fargeon, which he read, first to himself, then aloud:

"Capt'n. Chafferty requests the immediate presence on the parade-ground of the regimental guard to enforce discipline in his command."

Fargeon hurried off. Mac put on his sword and directed Morphy to do likewise, and then gave his orders:

"Fall in, Company K! Fall in, men; fall in!"

The men obeyed, and were marched to their usual

place on the color-line.   There, in full view of Company
C and of the relief-guard, they, at the word of command,
deliberately loaded their muskets with ball-cartridge.

Mac scanned his men narrowly as they charged their
pieces.   His own face was almost unchanged as he gave
the successive orders;   perhaps showing a slight flush
which his men, in after times, learned to recognize as
a battle-glow, while his speech took on a slow, cool, half-
persuasive deliberateness—a "battle drawl."   [We shall
all know it well a few pages further on.]

"Handle—cartridge! Tear—cartridge!"

Here he paused and walked along the front of the line,
to see that no man bit off the *wrong end* of his cartridge,
as reluctant members of firing parties (details for military
executions, for instance) have been known to do, removing the bullet, spitting it out, and loading only the
powder and wadding.

The men showed various sentiments in their faces.
Clinton Thrush was crying quietly—Mac knew he could
rely on him.   Mark was unmoved and business-like—he,
too, could be trusted.   Jeff Cobb, George Friend, and
Tolliver, the marksman, looked pale and troubled—they
probably had not made up their minds.   Caleb Dugong
was boastful and ferocious—he would fail at the pinch.
Well, the lieutenant could calculate on from twelve to
twenty shots, and more if the resistance was flagrant,
violent, and dangerous, including an appeal by the mutineers to muskets and bayonets.

Here is what had occurred in Chafferty's command.
The men, tired as they were, had been mustered after
dinner and marched out for a continuance of their "train-
ing down."   No sooner were they in column, and the
officers giving the marching-time with the usual "Left!
Left! Left!" than the men took up the cry with a sten-

5

torian "Rest! Rest! Rest! Rest!" that could be heard all over the camp. In vain did the officers command, 'Silence in the ranks!" When they were halted they were silent; when they marched they shouted. After Chafferty had tried speech-making, persuasion, and threats, all fruitless, to preserve silence whenever the men were started marching again, he sent off for aid to the officer of the day, as we have already seen.

Fargeon joined him in front of the recalcitrant line of men, standing with arms at shoulder, and the two engaged in a whispered conversation which Fargeon purposely prolonged until he saw Company K take its place and load muskets. Then he and Chafferty turned to Company C, and in a voice loud enough for the men to hear, Fargeon said:

"Capt'n. Chafferty, what lawful order have your men refused to obey?"

"Among others, an order to ground arms."

"Captain, you will please repeat the order in my hearing."

CHAPTER VI.

"GROUND arms!"

Not a man stirred.

Fargeon felt the blood leave his face and surge toward his heart till it seemed full to bursting. He turned slowly toward Company K, and, with a mixture of alarm and relief, saw Mac come running toward him. Was he coming to say that K would not use force against their fellow-soldiers? He walked forward to meet his lieutenant.

"Well, Mac!"

"Why, Captain, don't you see the dam' fool has given an order that cannot be obeyed? Men do not ground arms from shoulder arms! The first command should be to order arms—then ground arms! The men are right in standing still!"

"True enough, Mac! I'll tell Chafferty," and he was starting back when Mac recalled him.

"No, no, Captain! Don't let him try them any more —just tell him you will take the command of his company. You have the right."

Fargeon took the advice.

"Capt. Chafferty, with your permission I will take command of your company."

Both men bowed ceremoniously. Chafferty sheathed his sword, while Fargeon drew his and brought it to his shoulder.

"Attention—Company! ORDER—ARMS!"

Without a moment's hesitation, in admirable time the order was obeyed, each and all the musket-butts striking the earth together.

"GROUND—ARMS!"

Every man stooped forward, advancing and bending the left knee in proper form, laid down his piece, bayonet to the front; and recovered his upright position empty-handed.

"By fours, right FACE! Forward, file right — MARCH!"

He placed himself at their head and conducted them to the quartermaster's tents. There he called for picks and shovels, and ordered every odd-numbered man to take a pick and every even-numbered man a shovel—always looking for the first act of disobedience. Not one showed itself, nor even an instant's hesitation. Next he marched them to the sinks, and set them at the disagreeable job of filling up one and making another.

They went to work with alacrity, even zeal!

Fargeon walked up and down behind these strange "mutineers," pondering much, and feeling his heart warm toward them with every blow they struck and every shovelful they threw. At last he halted, leaning on his sword, near one who was working somewhat apart. The fellow looked up pleasantly, and Fargeon met his look with a slight smile. This was evidently enough to encourage the volunteer to relieve his mind. Never halting in his work, he spoke (the dashes represent shovelfuls of earth thrown out):

"Say, Cap,—do we fellers—look like we was—mutineers?"

"You don't work like it, anyhow."

"No, sir-ree!—Nor we ain't!—There ain't no order—
no lawful order—for anythin' that needs to be done—
that we don't stand—ready an willin' to do it!—No, sir-
ree!—We come out to fight—an' to drill—an' to dig—
an' we'll do it—till hell freezes over!—Yes, sir-ree!—
till the cows come home!—Yew jest try us!" Here he
paused for some sign of assent or dissent—which Fargeon dared not trust himself to give. The soldier, however, took encouragement (or obstinacy) from silence,
and continued:

"Wha' d'yew s'pose—an' wha' dooz anybody s'pose—
we came aout fer?—Fer thirteen dollars a month?—Not
by a jug-full!—not by a dam' sight!—Leave aour homes
—an' aour farms—an' aour folks—fer boys' wages an'
poor-house feed!— * * * * No! We come t' obey orders
—proper orders—live er die—an' git back home—if we're
lucky enough—jest as quick as Goddlemity'll let us—"

Another pause; Fargeon looking far away and winking
and blinking rapidly to keep a troublesome moisture out
of his eyes. His interlocutor perhaps saw the expression, for his next words were:

"Ye see, Cap,—it ain't every company—has got officers
—like Company K has.—Them a tryin'—t' make us—
ground arms—from shoulder! Chaff means well—so do
the lootenants—an' we're willin' to mind 'em—fer the
good o' the service.—But they ain't no call—t' try no
dam'—fool notions on us—reg'latin' haow much—flesh
we're to carry—on aour own legs!—Aour flesh an' blood
—b'longs tew us—till it gits shot away.—When they
try t' prescribe—aour fightin' weight—they've bit off
more'n they kin chaw—they've cut daown—more'n they

kin cock up—afore rain. No sir-ree!—Not fer all the wuthless Chaff—-that ever was blowed aout—of all the fannin'-mills in Ellenoy!"

Fargeon turned away and walked the length of the working line, and then back again, saying:

"There, men! Throw out what you've got loose, and square up the sides and bottom." When this was done:

"Fall in, Company K — Company C, I mean." He placed himself on their right, giving the alignment with his sword.

"Right—dress! Front! By fours, right—face! Forward—march!"

He took them to the place for leaving the tools; then to the field where they had laid down their arms; had them resume them, marched them to their place on the color-line; sent for the captain, and prepared to turn over the command to him. As he did so he heard from somewhere in the line:

"Three cheers for—"

"Silence in the ranks!" he shouted; and he was obeyed.

After transferring the command he went to regimental headquarters, and with a very little argument got an order published and posted limiting the hours of drill, and the loads to be placed on the men in drilling, parading, and guard-mounting. The "field and staff" were very glad to get out of their dilemma so easily.

———

"Mac, would our boys have fired on Company C to kill?"

"They wouldn't have had to, Captain. If the worst came to the worst, all I should have done would be to have K cover them with their muskets while the guard went up and disarmed them. If they'd resisted the guard—why, then, of course—"

"Then would our boys have aimed at their brothers in arms?"

"Some would and some wouldn't. I should have seen that all pieces were properly leveled, but some muzzles would have been dropped when the triggers were pulled. Mark Looney would shoot to kill, because I told him to. Chipstone, Cobb, Tolliver, George Friend, the two Thrushes, and a lot of others would do the same, because they see the necessity of discipline at any cost."

"Well, it's all over now, thank God! And we have nothing to reproach ourselves with. Thanks to you, we did just the right thing at the right time."

"Yes; but Colonel Y. R. Puller has half spoiled our work by a foolish speech he is making to everybody, saying that the boys ought to come straight to him when they have anything to complain of! I always knew he was a regular *politician*." [What contempt he threw into that last word!]

"But the boys must have some appeal from wrong orders."

"Yes; but it ought to go up through regular channels, as the phrase is; 'Respectfully forwarded, approved' (or 'disapproved,' as the case may be) by company, regimental, brigade, and division officers, clear up to the President himself, if either party desire it."

How delightful were all the duties of the rest of the day! Fargeon's heart was so light he could have sung aloud at every step; and even the steps themselves seemed to be on buoyant air. "Blessed are the peacemakers" rang through his heart unceasingly. Every face he saw was that of a friend and brother. The sun was softly bright, the leaves green, the breeze sweet—in fact, life was very much as it had been while Sara was there to glorify the world with her presence. By the way, there was her present still to be unfolded.

At the mess supper no one had any reason to be sad or glum, and the rebound of spirits made the occasion one of great hilarity. Before long Mac called Fargeon's attention to the express package, which had been again brought out and placed by his plate.

"Ah, yes, Mac; I thank you for reminding me of it— I might never have thought of it again!" And he took it up, scanned it once more with laboriously assumed indifference, and laid it down again.

Morphy ventured a remark:

"It's just the right shape and size for a fine revolver."

"Yes," put in Mac, "but it hasn't the weight."

"We're having the wait," said Morphy.

"I'll tell you what strikes me; it's an infernal machine, sent down by some rebel sympathizer with murderous intent."

"Yes, Mac; the intent to free the enemy from the three most valuable officers on our side; the three they're most afraid of—the captain, you, and me!"

"Well, we're ready to die. Captain, is there anything we can do to help you solve the mystery?"

"Now, gentlemen, don't you think it would be better that only one of us should perish? Just consider the interests of the Union cause! I ought really to return to my tent and open this alone."

"No!" said Mac stoutly. "Never shall it be said that I owed my promotion to the heroic self-sacrifice of my captain!"

"As for me," said Morphy, "the moment I heard the explosion in your tent I'd blow my brains out! Jine the

"TEAR—CARTRIDGE."—Page 65.

brass band, I mane, and blow 'em out through me bazoo. But I'll tell you how we can rejuce the risk to a minimum; we'll all crouch down so that only our heads stick up over the edge of the table." [He suited the action to the word.]

"Or, still better," suggested Fargeon, "put our heads down below and let nothing but our feet stick up."

"Oh, come!" cried Mac, "let us say our prayers and die together. Die first and say our prayers afterwards."

'Well, if I had a sword I should certainly proceed at once to cut the Gordian knot."

Instantly both lieutenants sprang for their swords, each striving to get his blade into Will's hand before the other. Both arrived together, and Will took both, carefully tried the edge of each, and asked:

"Are you ready, gentlemen?"

"All ready?" cried the impatient youths.

"Well, then, here goes!" He cut the string in one place with one, and waited for the explosion; next in another place with the other, and so on alternately until there was not a bit of it left entire. Still no catastrophe. Then with a bow and a smile he returned each sword to its owner, and turning to Mark Looney, handed him the package, and said:

"Be good enough to put that in my tent and not bring it out again until I tell you to. Now, gentlemen, what was it we were talking of before you were so kind as to bring me your swords?"

The laugh was certainly against the lieutenants now— but not for long.

While they were enjoying their first pipes after supper, chaffing each other on the manner in which the captain had turned the laugh on them, lo! the captain himself, puffing away at a handsome meerschaum and pretending to enjoy it. He would put the stem between his lips, fill his mouth with the smoke, remove the pipe, blow out the smoke as quickly as possible, and then repeat the operation—to the great amusement of all beholders. Even the imperturbable Mark was red with suppressed laughter—redder than usual.

"Bravo, Captain!" said Mac. "You take to it like a veteran—just as I did at nine years old. Morphy, how do you think our captain looks with a pipe in his mouth?"

"Well, Mac, if you ask me as a friend, I must say I think he looks like an angel."

"I'm afraid, boys, it's only the fallen angels who smoke—and don't need any pipes even then. No! come to think, there *is* something said in Holy Writ about praising with pipe and tabor."

"Of course! and tabor is Hebrew for tobacker! Might have known it!" [Great laughter.]

"Well, now," said Mac, "if any woman—any white woman under fifty—were to send me a pipe like that, I'd go and get my leg shot off so I could get discharged, go home and marry her, and live on my pension—twenty dollars a month."

"So would I, Mac," said Barney; "or even if she sent me a needle-case."

Fargeon now sat down with a rather listless air and handed over the pipe to be admired and criticised.

"By the way, Mac, what is it a sign of when you don't know—nor care much—whether you are holding your head up straight or letting it wobble around?"

"Poison, captain! Deadly poison!"

"Humph! And is it generally fatal?"

"Always! A single drop of pure nicotine on the tongue of an elephant kills him in eighteen minutes."

"And on a man—is it slow or quick? How long have I to live?"

"Middling quick. Not one man in ten—feeling the way you look now—not one man in ten lives to be over ninety."

"*Ninety!*" groaned Will.

"But, Captain," cried Morphy, "you don't seem to be very jubilant over the joke you played on us a while ago. Who's ahead now in that affair?"

"Gentlemen," replied Fargeon, with all the sad, weak, bilious bitterness of seasickness, "you are avenged! I am thinking how dreadfully long it will be before I am ninety, and, incidentally, how much it could probably cost me to hire somebody else to smoke that pipe for all those fifty odd years." And he looked with loathing at his beautiful meerschaum.

The nausea wore off, but a nervous, headachy feeling remained, which he felt must be walked away before sleep could be hoped for; so he wandered through the lightened darkness and busy idleness of evening in a camp of volunteers.

Every tent was wide open, and all were filled with groups of half-dressed men, variously engaged, clustering around candles held in the necks of bottles or in the sockets of bayonets sticking in the ground.

Single men were reading, or writing, or washing and mending clothes. Here was one serving another as hair-cutter; there a little party talking war and politics. Sociable groups were playing cards or draughts and looking on at the games.

Will lingered longest at the tent where Clinton Thrush —he of the fine pale face and natural musical voice— and his brother Aleck were singing (and teaching others

to sing) a new patriotic song which Clinton had adapted
from an old revival hymn:

Will joined in the singing, and many followed his example, so that the fine marching tune could have been
heard far, far out over the great rolling river. Then he
left them and strayed on and out, passed the line of
sentries, climbed the high Mississippi levee and descended its western slope to the very water's edge, stooping
and dipping his fingers in to feel the water passing from
right to left in its flow to the southward. The stream
was so broad that he could only tell it had a farther shore by

the slight irregularities in the forest top outlined against the starry sky.

"Reveille" (pronounced *revelee*) is a wild, romantic bugle sound, thrilling to the young soldier. In a large camp the bugler at general headquarters wakes the echoes at some appointed hour in the early dawn or before; and the buglers at other headquarters, division, brigade, and regimental, take it up in succession; each repeating the familiar notes in his own especial key. He wakes the echoes; and he wakes thousands of tired sleepers, unwilling to bid farewell to their short repose.

No use to rebel, no use to protest, no use even to grumble. Good-bye, needful rest; good-bye, forgetfulness of toil, pain, and danger; good-bye, dear dreams of home. Good morrow to hardship. The day has begun — for trying labor; for certain danger; for death to those whom the unseen, unheard messenger of fate has selected during the darkness.

Fargeon failed, for once, to hear reveille and attend morning roll-call, and (by Mac's orders) was allowed to sleep late. His agitating experience as officer of the day, queller of mutiny, apprentice to tobacco-smoking, midnight prowler and scribbler on the banks of the great river, made his morning nap a very welcome luxury, and he was only aroused by wild, wandering cheers, starting, dying away and breaking out afresh all over the camp.

Will sprang from his cot and began his toilet. Mac poked his head through the tent flap, and Will lifted his glowing face from the tin toilet pail and let the water drip, drip, drip from hair, eyebrows, nose, and beard, on the towel spread across his hands, while Mac asked in bantering tones:

"Dressing for the theater, Capt'n. Fargeon?"

"Well, Mac, not that I know of."

"You'd better; you've got to go."

"What do you mean? What theater?"

"Theater of war. The J. R. Graham takes the Sixth, the Aspasia takes the Twelfth, the Memphis takes the Thirty-ninth, and the Ruby takes the battery and the wagon train—all goes, bag and baggage, and three days' cooked rations."

The spread towel continued to catch the drops until there were no more to catch; and then Will buried his face in it, hoping that no perceptible pallor had intervened, and resolute that none should remain when he had done rubbing.

So death was at hand at last!

TO THE AMUSEMENT OF ALL.   PAGE 75

"Get there? Get where?"

"Nobody knows; but it can't be to the rear. It doesn't need steamboats to carry us there, being there already."

"When do we start?"

"Draw the rations now; cook and distribute 'em as soon as possible; dinner at noon and strike tents by bugle call at one. We ought to steam away by two."

"To the front?"

"Of course. I see two of the gun-boats are getting up steam to go along."

The thought of the gun-boats was comforting. Their huge cannon carry so far!

CHAPTER VII.

HERE was rivalry between regiments, and even companies, in the matter of striking camp. The tent-pegs were all loosened, and, at the bugle call, the great canvas town sank into nothingness like the baseless fabric of a vision. In twenty-eight seconds by the watch, Company K's men straightened up and looked about them—then burst into a cheer of exultation, for every one of its tents was down and tied fast in its ropes, while no other company in the brigade was within several seconds of the goal.

The baseless fabric of a vision, when it dissolved, left a multitudinous wrack behind, the comfortable paraphernalia which volunteers gather about them wherever they encamped for long. "Pulpits and pianofortes" Mac called the cumbrous and unmilitary contrivances.

"Looks like the sack of Jerusalem by the Romans, doesn't it, Mac?"

"I guess so—though I wasn't in service at that time."

"What ought to be done about it?"

"Load the tents and the cooking utensils in the wagons, and then muster the men with arms, blankets, knapsacks, and haversacks, and march away."

"Leave all the rest?"

"The whole kit and caboodle!"

It was but a short walk to the boat, however, and the officers allowed the men to load themselves down, even to the floor-boards of the tents being carried by many on their backs under their knapsacks and belts, while their hands and arms were miscellaneously overloaded.

"Now what do things look like, Captain?"

"DRESSING FOR THE THEATER, CAPTAIN?" PAGE 79.

"Well, Mac, a little like the children of Israel starting for the Promised Land, loaded with what they had borrowed from the Egyptians."

Mac chuckled. "Ya-as. Just so. It takes you literary men to state things about right."

To the infinite joy and relief of the rank and file, they had got marching orders "at last." To these heroic, unsoldierly volunteers, three months of drill seemed an unbearable affliction; although it is a space of time about long enough to get an old-world recruit through the awkward squad.

Handling the musket and bayonet, marching, wheeling, facing, ploying, deploying, loading, firing, charging, halting, dressing, skirmishing, saluting, parading, for days and weeks (not to say years); all for the single purpose of bringing men into a double line, shoulder to shoulder, facing the foe; knowing enough (and not too much) to load and fire until they fall in their tracks or the other fellows run away.

To such simple, mechanical, dull, dogged machine-work has the old art of war come down. No more "gaudium certaminis," no more crossing of swords or "push of pike," no more blow and ward, lance, shield, battle-ax, spear, chariot-and-horse; no more of the exhilarating clash of personal contest. *Nothing* left but stern, defenseless, hopeless "stand-up-and-take-your-physic"—fortuitous death by an unseen missile from an unknown hand.

Is not the time coming when the rank and file, the stepping-stones on the road to fame, will call a halt on their own account? When they learn good sense they will cry with one voice: "It is enough. We will have no more of it."

Whenever it shall become the rule that the man who causes a war shall be its first victim, war will be at an end. War flourishes by what Gen. Scott wittily called "the fury of the non-combatants."

But to the average American brutal battle is better than irksome idleness. This found fresh expression when the men of the Sixth were clustered in groups on the many and spacious decks of the Graham, filling every inch of space where a human being could sit, stand, or lie. The few Mexican war veterans laughed at the impatience of the new volunteers. Said one:

"Why, boys, wha' d'ye mean? Here ye've had it all yer own way. Plenty of grub, camp fixed up like winter quarters—couldn't live better at a county almshouse—

nothin' to do but play checkers and draw pay for doin' it! Ye'd orter be'n prayin' Heaven night an' day to have the War Department ferget ye. Yer best luck would be if the card marked Sixth Illinois was to slip out of the pack an' lay on the floor under Uncle Sam's chair till the game was played out."

"Oh, shucks! What in thunder did we come fer if they didn't want us! Might have staid to hum and 'tended to our little biz. 'List for a soldier and spend our time diggin' slippery-ellum stumps out of a Cairo bottom! Idle month after month; two dozen gone to kingdom come, an' goin' on two hundred sick or discharged for disability!"

"That's so, every time! It ain't right. If the head fellers don't know enough to git us to work they'd better resign, and we'll put in somebody that does."

"They want to get a good ready."

"Oh, shucks! They're like the boy that took a run of three miles to jump over a small hill, an' when he got thar he was so tired he couldn't jump over a caterpiller in the road!"

The first speaker disdained to argue. He only drew out his pipe, and, producing a plug of tobacco, proceeded to fill it.

"See that plug o' t'backer? We'll call that the Sixth Illinois."

Then cutting off a bit he added:

"An' that's Company K. Now see what next." He chipped the piece with his knife and ground it between thumb and palm to small fragments. "Now it's gettin' drilled, ye see, ready fer use." Then he poured it carefully into the pipe-bowl. "Now it's loaded onto the J. R. Graham, goin' to the front." He scraped a match on his trouser-leg and lighted the pipe. "An' now it's under fire and wishes it wasn't—wishes it had staid on the farm where it growed."

Loud and long they laughed at this graphic illustration of the fate of the volunteers, but the very laughter showed that they could learn nothing from it. Poor fellows!

Another group fell to discussing their company officers.

"Oh, Cap Fargeon means well. Cap's a good feller, an' a perfect gentleman, too, but he won't never make a soldier, Cap won't."

"No! He's be'n fed on spoon-vittles all his life—can't never learn to stomach bull-beef."

"Thasso! Takes Mac to do the hard chawin'!"

"Cap's fustrate for this camp-trampin' an' book-keepin' business—psalm-singin' an' moral suasion—mark time, present arms, right oblique, tick-tacks, flubdub an' folderol; but whar'll he be come to charge bay'nets an' the enemy in front?"

"Boys," cried Caleb Dugong (a "blowhard" and favorite butt of the quieter men, who saw through him), "would ye believe it, Cap wanted us fellers t'leave our tent-boards behind!"

"Well, Cale," said Jeff Cobb, ain't you got yourn behind now?"

"Oh, shut up! He wanted us to leave 'em in-camp. Said we was a-overloadin' ourselves an' couldn't stan' it. Now mine jest fits my back—kind o' holds me up. Blamed ef I don't believe I kin march better with it than without it."

"Say, Cale," persisted Jeff, d'ye know what I advise you to do?"

"No; what?"

"Why, whenever ye go into battle, carry that board along an' wear it jest where ye've got it now, an' ye won't never git wounded."

A general guffaw burst out at this "burn" on Caleb, which did not tend to improve his humor. But he was brave, at least among his friends, and not easily bluffed. He turned to Mark Looney as easy prey.

"What do you say, Looney Mark? You 'llow you've be'n to battles where Mac was a-fightin —ain't Mac jest about the right kind of a peanut fer a fight?"

"Oah—the liftin'nt's all roight," replied the discreet veteran.

"Well, how do you say Cap Fargeon'd pan out?"

"The caftain'd turrn as white as a shayt—"

"I'll bet ye!"

"An' he'd shiver an' shake fit to knock the tayth all out av his head—"

"I knowd it!"

"An' he'd shtan' there, pale an' shakin', facin' the music, whilst most av you red-faced divvles'd be out o' soight in the rayr. He wud—oah yis, he wud."

This quaint expression of confidence in their captain was greeted with low laughter and other marks of approval. Caleb tried to turn the tide.

"Tell me a brave man would git pale an' be a-tremblin' like that! Why, the wuss things git, the madder I git, an' the madder I git the redder my face gits."

"All right, Cale," put in Chipstone. "I'll stand by ye."

"'Course ye will!" said the other, in a gratified tone.

"'Druther stan' by you than by Cap Fargeon."

"That's right, Chips! I ollers knowd ye wuz a friend of mine."

"Well, it ain't that exactly; it's because I guess I'll git to live longer."

Another general laugh at the expense of the helpless Caleb.

"I guess yew fellers must a' found a ha-ha's nest with a

Mark leaned forward and covered his blemish with his hand.—Page 88.

tee-hee's eggs in it. Well, laugh all yer a mine ter. I'll bet any man five dollars ye won't never hear my teeth a-chatterin' under fire!"

"No, Caleb; not unless ye're tied there."

"What's the use of a scairt man, anyhow? Cap's chatterin' teeth'd scare the other fellers."

"Oah, whilst his tayth wor a-chatterin', av ye wor a-listenin' ye'd hear em' chatterin', 'Shteady, b'yes, shteady; doa'nt hurry—ye've time a plinty—fire slow an' fire low! Shteady!' That's the how they'd chatter. They wud; oah yis, they wud."

"An' where'd you be all the time, Looney Mark?" asked the angry bully.

"Oah—shtan'in' somewhere's thereabouts; or layin' down on me face takin' it aisy an' quiet-like, through havin' got through me job." .

"An' the rest of us'd be all runnin' away, would we? Is that what ye say, ye dam' little split-mouth Mexican Paddy? If I had such a mug as yours I'd lie on it all the time!"

A shocked and angry silence fell upon the group at this brutal assault. Some looked with contempt at the speaker, some with sympathetic curiosity at Mark, to see what he would do. He leaned forward, with his eyes fixed on the ground, and covered his blemish with his hand, while in his disfigured face a look of patient habitual endurance followed the discomposure; a look which might be interpreted, "I bide my time."

"Well!" cried Clinton Thrush, after a moment of thought, "I'd rather be Mark Looney than any man who'd make such a speech as that!"

"That's the talk!" added Chipstone. "Count me in there!"

"Why, fellers! Mark 'llowed we was all cowards but him!"

"He never said no such a thing!"

"An' if he had, what you said would go to prove it was true, regarding one of us, an' that's Cale Dugong. It takes a coward to make a break like that!"

Caleb was "squelched"—didn't open his lips for an hour, and was not spoken to again for a day or more.

Proudly and triumphantly, the Sixth disembarked when it reached its destination, with all its comfortable impediments. Gleefully it pitched its camp on the low bluff bank. Stoutly—though with some misgivings—the men took up the march next morning, loaded down with "pulpits and piano-fortes." Before they had gone a mile, however, some began to unburden themselves; Tolliver remarking: "I didn't enlist to be a pack-horse in Foot, Leggit and Walker's line."

If Colonel Puller had asked Mac's advice, the men would have been forbidden to carry anything but the ordinary load of a marching soldier—twenty to thirty pounds under the best circumstances; but no such orders were issued, and all Mac and Fargeon could do (without causing dissatisfaction, by putting restrictions on Company K different from those of other companies) was to tell the men the folly of starting out with a load they would have to drop. This advice was heeded to some extent at starting, and bore more fruit as the day wore on, for before noon there was not a floor-board in the company; and even other burdens were greatly lessened. The consequence was that at night K reached camp entire, not a man missing, after passing, during the afternoon, hundreds of exhausted stragglers from the leading companies, some of which stragglers never reached their destination until after dawn on the following day.

Very creditable was this to Company K, but perhaps not an unmixed blessing, for when the orders came next morning for the Sixth to deploy a company as skirmishers, "to feel the enemy," a very slight examination showed that K was the one best fitted for the job, and K was designated.

Fargeon found time to make a few hasty preparations for "whatever might happen." He wrote a farewell note to Sara—"to be delivered if I fall"—and inclosed it in a sheet containing directions for the disposal of his personal effects and his remains. He donned his oldest suit, so that his best might serve as a burial garb; and then thought of his own face, drawn and ghastly, showing through an open coffin-lid in front of Mr. Penrose's pulpit when the good minister should say, in sad, sonorous tones:

"Friends will now be afforded a last look at our departed brother. Pass up the north aisle, please, and round and out at the south door, where the line will be formed."

As this scene rose before his mind's eye he felt a choking in his throat and moisture on his cheeks. It was all reasonable enough; then why, in later years, did he laugh at himself with shame—keep the weakness secret, and never let it be known to a living soul till now?

To "deploy as skirmishers" (as the Sixth had learned the trick) is to separate the men and dispose of them at intervals of six paces, keeping about a third of them massed in the rear as a reserve. Company K had now about seventy-five men for duty; therefore, twenty-five being in reserve, the remaining fifty covered a front of about 900 feet in extent—about the space occupied by a regiment in "line of battle!" To "advance as skirmish-

ers" is for every second man to kneel, musket at "ready,"
while the alternate men move forward about twenty
paces, (keeping the line as nearly straight as may be), and
kneel in their turn, while their brothers go forward twenty
paces in front of them; and so on until checked by the
enemy or halted by command. [In retiring, skirmishers
keep the same order—half halting, face toward the foe,
while the others get to the rear of them.]

Behold Company K at length on soldierly duty! The
men flushed or paled, according to temperament. Sweat
trickled down their chests, tickling as it flowed. How
their hearts beat! How fast they emptied their canteens! How their hands trembled! As Tolliver afterward described his feelings:

"I couldn't 'a' loaded my gun then to save my life. I
couldn't 'a' steered a catteridge into the muzzle of a
bushel-basket!"

It was difficult to prevent them from firing whenever
they knelt down, albeit there might be no enemy within
three miles of them. They had strict orders against it;
yet they sometimes fired, and when one did so the conta-
gion was apt to spread along the line. The first offender
felt the stinging weight of Mac's curse; and then Fargeon and Morphy, taking their cue from him, and the
four sergeants learning their duty, aided in maintaining
the needful discipline.

Listen to Mac, stalking leisurely back and forth and
drawling out in a voice clear as a bell:

"Chipstone, don't get so far to the front! Your legs
are too long; try fifteen paces. More to the left, Clinton! You're always leaning too much to the right!
There! Steady boys! Kneel down! Caleb Dugong,
don't let me catch you cocking your piece! You've

started the firing once—do it again, and you'll hear me do a gong you won't like."

Fargeon listened to Mac with earnest attention, and tried to go and do likewise. He may make a soldier after all! True, they have not yet seen or heard of a rebel. Well, when that happens we'll hope for the best. He thought to himself:

"Now I ought to be hoping to find the enemy; that's what I'm here for. But I don't hope it—no—I hope I shall not hear or see one all day—or any other day— never while the world stands! I wish there were no enemy; no war; that I were at home where I belong." And a vision of a domestic fireside, a carpeted room, a shaded lamp, a well-spread board, a tea-tray furnished with a bell to call the maid, rose before his mind's eye, and sweet, friendly voices filled his soul. It was a long-forgotten parental tea-table, and his widowed mother sat at the head.

All vanished. Here again was the unfamiliar forest; the loaded, leveled muskets; the enforced seeking for what he feared to find.

Their advance had been through a wood, rather thick with underbrush; now there seemed to be a little light ahead—either a clearing or low ground.

Now listen to Fargeon:

"Forward, second line! Steady! Dugong, I have got my eye on you! Double-quick to your places, boys! There—not too far—steady—halt and kneel down. Is that a clearing ahead? Now, first line forward! Double-quick! Now down!"

Bang!

"Curse you, Dugong—what do you mean? And you a corporal!"

Had he really said a swear-word for the first time in

his life? He hadn't time to make sure whether he had
or not, for the trembling culprit spoke.

"Ca-cap! I heard 'em fire on the left."

"That's a lie! Not a man fired till after you did. Is
your piece loaded? No? Here—give me your ramrod!
now fire again if you can!"

"Sha-shall I go to the rear, Cap? I will, if you say
so—go to the guard-tent in arrest."

"No, sir! Go on and learn to behave yourself!
What's that—a fence? Halt at the fence—pass the word
to halt at the fence!"

"Oh, Cap! Gimme my ramrod, and let me load before
I go up to the fence! I'll get killed, sure!"

"Will you behave yourself?"

"Oh, yes, Cap! I won't fire till I see a reb right in
range."

"Well, take your ramrod! Hello, Mac! what's the news?"

"Did you say to halt at the fence, Captain?"

"Yes. Let's take a look. Here! what's the use of
standing up like that? Get down and let's take a sight.
Here seems to be a field of growing corn and woods beyond. What shall we do next?"

"Skirmish right on across the field. I *guess* we shall
find some rebs in those woods."

"How far do you think we've come?"

"Oh, three-quarters of a mile, or a little better."
[Fargeon would have guessed two miles.]

"No danger of our getting out too far? getting outflanked and gobbled up?"

"No, I guess not. We must take our chances. Can't
drop it this way."

"You think there are rebs in those woods?"

"Shouldn't wonder. We can soon find out by going
over there."

"Spoil the man's corn—and perhaps he is a Union man."

Mac either said "Damn the corn," or he thought it so hard that you could hear him think.

Just here a voice seemed to come from the sky.

"Hi! I see 'em. Men movin' in them woods."

It was Ben Town, who had climbed a tree, and whose example was soon followed by several others—so many, in fact, that orders had to be given for all to come down except Ben.

"Well, Captain," said Mac, "will you give us the order to advance? Whenever you're ready, we are."

"Why, Mac, if we go out in the open our men will be all exposed and sure to get hit."

"We've got to go if we want to find out anything."

"Suppose we fire from here, and see if we can't draw them out."

"Oh, they're too sharp for that!"

"Well, why not get a section of artillery and shell the woods?"

"Why, Cap'n Fargeon, we can feel 'em and get done with it long before we could get a gun up here."

"No, sir, never! I should call that a needless waste of life. Keep the men quiet here, and I'll fetch up a gun or two in half an hour."

He started on a run for the camp, and halted to speak to Lieutenant Morphy, commanding the reserves—all of which force was fuming with impatience and curiosity—and reached headquarters in less than ten minutes, much to his surprise, for he could not get rid of the feeling that they had skirmished over many times as much ground as they had really passed.

On reaching Col. Puller's tent Will opened his mouth to speak, and found, to his surprise, dismay, *horror*, that he could not utter a syllable! His mind was clear, his words were ready, but, miraculous to relate, his tongue "clave to the roof of his mouth," and the muscles of his throat refused to act.

"Why, Capt'n Fargeon! Are you wounded? Are you sick? What is the matter? Major, get the captain a glass of whisky."

Will could only manage a ghastly grin and an imbecile chuckle as he sank into a seat. The colonel poured some whisky into a cup. Fargeon took the cup with perfect composure, steadily added a quantity of water, and drank the mixture. He put his hand to his throat, found all apparently in order, tried once more to speak, and succeeded.

"Excuse me, Colonel. I suppose I ran too fast—never felt so before in my life; hope I never shall again."

Poor fellow! Many another citizen soldier has felt so; some as often as they took part in a battle; some only on their first experience.

He made his report and the suggestion as to the aid he would like to have in the shape of a cannon or two. The colonel, being green like himself, thought it an excellent suggestion. [It takes some years of war and the loss of many guns to teach the lesson that artillery is a very poor reconnoitering arm.]

While the colonel went off to brigade headquarters to ask for the guns, Fargeon retired to his tent for a moment to get some food. He fancied that the lightness of his breakfast might account for his extraordinary temporary paralysis of the throat. There he saw Mark Looney, told him of the experiences of the company thus far, and ordered him to help the company's cooks fill two cracker-boxes with food and bring them to the men on the skirmish line as soon as possible.

"Begorra, Captain—that's the best news I heard since

me stef-father's funeral! I was afeard I was goin' to be left out here in the coald! I was—oah, I was!"

"Why," said Will to himself, "I believe he'd rather go than stay here!"

"There," he went on, as he took his way hurriediy to the front, "that shows I am not *frightened.* A man in a panic does not have his wits about him and attend to business like that. Why, I can talk as well as anybody! I can sing." And he sang low, but clear:

"I wonder why all saints don't sing."

"Frightened! Of course I'm not! Only excited. Never felt better in my life! My heart feels warm—glowing."

Then, after a few steps:

"Great Scott! Can this be the whisky? Heavens and earth -I believe it is! Ho-ho! But I don't care! So *this* is what the joy of drink is like, is it? Contented self-conceit! Well, there is something rather pleasant about it—if it only lasted forever!

"Ha! What's that? Firing on our line? Can Mac have disobeyed me and pushed forward? And the guns just coming? Lives lost for nothing! Oh, Mac, I didn't think it of you—I didn't think it of you! My poor boys!

"God! How they rattle! Hark! What's that?" For he heard, far above him, a long, sharp wail, beginning high in the scale and nearly overhead; then lower, lower, as it died away in the distance behind him. "W-e-e-e-e-e-e-e-e-e-e-e-p," it seemed to say. It was the first hostile bullet he ever heard.

He walked on, but more slowly. He instinctively directed his steps behind trees that stood near where his way led. Then a bullet passed him at his own level—

"Whip!" Then another that lodged in a tree—"Hitt!"
Then something struck lightly on his kepi—it was only
a twig that had been cut off by one of the high-flying
balls, but, at the same instant, "Spatt!" a bullet struck
the ground at his right, and he rushed up to a tree in
front of him and leaned, panting, against it, with both
hands on the trunk. It was a white-oak, and the rough
gray bark impressed on his staring eyeballs a picture of
its long, pointed, diamond-shaped corrugations, which he
never forgot.

"Why am I halting here? Because I *cannot* go on! It
is settled—the long doubt is over—I am a coward. My
poor boys are in front of me; shame and disgrace are
behind me—are here with me. Yet I *cannot* quit this
shelter. God help me, I cannot! Oh, if I could take a
bullet in my hand—my arm—anywhere but in my face!"
He thrust his hand out as far as he could reach, absolutely expecting it to be hit.

"Oh, God! Send a bullet through my hand—my arm!
Then I could lose a limb and go back home—my dear
home—where I belong."

He brought back his hand against the tree trunk; and
between his thumbs pressed his forehead hard against
the flinty bark, and rolled it from side to side, as if to
get a little bodily pain to assuage his mental agony.

"How they screech and scream! Oh, my dear home!
I will never marry Sally. I will tell her how unworthy
I am—and then bury my shame in solitude."

"What's that? Who said 'Come on, Ed?' Why—
there's Mark—poor, simple-hearted little Mark—marching
forward as if on parade, with a cracker-box of provisions
on his shoulder, and Ed Ranny behind him! I am
saved. Thank God, they did not see me! I must get to
the line before they do, or die in my tracks."

7

He darted past the tree on the side furthest from Mark, put his head down and ran like a racer to the front. The motion, the effort of mind and body, gave him new life. He passed the place where the reserve had stood, and observed that they had moved up to the support of their brothers.

When nearly in sight of the fence he saw—almost stepped on—the body of a man lying on his face behind a log. The soldier's musket lay by his side; a corporal's chevrons were visible on his sleeve; and Will thought he recognized Dugong's stalwart form. Fargeon's heart seemed to stand still; but his legs kept moving and carried him whither his soul impelled. He was still afraid; but panic-stricken ("stampeded") no longer. He remembered Mac's saying: "The ball you hear never hits you; the ball that hits you, you never hear;" and tried, with some success, to gain comfort from it, aided by the wonderful fact that he was still alive.

The enemy had deployed a line of skirmishers and were advancing doggedly across the open, in alternate steps, as has already been described. Our boys were crouching and firing through the fence, with every advantage on their side. Some stood erect, firing coolly over the top of the rail. Mac walked up and down, talking incessantly, in his fighting drawl:

"Steady now, boys—don't waste your shots. Aim! aim now; aim every time, and aim low. Carberry, you fired almost before your gun touched your shoulder; might just as well have fired into the river! There! bully for you, Chip! You fetched him! They won't make another step forward, see if they do! What did I tell you? They are picking him up—that means they're going! Now, when they get started, over the fence and after 'em! Now's your time! Forward! FORWARD, COMPANY K!"

CHAPTER VIII.

A WILD cheer rose, and Company K swarmed over the barrier, firing and loading on the run as they went. Fargeon was with them, running, shouting, waving his sword, till suddenly he saw one of his men stumble, fall forward, and not get up again. The man next the fallen one dropped his gun and called to another to do the same, and the two, in less time than it takes to tell it, had their hurt comrade raised up between them.

"What are you about?" screamed McClintock with a volley of curses. "Drop that man, * * * and take your guns again!"

"Why, lieutenant—he's wounded—his leg's broke—and he's my brother, De Witt Clinton Thrush."

"I don't care if he's your sister! Drop him and take your gun!"

Poor Aleck obeyed; laid down his burden, tenderly kissed the pale face, rose with tears streaming from his eyes, loaded his piece, crying—still crying, went forward to the firing line, and cried and fought, and fought and cried, as long as there was any fighting to do. Country—duty—glory? Yes; but turning your back on an only brother, a heart's twin, moaning in deep distress and bleeding to death for want of your help!

The advance was tumultuous, yet not rapid, for the brave confederates fought well. With shrieking bullets, scattered puffs of smoke, and sharp reports, now soft- ened by distance, now near and deafening, the onward surge of Company K carried it some distance beyond where poor Clint Thrush lay moaning. He saw two of his comrades hurrying to the rear, and called to them with all his feeble strength, for help; but they paid no attention; they were nursing wounds of their own.

Mark Looney passed him going toward the fray, and Clinton begged piteously to be carried back.

"Arrah, me bye; tehk me canteen an' gimme yer gun an' yer cathridge-box! I'll jest give them divvles wan or two blessin's in yer oan name; an' thin I'll come back an' carry ye in like a lehdy a-ridin' in a coach an' four." And he too was gone.

An officer from brigade headquarters came to the fence and shouted for Captain Fargeon. Nobody paid any atten- tion to him, so he was forced, against his will, to come on into the melee, making a detour to avoid running over Clinton.

"Captain, I have orders from Gen. Peterkin that you are to halt as soon as you have developed the enemy's position, and retire at your discretion."

Fargeon called McClintock to him and communicated the message. Said Mac:

"Well, that means now. They are firing strongly from the woods; only, their own men being between them and us, they are forced to fire high."

"Very well, sir. You have the general's orders." And the relieved aide darted for the rear. Mac went one way and Fargeon the other, shouting, "Back! back!"

and motioning toward the fence; and the excited men reluctantly began their retreat, luckily, before the concealed portion of their foes got a fair chance at them. They brought in the confederate wounded (such as fell into their hands) with as much tenderness as was possible in the haste and confusion. The dead they left as they lay. Fargeon went to poor Clint Thrush, and, with help from Aleck and others, got him to the fence, where the boys quickly laid down a length of rails to pass him through. The transit was not made without some groans, and one cry that was almost a scream. Sharp bone ends were evidently loose in his flesh.

Then all the wounded were clustered together waiting for transportation homeward.

"I wonder if anybody will have sense enough to send us some stretchers! Oh, yes; here they come. Thank God, Dr. McShane knows enough to know that shots call for stretchers."

A feeble voice was heard from near by. It was Clinton's, as he lay by a tree, his head supported by his brother.

"Did we lick 'em, Lieutenant?"

"You bet we did! I counted three stone-dead. And just see our boys fetching in their wounded! One, two, three, four—right where we are."

Company K halted behind the fence and watched the opposite woods while waiting for orders. The pork and crackers brought by Mark and Ed were sparingly dealt out and contentedly munched, the prisoners who were not too badly hurt getting their bite with the rest. Canteens were generally empty before this, and certain men were now allowed to gather from their comrades as many as they could carry and go back to a little ditch they had crossed in their advance, fill them, and distribute them to their thirsty owners. Fargeon noticed Corporal Dugong very active and audible among the workers, so he must have been mistaken in the identity of the dead man.

The captain mingled with the men and ate a bit of cracker with a slice of co'd boiled salt pork (sweeter than fresh grass-butter) laid on it; took a pull at one of the canteens newly filled at the ditch (delicious nectar), and, looking round for fresh, new worlds to conquer, accepted the loan of Morphy's pipe, from which he took several cautious whiffs.

"Mac, what day of the week is this?"

"Let's see: we got our orders Wednesday, we sailed Thursday, we landed Friday, we marched Saturday—that's yesterday—to-day's Sunday, by my reckoning."

Captain William Fargeon, Sunday-school superintendent and temperance missionary, smiled grimly, then laughed aloud.

"What's the matter, captain?'

"Oh—nothing much," he answered; then, to himself, he added: "A fight, a swear-word, a drink of liquor, and a pipe—all on Sabbath morning!" and laughed again.

The men are resting gayly, at their ease, some in the shady corners of the worm fence, some under the trees hard by, among whose branches the cicadas are screaming their delight in the hot sunshine. It is scarcely more than twenty minutes since our boys leaped the fence to pursue the retreating foe, yet to some men it is a lifetime, to others the beginning of a long, slow, maimed existence.

In front, the young corn spreads its deep green far and wide, broken and disturbed by the deadly work that went on in and through and over it a little while ago.

Somewhere in its expanse, at some unmarked spots, lie three prostrate human figures. Enemies? No; former enemies, now insensate clods, to be neither hated nor feared.

The rest following a small affair, wherein we have had a success, or at any rate no serious loss or disaster, is a delightful interval to those alive and unhurt. One more yawning chasm past, one less deadly peril before us of those marked opposite our names in the illegible book of fate; a hard duty done this day, whether any one except us ever knows it or not; and perhaps a little dearly-loved honor and fame added to our few treasures. Something to talk of in camp; something to write of to the dear home-folks, now further away than ever. Something to remember to the day of death, be it near at hand or dim in the future. A great rebound of spirits from the terrible tension of the ordeal—a hilarity that seems natural even in caring for the suffering wounded or the quiet dead.

"Well, Clinton, old boy! Your turn to-day, mine next time. How do you feel?"

"First-rate, Captain."

"I guess Clint will come out all O K," said Aleck, who now had his arm under his brother's head as it lay on the stretcher, and was wiping off the sweat-drops of pain and weakness as they gathered on his forehead.

"All right? Of course he will! He'll be singing in the quartet again before we know it."

"I wonder if those fellows have any brothers on the other side!" said Clinton, turning his head with difficulty to where the wounded prisoners sat or lay in a row.

"Might be," said Fargeon, while the laugh died from his face. But his blood was flowing too free for long regrets. A smile chased away the pain and he added: "They had no business to be rebels—and then to come out and try to fight Company K!"

"Bully for you! Bully for all!" quavered Clinton. "What became of my gun?"

"Oh, little Mark got it," answered Aleck, "and * * he used it too!"

Fargeon had taken off his kepi.

"Why, Captain, did you get hit? Your forehead looks as if it had been grazed by a ball."

"No, no!" answered Will hastily, while the abraded forehead flushed up to the roots of his hair. "Brushed against something in passing."

The stretcher-bearers were now told off to help the hospital men, and our wounded carried to camp.

"Set the stretchers down at the hospital tent, and get four more and hurry back for the wounded rebs. Don't wait for these to be unloaded," shouted Mac.

"Four? Why, there are five to go," said Will.

"Oh, there's one who won't need a stretcher."

They went over to where a fine specimen of humanity was lying (and dying), a little apart from the rest. Young, strong, handsome, high-bred—curls, that might have been the pride of a doting mother, clustering round a brow that might have been the hope of an ambitious father. Eyes fit to shine as the heaven of love and trust to some happy bride, the light gone from them forever; the lids drawn back and the balls sunken so that it seemed as if their owner had been born blind. A bullet had torn clean through his lungs, and the breath made a dreadful noise escaping through the wound at every exhalation.

Fargeon wiped away the bloody froth that oozed from the wounded man's lips and over his downy beard, and tried to pour some drops of water into his mouth, but it ran out unswallowed. He asked the others the name of the dying man, and found it to be Huger. [Pronounced Hujee.]

No more "joy of battle" for Captain Fargeon. He walked away along the line, trying to forget the dying boy, and listened to the usual free comments of the private soldier.

"Now, why don't our boys back in camp move up and charge them woods? We've done our part, and now the big-bugs that sent us out ain't ready to follow up our victory!"

"Oh, dry up, Eph! What do you know about war? Ye don't know no more about war than a fish knows about water! War's jest pushin' men out to git killed and then pullin' 'em back to die of old age. Kind o' 'mark-time march;' keep a-steppin' an' never git ahead none."

In spite of the relaxation and repose, watchful eyes were always directed toward the front.

"Hello! They're sending out a flag of truce!"

The cry came from several parts of the line at once; and Fargeon ran to McClintock for advice, as usual.

"Sarg'nt Coggill and Chipstone, leave your guns an' go out—double-quick—halt them where you meet them, and find out what they want. Tell them if they come any nearer we'll fire on them, flag or no flag. One of you stay with 'em—Sarg'nt, you stay with 'em; keep your mouth shut and your eyes and ears open. Chipstone, you bring back the message."

The emissaries started, and our boys began to perch themselves on a fence.

"Down! Git down, all of you, you fools! Do you want to let them know how few there are of us? Let 'em think there's a battery and a whole brigade in line of battle right here, if they want to."

Soon Chipstone came running back.

"They want to see an officer who can treat for a truce to bury dead and care for the wounded."

"What's the rank of the officer with the flag?"

"I—don't know.   He had no shoulder-straps."

"No; they don't wear 'em.   You go back and find out."

Soon he made the journey out and back.

"A captain and a lieutenant."

"Well, Capt'n Fargeon, you will probably meet the captain, and take either me or Morphy with you."

"Oh, come along, McClintock.   We'll see what they want."

"Well, sir, will you instruct Lieut'nt Morphy to take charge of our men—to keep them hidden and watchful in front and on flanks?"

Morphy got his orders, and the others started.

"Mac, could it be that they are moving to cut us off?"

"No, not while the flag of truce is out.   They ain't Injins."

As they walked on, he added:

"Same time, this flag of truce is a mere pretense. They want to find out if there's a chance for a rush on us, to retrieve their little repulse of this morning.   Now, suppose your two guns were there and only K company to support them, and they found it out by this smart trick, and had a regiment in the edge of those woods—"

"Well, what then?"

"Why, the confederacy would be two guns ahead to-night.   Guns without infantry to back them are as helpless as baby-carriages."

They approached the two officers and the sergeant bearing the flag—a handkerchief tied on a gun-rammer.

The captain was a tall, pale, rather elderly gentleman, silent and rigidly grave. The lieutenant was the typical southern officer; thin and sallow, smooth-faced except a fringe of mustache over a sharp mouth, long black hair brushed behind his ears and falling to his collar; level brows and black eyes that shone with fierce, untamable light.

The four officers touched their caps as they met. The confederate lieutenant spoke:

"Gentlemen, I make you acquainted with Capt'n Huger, of the Lou'siana Fire-Eaters. I am Lieut. Judah, of the same reg'ment."

As the junior officer had spoken, McClintock replied, introducing Captain Fargeon and himself. Then the southerner went on:

"Gentlemen, as we were ovahmatched—I would say out numbahed—in our little affaiah of this morning, we thought best to retiah, and, in disobedience of the ordahs of Capt'n Huger and myself, some of ouah dead and wounded were left on the field."

The northerners bowed.

"Now, sah, Majah Leroy commanding the fo'ce in your immejate front, sen's his compliments and requests the cou'tesy of a truce fo' two houahs to cayah fo' ou' wounded and bury ou' dead."

Fargeon made an inclination to Mac to authorize him to reply, and he did so.

"Lieutenant, we have already cared for your wounded; and as to your dead, we are willing to send them over to your line by details of our men; or, according to rule, to forward your request to our commanding officer."

"Very well, sah. Do you mean that you will insist that yo' men shall be allowed to bring ou' dead quite

to ou' own lines, sah? Or that we shall leave them unburied, or come and take them by fo'ce, sah?"

"As to coming to take them by force, you know, Lieutenant, you didn't need a flag of truce to authorize you
to do that."

"By God, sah, if I had my way we would have had no
flag of truce, sah! We'd have had our battle-flag, sah,
to recovah ou' dead, sah!"

"We should have been glad to see you, Lieutenant.
There's room behind our lines for the rest of your force."

"By God, sah!—"

But the silent gentleman at his side laid his hand on
the youth's shoulder and quelled him by a look. Fargeon now interposed.

"Pardon, gentlemen, I think we should feel authorized
to have your dead brought to this place, and your men
allowed unmolested to take them into your lines."

The elder man, to whom Fargeon had addressed himself, bowed a silent assent to this.

Mac wrote a few lines in his book, and, tearing out the
leaf, gave it to Chipstone to deliver to Lieut. Morphy.
In a few minutes eight men were seen to leave the fence
and begin searching about among the corn-hills. Before
long three bodies clad in shabby gray, dirty and blood-
stained, were being slowly dragged toward the little
group, their helpless heels leveling the corn-plants as
they passed, their hatless heads dropped back, their
white mouths wide open, and their dead eyes staring hid-
eously toward the pitiless sky.

Captain Huger stood with his back to the work, but as
each corpse was laid down he gave one quick, searching,
agonized glance, and then turned instantly away.

"That is all, gentlemen."

The old captain heaved a long, deep sigh, seemingly of relief and hope.

"Are all the six others whom we miss, wounded and in your hands?"

"We have six in our hands, wounded or not."

"Are there any prisoners not wounded?"

"One. I have not yet taken his name."

"Can you describe him?" asked the lieutenant. But Captain Huger shook his head, intimating that he knew it was not the man they had in their minds. So the lieutenant changed the question.

"Can we obtain him by parole, exchange, or otherwise?"

"Personally we have nothing to say about parole or exchange."

"If we could lay our hands on him he would be shot at sundown."

"Then of course he can in no case be paroled or exchanged."

The Confederate lieutenant here whispered a few words to his senior, who replied with a nod; then turned his back and stood like a statue.

"There is one man in yo' hands, gentlemen, I wish informally to ask about, undah circumstances—"

"Do you mean Private Huger?"

"I do, sah."

"He is wounded in our hands."

"Severely?"

"Mortally."

A dreadful silence fell upon the group. No one knew how to break it. Fargeon, with a question in his look, pointed to the heroic figure beyond; and Judah answered with a nod that seemed to say, "Father and son."

The grief-stricken father never raised his hand to his eyes; but his frame wavered a little, and from time to time he bowed his head and shook it slightly, when one or two scattered drops would shine for an instant in the sun as they fell to the ground.

At last Mac spoke:

"With Capt'n Fargeon's permission, I propose that if Private Huger shall have died before the flag is withdrawn, we shall deliver his body as we have the others."

"Very good, sah. And if not, sah?"

"Then I don't know what more we can say," said Mac; to which Fargeon added:

"Except that we shall treat the rebel wounded as we do our own."

Judah flared up again in an instant.

'I'll thank you, Capt'n Fargeon, not to presume upon the protection affo'ded you by a flag of truce! I'll thank you, sah, to speak of Confederate soldiers befo' Confederate officahs with propah respect, sah!"

"Lieutenant, it was quite accidental. I will repeat the remark in the form I should have given it at first: We shall treat wounded enemies as we would wounded friends."

"Very well, sah. I am moah than satisfied. You speak of us as yo' enemies; I reg-yahd that as the most honorable name you could bestow, sah!"

Fargeon answered with a good-humored smile. How far he was from looking at them as they seemed to look at us!

Said Mac, listlessly plucking a corn-leaf and tearing it into long, thin, green ribbons:

"I need not say that if Private Huger shall live long enough, we shall be glad to favor an exchange for one of our men, if you have one to offer."

"A wounded man, sah?"

"No; a well man."

"Well, sah, I assume to say that that would be an
exchange giving you-uns an advantage which Capt'n
Huger would decline to give you, sah."

"Then, gentlemen, as we have no more immediate business, we propose to withdraw."

"And how about ouah flag, sah?"

"We shall consider it withdrawn within half an hour
after we leave you, unless we in the meantime act under
it as proposed."

"Very well, sah! Capt'n Huger, the gentlemen are
ready to retiah."

The dignified father turned toward them, his face like
that of a stone image. Fargeon impulsively extended his
hand, but the other seemed not to see it. He touched
his hat, turned on his heel again, and stood motionless
while our men retraced their steps, pushing down their
sword-hilts so that the scabbards should not drag against
the corn-blades.

Our wounded had been sent in and the stretchers
brought back for the rebels. All were loaded except
Huger, who was still alive, though nearly done with his
struggle. Mac went to the stretchers and made a slight
examination of the sufferers. Then he said to one of them:

"Get up and walk."

"Oh, Lieutenant, my arm's shot to pieces; I can't
travel."

"You don't travel on your arm. Get out of that. I
want it for Huger."

"Oh, for Cap Huger's son? Surely I'll get up. Could
ye give me suth'n' to tie my arm so it won't hang down?"

"Get up! I ain't here to wait on you," and he made
as if he would tip the man off on the ground.

"Oh, hold on!" cried Fargeon. "I can't stand that!
Here, boy, let me tie my handkerchief in your button-

hole; now let me slip your wrist through and clasp your hands together—so!"

The fellow submitted in wondering silence, and then got up and sat down on a log, nursing his unlucky arm as if it were a pet dog.

They lifted Huger on the stretcher. Mac looked at him critically.

"Guess we'll call him dead, captain, and give his friends the job of burying him. What do you say?"

"I say yes."

"All right, then. Here, Mark, you and Chipstone and Bob and Coggill carry this body over to the men at the flag. Remember it's a dead man—never anything else— you remember?" And he winked at them individually and collectively.

Fargeon saw them reach the place; saw them lift off the load and come back with the stretcher; saw that there were only two figures instead of three visible at and about the flag; and felt what he could not see—the desolate old man prone among the corn-hills, with his son in his arms. One more embrace, after so many, to the baby, boy, youth and man.

"Now, Mac, what do we do with our dead man? Who was it?"

"One of our men killed? First I've heard of it. Must be out on the flanks somewhere."

"No; right near here. I passed him as I came up. Here—I can find the very log he lay behind, in half a minute."

"Well, let's be quick," said Mac. "I'm expecting some shells over. Of course you noticed that their white flag was tied onto a gun-rammer."

Will was ashamed to confess that he had not noticed anything of the kind.

CHAPTER IX

BURSTING SHELLS.

FARGEON and McClintock found the gap in the fence, debated which way from that had been the point where the former had rejoined after his trip to headquarters, started back, and soon came upon the very log. Will approached it with awe-struck seriousness, ready to turn over the corpse and look in the face of a dead friend. There was nothing there.

"No body—nobody!" cried Fargeon, whereat Mac laughed.

"What does it mean?" asked Will, standing on the log and looking about to see if he could be mistaken. No! There in the distance stood the memorable white-oak! Then he got down where the man had lain, and found dim foot-tracks, and marks that might have been made by the toes of boots. Also a dint that might have come from the butt of a musket. Then he cried to Mac to come and look—at not less than a dozen cartridges, partly hidden under the log.

"It means a skulker," said Mac. "A corporal, too, you say? If I can prove it on him, I go for tearing his stripes off in the face of the whole regiment; then having him bucked and gagged, put on police duty for a month and docked of a year's pay! That's a thing that's *got* to be squelched!"

"Why, Mac—is it common?"

"Common? Don't ask me! Every battle is fringed with 'em. The fine fellows get killed and wounded and the skulkers live forever, and their widows draw pensions afterward."

"I guess I can pick him out, Mac. I'll let you know if I succeed."

He strolled off to the line and joined one group of gossipers after another, telling them a little of the scene at the flag of truce, concerning which they were extremely curious.

"Cale Dugong, where were you in the fight?"

"I was right in over yonder, Cap, or a leetle more to the left. I was just telling the boys how I knocked over two of the Johnnies—I shouldn't wonder if one of the wounded men see me aim at him. Maybe not, though. But I know one of the killed did; and it was the last thing he ever did see, too."

"Which two of our men were you between?"

"Oh, I started in between Eph Tolliver an' Tom Looser, didn't I, boys?"

"Yes; that's the way we stood coming up through the woods, an' after we got to the fence, before the rebs come out."

"Well, there's where it was, then. After the reserve jined, I dunno who I was with, I was a-firin' so fast. I bet there ain't a man in the company fired more cartridges than I did!" He opened his cartridge-box, and, to be sure, it was half empty.

"Maybe that's because you fired so often before you were told to fire! Step this way, Caleb: I've got to have a talk with you."

Caleb obeyed, his face turning rapidly from "red as a beet to white as a sheet," the boys said, winking at each other as he disappeared in the wake of the captain.

They walked to the log in grim silence.

"Pick up those cartridges and put them back in your box."

"Why, Cap—"

"Silence, sir! Now throw some leaves over where your toes and the butt of your gun scratched the dirt. Hide your shame!"

Caleb obeyed.

"What ye goin' t' do to me, Cap? I was sick—honest, I was." And he proceeded to give some plausible functional reason for his defection.

When he had done, Fargeon pointed back to his place in the ranks, saying sternly:

"Private Dugong, go back to your duty."

"Ain't I a corp'ral no more, Cap?"

"No. We don't want skulking corporals. If you resign and rip off your stripes, all right; if you don't, it will be done for you. If you are brought before a court-martial, you may be shot for leaving the ranks under fire. Your life depends on your future conduct."

He left Caleb sitting on the log, helpless with fright. The culprit soon braced up, however, and blustered back into his place.

"Well, I won't stand it! I'll go back to the ranks! Any private could make a mistake an' fire without orders, an' nobody'd say a word to him; but let a corp'ral do it wunst and he gits abused like a dog! Yes, sir! You needn't call me Corp'ral Cale no more!" And they did not.

Fargeon told Mac what he'd done, and the latter remarked:

"Well, that's good in one way, anyhow, even if it's bad in another. It gives us another chance to promote a man. Clinton Thrush is a sergeant; he'll be off for a long time, if he ever comes back. We can promote a corporal to his place and raise two men from the ranks."

"Hard on Clinton."

"No! He ought to be a lieutenant by that time. Lots of vacancies coming; not to speak of new regiments."

"I'd like to see little Mark a corporal, for particular reasons."

"Mark'll be one, of course, though we'll lose him as our orderly. Ought to have been one from the start, knowing as much as he does. How would Clinton's brother Alec do for a sergeant, and Chipstone for a corporal?"

"Couldn't be better."

Orders now came from headquarters to return to camp at once. [The two guns had been overtaken and turned backward.] Word was passed along the line to come to "attention" and "prepare to retire as skirmishers;" but before the order could be obeyed a flash in the opposite woods sent across the corn-field a slight gleam visible in spite of the sunshine. Soon followed the roar of a distant field-piece, and, almost at the same instant with the sound, the shriek of a near shell passing over their heads; then among the trees behind them there was another great bang as the shell burst; then a humming, as of a hundred gigantic bees, from the fragments of the shell as they flew through the air, hunting the neighborhood for victims.

The men in the immediate vicinity dropped flat down as if they had been struck by lightning. It seemed impossible for human nature to stand up before and beneath the yelling, flying beast. Fargeon dropped among the rest. He felt as if he could not hug mother earth closely enough—he would have liked to dig a hole, with his nails, to hide in. Almost before the echoes of the first shot died away another rang out, with the same series of sounds. The shriek of a shell is more appalling than the scream of an angry horse.

Will knew that something must be done, but what? He wished he could ask Mac. As he framed the wish he heard Mac's drawl above him; raised his head, and there was the bold fellow erect and cool, standing on the top rail of the fence, steadying himself with his left hand on a fence stake, while he peered under his right at the opposite woods.

"Two pieces—that's all. I wish I knew how much infantry they've got! Can't have been much while we were fighting, or they'd have come out and supported their skirmishers. No matter, though. We couldn't venture to go for the guns with only one company. It would take all our men to drag the pieces—allowing for losses before we got hold of 'em. If I had a regiment I'd try it; I would! That is, of course, with your consent, Captain."

Will got up and began to brush the dust off his clothes, but by this time the first gun was reloaded, and again he saw the flash and heard the shriek, the double explosion and the humming—heard them from the ground as before; Mac still perched high above him. The third missile struck in the corn-field, the fertile soil being too mellow for a ricochet.

"They are getting the range," coolly observed Mac. "Let's get back, Captain, whenever you are ready."

"The sooner the better," said Fargeon, now shamed

out of his nervousness. "If you'll go to the right I'll go to the left."

"Very well—oh, I thought you said I was to go to the right."

"Do; and I will go to the left."

"Yes, Captain; but you are going to the right now."

"Surely, surely! There; I'll go to the right and you the left. I forgot that I should always talk of right or left as if we were facing the enemy."

The long, straggling, scattered line now worked slowly toward camp, the halting portion of the men always selecting trees, and peering out from behind them as the moving men retired past. The shells still rang merrily, and the tree-tops suffered some damage, but nobody was hurt. Will asked Mac if it wasn't wonderful.

"Naw!" answered Mac contemptuously, true infantryman that he was. "Artillery scares, but doesn't kill. It's only the musket that means business." And he tramped back and forth along the line, talking incessantly, as was evidently his habit in action.

As the sense of danger again wore off, Will's spirits took another rebound, and he moved and talked as Mac did, just as if there were no peril in shells. Then he heard a man near him cry out "Ouch!" and saw him drop his gun and begin squeezing the right hand under his left arm as a boy might who had pounded his thumb with a hammer. One of the buzzing iron bees had evidently stung. Will picked up the gun, and caught a glimpse of the hurt hand as the man hurriedly and anxiously inspected it. It was a mere glimpse, but it showed a broken bone, and bloody skin and flesh both fat and lean. Will told the sufferer to hurry on to camp; and himself resumed his tramping back and forth, carrying the gun and feeling a little nausea.

A new depression seized him; his mind's eye saw only the horrors of the day, and his mind's ears heard only the bubbling escape of air from Private Huger's breast. His fancy pictured this last wounded man going through life with a maimed, misshapen, hideous, useless right hand; a burden to himself and the world. The cannon firing behind them suddenly stopped.

"Now, look out for them, boys!" shouted Mac. "Every man take a tree when he halts, and give 'em 'Hail Columbia' if they're tryin' for a rush."

Will repeated the order, and as Mac didn't take a tree he did not either, but moved back and forth as before.

"Cap Fargeon don't take no tree," he heard one halted man call to his neighbor.

"Cap hain't got no use for no tree," called back the one addressed.

Once more a happy glow filled his heart, and he felt a lump rise in his throat and dew start to his eyes. He loved the men who had praised him. He loved all the men in his company. Then he thought of their being food for powder; the mere sport of fate. "The best fellows get killed; while the skulkers live forever, and their widows draw pensions afterward," Mac had said. Oh, how can a just God permit such things? So did pleasure and pain follow each other across his abnormally excited soul.

No enemy appeared, and soon the movement became a mere scattered tramp to the rear. Fargeon approached McClintock and they walked along together.

"They got their full ration in the corn-field," said Mac.

"Yes— poor devils!"

"If we hadn't met their flag of truce where we did, they would have found out how weak we are, and tried to get back at us, for keeps."

They walked on in silence, Will thinking of Private Huger and his father.

"Oh, Mac! can't this business be stopped?"

"It ought to be. It's a cursed shame."

"Think of that poor old Capt'n Huger!"

"Ya-as. The old cuss ought to know better. But, then, both sides do it when they get a chance."

"Do what, do you mean?"

"Why, use the flag of truce to snoop information."

"Oh! that was not what I had in mind."

"What then?"

"Oh, the whole beastly job – the slaughter, the wounds, the maimings, the bereavements."

"Oh, I see! Well, how can we help them?"

"Just look at it! Take that young Huger, cut off in his prime and promise, shot through the lungs in a corn-field by a man that had nothing against him—Chipstone, as good a fellow as ever lived, without a hard feeling in his heart toward any man on earth; I can see that Chip feels it. He looks like a ghost, and hasn't opened his lips since we picked up the poor boy."

"Oh, Chip'll get over it."

"I hope he will; or I'm afraid he will; I don't know which."

"Let him go and take a good look at Clint Thrush's leg. That'll help him."

"Oh, my God! It makes me sick." Will threw his disengaged hand up toward the unanswering sky.

"Well, how are we going to carry on war if you look at all those things?"

"It ought never to be carried on at all!"

"Oh, of course! Bad the best way you can fix it. But that's none of my business. Our job is to make war; somebody else's job is to make peace."

"I wonder there aren't lots of our fellows poking over to see what the firing is all about."

"Like as not they never heard a thing—except these last cannon-shots."

"What? That fusilade not heard in camp?"

"No. You see the wind is in our faces as we go back. And then the air is dry and thin; that makes a wonderful difference. If it had been rainy they might have heard the muskets in spite of the woods."

"Well, that young aide-de-camp must have told we were engaged."

"Yes, he told it at headquarters of course; and then probably the stretchers were started and the brigade was called out under arms on the color line. No chance for anybody to wander in the woods after that. Still, as you say, there ought to have been messengers constantly going and coming—would have been if headquarters amounted to shucks."

"To be sure, he brought us orders to retire."

"Ya-as, but how did they know we *could* retire in proper order, bringing dead and wounded. Suppose we'd met a regiment, instead of a company, and they'd outflanked us and wrapped us all up!"

"The prisoners we sent in told the story."

"Thanks to our good luck and good fighting. not to their good management."

So they tramped along through the scattered underbrush, spotted with sunshine and shadow.

Meanwhile an unlooked-for glory and pleasure was in store for them.

CHAPTER X

HONOR AND OBLIVION.

OMPANY—HALT! By the right flank, close intervals—MARCH!"

The skirmishers were coming in sight of camp. They faced into line (fronting toward the enemy, of course), and re-formed, re-counted and re-dressed the ranks disordered by their losses.

The officers drew swords. "By fours, right—FACE! Right shoulder-shift—ARMS! Forward by file right—MARCH! Left—left—left—left."

As they neared the camp they saw that the three regiments of the brigade were under arms on the color line, standing at "rest." [They had been called out, as Mac had guessed they would be, at the sound of the cannon.]

A wild "Heigh!" started spontaneously from the long brigade line when the head of Company K came in sight. Again and again it rose, springing up in one part of the line after another, and always spreading along the ranks from end to end, while the men swung their caps or raised them high in air on the points of their bayonets.

Somewhere in K's rank was heard a strong voice (alas!

not Clinton Thrush's!) starting the company song, to which all burst into chorus at the proper time:

"Company K has shown the way.
　BULLY FOR YOU! BULLY FOR ALL!
Your turn's a coming some other day.
　BULLY FOR YOU! BULLY FOR ALL!"

The other companies of the Sixth took up the song, and then the rest of the brigade caught on in a hearty though desultory and irregular fashion. They paid small attention to words. "Company K! Company K!" was good enough for the song, and "Bully for you! Bully for all!" was always ready when anybody thought it was time for the chorus.

Fargeon was going to lead his men straight in, past the right flank of the brigade, but as he approached he saw the commanding officer (lieutenant-colonel) of the nearest regiment motioning him down toward the left flank. Not knowing just what he would be at, Will changed direction to the right, and soon found that K was to be highly honored.

The lieutenant-colonel brought the regiment to "attention," with arms at shoulder. Then, to the surprise and delight of the home-coming skirmishers, he cried:

"PRESENT—ARMS!"

Fargeon turned to the happy, excited faces of Company K, and called "SHOULDER—ARMS!" [The marching salute was with arms at "shoulder."] Tears of gratified pride rose to his eyes—why, he did not know. The springs of smiles and tears lie close together.

The other regiments in turn were called to "attention," and the salute repeated; and the Sixth, when its turn came, gave three regular cheers and a "tiger" to its distinguished brothers.

At last K reached its tent-street. The coats were old;

the caps, once so jaunty, were in all possible shapes of crushed, misshapen disfigurement—the whole uniform was shabby, with various shades of faded blue and various signs of sun and rain, wear and tear; but yet its wearers were clothed with honor and distinction. Company K had fought, suffered, triumphed, and had brought in prisoners and trophies.

"Company—HALT! Break ranks—MARCH!" And with a last "Heigh!" and the usual slapping of musket-stocks, the boys darted into their tents, laid aside their arms and accoutrements, and flung themselves flat on their backs for welcome, grateful rest. They had not known till now how tired they were. The absence of their comrades under arms on the color line, gave them an interval of delicious solitude; utter silence reigned; their eyes closed as if by magic, and some were asleep almost on the instant.

But George Chipstone lay staring at the canvas above him as if he could never sleep again.

Fargeon had noticed that Colonel Puller was not with the regiment under arms. In fact, all the regiments were in charge of lieutenant-colonels. He went at once to the colonel's tent to report, but learned from an orderly that his commander, with the other colonels, was at brigade head-quarters, where some festivity was in progress on the occasion of a sword presentation to the valiant Y. R. Puller, of the Sixth Illinois. A committee from his home district had arrived, which would have taken him greatly by surprise if he had not known all about it beforehand, and now he was entertaining the delegation at headquar-ters, where speeches were being made, toasts drunk, and a "good time" was enjoyed at a spread given by Colonel Puller to the general, his staff, the visitors, and other invited guests.

Will made his way to brigade headquarters—a neighboring farm-house—and heard, from the open windows, sounds of merriment that jarred on his ears; that festive volubility which is so repulsive to a sad and sober listener. He sent in his name to Colonel Puller; no answer came out for a long time, because the messenger dared not interrupt the speaking; and when word did come it was:

"Colonel Puller sends his compliments to Capt. Fargeon, and requests him to call at his quarters in an hour."

He went back to his own tent sick at heart, the reaction from excitement and tension of nerves taking full possession of soul and body. He threw himself prone along his rude couch and pressed his eyeballs hard with his fingers. "Who am I? Am I Will Fargeon, or am I a Sabbath-breaking, tobacco-smoking, swearing, drinking, murdering ruffian? Who was it storming up and down that man's corn-field, glad to see my friends killing other people's friends? Glad Chipstone's bullet plowed through the lung of that splendid old man's splendid son! Glad my men fired low and sure while theirs fired high and wild! Glad about those corpses with flies sucking the unshed tears from their eye sockets!

"That was just about church-time; when Sally was sitting at the sweet-toned organ, playing soft and low; while the sun was throwing through the stained glass that special ray that always makes her hair look like an aureole. I can hear her voice chanting, 'And on earth peace, good will to men;' while I was screaming through the din, 'Fire low, men! Aim every time!'

"Is it all a horrid nightmare? No—there is the wall of the tent; I can feel the roughness of it with my fingers. What a looking hand! How horribly shabby I am all over! On earth fire low—peace—aim your piece every time. That's a pun, isn't it?" And he fell asleep.

"Hello!" called a vinous voice in spirituous accents. "Hello! Capt'n Fargeon, I believe."

"Ye-es, sir; I believe so too."

"Well, Captain, I represent the 'Fulcrum,' as you may have heard. I just asked Colonel Puller *who* had the honor of commanding our force in the little ruction this morning, and he named you." [Silence.] "Now, Cap, I being who I am, and you being who you are, you may readily fancy my object in disturbing your rosy slumbers."

"And what can I do for you, Mr. ——?"

"Call me whatever you please, Cap—it's all one—when you talk to me you talk to the 'Fulcrum.' That is, I presume, a sufficient introduction. You had but one company, I understand; and I suppose the force you met outnumbered yours two to one, eh? Or was it ten to one this time?"

"Mr.—Mr.—Fulcrum, I may be wrong, but as I understand my duty, it is to make my report in the first instance to my immediate superior, Colonel Puller."

"Oho! Red tape, eh? First lesson in tactics for new beginners is red tape!" [Silence.] "Now, once more, Captain, and for the last time, I ask if you will furnish the public through our columns the details of your alleged skirmish of this morning."

Will slowly rose, slowly pulled aside the tent-flap, pointed in silence toward the outside, and waited till the upstart, with a contemptuous snort, departed.

All was dark, dismal, disgusting, degraded—well-nigh intolerable. Will said to himself:

"Lucky there's no whisky at hand—I should be almost tempted to take some to put me back into that contemptible state of ignoble self-complacency."

Suddenly he bethought himself of his pipe. He found it and filled it; then, looking around for a paper to light at the camp-fire, his eye fell upon he letter to be delivered "if I fall," and he hastened to crumple and burn it, as if it had been something to be ashamed of.

After Fargeon had made his report to Col. Puller, the latter joyfully welcomed the young dispenser of fame, and submitted to the inevitable interview with scarcely disguised gratification, flattering frankness, and unlimited whisky and cigars.

Fargeon was very glad of this, for he would have been sorry to be the means of depriving his brave fellows of the solace that flows from public mention of public service. As to his personal share in the skirmish, he held it in very humble esteem, and would try not to grieve if the offense he had given should result in his being deprived of anything beyond a bare mention of his name as commanding the fighting force. He knew that some bright eyes would glisten, and some friendly faces would smile with approval, on merely knowing that he was on hand and had his share in the manly fray.

Then he let his fancy roam a little along the road to fame—so easy for the eyes of the soldier, and so hard for his feet—and read in advance the letters and newspapers that were to reach him through the mails of the next month or two if he should live so long. Sara Penrose? Surely; sweetest and best of all. Her father? Yes; urging that to God should be given the glory. Families of his soldiers? Yes, indeed! Business friends? Probably some; perhaps even one from Mayer Moss-Rosen, his close competitor in the bitter rivalry of trade. How gratifying and consoling *that* would be!

To return to our resting boys: The men of the brigade under arms were relieved from their tiresome confinement on the color-line; not as soon as they might have been, but as soon as the attention of the brigadier-general could be drawn from Puller's hospitable board and turned in their direction. Then the rest of the Sixth swarmed over Company K's quarters and put a speedy end to all repose.

Over and over did the men have to tell of their "baptism of fire." Cale Dugong was perhaps the most graphic and soul-satisfying narrator; George Chipstone the least, for he lay in his tent and scarcely opened his lips.

"Killed a fine young chap," said the others in a whisper, to account for his "horrors."

"Well, what of it? That's what we come out for," said Dugong. "I expect I killed two. Seen 'em drop, anyhow, an' I'm glad of it!"

When Mark brought up the officers' supper he mentioned Chip's predicament to Captain Fargeon, and the captain thought he ought to do something for the good fellow. He had Mark send him up.

"Chipstone, you and Clinton are great friends, aren't you?"

"Yes, Captain," answered the other in a hollow voice.

"Let's go over to the hospital, and cheer him up a little. You get his things together and bring them with you. I'll pass you along."

As they walked Will said: "A Chicago newspaperman is in camp. I suppose our friends at home will get news by day after to-morrow of the good job we did to-day."

No answer.

"Those rebels seem to think they are going to destroy the great United States of America! We have *got* to teach them that it can't be done, while any of us are living. You and I may fall; some other good men will step into our places. The southerners will find they've 'bit off more than they can chaw,' as the country folks say. *They* began it, but *we'll* stay and finish it. Don't you say so?"

"Oh, I suppose it's got to be done by somebody."

"Of course it has! And the bitterer the lessons we give them, the sooner they'll learn the great truth. Did you notice how savage that rebel lieutenant was?"

"Wasn't he!"

"Slave-holding seems to have made those men crazy with pride and foolishness. Now, I haven't got anything against that fellow, but I can see that nothing but blood-letting will give him common sense."

"It's no use to go easy on 'em."

"No. Any kind of half-way fighting would be sheer cruelty. It would be like the fellow who was too soft-hearted to cut his dog's tail off all at once, so he cut it off an inch at a time."

Chipstone gave a half laugh at this illustration, and they reached the hospital—a neighboring barn pressed into the service. Long rows of cots covered the floor in every direction. They were chiefly occupied with sick men, as the visitors observed as they passed and asked the way to the corner devoted to the wounded.

The great doors at each side of the barn were wide open, the breeze swept through, and the low-descending sun shone kindly in with level rays. Attendants moved about here and there, carrying to the disabled soldiers such rude comforts as a field hospital affords. Pale faces looked at the visitors, and two or three voices called to them:

"Cap, got any newspapers?"

Will was sorry he had no reading matter to relieve their tedium, and made a mental note of what should be his first care on the morrow.

They made straight for the cots devoted to their own

9

companions, and the eyes of the Company K boys lighted up at their approach, and even the wounded confederates seemed to smile at their late antagonists. Familiar voices greeted them: "Hello, Captain! Hello, Chipstone!"

Both gave a hearty hand-clasp to each prostrate comrade. Clinton Thrush was the most seriously wounded, and another—the man who had his hand hurt—sat by his side waving a leafy branch to keep the flies off his exposed and bandaged leg. Clint knew them, but fever had come on, and he talked incessantly and incoherently, in a voice of weakness and excitement.

"Bully for you! Bully for all! Company K in the corn-field. Says Mac, 'Forward, boys!' and I heard him say 'Forward boys!' and I did forward boys! Cap, I'll leave it to you if I didn't forward boys when he sung out 'Forward boys!' First thing I knew I didn't know anything! Give a man all the appellations in the world and take away his consignments, and what'll he offer at next? But *then!* Aleck is my brother. That's nothing against him. Mac had no call to be hard on Aleck for being my brother. Oh, Captain—you'll stand by Aleck, if he *is* my brother, won't you? Don't let Mac hurt him for being my brother. Him an' I are all the boys mother's got—except the girls. Oh, mother! Oh, mother!" And he began to cry in a foolish fashion.

To divert his thoughts, and if possible calm his shattered nerves, Will began in a gentle voice:

<blockquote>"Our God he saw us from on high."</blockquote>

And almost on the instant the poor fellow took up the melody, and in a voice like his own clear tenor, only sublimated, as if made of the breath of Heaven itself, he sang and sang until every other sound was hushed into silence; and still the sweet, touching strain soared

THE GREAT DOORS WERE WIDE OPEN.—Page 129.

aloft and floated out into the fading, dying day. Never afterward, never as long as he lives, can Will sing that strain; nor can he even hear it sung without a choking in his throat and a rush of tears to his eyes.

An attendant brought the sufferer a soothing drink, and he became calm and quiet. Will let go his hand and turned to talk with the surgeon, who was attending the confederate wounded.

"Captain," said the doctor, "I'm glad to see you. The boys are all doing well except Clinton. We are going to try to save his life and maybe his leg, but I don't know about it. If he were at home, in his natural climate and surroundings, he would be all right. But here —blood thinned by hot weather, hard work, and poor food—"

"Why not send him home at once, doctor?"

"Oh, of course we can't send every wounded man home. Ambulances can't be spared, nor attendants provided for individual enlisted men, sick or wounded. They have to be treated together."

"Great heavens! Must the brave boys stay here and die when they might go home and live?"

"Well, how would you fix it?"

"Oh, I don't know! Any way to save lives and limbs. The whole State of Illinois ought to come down for them if necessary!"

"The state won't do it, and can't. If she'll send us well men to take their places when we lose them, that's all we can ask."

"When will you decide about Clinton?"

"In the moring we shall know. We won't amputate if we can save'the leg, and we won't amputate if it isn't going to be any use."

"How—any use?"

"Well, if he can't live anyhow. In Mexico we didn't have much luck with large stumps. So much against the patient; so many died of trouble with the stump—they call it blood-poisoning nowadays—that we got to feel as if we might as well let them die without the knife as after it."

"Clinton's brother Aleck ought to be with him."

"Well, why not have him detailed as hospital nurse?"

"The very thing! I'll attend to it to-night."

The doctor smiled enigmatically, but did not say anything more. Fargeon spent the next hour passing from cot to cot; chatting with the men, making memoranda of their little needs and wishes, comforting and encouraging them in every way; his own spirit growing calmer and happier in this congenial task. It was the pleasantest hour of his day, this stormy Sunday.

"Here's where I belong," said he to himself. "Saving life, instead of destroying it; giving comfort and consolation; making peace, instead of war. Blessed are the peacemakers. Oh, how I wish I had such a job as this instead of that other—that infernal corn-field!"

As they walked back, Chip said: "What did the doctor say about Clint?"

"Very doubtful."

"Which, leg or life?"

"Both. If the fever goes off, the leg must probably *come* off; and if they amputate the leg, he'll have a poor chance to get over it."

"Great God! Is that so?"

"Yes. Likely that bullet has silenced Clinton Thrush's singing for good."

"Curse the bullet—and the man that fired it!"

"And those who sent him to fire it," added Fargeon.

As they walked on in silence he said to himself:

"I guess Chip is all right again."

When he spoke to Mac about sending Aleck to serve in the hospital, the lieutenant gave a snort of dissatisfaction.

"Why, Aleck Thrush is one of the best men in the company! If they call on us for a hospital detail we can pick out men who will be no loss; but Aleck Thrush—! The hospital's the place for the trash that haven't got snap enough to fight—the grannies in trousers—but Aleck, he's a *man!*"

"All the same, Company K won't keep him away from his brother while I have anything to say about it." ("But I guess I won't go into the hospital service myself just at present.")

Next morning was rainy, but the requisition in Company K for an enlisted man to serve as hospital attendant came promptly, and Aleck was sent. He carried with him every old newspaper there was in the whole brigade. The poor fellow's trembling delight was a sight to see. He sang for joy and set off for Clinton's bedside running like a deer.

"See him scoot! Aleck always was the beater to run; he beat us all in a foot-race like we was standing still; but I'll bet this time he's a-beatin' himself!"

Speed uselessly made. Aleck might as well have run in the opposite direction. Before he reached the barn-hospital he met four men carrying a stretcher, using their disengaged hands in restraining the weak, frantic struggles of Company K's first martyr—the brave fellow, the good man, the sweet singer, De Witt Clinton Thrush. His ravings had become a terror and a danger to the other sick and wounded, and he was being carried away out of their hearing.

"Christ! Is that my brother? Here, Clint! Old

boy, don't ye know Aleck? There, there, there, there!" The soothing tones reached the sufferer's ears and heart, and he threw his arms around Aleck's neck and tried to climb off the stretcher by their help, while the wounded leg bled afresh.

Expelled from the hospital, surrounded by sighing woods through which the rain dropped drearily, no shelter in the world open to him to die in, home and mother and sisters five hundred miles away!

Late the next afternoon Aleck crept back to camp with a piece of board he had somewhere found; and all night he hacked and carved at it until he had made a deep-cut and legible inscription to distinguish his brother's lonely grave. Our forces did not hold this position; and after we retired it is probable that some enemy found the spot and destroyed the simple record, or perhaps the wood-fires burned it, or hogs rooted it up. But what difference did that make? Nobody ever went back to look for it.

A mail from home! Oh, joy! Oh, love! Oh, curiosity! Oh, wild excitement! In every place that offers anything like privacy in the rude publicity of camp-life eager faces bend over letters. Lavish dimes (from the private soldier's scanty purse) are spent for every newspaper that has reached the sutler's tent for sale.

"Dear, dear, dear soldier—otherwise known as William Fargeon, captain of Company K. * * * To tell you what happens (of interest) in Chicago while you all are away making the only news we care about, wouldn't take a page. To tell you all that doesn't happen would take a quire, a ream, a prairie of foolscap. * * *

"Dear old Colin Thorburn comes often. I think he feels as if he were responsible for your leaving us, and calls as a kind of expiatory duty. Last night he sang

> "There is nae luck aboot the hoose,
>   There is nae luck at a',
>   There is nae luck aboot the hoose
>   Syne our gude mon's awa,"

in a cracked old voice, so gentle and sympathethic that it wrung tears from the eyes of a poor goose who is too, too fond of you.

"I have come to the conclusion that woman is an absurdly incomplete being. I think that if Eve had been made before Adam she would have spent all her time moping about the garden, crying, 'Why—is this all? Nothing but sun, moon and stars, sky and earth, animals, flowers, fruits, and *me!*' (She wouldn't know grammar yet, poor thing!) 'I don't think much of such a show as *this*, and I want my money back.' * * *

"Oh! Merciful Heaven! Here comes the Fulcrum saying that the Sixth has had a fight and that some men were wounded! Oh, I hope you were not in it! I am sure you were not hurt or they would have said so. They only mention Col. Puller, and say that he was *not* hurt. How my heart beats! I hope you were not in the fight at all—I don't know why—it is a useless thing to wish or to hope. It is what you went for!

"How unhappy I am! I am leaning back so that my tears shall not fall on the paper. There—I have leaned forward so that some *should* fall on it. Do you see those two crinkly spots? Those are tears, dear, shed for you. Now I must stop before I write down past them.

"Your sorrowing, loving,

"SALLY."

As soon as Fargeon could look at Sally's letter with any eyes but those of tenderness and happiness, he began to wonder at the fact that there should be any doubt as to whether he had been wounded, or had even been present at the skirmish. He secured a copy of the paper which had sent down the correspondent whom he had met. He got it, he read the narrative it contained—read it with amazement.

"DID WE LICK 'EM, CAPTAIN?"

PAGE 101.

CHAPTER XI.

T the time of the war, Chicago was already great—even down to her daily press. It was the Fulcrum which had sent forth the reporter whom Fargeon had met and had offended; and he pounced upon the Fulcrum with all the eagerness of a young citizen-soldier looking for the home-picture of his maiden fight.

First there was a column and more of the "sword-presentation ceremonies," including a full report of the "impromptu remarks of our correspondent." Then followed a short statement of the "affair." This is the substance of the tale:

———

Col. Y. R. Puller, of the Sixth, had been surprised by a demand for a detail of skirmishers "to find the enemy," on the very morning after his arrival. But when did that brave patriot ever hesitate at the call of duty? He instantly deployed a company for the service, perilous and bloody though it promised to be, and as the result showed it was destined to be in fact. And right well was that service performed! The brave colonel "found

138

the enemy," as he had been ordered to do—found them in force, not only infantry, but artillery! Yet he managed by his admirable arrangements and gallant fighting, to inflict loss far in excess of what he sustained. Four rebels were left dead on the field; five prisoners, most of them wounded, fell into our hands. Including the dead and wounded carried off by the retreating foe, their loss could not have been less than forty or fifty, while our entire loss was only five wounded. Fortunately Col. Puller was not himself among the wounded, for the army and the country could ill spare officers of his caliber. Whenever Col. Y. R. Puller leaves the field it should be at the call of his fellow-citizens of the ninth district, who think that he can do more service to the great cause in Congress, battling the fire in the rear, fighting the insidious enemy at home, than at the front, facing the more honorable and less dangerous foes in the field.

That was all. The gentlemanly dispenser of fame and maker of history had avenged his affront by omitting all mention of the real fighters, wounded and unwounded, in his words sent home for the eager perusal of their families, friends, and neighbors. He had managed to wound the unwounded, and to withhold balm from the hurts of the disabled.

———·

That particular movement southward, wherein Company K took its baptism of fire, turned out to be "one of our failures." The brigade was ordered back to Cairo, and back it journeyed, leaving to our enemies our footprints and the graves of our dead.

In the twenty-mile march it made to reach the steamboats, Company K was again honored with the post of danger and distinction, this time the rear guard. Confederate cavalry followed us sharply, and for many hours our boys kept up a running fight; suffering some loss, but inflicting more on the brave southern horsemen, many of whom were seen to fall, and some of whom, dashing recklessly through our line, were "gobbled up," horses and all; the men to be marched in as prisoners and the horses to be used to carry our wounded. The temptation to describe this day's fighting must be resisted; because, in cold blood and black and white, it would seem to a reader too much like the corn-field job to bear the needful detail.

So, too, the resumption of camp life at Cairo. As the men said: "Same old story, only wuss an' wuss, an' more of it."

When the snow was half mud, and the mud was half water, and the three were combined into an enemy more invincible than an army with banners, an enemy which not merely invested but infested Cairo, Will Fargeon yielded to the pressure of circumstances and of home urgency, took a leave of absence and the noon train for Chicago.

What a lot of miles! 365—one for every day in the year—but they were homeward miles, and sweet to the soul. Did a fellow-passenger yearn for communion of spirit? Well, it was grudgingly given, for the moments of anticipation were too near absolute fruition to be wasted in talk when fancy might be running riot in thoughts of to-morrow.

"Centralia! Twenty minutes for supper!" Snow, mud, darkness, glaring refreshment-room.

"Rosbeefmuttonchopscoldamfish!" Not alluring to the common Christian, but quite so to the camp-weary campaigner—if they would only hurry through it and move on!

Rumble, rumble, rumble; sit awhile, stand awhile, walk awhile—always rumble, rumble, rumble, and always the rosy dream. Not an unhappy minute except when stopping at stations. (Then rises a chorus of snores.)

Nine o'clock; time to wind his watch. Ten o'clock, eleven o'clock. Already? It seems impossible that these hours should be so full of delight and yet pass so quickly. Midnight—"Tolono! Ten minutes for refreshments!" He crossed the dripping platform, shining under the lamps, and smiled as he heard the man ahead of him give the wholesome order: "Piece o' pie, cup o' coffee, and a paper o' chewin' tobacker." Then the long ten minutes of stop came to an end and the short hours of progress began again.

Well, there was a to-morrow coming—a Chicago to-morrow. He ought at least to try for a little sleep. Gripsack pillow is soft enough, army overcoat is warm enough, double seat is long enough—but heart is not calm enough. There is too much joy in waking to get to sleep. Rumble, rumble, rumble; more walking up and down the long-drawn aisle of the passenger coach. There were a mother and child who had got on at Tolono; and the baby cried until the mother was forced to cry too. Very good—here was Will's chance—he always was lucky! So he took the child without asking leave, raised it high in his strong arms and resumed his walk. Not another sound from the infant; it was fast asleep. The mother would have taken it from him; but no, she must put up her feet, cover her head in her shawl, and sleep, too.

"Kankakee!" Only fifty-five miles more; of course it would scarcely pay to go to sleep now, so he would sit down, make himself into cradle-shape for the baby's sake, and watch the snow-flakes as they flitted past the window, showing for an instant in the light of the car lamps.

What's all this? Why—why it's broad daylight, and the mother, up and refreshed, is trying to remove the sleeping baby from his arms without waking either of them!

The late winter sunrise is shining over the black and wrinkled face of Lake Michigan as he enters his native city. Sweet, sharp, frosty air fills his nostrils and refreshes his heart. When he alights from the cars he stamps hard on the frozen soil; joyful to feel that it does not sink mushily under his heel. He hears the ringing, steely sound of sleigh-bells in the air. Inside the station he sees men capped and muffled against the cold, and through the doors he catches sight of horses' heads all white with their congealed breath. All is fresh, cold, wholesome, and exhilarating!

After caring for his scanty luggage he turns up the high collar of his long blue army overcoat with its broad-shouldered cape, seizes his sword and sword-belt with one hand, pulls down his kepi with the other, and prepares to face the sweet, dry frost.

"Richmond House!" "Adams House!" "Briggs House!" "Sherman House!" "*Tree*-mont House!" "Massasoit House!" shout the representatives of those hostelries.

"*My* house!" cries the deep, sonorous, clerical voice of Mr. Penrose, who comes pushing his way through the crowd, closely followed by a lithe little figure all in furs.

The sword falls clanging to the ground, for the indiscreet preacher seizes one of his hands, and *somebody* has to have the other! *Somebody* wants to call him her soldier—her hero—her own love; while he wants to take *somebody* bodily into his arms and hold her there forevermore.

For manifest reasons all these natural and blameless

wishes must be suppressed. Even the silent hand-clasp and the long, loving look do not pass unnoticed. Cordial glances and sympathizing smiles center upon the little group, telling that more than one looker-on takes delight in the joy of the returned volunteer and his trembling, tearful, smiling welcomer.

"Oh, you bearded warrior! I didn't know you! You bronzed veteran—I want you to be introduced to me again!"

"If I am changed, it is only on the outside. My heart is just the same." Then to Mr. Penrose: "Oh, my dear friend, don't trouble yourself with those things—there, the sword is falling out of the scabbard—let me relieve you of it."

"No, no! I am proud to carry it!" And getting the weapon right end up at last, he marched forth in triumph. "Here's the covered sleigh. You and Sally can ride inside and I will drive."

*   *   *   *   *   *   *

"There, there, Capt. Fargeon! That will do. How bold soldiers are, to be sure!"

"But I may keep my arm around you, surely!"

"Well—if you'll be very discreet—since arms are your profession. But, oh, how changed you are!"

"Yes, I suppose so. Either I have changed or the world has changed; all looks so different to me in these few months. All but you, my sweet love!" * * *

"Now, now—didn't I tell you to be discreet?"

"How am I changed?"

"Oh—take your face further away, so that I can see you. There! You are very brown, and very thin. A deep wrinkle has come between your eyebrows; and your eyes, when they are not actually smiling, are sad. Your beard and mustache hide your mouth, but from your voice I'm sure your lips have grown grave, and—almost stern."

"My eyes have looked on blood and death. My ears have heard awful sounds—minié bullets—the screaming of shells and the groans of dying men."

He turns away his face and a far-away look comes into his eyes as the past comes back to him.

Sally puts up her little mittened hand and pulls his face toward her again, saying in a soothing tone:

"Never mind now, dear! Never mind now. Forget it all for awhile." And he gladly obeys her.

What a breakfast Mrs. Penrose gave him! How good the home-made bread and sweet butter tasted! So good that Will wanted to make an entire meal on them. And then when the broiled whitefish came on it was so miraculously delicious that he was sorry he had eaten anything else.

Yes, the world was changed. Everybody looked only at him, listened only to him. The boy—*spes gregis* in the Penrose fold—never took his eyes off him, and never opened his lips except to express silent awe and wonder —and to eat when he happened to think of it. Even the irrepressible Lydia was abashed for once in her life.

Lydia, when he saw her last, had scarcely yet got used to long dresses, which she said made her feel as if her skirts were coming off. Now she had blossomed into a girl as pretty as her sister was beautiful. Then she had been still "Bunny;" and even yet, as of old, her dainty upper lip usually showed those two dainty upper teeth in a rabbit-like fashion. But now she was "Lydia" (except when some one forgot, or wished to tease her), and made spasmodic efforts to subdue that rebellious lip—to "hold her lip," as Spes Gregis rudely and slangily expressed it.

She had also nearly outgrown her old condition of chronic protest against the domination of the masterful Sara; so calm, so indomitable because irresistible, to her younger sister as well as to the rest of the world. Having a sphere of her own, she could let Sally reign supreme in hers.

"Well, Miss Bunny, how has your world gone on since I went away?"

Lydia's lips suddenly closed, and she began looking all about the floor and even under the table. The others laughed, and Will asked:

"What is she looking for?"

"I am looking for Bunny, Capt. William Fargeon. I thought you had perhaps lost your pet rabbit."

"I hope I haven't lost my pet little girl."

"Well, if you haven't you soon will if you call her by a horrid nickname."

"Any name would be sweet that had ever been associated with you."

Lydia tossed her lovely, curly head, but deigned to smile as she replied:

"You *had* to say it, but I thank you all the same. Please try *Lydia*, and see if the rule about sweetness won't hold good."

"The fact is, Will," said Sally, "I favored the name-reform movement because I have seen how bad it is to grow old with a nickname. We know two middle-aged ladies, regular mothers in Israel, who are called 'Chips' and 'Pinky' and always will be, by reason of the early errors of fond, foolish, misguided parents."

'And Bunny blacked her teeth," cried Spes Gregis.

This brought new laughter and the explanation that Lydia, in despair at the obstinate forgetfulness of her family and friends, had daily stained her teeth with ink until she thought the reform was effected.

"Now, Brother Fargeon, I presume you would like me to give you a full account of the progress of the Lord's work in this part of His vineyard."

"Oh, I have no doubt it is going on as it should."

"To begin with your own especial garden, the Sabbath-school, you will remember that last year, just previous to our Christmas-tree, the average attendance rose to three hundred and eighty-four and a quarter; and, after the festivity, fell off to seventy-eight and two-thirds, a loss of eighty per cent. This year I am grieved to say that the highest average before the tree only rose to two hundred and six and two-fifths; but I am glad to be able to state that the *proportionate* decrease was less, following the festivity, than the year before, being only to fifty-two and one-third, which, throwing off the fraction of a child—"

"But, papa, why do you throw off the fraction of a child? "Isn't a third of a child worth saving?"

"Lydia, my daughter, no levity, if you please. Let me see, where was I?"

"You were cutting up a child into fractions."

"Lydia!"

"Call her Bunny, father, and see how quick she'll stop!" advised the experienced Spes Gregis, unheeded.

"But perhaps it was a fractious child," persisted Lydia.

In the laugh which followed this jest Sally managed to "head off" the earnest pastor from his salvation statistics, saying:

"Well, papa, the amount of it is that the Sunday-school doesn't do as well as it did when Capt'n Fargeon was Superintendent Fargeon. But I, for one, would rather have him captain."

"Doubtless, Sally. He who doeth all things well will not leave Himself without a witness, nor let His sheaves go ungarnered, because one of His servants is called to another field. But to resume—"

"Of course," said Fargeon. "He can get along without me—or any of us—if He tries hard."

A silence that followed this suggested to Fargeon that such expressions jarred on their reverent ears, and he hastened to add:

"It would be the height of arrogance to count one's self necessary to the work of the church. Now, Mr. Penrose, did you think of taking a walk city-ward this morning?"

"Why, yes; I shall be very happy to accompany you. And we can continue our talk on this great theme as we walk. Let us sally forth."

"Going to leave us already?" cried Sara, in pleading tones. "You ought to think of Sally first, and sally forth afterward."

"Oh, ho!" cried Spes Gregis. "That joke came over in the ark. We will soon be hearing how all the pigs in the pen rose."

"Stop squealing, littlest pig," observed the polite Lydia.

"Business first, pleasure afterward, Sally. Being here with you—with all of you—is *too* joyful! I must dilute it a little, so as not to grow drunken with delight."

"If I were invited to walk with you—"

"But, Sally," interposed her mother; "your daily tasks—"

"Oh, mamma, duty is nowhere with me to day! I am not a pattern; at this moment I am a reprobate! I am utterly bent on a wicked, violent, unscrupulous, outrageous course of turpitude! I will not sweep and dust the parlor, and I will not give Lydia her music lesson, and I will go out like a raging lion seeking whom I may devour somebody! I will walk down town with papa and Capt. Fargeon, even though I have to be brought back in fetters and manacles!"

"Fetters and manacles are the same, Sally."

"Bunny!—middle-sized pig!—don't talk on subjects you know nothing about! I am usually harmless, but dangerous when roused. Papa, wait till I put on my things."

"But, Sally dear," began her mother, between laughing and fault-finding.

'Avaunt! Exemplary person, I know you not!" And she threw up her little hand like a tragedy queen or a statuette of liberty, and ran out of the room.

"It is weeks and months—years, I might say—since we have seen our dear angel so gay," said the minister. "You must make allowances for her, captain."

"Allowances!" cried Will, and then paused, at a loss for words to say how irresistibly lovely she seemed to him.

––––––

Down the old familiar plank-walk they sped through the bracing air. The boards cracked and resounded under their tread. The sun sparkled on the icy waters of Lake Michigan. Each of the men gave an arm to the young woman (the walk being slippery with frost), and her feet scarcely touched the ground, her steps keeping pace with the dancing of her happy, innocent heart. She had long been accustomed to feel the eyes of men (and women, too,) constantly fixed on her exquisite face as they approached. Now she was delighted that it was Will in his uniform whom all looked at with flattering, welcoming attention.

And Fargeon? Well, he was far from a vain man, but it was not a disagreeable thing to find face after face, whether of friend or stranger, man or woman, glowing and smiling at him. Some men and boys, meeting his answering eyes, took off their hats and swung them in flattering salutation. Those who recognized him shouted his name. One elderly woman—perhaps a soldier's mother—seized his disengaged hand and detained him long enough to press it to her veiled face, and then hurried on without a word. A little school-girl, sachel on arm, after he had passed her, made haste and thrust her mittened hand into his glove and trotted by his side, looking up at him in undisguised admiration. By and by, when they came to Quincy street, she seized his hand with both hers and hung back, saying, "Good-bye, soldier!" He stooped and kissed his rosy admirer, and when he walked on his eyes were full of tears. Said he huskily:

"Sally—it almost pays for all!"

The happy Sara could only press her handkerchief to her eyes and bury her face in his sheltering cape.

They turned westward from Michigan avenue, and as they passed Dearborn street they came upon a little crowd clustered about two men struggling and fighting in the snow in front of a grog-shop. A poor woman was screaming: "Oh, he'll kill him! He's killin' my man!"

"Where are the police?" angrily cried Mr. Penrose as he edged away.

"One moment, Sally," said Fargeon, disengaging his arm.

"Oh, Will! Come away! Let us find a policeman— let the police attend to that."

But he paid no attention to her; elbowed his way into the crowd; thrust aside the inefficient, fussing spectators, all afraid to interfere; seized the uppermost man, who was raining blows on the bloody, averted face of his prostrate foe—seized him with both hands and dragged him off, and with help of knee and foot flung him into the street.

"Go on now! Go on about your business!" he said sternly, advancing toward the fellow as he struggled to his feet.

The wretch cursed him and made as if he would have jumped at him; but the crowd, emboldened by leadership, closed around the fellow and forced him away, one of his friends saying in an expostulating tone and a rich brogue:

"Arrah, Dinny, go on wid ye! Wud ye be afther shthrikin' the so'jer?"

Will looked back to see that the wife and her friends were taking the vanquished combatant out of harm's way, and then hurried on to rejoin Sally and her father.

"I think the constituted authorities are bound to deal with such things," said Mr. Penrose.

"Yes, they are; but I guess the under fellow would have been killed before any constituted authorities got here."

"And you might have been stabbed or shot, Will."

"Not likely."

"But, to resume," said the minister, resuming accordingly, and detailing wise views at some length, while the young folks walked on in silence, until Sally suddenly broke forth, squeezing Will's arm:

"How changed you are!"

"Ha, ha!" he laughed. "I suppose I am. A year ago I should have hunted for a policeman if it had taken all the morning, and then entered the complaint, followed up the trial, secured the conviction of the murderer—also his conversion before execution—buried the dead and provided for the support of the widows and orphans."

"Will, dear, this was better."

"Thank you, Sally. Glad you like the religion of force."

"Oh, I feel as if nothing could hurt you; as if you were invulnerable. Why isn't your name Achilles?"

"Ah, I see you haven't forgotten our old reading-club evenings."

"No, indeed! And I think I'll begin calling you Achilles—Killie instead of Willie!"

"Well, now, Sally, here's the counting-house door, and I've got to leave you and plunge into a fight where Achilles himself would be helpless."

"Oh—that horrid *business!* Mean, narrow, sordid!" After a pause she added: "It was *an arrow* wound that killed Achilles!" They laughed.

"But not a *sword did,*" said Will; and even Mr. Penrose had to laugh at the classic joke (when it was made clear to him) before "resuming" the previous subject.

So the lovers parted, each thinking how witty and how classic they both were, and that no matter how dull the lives of common folks grew after marriage, *their* married life would be one long, happy, gay, intellectual paradise.

But now the captain fell into sore trouble.

CHAPTER XII.

THINGS were blue, very blue indeed, at Fargeon & Co.'s store. Will's partners were pale and thin; more worn down than Will himself. The pinch of war had already come, while the drunkenness of inflation was not yet. Customers' notes were uncollectible, and their own obligations necessarily postponed in consequence. They had taken some government contracts which they were filling at a loss, because goods were rising in price at the East, though not yet higher in Chicago. At the same time, their chief rival, Meyer Moss-Rosen, was said to be doing well, now that the great Fargeon was no longer personally an active competitor.

Before noon Fargeon was inclined to wish himself back in camp with his poor, simple-hearted, single-souled soldiers. Instead of having, as of old, to tear himself away from his business, he had to force himself to stay among its discouraging, confounding, confounded intricacies. In a month or two he could have got into harness once more; could perhaps have peered into the future and foreseen the towering rise in prices that was bound to follow the issue of greenbacks. If he had not thrown himself into the gulf of war, he could, like others, have flown high upon its vapors. He, like others, could have made millions in the days when "the biggest fool was the wisest man of business," because wild speculation, piling up mountains of debt, buying, begging, borrowing, stealing—anything to get hold of property—during the huge inflation of 1862-65, was for once in the country's history the sure and only road to wealth.

The monthly trial-balances which had found their way to him in camp had half broken his business heart; now the actual, physical contact with the reality went near to finish him. Such prices as goods were marked at for sale! Not because they were worth the new values, but simply because nothing less would bring the firm out whole.

"Uncle Colin, what do you say to all this?"

"Aweel, ma lad, be it peace or be it strife, the warld's na changit. Fast bind, sure find. Brag's a gude dog, but haudfast's a better. Wha gangs a-borrowin' gangs a-sorrowin'. Mind ye this: whate'er the pace, slow and steady wins the race. Mackerel skies an' gray mares' tails mak high ships carry low sails. Never syne the warld standit was the sky mair clapperclawit than noo, an' wae's me for the ship-man that heeds not they signs. Ye maun buy what ye see the surety o' sellin', an' mak nae promises that ye see nae surety o' keepin'. Thae preenciples hae guided me, an' hae stood me in gude stead a' my life, when ither men—aiblins better men —went doon. I just tuke heed that the day's refection should bear the morrow's reflection. That's a' the wit your Uncle Colin knaws—but ye'll gang yer ain gait. You Yankees are neither to haud nor to bind."

"Surely, surely, Uncle Colin," Will hastened to answer, "those are the lessons I was brought up on. The other fellows seem to have learned some new ones, but if they are good sense—why, I have been out of school while the old wisdom was rubbed out and the new written on the blackboard."

One little circumstance, corrective of any lingering tendency to puffed-up-ness on Fargeon's part, was the comparative indifference which business men felt and showed for his war record. William Fargeon had gone off to fight—a very proper and creditable thing for William to do, but—business is business.

"Well, Meyer, how goes it?"

"Why, William! is that you? Glad to see you back! Let's see—two arms, two legs, one head—goods seem to agree with inventory and sample so far."

"Oh, yes; I'm all here yet."

"Well, that's first-rate! Been in any battles yet?"

"Some skirmishes."

"And never touched, eh?"

"Not yet."

"You're in luck! Well, you always were a lucky cuss. Shouldn't wonder if you came out safe and sound after all! You'll save the Union and be back again, under-buying and under-selling the rest of us, like old times, before we know it!"

"Can't most always tell what we may least expect. What do you think of trade?"

"Oh, don't ask me." [Fargeon was not a purchaser, so the most bearish views were in place.] "Some pretend to think they can see their way out, but hang me if *I* can."

"'It is naught, it is naught, saith the buyer, but when he is gone his way then he boasteth.'"

"Ha, ha! You always were a cuss at quoting Scripture! I'd like to see the buyer that can boast nowadays. I buy a bale of goods, sell it at what looks to be a profit, and hang me if it don't take every cent I got for it to buy another like it!"

"How are collections?"

"Collections! There ain't any. *Nobody* pays in anything but promises."

"Come over and buy us out. I'll take your promises for every stitch we've got."

"Buy you out? Yes, if you'll take pay in the bad debts we've got owing to us!" He laughed and turned away to hide the flash that came from his shrewd eyes at the thought of getting hold of that great mass of goods at last year's prices.

"Think it over, Meyer."

Meyer Moss-Rosen did think it over. Little sleep did he get that night, and before morning he was a millionaire in his waking dreams.

"Oh, Sally, how tired I am!"

"Why, Will, *dear* Will, you look perfectly worn out! What have those horrid, sordid, low counter-jumpers been saying to my splendid soldier?"

"The truth, I believe."

"Never mind them, my poor dear!"

"But I must mind them, love. I owe vast sums of money that must be paid."

"Well, I have hundreds of dollars of my very own. That will help. And how much is your pay as captain?"

He laughed almost gayly, as he replied:

"Oh, you blessed little simple-hearted financier!" (squeezing her pretty chin until its dimple was as profound as her wisdom). "Your hundreds of dollars, added to my pay as captain for a hundred years, would just make a little bit of a beginning toward paying those debts, if no interest were charged meanwhile."

"Interest?   Our whole interest is in you!   We owe you soldiers all our interest in life!"

"Well, how about the principal?"

"Oh, bother the principal!   Don't tell me that people who don't go to the war are going to demand money from those who do!"

"Oh, won't they, though; that's all!"

"Well, Captain Fargeon," broke in Mr. Penrose, "now let me tell you what I've been doing for Company K this morning."

"Again have you come to our rescue, Mr. Penrose?   I remember how you got our outfit."

"A hundred double blankets, twenty camp-kettles, ten axes with helves—" began the minister.

"Father!" screamed Lydia, clapping her hands to her ears.   "Father!" murmured Sally, doing likewise.   "Now, my dear!" expostulated Mrs. Penrose, while the boy made a pretense of hiding under the table—from which demonstrations Will guessed that Mr. Penrose must have mentioned the matter before.

"There, Captain; that's the way they gibe and jeer at me whenever I allude, even in the most casual manner, to the little service I was able to render you—buying the things you wanted, whereof, by the way, I unluckily lost the list.   One would think that I had frequently spoken of the circumstance, while in fact the case is quite the contrary.   And such is the gratitude of republics!   But to resume: You know it was the Fulcrum which sent down its reporter on the sword-presentation occasion. Well, the Rostrum is bitter as ever against the Fulcrum, so I went to see its editor, whom I know well, and told the story of your skirmish and the shabby way in which the Fulcrum behaved about it."

"You did?   You frighten me!   Where should I stand

in the army if I were to show up as using my leave of absence to hunt for newspaper notoriety?"

"Oh, I took care to say that I called without your privity, and they promised to make that plain."

"And what did you tell them?"

"Simply and truly that the reporter had taken offense at your proper reticence, and had vindictively and wantonly suppressed the identity of the fighters."

"Mmm! Well, it's the truth, anyway. Poor Clint Thrush!"

"They are crazy to get hold of the thing, and are going to send a short-hand man here to-night to get your story of the battle—"

"Skirmish."

"Well, whatever you call it. But to resume: They say that they will have something simply terrible—a *scoop*, I think they call it—on, or in, or over, or under, or somewhere about the Fulcrum. I asked in vain for further information as to the nature of 'scoop'—whether it was anything explosive, or poisonous, or disgraceful, or in the nature of a legal or punitive process; they only laughed, and said it was worse than any of those, and advised me to wait and see if it didn't make the Fulcrum people lie down and howl and feel sorry for the day they were born!"

"Oh, a 'scoop' is only the seizure of an interesting item by one journal to the exclusion of another."

"Ah! is that all?" said Mr. Penrose, rather crest-fallen. But to resume.

———

War correspondence had not then risen to the high art it afterward became. Fargeon (through years of practice as philanthropic platform-speaker) was expert in the putting of things into simple, graphic language, and he was able to talk to the Rostrum's reporter half an hour in a flow of homely narrative that placed the events of the corn-field before the reader like a photograph; while, at the same time, partly by instinct and partly by design, he managed to keep himself almost out of sight in the picture.

In reply to a direct question regarding his interview with the Fulcrum's representative, he said:

"Oh, I have no disagreement with the young man. If he had come to me an hour later, after I had reported to my commanding officer, I should have told him the same story I have told you. But I suppose he knew his business, and took what would interest his readers."

The modest tale, pathetic, touching, harrowing, inspiring, made a sensation. It was an education to its readers concerning the realities of war from the point of view of the front-line men. Hitherto they had been confined to the old-fashioned, upholstered, historical form—charging battalions, triumphant tactics, masterly combinations, and other stuff, chiefly manufactured at headquarters after the musket-carriers had won or lost a day. For example:

"Gen. Rearview now observing a wavering on the left, led forward the brigades of the reserve, and right gallantly did they spring to the rescue. Passing through the decimated ranks of their comrades, and over the bodies of the fallen, lying so close together that it was difficult to avoid stepping on them, they soon crossed bayonets with the foe."

Here, on the other hand, was a narrative of what Brown and Jones and Robinson did and tried to do; how they loaded and fired and bled and died, and how they felt about it; how prisoners are taken, and dead and wounded are cared for; and, incidentally, how the

Fulcrum failed to get hold of the matter. It was break-fast-table-talk in the morning, and town-talk by noon; and the Fulcrum "couldn't stand the pressure," but sent one of its editors to Fargeon to try to set itself right.

"Capt'n Fargeon, it appears that you think you have a grievance against the Fulcrum."

"You are mistaken, sir."

"Well, to read what the Rostrum says this morning it looks that way to a man up a tree."

"The Rostrum got nothing from me except the account of my company's skirmish, and the fact that your young man asked me to make my report to him before I had seen Colonel Puller."

"You did not inspire the attack they made on us?"

"Not in the remotest degree."

"Well, now we propose to do full justice to you, and shall be glad to publish whatever you have to say."

"Thank you."

"What shall it be?"

"Nothing."

"Why, you know the Fulcrum has a good deal of influ-ence on the public mind in Illinois." [No reply.] "We really desire to give you a chance to place yourself in the light you would wish to appear in."

"Thank you again. Whenever I wish to make any per-sonal explanation through your columns I shall certainly call on you." [A beaming smile reinforced this asser-tion.]

"Well—now—" [evidently disconcerted] "is not some-thing due to us, in view of the virulent attack the Ros-trum has made?"

"I'm sure I can't say." [More smiles.] "It's none of my funeral."

"Why shouldn't you treat us as well as you did the enemy?"

"What?   The rebels?"

"No, the Rostrum."

"Oh, I beg your pardon.   I do say to you exactly what I said to the Rostrum; that is, that Company K, of the Sixth Illinois, largely a Chicago regiment, did its duty, did its best; and that Private De Witt Clinton Thrush, of Kingsbury street, was killed, and Privates Robinson, Alger, Corson, Bryan, and Taylor were wounded, and that four rebels were killed and four wounded that we know of—and that I shall be glad to have the friends of the company, especially of the soldiers named, made aware of these facts."

"And that is all?"

"That is all I have told and all I have to tell." [Smiles--always smiles in plenty.]

A very crest-fallen editor soon departed from Mr. Penrose's door and returned to the office of the Fulcrum; while Will and Sarah went forth for a long and lovely walk, during which they talked over the "interview" with much happy laughter and many congratulations regarding the day's doings, especially the discomfiture of the Fulcrum.

When they returned, two hours later, behold the same gentleman, reinforced by a short-hand writer, impatiently waiting for a second interview.

"Captain, since I saw you we have telegraphed Col. Y. R. Puller, and ascertained that it was Company K which covered the retrograde movement, and had another fight with the enemy."

"That is the fact, sir."

"Now, will you be good enough to dictate to my reporter an account of that operation—that is, if you have no objection?"

"Certainly not."

"You won't? Now let me tell you, sir, that the Fulcrum is not to be trifled with! It is a power in the land, and can make and unmake such men as William Fargeon, late trader, now company officer of volunteers!"

"Very possibly. It is also possible that you misunderstood me. I meant to say that I certainly had no objections to stating the facts of the operations of the day you speak of for publication in the Fulcrum—seeing that I have long since reported them to my commanding officer." [Smiles as before.]

"Oh—I beg your pardon." [Quite humbly for an editor.] "Then at your convenience the reporter will take down all you have to say; and, Captain [with condescension], "I assure you, the more the better!"

The Fulcrum of next morning had two columns to the Rostrum's one concerning Company K's doings; and in order to out-Herod Herod, and quite leave the Rostrum in the shade as a friend to the volunteers, it pursued the unpleasant course of plastering Fargeon himself with fulsome praise: "The modest hero and patriot." "But for the enterprise of the Fulcrum in telegraphing to Cairo for the information the world would never have known even that that splendid company had rendered the valorous and dangerous service so graphically set forth in our columns this morning. Its captain, a true Chicagoan, was far too modest and retiring to volunteer the information."

So were all wrongs righted, and honor given to whom honor was due.

Fargeon had no end of "glory" in the days following. Invitations showered on him. Mr. Penrose's church was crowded with people anxious for a glimpse of his shoulder-straps. Sally Penrose was happy and proud and smiling and talkative. She accepted congratulations without reserve. Oh, no, she could not say when "it" could be—perhaps never—but she could hope—all could hope and pray for Captain Fargeon's safety, and that even if wounded his precious life might be spared. Then she added to herself: "He doesn't seem to be in a dreadful hurry to marry me. I thought men always were. I'm sure in novels girls are everlastingly pressed to name the day! Perhaps I am too repellant." So she tried hard not to be. And she was utterly, entirely, absolutely, perfectly happy—almost.

"Gabriel," said the editor-in-chief to the managing editor of the Fulcrum, "it was Parson Penrose that started that thing in the R., wasn't it?"

"Yes."

"That d—d old cuss has had a good deal of free advertising from us, hasn't he?"

"No end of it, for years—ever since he came to that church."

"Well, stop it."

So the word went down through the establishment, "Drop Penrose." And his name was never again mentioned in the Fulcrum. No more reports of sermons. No more sketches of "remarks." No more of the thousand and one little recallings of him to the public heart, which had been sweet and dear to the good dominie through all the years of his able, earnest, hearty, valuable, toilsome, ill-paid service to the cause of religion, temperance, patriotism, charity, and morality.

But to resume.

CHAPTER XIII

ERHAPS he'll ask me to-day!"
But he didn't.

"Good evening, Mister Captain William Fargeon, Esq. How are things at the store? Any better?"

A sad smile, a sigh, and a little, quick, almost imperceptible shake of the head—more like a shiver than a negation.

"Oh, dear; Willie—or, if you like it better, oh! dear Willie—why are you not like a novel hero? Why don't you sink gracefully on one knee, gesticulate loudly with your right hand, and say: 'Miss Penrose, I am a capitalist, wealthy, affluent and rich, with a large fortune and plenty of money besides. Take this hand! Be mine!' That is the nice way to behave!"

"Delightful! Only I should have to finish my speech by adding that my other name was Ananias."

"Well, now, Achilles Ananias William, do tell me exactly how it is. I can bear it. All my life I have had so many disappointments that nothing can surprise me except an—appointment."

"Oh, Sally, as things stand, I have less than nothing.

The best news I could have, would be that somebody would take all we have and pay our debts."

"Well, dear, what difference should that make to us? I never loved you for your money. When you had most I liked you least. And now the reverse is true." [She meant the converse.]

Will's reply to this was not in words. It was gratifying, even consolatory; but it was not an acceptance of her flattering advances.

"If my time was not otherwise pledged, I could do as I did once before; get an extension of credit from my creditors, and think and work and strive and contrive until I had again paid every cent I owe. But now I suppose I must leave it all at loose ends—go off to the front —give to the great cause the time I owe to those who have trusted me—hear of their trust's being disappointed —and almost wish a heaven-directed bullet might wipe out the score."

"Oh, don't—don't talk so! You are horrid! How you overestimate money and underestimate life—and courage—and love!"

"Shouldn't we rate highest what is most in demand and least in supply?"

"Well—you seem to do so, at any rate." [A little air of injury and offended pride had to be charmed away.] "Uncle Colin Thorburn is coming this evening. Let us talk to him, and perhaps he can build you up a bit."

Thorburn had the old-time and old-world view of things.

"The deil is gaun ower Jock Wabster. Ye canna whup the dom secesh—it canna be done—heest'ry shows that whaur a' the folk in a gret deestrict o' country are banded thegither to set up for theirsels they canna be o'ercome."

"You thought we ought to try."

"AULD COLIN 'LL SEE YE THROUGH."—Page 166.

"Sae ye should strive, an' sairly, an' sae ye have striven. An' Bull Run's the upshot! I thocht that a gude show o' force and speerit wad haud the Southrons back frae fechting; but it didna—it didna—an' noo, the deil's gaun ower Jock Wabster."

"Well, Uncle Colin, you say the South cannot be overcome: I say the North cannot be defeated. We are bound to maintain the Union, and we will do it, too! But that's aside from the matter of making my store pay its debts."

Then, upon solicitation, he told the old man just how things stood—how the stock on hand was inventoried, how much the good bills receivable amounted to, and how much the delayed, doubtful and bad; then, the awful sum of the bills payable—some past due and un-paid—"Six figures and neither of them a one."

"Aweel, ma lad; gin ye'll stay and settle up the thing yer ain sel'—"

"That is out of the question."

"Then leave orders to buy nothin' an' sell everythin'—and auld Colin'll see ye through."

"What?"

"I lo'e the Union, whaur I hae made ma fortin'. I'm ower auld to gang doon a-fechtin' for it—but I'm no too auld to care for a fine young sprig that I lo'e like I'd lo'e my ain son if I had ane: So gang yer gait. Gie me your poo-er of attorney to close up yer matters, an' I'll gie ye ma obligation to pay evera cent ye owe in the warrld."

"Impoverish yourself for me?"

"Aiblins aye, aiblins no. Dinna fash yersel' aboot that. I might come oot squar. I might e'en save a wee bittock for a hansel for you and the bonnie lassie here whan a's said an' done."

The bonnie lassie went up to the old man and gave him a kiss and hug that showed what she thought of him, even if it did not altogether balance the magnificent offer he had made.

"Well, Uncle Colin," laughed Will, "I might as well let my creditors suffer as strip you; but I thank you all the same."

"Na, na, ma lad.   Ye're no the mon to tak their ain frac them by force, when ye can tak mine frae me by ma frae will.   An' then as to streepin'—I'm no sae easy streepit. It wadna streep me.   Auld Thorburn could pay it a', an' yet no gang wantin' a bite an' a sup in his auld age."

"What!   Those bills payable?"

"Aye; thae bills peeable.   Colin's nae booster, an' ye're the only mon and Sally's the only woman in the warrld he'd tell it til; but noo ye ken the truth, the vara truth."

"Well, well!" cried Fargeon.   "That is good news! That is another instance to prove what I always believed —that a good life well spent is sure of its reward."

"Aye, lad, sure eneuch—if not in this warld, in some ither."

"No, no; I mean right here and now.   Mankind does not take benefits from men without repaying them."

"Aye, aye, lad.   Gang yer gait an' think sae whilst ye can."

"Why, Uncle Colin!" said Sally in expostulating tones. "How dismally you talk!   We love to reward our benefactors.   Just see how all the land is trying to be kind to the soldiers!   There is nothing too good for them."

"Bide a wee, lass, bide a wee.   The war is only just begun—gratitude is weel said to be a lively sense of future fayvors—bide till the fayvors are a' rendered, then mark how sune they'll be forgot!"

"Oh, it's not so! It's not so! I won't listen to such horrid talk!" And she covered her ears with her hands.

"Aweel, ma bonnie lass; gin ye list me or no, ye maun learn by exper'ence an' no by ma puir guess-warrk. An' ye'll learn that to mak' the warrld pay its debts, ye maun haud an' bind it hard an' fast before ye do your part of the bargain."

Then he told them a fable. Once there was a "puir simple body" who thought, as Sally thought, that mankind would care for its servants, small and great. He tried many experiments in the line of rendering public benefits which nobody seemed to appreciate; he himself growing poorer and poorer as time went on. At last, one day, when he was starving, he observed that a certain park gate was an obstruction to travel, thousands of persons being obliged to open it for passage every day. He seized his opportunity, posted himself at the gate, and, with a bow and a smile, opened it for every comer, large and small, high and low, rich and poor. Then his wants were relieved, for they put him in a mad-house.

After Uncle Colin had departed, the lovers talked over his munificent offer, and his great fortune, hitherto unsuspected. Sally urged her hero to accept the proposition, so that his soul might be freed from these sordid cares—free for war, and friendship and affection.

But at the same time her gratitude to the old man was sadly interfered with by her indignation at his cruel, hateful cynicism—his skepticism regarding the undying gratitude in store for the volunteers. Her father agreed with her.

"Capt'n Fargeon, I hope that neither you nor any other volunteer will give weight to such words—unpatriotic I should call them, but that Brother Thorburn is an alien. Coming from the mouth of any American, I should feel impelled to rebuke them as being unjust toward man and blasphemous toward God.   If I err not, He would pour out the vials of His wrath on this nation, were it ever to justify the gloomy prophecies of Brother Thorburn."

Will thought of the "squeeze" he was undergoing in his business matters, sighed and shook his head doubt-fully. Sally looked at him with anxious, sympathetic eyes, yearning to reassure and comfort him.

When they parted (for he had insisted on transferring himself to his own lodgings) she fairly clung to his neck with her white hands, as if she could not let him go, or as if she had something more to say. She did let him go, and she did not say it, whatever it was. But when he had shut the gate and was walking away she called after him:

"Will Fargeon—you —are—an—awful—goose! "

And then she slammed the door and fled to her own room like a scared fawn—only fawns cannot blush.

―――――

"An important movement on foot. All officers on leave ordered to rejoin their regiments at once."

Such was the startling head-line Mr. Penrose read out from the Fulcrum at breakfast next morning.

The cup of milk Sally was raising to her lips fell to

the table and broke, and its contents streamed down her dress. Lydia, who sat beside her, hurried to wipe off the fluid, Sally not making a motion to help. She only said, in a thin voice not her own:

"I'm afraid—my gown—is spoiled."

And then they laid her gently down on the sofa, happily unconscious of the dreadful news and of the agitated scene enacting around her. The agitation passed; her pulse returned; her breathing became stronger and more regular. At last the great lids lifted from her soft eyes, and after a moment of death-like wandering, they fixed themselves on her mother's face bending over her.

"Oh, mamma! it's nothing. Of course I knew it must come, some time. This is the end—that's all." And she burst into a storm of tears and sobs.

Later, even this abated, and she grew calm, and insisted on the others finishing their breakfast, a command which the dominie was only too glad to obey—had been awaiting some time, in truth.

"Father, please ask Capt'n Fargeon to bring Mr. Thorburn with him when he comes. I want to see them together."

"But, my love, I don't like to leave you so ill."

"Now, father, don't do as you did that other time-- made a failure, so that I had to go to the station to find Mr. Fargeon!"

She tried to smile, and did manage to put on a little bit of the appearance of strength and courage.

All the gentlemen came up to mid-day dinner and she welcomed them with a sad smile. She could not sit at the table, "to spoil your appetite with my foolishness," she said; so she lay on the lounge, a vision of beauty, and tried to eat a little from a stand placed at her side; her own and her lover's eyes meeting and dwelling together without any pretense of secrecy. Such moments, like those of death, are far above disguise and shame-facedness.

During dinner came the usual daily letter from Mac, written in his strong, stiff, unaccustomed, soldierly hand, beginning, as always, "I have the honor to report," and containing the "sick report" and "guard-house report," the "general orders," if any, and the "watchword and countersign," and nothing else, before the military close, "I have the honor to be, very respectfully, your obedient servant." But to-day Fargeon's eye was caught by an enigmatical postscript: "I beg leave respectfully to ask your attention to the request I had the honor to make to you before you left camp."

"Now what on earth did Mac ask me to do for him?" And he passed the letter around the table for suggestions.

"Possibly he needs something which might favorably affect the moral nature of the men," suggested Mr. Penrose, privately thinking of a large number of copies of a bound volume of his sermons, which were still uncalled for.

"More likely something good to eat," ventured Spes Gregis.

"I wonder if his wardrobe is fully supplied," said Mrs. Penrose, her very fingers itching to be called upon to sew, or knit, or work, or crochet something that could add to a soldier's comfort.

"I'm afraid it was only to urge you to hurry back," cried Sally. "That is what I should ask if I were there. But I'm not; I'm here, and I don't want him to have his wish!"

Lydia was the only one who had not spoken. The letter rested in her hands, and her glowing face bending over it suddenly recalled the whole matter to Fargeon.

"Why, Lydia! How stupid of me! Of course I know now—it was that I was to beg, borrow, or steal a portrait of the young lady who made that needle-case! The one I had was lost during our expedition."

All eyes were turned toward Lydia, who blushed and bridled, and then suddenly buried her face in the hollow of her arm and began to cry.

"Why, Lydia, what is there to cry about?"

"You can simply decline, my daughter, if it is so distasteful to you."

"Certainly, there need be no distress over the matter. I can explain that I forgot the errand until just as I was starting."

"Never mind, Bunny! Don't cry. I'll send him mine, and so it'll be all right," remarked Spes Gregis, to clinch the matter.

"Let me be! Go away, all of you! I'm only crying because I didn't know in time to be taken in my new hat."

Then it was easily settled, that the very best of the old pictures should go, now, to be followed by one taken in the new hat at the earliest opportunity.

They talked everything over after dinner. Events seemed to combine to force Will to accept Thorburn's kind offices, and he reluctantly concluded to do so. Will's junior partners were only too glad to have the shrewd old Scot to share their responsibilities; and the needful documents were executed in time to let Will spend some quiet hours at the parsonage, Thorburn considerately declining to be one of the party.

"Good-bye, Uncle Colin. Take care of Sally while I am down tending gate, like the fellow in the fable."

"God guard ye, ma lad! gin ye win safe hame. I'll see that ye'll no hae to gang til the mad-hoose after a'."

Needless to try to tell of Will's parting with the others. It was like the tens of thousands of other partings of those days at the North, the South, the East, and the West. But after the last kiss, the last word, the last embrace, Sally called her lover back to whisper something in his ear—then changed her mind and pushed him away, saying:

"No—I won't tell you after all!"

Meyer Moss-Rosen had been aching to see Will again on the subject of the purchase of his business, but he did not dare to make the first advances. He absolutely kept away from the Fargeon store, but oh! how his eyes kept watch of his own doors, hoping to see Will appear! Now, when his rival had been suddenly called away, he cursed his caution, and wished that he had braved the loss of a few thousands, rather than that of the whole huge prize.

But he soon found that all had turned in favor of his grasping hopes. Fargeon was gone; but he had left his affairs in the hands of old Thorburn—shrewd and cool-headed, but a foreigner, a conservative, an unbeliever in miracles, a believer in precedents, a skeptic as to any profit being possible out of great, immeasurable disaster.

To pass quickly over a dry bit of our story: Thorburn sold and Moss-Rosen bought the entire assets, accounts, stock, leasehold, good-will, and fixtures of the Fargeon store, the consideration being the assumption by the buyer (with ample security) of all the debts owed by the Fargeon firm; also the employment of the Fargeon partners and employes at fair wages for considerable lengths of time, dependent on good conduct and faithful service.

Thorburn was so overjoyed that he could not refrain from telegraphing the news to Fargeon, paying dollars for the long message; to which Will replied tersely, "Thank God and thank you," and signed it "Gate-opener."

A year later the thing sold was worth above its price $100,000 (in greenbacks); two years and a half later $250,000 (in greenbacks); and, fifteen years after *that*, greenbacks and gold were interchangeable commodities, dollar for dollar. The miracle happened; all precedent was denied and all "heest'ry" defied. The purchase w. s Moss-Rosen's first great step in the vast fortune he accumulated—millions—which he held fast up to the time of the great fire, and might have kept to this day if he had not (in the slang of the time) "wanted the earth."

The good old man who had been the unwitting agent of Fargeon's financial mistake never forgave himself his share in the blunder. "Me to fancy, like an auld fule as I am, that a Yankee ell could be gauged by a Scottish thumb!" And he tried, with his latest breath, to atone for the error, as we shall see hereafter.

"Sally, dear, I suppose you are growing accustomed to these ragged note-book leaves, scribbled over at all kinds of moments (with words of *no* kind of moment) and torn out to send to you. Well, this one will surely be wildly illegible, for as I write it I am standing on the rear platform of the hindmost car in the train which is carrying me south to—who knows what? The great, pure, pale moon is almost setting in the west. Good-bye moon! You have shone upon the happiest nights of my life—those of the past week, spent with my sweet love. Now the rude day is dimming your peaceful light in unfriendly glare! Heigh-ho!

"Now we are halting awhile in the open prairie. How the frogs are trilling their ceaseless, senseless song in the invisible ditches at the side of the track! R-r-r-r-r-ee! R-r-r-r-r-r-r-ee! Trills near and trills far, following, crowding upon one another, overlapping and making the sound continuous as a whole, though dominated by one brazen-throated denizen of the nearest puddle.

You may guess, from the unseasonable place and hour at which I scrawl these lines, that this has not been a very restful night. Well, who could sleep—who *would* willingly sleep—under my present circumstances? Just parted from the loveliest, dearest, sweetest of women; the one woman whom * * * *

"What? The moon is gone. Thus perish the fairest of earth's visions.

"Now we are rumbling on again. The dawn is reddening the east. So flat is the prairie, and so low the train, that my horizon is formed of the tall grasses only a stone's throw off—all the rest is starry sky, reddening, always reddening to the sunrise. Long level streaks of fire fringe the under edges of low-lying clouds in the east. As it grows lighter, I see that the prairie around me is covered with a lake of heavy, white mist. Ugh! It looks so cold that I shiver! And here comes the brakeman to put out the light by which I have been writing. Good night, dear—or rather, good morrow "

CHAPTER XIV

AC, where have you been?"

"Away out in the bow, Captain."

"On the lookout for rebs?"

"On the listen. Come forward and hark. There; now we're out of the noise of our own boat. Hark!"

Boommm!

Boooommmmm!

"What's that?"

"Gun-boats shelling Fort Donelson."

"Can they take the fort?"

"Naw!" [The *no* contemptuous is *naw*.] "Artillery can destroy, but it's only infantry that can capture."

"Mac, do you know, I half suspect you were born in the infantry." After waiting in vain for a laugh at this poor joke he changed the subject.

"Who is this Grant, anyhow?"

"West Point and Mexico."

"Is he all right?"

"I guess so, if he'll keep straight. He was a bully good company officer; but I hear he went a little wild after he came home from Mexico."

"Will he do any good here?"

"Well, he took Fort Henry the other day with a hurrah, after the gum-boats had tramped it all out of shape. Now he's after bigger game—their whole army and Donelson itself."

At last the Saginaw ran her nose into the muddy bank and the Sixth Illinois disembarked, looking in vain for the Silverheels with the regimental baggage. When they could wait no longer, the men marched along the rear of the earlier comers to their designated camp; alas! no camp! "Foot, Legget and Walker's line again," they said.

As they plodded wearily on, "hunching up" their heavy cartridge-boxes, and changing their heavy muskets from one shoulder to the other, they could hear the novel, thrilling sounds on their left—distant musketry and field artillery, and always the sullen thunder of the fort and the gun-boats.

Weary miles are passed. Night falls, and the gleam of camp-fires lights up the tents of the troops already encamped.

"Say, fellers, ain't we most thar?"

"Never you mind, Johnny, my son. Jest you 'tend to business, an' keep a-puttin' one foot afore the other."

"Ah, yah! Thankee fer nothin', Jeff Cobb. I've been a-doin' that so long I'm tired of it. I b'lieve I'll try puttin' one foot behind the other for awhile." And Johnny turned around and walked backward until the man following him threatened to step on his toes.

"Whar in thunder is our tavern? Blamed if I don't think we must 'a' passed it unbeknownst."

"Nary. We'd 'a' knowed it by the smell of the beef-steak and fried onions they're a-gettin' ready for our supper."

Somebody struck up "The Lord, He saw Us from on High," and for a while the way was lightened with the inspiring music. A melting snow began to fall, and the cheery voice of Mac rang out through the darkness:

"Secure arms! Git yer gunlocks under yer armpits, boys! Ye may not want 'em, but when ye *do* want 'em ye want 'em *bad*, and ye want 'em *dry*."

A voice called out, "Who's dry in this crowd?" and another answered, "I be—ef ye've got anything in yer flask wuth drinkin'," which raised a low laugh.

The mud was terrible, especially for Company K, which had to tread where the other nine companies had preceded it. Feet floundered and slipped hither and yon. Shoes were loaded and invisible; trousers solid with mire as high as the knees, and plastered up to the waistband, above which coats were spattered to the collar.

Fargeon himself started, "Bully for you, bully for all," and again there was a short space of relief from tedium.

At length they left the soft, slippery road, and halted in a forest of evergreens, where the foliage looked inky black in contrast with the snow that covered the ground and loaded the branches. The night was dark, moonless and starless; and if it had not been for the snow they would have had almost to feel their way. Will groaned in spirit as he thought of the cheer, the moonlit beauty, and the paved streets of Chicago, the floored and roofed houses, the loaded tables, and the lighted fires and lamps.

"Mac, what does this mean?"

"What does what mean, Captain?"

"Why, this; no tents, no blankets, no food, no fire, no axes—no anything but cold and wet and misery!"

"Well, Captain, it means *war;* that's all."

Will kicked the toe of one boot against the heel of the other, alternately, to restore circulation, and then mused aloud:

"It seems incredible! Here am I, a free American citizen, unconvicted of crime, with money in my pocket, and yet I can't leave this—this infernal *purgatory* to get warm and buy a meal of victuals and a night's lodging, to save my life."

Mac smiled grimly for a moment and then rejoined:

"You are not a free citizen. You're a soldier; and you don't come out to save your life, but to spend it—lose it, like enough."

However, a few axes are soon borrowed from a neighboring battery camp, and then how the boys leap and fly to the work! Scarcely is a tree felled before it is stripped of bark and branches by strong hands pulling, twisting, tearing at everything that will come off by help of knives, bayonets, stones, or any other substitute for the friendly ax. The first flames light  the choppers to redoubled efforts, and before midnight every company has its fires and its store of fuel laid by for all-night cheer. Even the butt ends of the burning logs hiss and sing almost like the comfortable tea-kettles of home.

Lucky the man who finds himself at last lying upon two sticks of somewhere nearly equal size, which keep his body at least partly clear of the cold snow; his wet feet toward a fire, his musket in the hollow of his arm, his cartridge-box under his head, his haversack spread on his stomach, and its last bits and crumbs finding their way into that long-suffering organ. Those who have no remaining bits and crumbs will know better how to husband their "three-days' cooked rations" on future marches; not throwing away a hard-tack merely because it tastes moldy, or a bit of pork because it smells tainted.

But he who has food is only half blessed if he have not also his tobacco; and he who must fast is not utterly forlorn if he have his tobacco. The luxurious cigar, the comfortable pipe, or even (boldly be it said) the consolatory mouthful! Call it not a "cud," or a "quid;" call it rather a drop of the balm of forgetfulness; a bud of the lotus, which, when Ulysses' fellow-voyagers tasted, they were cured of their homesickness. Spurn, if you will, the churl who has less excuse for resorting to it, but do not begrudge it to the cold, wet, tired, hungry, home-sick patriots of Company K.

About midnight some officers pass along the line, calling:

"Fires out! Fires out! General orders says extinguish all fires!"

"What in God's name is that for?"

"The light will draw the enemy's fire."

"Ah, yah! If we can stand it, he can."

"Fires out, I tell you."

"Hell fires out! Nothing out! If General Orders wants our fires put out let him come here and—spit on 'em."

"What regiment is this? I'll report you!"

"The Forty-'leventh Froze-to-death. Give General Orders the compliments of the Forty-'leventh Froze-to death, and tell him if he'll send us some tents and some-thing to eat we'll put out our fires."

"Where are the officers of this regiment?"

"No officers present, but you. We're all men out here

in the snow; and we'll keep our fires till the tents
come."

"That's what I call a mutiny!"

"Call it a matinee if you're a min'ter. Only move on
about your business."

"Officer of the guard! Where's the guard of this regiment?"

"Out in front, where it belongs, you fool! Out in
front, where you don't never go! (General laughter.)

The *vis inertia* of a great line of prostrate men, half
seen by the fitful fire-light, half hidden in the dense
darkness of overhanging foliage, was too much for the
troublesome emissaries of authority. They could not
even say where the voice or voices came from; so they
seemed (as in a sense they were) the voice of the regiment at large. They gave one parting threat:

"If these fires aren't out in half an hour the provo'
guard will come down and arrest every man that refuses
to obey orders."

Then they disappeared, pursued by jeering laughter.
The fires were kept going, and the provo' guard did not
come.

From one o'clock to four, Capt. Fargeon slept almost
constantly, only waking when some man, more uncomfortable than the average, would get up and throw a stick
on the fire, rousing clouds of smoke, all alive with
sparks, swirling toward the sky, in graceful spirals that
died away among the tree-tops.

At about four the first deep slumber gave way to
anxious thoughts, and after one or two uneasy lapses
into dreams and half-forgetfulness, he found himself
broad awake and watching the snow-flakes which had
again begun to fall.

With yawns and stretchings he rose from his rigid

couch and moved his stiffened joints, feeling so purpose-less and spiritless that he wished he could longer have remained oblivious to his painful environments.   But the sight of the well-known figures of his own beloved Company K men put from his mind all thought of self, and awakened in him a full, keen sense of his responsibili-ties.   He tramped along the irregular line till he came to the beginning of Company I's men; and then he turned back, hunting for McClintock, his guide, philosopher and friend, his ever-present help in time of need.   At length he saw the calm, bronzed face that was always restful to his eyes.   Mac was sharing the blanket of two sol-diers, each of whom had evidently been so anxious to ac-commodate the great lieutenant that they had gradually robbed themselves of their precious shelter for his benefit.

Mac was sound asleep.   His strong chest rose and fell in slow, rhythmic motion, undisturbed by the slight crackling of the fire, the hissing of the end-logs, and the loud chorus of snores that rose into the still air from the recumbent groups.   Will was loth to rouse him, and stood for a long time with his back to the blaze, enjoy-ing the genial warmth and the sight and sound of rest and recuperation all around him.

"Sleep, the leveler!   Every one of my poor boys is just as happy as any other sound-asleep man on earth! There is nothing more beautiful—but death."

At length Mac stirred, yawned, turned uneasily, and opened his eyes.

"Good morning, Mac."

"Good morning, Captain.   Anything up?"

"Nothing, except me.   I'm thinking about the boys' breakfasts."

"That's so," said the other, instantly ready for duty,

sitting up and spreading the blanket over his two companions. Then, as he arose, he added: "Of course the regimental commissary didn't get anything last night, and I don't know where the brigade commissary keeps himself."

"I'd like to beg, borrow, or steal a few rations just now."

"So would I. I guess I'll feel my way back to the artillery camp we passed. The battery boys are always best off. With all their guns, caissons, limbers and one-thing-another, they have more transportation than anybody else."

"Good enough! I'll go too."

"Halt! Who goes there?"

"Friends."

"Advance one friend and give the countersign."

"We haven't the countersign. Please call the officer of the guard."

"OFFICER OF THE GUARD! POST NUMBER FOUR!" The officer came.

"We are from the regiment that got in late last night, and we want some help—the Sixth Illinois."

"What! the Sixth! Come along in, gentlemen! This is Taylor's Battery, right from Chicago, where you belong! What can we do for you?"

All was lovely. There were cooked rations on hand enough to justify the loan of a substantial breakfast for Company K, and there were rested and refreshed men astir ready and willing to "pack" the victuals over. Our lucky friends walked back (after a long, blissful drink of hot, black coffee), munching hard tack and boiled salt pork that "went to the spot," as the phrase goes, and then amused themselves by stealing along the sleeping line of Company K, slipping two biscuits and a bit of pork into every sleeper's haversack; not forgetting the men on post, sleepy, tired, and grateful.

By this time it was almost six o'clock, and, though dark, near enough to dawn to tell which way was east.

Reveille was sounded by bugle at brigade headquarters, and by drum and fife at each regiment. The drum-and-fife tune (as expressed by the words the men had fitted to it) ran thus:

The men began to squirm and yawn and twist and turn; while hoarse coughing, hawking, and other catarrhal sounds bore testimony to the injuries which had resulted from the night's exposure to cold and wet. The more hardy spirits gave vent to their feelings in curses or jokes, as their various dispositions inspired them. Quoth Jeff Cobb:

"Hello, Maria Jane! The baby's pulled all the clothes off in the night." [He added some imaginary domestic baby infelicities.]

"Tell ye what, fellers, I didn't never in my life feel so old as I dew this minute."

"That's all right, Cy. Don't ye know the reason why? It's 'cause ye never was so old."

"Ice-cream for breakfast, all except the cream part," cried Tolliver.

"Oh, Lord! Darn a volunteer, anyhow, and darn any man who wouldn't git up in the middle of the night to darn a volunteer."

"Gabr'el, blow yer trump! I don't want this world to last any longer."

"If any man names hot griddle-cakes, with butter and honey, shoot him on the spot."

"Ya-as, an' if ye can't hit him on the spot, shoot him in the head."

Fargeon's and Mac's little joke soon began to come to its point.

"Tom Lightner, ye infernal cuss, what ye eatin'?"

"Oh, nothin'. I ain't waked up yet. I'm sound asleep an'

dreamin' I'm eatin' a bully good breakfast."

"Why, look a-hyer! I'll swear I eat up every scrap last night the' was in my haversack, an' hyer's pork an' crackers! Seems like the Bible yarn consarnin' the Widder Cruse's oil-jug."

"Say, boys, feel in yer haversacks."

"Great Scott alive!"

"Glory hallelujerum!"

"Ah! that's sweeter than a pretty gal playin' the pie-anner with her hands crossways."

The captain and lieutenant stood, coat-tails in hand and backs to the fire, gazing up into the tree tops in pretended unconsciousness of the excitement, while man after man made his joyful discovery and expressed his sentiments, until Jim Flynn exhausted the subject and capped the climax of eulogy:

"Tell ye what it is, fellers; it's better than a punch in the eye with a cotton umbrella!"

"Boys!" cried Corporal Chipstone, "that's the kind of officers Company K's got! What ye got to say to our officers?"

A wild "He-igh!" arose on all sides which attracted the attention of the neighboring companies; and K's men were proud of their superiority over the rest, whose fast was not broken for an hour and a half—a weary hour and a half, during which food was got from the brigade commissary and cooked.

"Where did you K men get your grub before the rest of us? That ain't no fair shake."

"Oh, our company officers sat up all night makin' pine cones and spruce gum into good hard tack and boiled salt pork. *That* ain't no trick at all when you once get the hang of it! If we'd a-slep' an hour longer they'd have finished it up into fricasseed chicken an' punkin pie; but we tol' em we wouldn't wait—we'd take it in pork an' crackers."

"Never mind! We'll ketch K in a tight place some day."

"Hope so—water-tight, anyhow."

Company K took its share of the nine o'clock breakfast, but stored most of it in haversacks, having largely satisfied nature's immediate cravings three hours earlier. At about eleven the drummer beat the "long roll."

"Fall in, men! Roll up your blankets and fall in!"

The long line was soon in place.

"Attention, battalion! Shoulder—ARMS! By fours, right—FACE! By route step, forward—MARCH! Right shoulder shift—ARMS!"

Another hour and a half of marching through the sodden snow brought the Sixth to its destined place beyond the furthest out of the troops who had preceded it.

What next? Where's the enemy? What's before us? What's behind us? What's out there on our exposed right flank?

God knows! A private soldier is like a blind horse in a quarry; a precipice on every side and a lighted blast under his feet; his only comfort the bit in his mouth and the feeling of a human hand holding the reins over his back.

Was it truth, or only an *ex post facto* superstition founded on later events, that Jim Flynn and Harry Planter were gayer than usual—the very life of Company K—this morning?

CHAPTER XV.

ATTALION—halt!"

"Close up, men; close up!" and the men, as usual, trotted forward to their places, always "hunching up" their heavy cartridge-belts—haversacks were unluckily very light by this time—and there was a constant sound of musket barrels clashing together as they shouldered each other in the snowy road.

"Front! Right — dress! Front! Order—arms! Stack—arms! Rest!"

"Looks as if we were to form the right of the line," said Mac.

"How do you like our position here?" said Fargeon.

"Here? Thunder! This is no *position* at all—only a trap. It's what we call a 'flank in the air.' No cover and no reserve. Rebs coming in force from the right would have a regular picnic—double us up, one regiment after another, as fast as a man can walk, don't you see?"

"Yes, I see," said Will, looking anxiously toward the unknown right.

"First thing should be to deploy a company as skirmishers to find what there is over there; next, put somebody back in support."

"I guess I'll step over and speak to Col. Puller about it."

"Good enough—if he were a soldier, instead of a politician."

"Can't a soldier be anything else, Mac, besides?"

"Yes; but not a politician."

Will smiled at Mac's well-known dislike of "politicians" (especially his own colonel), as he went over to quote Mac's shrewd counsel—with full credit to Mac—which the colonel forthwith carried to brigade headquarters and repeated as his own ideas.

Within an hour the Sixth was formed "in echelon of companies"—each company thrown back about thirty paces behind its left-hand neighbor—to protect the right of our line; and Company K, its blankets laid aside, was deployed as skirmishers, and pushing out into the unknown wilds to seek a foe. They found a friend instead, in the shape of a swamp practically impassable; but the swamp was some half a mile away from the Sixth, and a road ran along its edge, at right angles with our general line of battle.

Here they halted, scattered in skirmishing order, trying their best to be comfortable. Each man selected some tree or stump, and cleared away the snow behind it to leave him a spot wherein to sit, stand, or lie, or stamp about for warmth and a pretense of drying his soaked and usually ragged shoes.

"Unless old Simon Bolivar Buckner is a fool, he will try a flanking movement by this road," said Mac.

"Where did he learn soldiering?"

"He's a West Pointer, too; and was with us in Mexico."

"How will he go to work if he concludes to try it on?"

"March right down this road, by the flank, 'left in front,' until he meets some force that persuades him to deploy."

"That'll be Company K, as skirmishers, won't it?"

"That's what's the matter."

"And if Company K weren't here—what then?"

"Oh, then Boliver 'd have a picnic; get down abreast of our 'flank in the air,' right face into line of battle, and double us up in spite of thunder."

"But we're here, Mac."

"You bet we're here!"

"I hope he won't come."

"Oh, we won't really fight him after he forms line of battle. While he marches by the flank, we'll face him. When he gets deployed, our business is to light out."

"Mac, I guess I'll send word to the colonel, to tell him what we've found out."

"Oh—well—but it's his business to send or come to us for the news."

"Likely he doesn't know enough. Anyhow, he'll be pleased with the attention."

"He'll never be pleased with anything we do."

"Why? Jealous of you, you war-worn old regular army veteran?"

"No; though he may possibly guess what I think of *him*. No; the trouble is the praise the Chicago papers gave Company K for the two Grand Hill skirmishes— leaving him out in the cold."

"Oh, he's forgotten that long ago."

"Forgotten it? Capt'n Fargeon, you just wait and see how much of it he's forgotten."

So Will wrote a few lines to tell Colonel Puller the state of things, and dispatched them to headquarters. He began to hope there would be no fight that day. It was getting well on into the afternoon. Oh, if the day might end in quiet! Some men arrived from the regimental commissary with K's share of the noon rations. They were received with the customary "Heigh! heigh!" which changed to jibes and jeers when the food was found to be uncooked.

"They think we're maggots and can live on raw pork."

Then he watched the efforts of Mark Looney to start a fire. It seemed as if the chilly dampness had infected every particle of matter in the whole region. "Dry leaves" were soaking wet. Match after match was fruitlessly tried.

"Have you plenty of matches, Mark?"

"Yis, Caftain. I'd a box av 'em this morrnin'."

"Take care of them! They're precious."

"The' are that, sorr!"

Finally Mac lent a hand. He lighted his pipe and puffed it into a fine glow, then inverted it over a promising mass of splinters, and they, tenderly nursed by Mark's breath, at last consented to blaze. While the fluttering baby flame was growing by the addition of the least refractory stuff they could find, Mark cut and slashed the great slabs of pork into rashers (rations?), and many jack-knives made ready many long twigs whereon the meat was soon sizzling, spreading around the most delicious, appetizing odor a soldier's nostrils can inhale.

Alas! The smell was all the boys were ever to get of that feast; for just now Mac's soldierly instinct was roused to cry out:

"Don't forget what we're here for, boys. Remember the rebs!" And his cry was answered by a shot from the front, the bullet whistling noisily over his head.

Instantly every man was on the alert; even little Mark running to where he left his musket, and peering out from behind his tree, forgetting fire and food.

"Save your fire, boys," said Mac, falling into his usual battle drawl, "and remember your orders. If it's a picket or a skirmish line, stand fast till hell freezes over. If it's a line of battle, give 'em one shot, slow and low, and then skedaddle. No running from skirmishers, and no standing against a line of battle. You hear me?"

Seeing Mac walking boldly over to his post on the left, Will left a friendly tree from which he had been peeping (like the privates), and made his way, hurrying and stooping, but with reasonable coolness, over to his place on the right.

Bang! bang! bang! went the guns of his men near the road, the very point he was making for. A dozen answering reports came from the front, accompanied by the sound of flying bullets, one of which seemed to have been aimed at himself.

"What is it, Tom?"

Tom went on reloading as he answered:

"Looked like a picket guard, Captain—just a squad in the road. One man got hit, and they picked him up and started back."

A dead silence follows this, and Fargeon looks at his watch. Four o'clock. It will be dark in less than an hour—all may yet "blow over."

No. Before 4:15 a rattling fire made itself heard from our own line, far on K's left. It was rapid and simultaneous, and indicated that the enemy was upon them in force—no mere skirmish line. Scarcely had this died

away when a roar of confederate musketry from K's
front set all doubts at rest.   It was certainly a regimental volley.   Almost immediately the men at his end of
the line caught glimpses that drew their fire, and they
were answered by another volley, fired by a full regiment
apparently, yet harmless.

"Back men!   Back!   Double-quick!"

They needed no second order.

Here a dreadful thing happened.   The rear companies
of the Sixth (in echelon) opened fire, and, careful not to
fire on each other, aimed too far to the right and sent a
good part of their bullets into the left wing of Company
K.   Curses filled the air, and Mac and his men, thus
taken between two fires, came running from the left over
to Will's quarter, whence all, in a confused mob, made
for the rear, or the swamp, or any place where they
should not be slaughtered by both friend and foe.

"Anybody hurt, Mac?"

"Jim Flynn killed and Harry Planter wounded."

"Where's Harry?"

"The rebs have got him by this time."

"Good God!"

The persistent rattle of musketry and frequent roar of
artillery indicated strong fighting along the front of the
Union line, and the increasing distance of the sounds made
it appear that the enemy was gaining some ground.
Time passed and with darkness the cruel noise died
away.

Company K was scattered widely through the swamp,
without any semblance of order, each man hiding or trying to get farther into the underbrush.   Will and Mac
were squatting, concealed in a spot whence they had seen
the enemy in considerable numbers passing down the road,
and none seemed to return.   They would have lain down,

13

but the standing water was over shoe-top and level with the snow. When the enemy had passed them and night was near, they were startled by a noise behind them, and Mac hurriedly drew his pistol and cocked it.

"Liftin'nt, wud ye kindly lind me a hand?"

It was Mark Looney who approached, dragging his piece with his right hand, while his left was buried in his breast.

"It's in me lift arrum, liftin'nt. It seems to be blay·din' bad, an' I'd like to jist git a bit o' stuff 'round it." As he lowered his arm the fresh blood trickled from his sleeve.

In the gathering darkness they ministered as well as they could to the poor fellow's needs, while, in spite of himself, his teeth chattered and every limb shook with pain, cold and exhaustion. The blood persisted in drip, drip, dripping, as if an artery had been cut.

"Mac, this poor boy'll die in the water and snow. What shall we do?"

"The road's our only chance. Let's risk it; the enemy is off now for a while at any rate."

"Good enough! Can you walk, Mark?"

"I'll thry, sorr." And he did try, still dragging his musket, until Fargeon insisted on taking it from him.

"Now, Captain," said Mac, "give me the gun, and you and Mark stay back, while I push on toward the rear. I'll whistle and keep whistling all the while, unless I hear or see something. When you don't hear me whistle, you get out of the road."

Mac started off, and Will helped Mark along as best he could, the wounded man's hard breathing growing shorter and harder in a manner that showed that this march of his would be a short one—perhaps his last.

They soon lost the sound of Mac's whistle, and shrank

into a fence-corner to wait for the foe. None came, and they concluded that Mac had overestimated their speed and simply walked out of hearing. It was now almost dark; still, they could hardly spend the night there, so they began to stagger slowly down the road once more, and accomplished perhaps another quarter mile before Mark gave up entirely.

"Thankin' ye kindly, Caftain, for all your goodness— I've got to give it uf. Ye'll fush on, av ye flaze; and, caftain, dayr, there's wan or two things in me focket I always kef' ready for whin me time kem. The d'rections is wrote on 'em—ye'll see when ye get to a light."

"Why, Mark, do you think I'd leave you?"

"Oah, yis, Caftain, it wouldn't be right fer ye to be took fris'ner along wid me—an' it'd be no good, nayther. Noa, it wud not."

"Now, Mark, I'll never desert you while I live; and as to being taken prisoners, I'd rather see you and me alive in the enemy's hands than dead out of them. So I am going to light a fire, hit or miss, rebels or no rebels, capture or no capture, sink or swim, live or die, survive or perish; here goes for a fire."

The darkness was now impenetrable, but he scraped away the wet snow, as well as he could, from a sheltered nook, while Mark, with his single hand, tried feebly to get together some moderately dry fence splinters, and picked up a few dead leaves and rubbed them on his clothes.

"Well, my boy, those feel pretty dry. Now, where are your matches?"

"In me focket, Caftain."

"Why—your pocket feels wet. And the match-box feels wet."

"I didn't lay down on that side," wailed the sufferer,

who had taken heart of grace at the prospect of a little warmth and light. "Could me wownd have bled onto 'em? Oah, I'm afrehd—I'm afrehd soa."

"I pray God they'll light!"

"Ah-min!"

Will rubbed a patch of fence-rail fiercely with his sleeve to dry it, selected a match and carefully scraped it. No light. But that might be an accident. Another careful scrape—no doubt now but that the chemicals had crumbled off unlighted; he could feel them in his fingers. Another match he tries in the same way, with the same result, while Mark grows sick and sicker with apprehension.

"Thry two to wanst, Caftain," he whispered, vainly trying to steady his voice.

No result.

"I guess I'll try one on the inside of my coat, as men light their pipes in the wind."

Vain again, and vain when he tried a dozen in similar fashion.

"You haven't another box, have you, Mark?"

"Nary a wan at all, Caftain, but the wan."

"Now, Mark, you take these three matches and try them together on the inside of my cap, while I hold it solid with both hands."

"The' moight burrn yer caf, sorr!"

"I hope they will—then we'll have a fire sure enough."

Mark's trembling fingers only made the same desperate effort that so often failed before, and it failed again.

"Av I had me ould musket now—I'd jest break a cat-tridge—an' lave in a little powdher an' the waddin'—an' shoot 'em into some laves—an' the'd burrn—the' wud— Ochone the' wud—oah the' wud!" [For once Mark's plaintive diminuendo was appropriate to the occasion.]

"Now," said Will, "I think I'll save the rest of the matches and dry them before we risk another trial."

He said it in as cheerful and hopeful a tone as he could command—even unconsciously forcing a false smile in the darkness—all to keep his suffering friend from knowing that there were no more. Those three were the last. The soldier's life-blood had destroyed the means of saving his life. Mark must have suspected that the matches were gone, for he murmured in a broken voice "Ochone—Ochone."

Then Fargeon laid Mark down on his well arm, lay down behind him, and embraced his shivering form, "snuggling spoon-fashion," as the children phrase it. His right arm was under Mark's head; his left strove to make one coat cover them both. As to their soaked and benumbed feet, they were past praying for.

"Caftain, dayr," said the thin voice, grown perceptibly weaker even since it spoke last, "d'ye think it's much afther midnight by this?"

"Oh, a long time!" ("God forgive me—it's not nine yet.")

Will thought the sufferer's weakness had brought on hiccoughs, but soon knew that these were half-suppressed sobs that he heard and felt. When he could disguise them no longer, Mark burst out:

"Caftain, dayr—ye'll not tell the byes that I got kilt with a dommed scratch afther all, comin' from our own min—an' died a-cryin' loike a ba-aby!"

"Never! I'll tell them you got your wound like a soldier and bore it like a man, and got well and wore shoulder-straps, like a hero—as you deserve!"

He beat the poor benumbed body and limbs and hugged the frowsy head; his own spirits rising in this congenial life-saving task—rising in direct proportion to the demands making on them. He could have been gay and happy if it weren't for his feet.

The hours of that night ought, perhaps, to be dismissed without a word; for a chapter or a volume could not depict its length and its misery.

Nature sets a kindly limit to distress, by the interposition of a barrier of insensibility, which says to pain, "Thus far shalt thou go and no further;" and this mercy soon came to Mark's relief and he ceased to suffer, though not to moan "Ochone" and shiver. But Fargeon remained conscious of his wretchedness. A text came to his mind: "In my Father's house is enough and to spare, while I perish with hunger."

A scene rose in his memory; a vision of the warm fireside of Mrs. Penrose's comfortable dining-room; a fire in the grate; whole boxes of matches on the mantel; a bright light shining on Sara's face and on a well-spread tea-table redolent with good things to eat and drink—all warm! warm! His nostrils expanded to inhale the aroma of tea, the comforter, only to find themselves filled by the smell of cold, stale tobacco smoke and other squalid things hanging about poor Mark's hair and clothes.

CHAPTER XVI.

LL night long, at stated intervals, the long, low thunderous groan of a gunboat cannon came to Will's ears from the distant river. It was almost a comfort—a sign of life in the midst of awful loneliness and desolation.

After midnight the stars came out and the cold grew more bitter. While Will was trying to accustom himself to an endless darkness and a limitless suffering, three figures might have been seen creeping cautiously along the edge of the road, peering sharply into it and into the neighboring shadows. Two carried swords and one a musket. One of the sword-bearers was whistling low and constantly—

"I wonder why all saints don't sing."

the tune Mac had whistled when he left them last night.

"Oh, Mac! God bless you, Mac! Is that you?"

"Great God, Captain! You here? And alive and able to speak to me?"

McClintock, Morphy, and Chipstone were the angels of succor. But how inadequate are words to do more than dimly suggest the flood of feeling that surged up in their breasts at this meeting! All were visibly moved; even imperturbable Mac showed emotion. All—that is, except poor Mark. He was long past joy or pain. Unconsciousness had dropped the curtain between his nerves

and their torturers, and if help had not come it is doubtful if he would ever have felt another pang. Tenderly
they disengaged Will from the inanimate Mark, scarcely
more helpless than his captain. Joining hands, the two
lieutenants raised the little hero between them in the
fashion so familiar to soldiers. Corporal Chipstone took
his musket on his left shoulder, passed his right arm
around Will, and helped him forward until circulation
was somewhat restored, so that he could readily keep
pace with the rest.

A fire! A blessed fire! A heavenly warmth—to save
life and restore benumbed flesh and blood, and bone,
and nerve, and brain! How he coughs and sputters the
smoke, as he hugs the blaze, and his clothes give off
clouds of vapor! No need to offer food; no use to ask
questions; no need to talk—nothing but sweet, holy, heavenly warmth now for a long, long time; to be drunk in
at every pore, with eyes closed in utter comfort; a whiff
or two from the pipe, warm and moist from Mac's lips
—and, at last, slumber—even dear, balmy, blessed sleep
—steals over the senses, and begins the repair of the
most ragged and frayed edges of the sufferer's being.

Yes, it is not another of those false, deceitful dreams.
It is a real fire that salutes Will's reopening eyes. *Now*
they may give him a toasted bit of biscuit and talk to
him slowly and distinctly, asking no questions yet. So
Mac tells of his walking and whistling, and his turning
back and searching in dismay for the hidden comrades;
going on and on until he was challenged by a confederate sentinel; then his return and building a fire, divided
between hope that they had got over to their friends, and
fear that they had been taken by their foes; then the
final effort which had brought the joyful rescue.

Will raised himself sufficiently to look across and see

that Chipstone was holding Mark's head in his arms, while his shoes were steaming beautifully in the warmth of the fire.

"Is he alive?"

"Yes," said wide-awake Morphy. "He spoke awhile ago—asked where you were, and then dropped off again with that same little smile you see on his face yet—if you call Mark's smile a smile."

Will a match ever again seem to Will like a simple stick of wood and chemicals? Never! It will always be a "Mark Looney," a humble little red-headed soldier, ready to try to do its duty and perish in the doing.

"What's that light over there, Morphy?"

"Daybreak, by God!"

"That's so!" cried Mac, starting up from a doze. "Come, boys, let's get over toward the regiment."

"Hadn't you better go on ahead, Mac, and see that Company K gets into shape and gets something to eat? I guess most of them have got in."

"Oh, Captain—s'pose you send Barney to do that. I'd rather not leave you and Mark."

So Morphy left them, and they roused Mark sufficiently to get him to eat a bit of biscuit, toasted, and soaked with snow-water into softness.

Will rose with difficulty, and left the blessed fire with regret, a long, strong shudder seizing on him as he faced the morning breeze. He thought the motion made him feel colder than ever! Mac and Chip gripped hands to pass under Mark's knees and gripped elbows to support his chest under his arms.

At the end of a mile or so of difficult walking, they came upon a pleasant scene—Col. Puller and the regimental staff gathered near a fire (a full half-mile to the rear of yesterday's line), and preparing for a breakfast *al fresco*, from which repast a refreshing odor of coffee and fried pork saluted their eager senses. They laid Mark tenderly down, and stretched and rubbed their stiffened arms.

"Good morning, Colonel."

"Good morning, sir."

"We began to think we should never see a friendly face again, or smell that delicious odor of Christian food."

"Where is your company, Capt'n Fargeon, and why are you not with it—you and Lieutenant McClintock.!"

"Company K was scattered and driven far to the right by the fire of the enemy in front, and—I am sorry to say it, Colonel--by the fire of your own command in our rear."

"I learned from one of your own men—the same man by whom you sent me a very curt and incomplete report in the afternoon—that your company retired in disorder before the enemy. And now, after a large part of it has straggled into my regiment, *you* appear; you and your first lieutenant bring up the extreme rear—with a cock-and-bull story of having been fired on by your own regiment."

Will stood dumfounded by this assault.

"Lieut. McClintock, have *you* anything to say in explanation of this state of things?"

The lieutenant silently shook his head.

"Both you gentlemen will go to your quarters in arrest."

"What!" cried Will.

"I presume you understand English, Capt'n Fargeon, and that you know your duty under present circumstances."

With an unmoved face and undisturbed voice Mac said:

"You will not object, Colonel, to our carrying Private

Looney to brigade hospital before our arrest takes effect?"

Puller turned to consult his adjutant—his monitor in all matters—and then said:

"I have no objection to your caring for Private What's-his-name or any other private business; but you may remove your swords before doing so." Then, turning to Chipstone: "Take the swords and report at your company at once."

Silently the captain and lieutenant took off their swords and handed them to Chipstone. Then they raised unconscious Mark once more and resumed their toilsome, labored march in the direction of the hospital. When they were out of hearing, Mac said quietly:

"Now, what do you think about Col. Puller's memory, Captain?" But Fargeon walked on as if he heard not.

At length they saw before them a large hospital tent. They walked up toward the open door, where sat a short, dark man in plain clothes and a slouch hat, smoking a cigar. Mac began:

"I beg your pardon, sir—why, Captain—General Grant!" and he stopped.

"Good morning, sir. Are you looking for me?"

"No, General, we are looking for the hospital. This is Capt. Fargeon, of the Sixth Illinois. I am Lieutenant McClintock, of the same regiment."

"Ah, McClintock. Yes, yes, Mexico; I thought I knew you. I am glad to see you, Lieutenant, and to know you are again in the service."

"General, this is Mark Looney, whom you may recollect."

"Very well, indeed; very well, indeed. Is Mark badly hurt?"

"Severely, not dangerously—only he has been freezing and starving all night. We were picketing on the ex-

treme right and were driven out by the fire of our own
men behind us."

"Ord'ly, is there any of that coffee left? Bring three
mugs of it for these gentlemen." He stepped up to
where they had laid down Mark. "Mark, do you remember your old lieutenant, Grant?"

Mark nodded and smiled slightly, but did not try to
speak.

"Ord'ly, give Dr. Hardy my compliments, and ask him
for a stretcher; then get three more men and carry this
man to the hospital."

They dipped a bit of biscuit in the coffee and placed
it in Mark's mouth, while they blew and sipped their
own beverage in luxurious refreshment.

"I haven't heard any intelligent account of the affair
on our right. How came you there, and what occurred?"

Will gave a short, lucid statement of the events we
have narrated, beginning with giving Mac full credit
for the suggestion which led to their being pushed out,
and ending with the disaster they had met with.   He
did not say that they had rendered any especial service,
but felt that the older soldier must see that such was
manifestly the case. Grant smoked and listened in utter
silence; not even an occasional grunt of recognition indicating that he saw the whole scene as it had occurred.

"Where are your swords?"

"As we passed regimental headquarters, Colonel Puller,
for reasons best known to himself, placed us both in
arrest."

"And had you give him your swords?"

"Not exactly; only send them to our quarters, while
we looked out for Mark."

[Puff, puff.] "Well, gentlemen, you know the duty
of officers in arrest."

"Yes, General; we are on our way to our quarters."

"Good day, gentlemen!"

"Good day, General."

They departed—but we will remain.

"Ord'ly, give Colonel Puller, of the Sixth Illinois, my compliments, and say that I would like to see him at twelve o'clock."

Then the general strolled over to the hospital and had a talk with Mark, now cared for and comfortable.

Colonel Puller arrived, punctually to the moment, in full regimentals, with sword, sash, and spurs, much excited and pleased by the summons, and primed with a glowing account of his own services of the previous day. He shook hands with the silent, sphinx-like figure sitting on the camp-stool (smoking as usual), and observed that he was glad to see General Grant looking so well.

"Colonel, in advance of regular reports [puff, puff], I should like you to give me an account of the affair of last night."

"Well, General, I am glad to be able to give you one."

[We must abbreviate.] The colonel had observed that our flank was unprotected, and, with the consent of his brigade commander, threw his regiment into echelon of companies, and deployed a company as skirmishers to give warning of any threatened attack. About four o'clock the skirmishers were driven in with some loss, and then the enemy made a most furious and premeditated attack upon that part of the line. For over an hour we withstood the onslaught of vastly superior numbers, repelling one assault after another in the most determined manner, completely decimating their ranks, while our own losses, though considerable, were small by comparison. Finally the enemy retired in confusion, almost decimated. Darkness prevented the pursuit which the colonel had planned, not only to order, but to lead in person.

[Puff, puff.] "What kind of country did you find on your right?"

The colonel had found a road bordered on the far side by a swamp.

"Did you go out to see what your reconnoissance had developed?" The colonel did not.

"Did you send?" No; the commander of the skirmish company had reported very fully.

[Puff, puff.] "Did the enemy use the road in an effort to take us by surprise?" The colonel thought that they had marched nearly their whole force to that point with that purpose.

"What prevented them from succeeding—as the troops that were to fill the gap failed to reach there?" The fire of the skirmishers, which the colonel had placed there for that very purpose, succeeded by the fire of his echelon companies, and, later, by the other regiments of the brigade.

"The skirmishers did well, then?" Up to that point, admirably, in accordance with the colonel's orders. But later, when seriously attacked, they fled in confusion.

"The skirmish line retired before the attack of a line of battle?" The colonel regretted to say that they did.

[Puff, puff.] "When did you learn this?" The colonel was apprised as soon as it transpired.

"Before the engagement began?" At the very beginning of it.

"From whom?" From a member of the skirmishing company.

"The first man of them to report?" The very first. The colonel had felt obliged to place in arrest the captain and first lieutenant.

[Puff, puff.] "Did you so direct the fire of your right

"My remarks are not drifting, Colonel."—Page 208.

flank company as not to injure your own skirmishers?"
The colonel had trusted to their own judgment for that.

"Did you tell them where you had placed your skirmishers? Did you give any orders or take any steps to
avoid shooting your own men?" The colonel could not
quite follow the drift of General Grant's remarks.

[Puff, puff.] "My remarks are not drifting, Colonel Puller. You seem to have sent out a company of skirmishers to reconnoiter, and not to have gone or sent to learn
what they found out; then to have left your line of battle uninstructed as to their duty regarding those skirmishers, wherefrom disaster resulted to them; then to
have placed two deserving officers under arrest upon the
unsupported statement of one skulker."

The silence that followed this was marked—almost
obtrusive. The quiet veteran smoked on unmoved.

"Have you anything further to add, sir?"

The unhappy colonel choked and gasped for breath,
but was speechless.

"Mr. Badger, one moment, if you please. Be kind
enough to write a general order" [Puff puff]. "'Captain
Fargeon and Lieutenant McClintock, of the Sixth Illinois Volunteer Infantry, having rendered distinguished
service in the affair of yesterday, and having been unad-
visedly placed in arrest by the colonel of their regiment,
are released from arrest and restored to duty.' Have
that repeated and sent out at once—or stay. Colonel Puller
should you think proper to demand a court of inquiry on
your part in this matter, I will readily grant your request
and make it part of the same order."

"Ge—General Grant—I beg for time to talk with my
brother officers."

"Very well, sir. Good morning, sir. Send out the
order, Mr. Badger."

The Sixth, still shelterless, had been provided with axes during the day, and was now building for itself a long, double line of "brush-houses," made of boughs supported on poles held up by crotched sticks—a poor camp but better than none; far better, even in case of rain. In front of one of these hovels, at a good fire (for it seemed as if they would nevermore be tired of warming themselves), sat Fargeon and McClintock, brooding over the coals and their own wrongs.

To them arrived Colonel Puller in trembling haste.

"Captain! and Lieutenant!" (extending a hand to each which they failed to notice). "You'll be glad to hear (but not half so glad as I am to say it) that I find that I was entirely misinformed regarding your share in last night's action!—entirely! I ought to have thanked you instead of—doing what I did."

They were as unresponsive as Grant himself.

"Now, I want you to regard those few words as unsaid —forget them as if they had never *been* said. You are relieved from arrest and restored to duty."

After a pause, Mac spoke:

"Thank you, Colonel Puller. I believe we prefer to demand a court of inquiry."

"Oh, Lieutenant—oh, Capt'n Fargeon—don't, I beg and pray, *don't* ruin me! What will be said at home? Where would it place me in the eyes of my congressional district—all for a hasty word or two?"

"Unpremeditated was it, Colonel Puller!"

"Premeditated! My dear lieutenant, what can you mean?"

The colonel laughed uneasily, while an added flush showed that the shot had not missed.

No, the gentlemen did not care to smoke. And they would prefer not to dine with the colonel's mess, under

14

the circumstances. Besides, Captain Fargeon could hardly stand on his feet. Yes, he should be glad of a call from the regimental surgeon.

"To tell you the truth, gentlemen, I have had a little talk with General Grant—a very nice talk on the whole —and he has consented to issue a general order speaking highly of you, and relieving you from arrest."

The others straightened up in their seats, leaned forward, stretched out their arms and shook hands—with each other.

"Now, gentlemen—Lieutenant, you know I am not up in military verbiage as you are—I suppose you can't persist in your own arrest after being relieved in general orders."

"Well, Colonel Puller, we are not officially apprised of our relief until the general order has been read aloud before every regiment at dress-parade."

The colonel departed, very downcast, and forthwith made his own headquarters a little purgatory, and his adjutant temporarily sorry he had ever been born. But the adjutant (who privately hated his colonel) got fully even with him at dress-parade that very afternoon, as the next chapter will show.

CHAPTER XVII.

IT is not difficult to imagine the deep indignation the men of Company K felt when they learned of the vile treatment meted out to their officers. There were symptoms of a roaring row when Will and Mac dejectedly approached the laboring company. Wild cheers greeted them, followed by resounding groans unmistakably meant for the objectionable colonel. By great effort the arrested officers calmed the tumult, and got the men to give to poor, unoffending Morphy the obedience he had a right to as the commanding officer, and deserved as a good one and a good fellow.

Four o'clock P. M. arrived, and with it dress-parade, and with dress-parade the reading out of general orders. Now came the adjutant's revenge. He read out the expiatory order so that nearly everybody could hear it; then paused for the cheers which he knew would follow. Follow they did, beginning with Company K, and spreading until the whole regiment had take them up; Company A, which had committed the cruel blunder while in echelon the day before, showing special anxiety to make themselves once more "solid with K."

"Colonel," whispered the adjutant, "it would now be proper to send for the captain and lieutenant before proceeding with the parade."

Colonel Y. R. Puller's Curses, "not loud but deep," must be omitted. Fargeon and McClintock were summoned and arrived, the captain leaning heavily on his lieutenant and on a stout stick. Yet both men looked handsome, dignified, and business-like as they were led up to the colonel, who shook their hands with misplaced effusion while the cheers were renewed, K going quite wild when they rejoined its ranks, the men tossing their caps and catching them on bayonet-points in a general scramble.

Puller, as colonel of the Sixth, was essentially "done for." Still he floundered and struggled a good deal. At the headquarters mess that evening he tried the force of eloquence.

"Fellow-comrades, the more I think of the way we've been tampered with by General Grant, the more I don't like it. How are we to maintain any *espritt dee corpse* in our regiment if our best efforts are to be prostituted by having such a stamina put upon them?"

His staff did not know.

"I would suggest," said the lieutenant-colonel, "that you either resign or ask for a court of inquiry." [The lieutenant-colonel was wild to get command of the regiment.]

"Yes," said the major, "that might give Gen. Grant a lesson." [The major wanted to be lieutenant-colonel.]

"And if Grant were out of the way, you ought to get a brigade," put in the adjutant. [He also longed for a step in rank.]

"Well, fellow-comrades," answered the colonel, who

fully appreciated the feelings animating his subordinates, "I'll think it over. It might, as you say, give *General* Grant a lesson regarding such high-minded outrages attempting to be put upon volunteer officers by regular officers. I should not be surprised if the matter went to Washington. If the government declines to take it up, Congress could very likely be induced to do so. I know one thing, and that is, that if *I* were in the halls of legislation every volunteer officer in service might be sure of one voice that would never bend the knee, one tongue that would never bow, one hand that would never be silent, where they needed the protection from the overweening, high-minded pertubation of West Point!"

Next day a general advance is made on all parts of the line not already in contact with the enemy's works. The Sixth gets more than a mile forward, and begins a parallel; and the "flank in the air" now rests solidly on the river above (southward of) Fort Donelson, just as the other flank rests solidly on the same river below (northward of) the fort. A semi-circle of converging fire is narrowing about the doomed foe. A confederate battery low down on the river-bank makes sad work with the gun-boats, but still they keep "pegging away," and command the river sufficiently to make the escape of any considerable body impossible; though the confederate Gen. Floyd and a few more do get across, leaving Gen. Buckner to bear alone the burden of defeat and ruin.

Will moves with his company, or at least not far away from it, though his legs and feet are very stiff and painful.

In the advance of the command they find the body of poor Jim Flynn, stripped to his very socks. They bury the hapless martyr; and the burial party, by Mac's orders, refuse to say whether the fatal bullet came to him from the front or rear. Harry Planter has disappeared as utterly as the pork and coffee—and Company K's blankets. ——

No lack of news along the line on Saturday, February 15, 1862. A flag has come in from Gen. Buckner, bearing proposals for capitulation and asking terms. Grant has named "unconditional surrender," adding, "I propose to move at once upon your works."

During the engagement on the right, Smith's division on the left had dashed in and taken a line of the enemy's outworks; and now the division to which our friends belong has been brought round and massed in that (reversed) entrenchment, in grim preparation for delivering an assault on the main works, if it shall be needful.

Strange to say, this change in what he called "the situation" did not make Colonel Puller any more contented with his lot. Even the rare privilege of leading (that is to say, following) his men up that deadly slope—perhaps underlaid with hidden percussion shells, certainly swept by a storm of missiles—failed to calm his spirit, perturbed by the official snub he had received. But just how to reopen the subject he did not quite see.

His lieutenant-colonel—one Isaacs, a "politician," yet a brave fellow and really a fine officer, who had served in the state militia—saved him the trouble by leading up to it himself.

"Well, Colonel, what did General Grant say?"

"Why, Isaacs, I haven't moved in the matter—yet."

"Now, if I were you, Colonel, I wouldn't hesitate. Go in boldly—heroically, I may say—throw aside all fear of consequences—beard the lion in his den."

The doughty colonel tapped the table with his knife, considering how he could best—that is to say, most reluctantly—follow the advice.

"You know, gentlemen, that I would rather lead that storming party a thousand times—yes, I speak within bounds and mean what I say; would rather lead *one thousand* storming parties—than do what you sudgest."

"Oh, we know all about that!" protested Isaacs, with only a scarcely preceptible wink at the major. Then he went on:

"You know, Colonel, this may be your last chance to render this service to your country. A bullet in your body this afternoon wouldn't help the cause a mite, while a word spoken in season might lead to great results."

"It will stir up a good deal of a foment. But if you consider it a matter of duty—"

"Duty before pleasure, every time! Move on General Grant rather than on Fort Donelson. If the whole volunteer force is to be made into a door-mat for the regulars to wipe their feet on, why, we want to know it!—that's all!"

"I'll do it!" said the colonel, with fierce determination. And he strode forth, courage and self-sacrifice expressed in the very squeak of his boots.

"Maje, my boy! that makes me colonel of the Sixth! And like enough this afternoon will make me an angel, and you the colonel!"

"General Grant, on interviewing my fellow-comrades, I am advised that it is best to take up with your sudgestion, report myself in arrest, and ask a court of inquiry regarding what we consider your very high-minded subvention in the discipline of my regiment."

"Well, Colonel (puff, puff), you can have your court (puff, puff), but I do not insist upon your arrest meanwhile (puff, puff). You may return to your regiment (puff), and I will order the court." [An infinite succession of puffs.]

"Excuse me, General, but under the stamina of your general order I cannot consistently appear at the head of my regiment."

"Return to duty, Colonel Puller, you are not in arrest."

"General Grant, as a protest against such a stamina as it has been to me to hear that order read at dress-parade, I would rather resign my commission than continue in command pending my justification."

"Let your resignation come up through the proper channels, and I shall act upon it."

The doughty colonel thought all went off pretty well; only once, when he repassed a tent where he had already called, he was disturbed by hearing loud laughter within, scarcely in keeping with the seriousness of the occasion. Then, too, his sensitive ear seemed to detect snorts of merriment as he passed groups of privates of his own Sixth Illinois Regiment, standing, sitting, crouching, lying, or lounging in the wet, muddy, dismal, ill-smelling, deadly earth-work.

"Old Wire-puller knows which side his bread is buttered on. He wants to go home and not wait for any pie."

"I knowed Wire-puller was a politician, quick as I seed how his eyes bug out."

"He reminds me," said Tolliver, perhaps the wittiest man in the regiment, "of a house that's all front door—the minute you lift the latch you're in the back yard."

All laughed. In fact, all were accustomed to laugh whenever Tolliver spoke. As soon as they saw his right eyebrow mount to the roots of his hair, while his left drooped so that the bright glance could be but barely seen through its shadows, they knew "suth'n wuz a-comin'."

"Ah, yah! Say, fellers, why don't we all resign?"

"I'm only sorry for one thing, an' that is that I never thought to enlist as a major-general, instead of a high private in the front rank. Now thar's ole Grant—ain't it awful easy for him to assault Donelson—'move on your works'—him a-holdin' down a camp-stool, away out of range in the rear?"

"Oh, you dry up, Jeff Cobb! He's in the right place, and the right man in the right place too."

"Well, Chip, I s'pose so. But do you know what I think when I read the papers? I think the folks at home are a-makin' a leetle mistake. They think *he* is where *we* are, and *we* are where *he* is. Now, there's him drawin' steenty-steen thousand a year, on a camp-stool, out of range; and here's me, all the same except the money, the camp-stool, and the range. I can find plenty in print about the brave and heroic Gen. Ulysses S. Grant, but nary a word about the brave and heroic Private Thomas Jefferson Cobb."

"Don't you be scairt, Jeff. Your name'll be in the papers soon enough."

"Ya-as—but it won't be in the head-lines. Them noospaper colyumes is like a coal-shute." [Jeff was a miner.] "The big chunks go thunderin' down on top of the screen whilst the little ones slip down through, 'most out of sight, in the lists of killed an' wounded."

"Wal, it's all one—er will be in a hundred years."

"Ya-as—only there'll be more Grants and fewer Cobbs."

Will got an ambulance to carry him as near to the earth-work as wheels could go; then a couple of men helped him to hobble to his post.

"Captain, you belong in the hospital, not in the assaulting column."

"Yes, Mac, I suppose so. My knees and ankles do feel pretty queer."

"What does the doctor say?"

"'Inflammatory rheumatism' was the sweet little speech he got off when he made his examination."

"What would he say about your spending the night in a trench—or even in the brush-house?"

"Probably 'fool,' with a past participle before it."

"Well—why don't you go along to the hospital?"

"And give *General* Grant a lesson?"

"Ha, ha! No, not exactly. Give yourself a rest."

"We'll see when the job is done."

And he looked anxiously across the space they would have to charge over.

He was dreadfully frightened. He could not see how it was possible to live through an advance across that rising ground and reach that horrid inner line of works under a plunging fire of musketry and artillery coming from them and from the fort itself, visible beyond them. True, our artillery had silenced the fire, and could silence it again whenever it broke out; but our artillery must be silent when the assault is made. And then—

Why should he go? He was surely a very sick man; nobody on earth who knew his condition would say it was his duty—nobody except himself.

If he were fearless, like Mac or Mark Looney, he wouldn't go. But now, afraid as he was, he *must*. He dared not stay behind, for fear it should be from the wrong motive.

And then his dear boys—how could he see them leave him and run into that maelstrom of mortality without him? How could he see them go down, one by one, and blot the ground with dreadful little blue heaps, he not even knowing which men were dead and dying? And how

explain to the rest of the world why his life was saved
when the others fell?   He heaved a great sigh:

"I'll be with you, Mac, when you start, anyhow."

"Well, Captain, I s'pose it's no use talking. But promise me one thing; that if we don't assault to-day—and
it begins to look as if we shouldn't—you'll go to the hospital for the night."

Will gave a reluctant consent to this, and when it became evident that "it," would not be to-night, he let the
ambulance carry him back to the hospital.

"Good enough!" said Mac to Morphy.   "Now ten to
one the assault will be ordered for daybreak, and be over
before Cap knows anything about it."

The men were allowed to go back to their tents and
shelters to eat and sleep.   Reveille would sound at five
(breakfast to be made ready beforehand); the whole army
being called to arms to support the assaulting division
when it had effected a lodgment, or to receive its
bloody fragments if it failed.   The division was to be in
the outwork at six, field and staff on foot, men in light
marching order—no blankets, no knapsacks, no haversacks—nothing but arms, ammunition, and canteens, full
of whisky and water if they wished it.   They were raw
soldiers, but well they knew what all that meant—chosen
victims, fatted and decked for sacrifice!

Half the men of the Sixth were writing letters that
night.   Pens and ink, pencils and paper were borrowed
and lent on all sides.   Candles stuck in bayonet sockets
were flaring everywhere.   No guard detail was demanded.
Nobody found any fault with anything they did.   Surgeons, chaplains, and other friends were burdened with
dingy letters and little packages, to be reclaimed to-morrow night or forwarded as addressed.   Watches, keep-
sakes, money, photographs—anything and everything a

man does not care to have buried with him or stolen from his body by the foe—were laid out for the dear ones at home. God! If I wanted to magnify the pathos of all this, what could I say that would not belittle it?

It seemed as if almost as soon as the camp had put on its night-quiet the company cooks were at work at the breakfast ration; and not long afterward the bugle at headquarters and the drums and fifes of the doomed regiments sounded the call to the opening of the dreadful Sunday. Then by degrees, yet rapidly, men began to gather around the camp-fires and prepare themselves for the work before them.

"Say, fellers, what's the use of eatin' so much? Jest wastin' good victuals an' makin' more work for the bury-in' squads."

"Oh, yes, Hiram—but I notice you don't hang back from the pot none to speak of! If you'd put all that stuff outside instead of inside, no bullet wouldn't never hurt ye!"

"Well, ye see, Jeff, I'm built like a camel—got three stomachs; one for ornament, one for use, an' one for some other time."

"Ah, yah! Th' ornamental one must be the insidest one of all!"

"Oh, Lord, boys—I wish I was in dad's barn!"

"Wha'd ye want t' be in the barn fer, Jeff?"

"Why, ye see, 't ain't more'n twenty rods from the barn to the house, 'n' I could jest run inter mammy's room an' hide under the bed."

"There's the long roll! Boys, say yer prayers. Somebody say one fer me, so I kin go on eatin'."

"Fall in, Company K! Fall in! Fall in!"

"Oh, yes," cried Jeff Cobb, the irrepressible, "we'll be a fallin' in in about an hour's time." Then he began to sing in a sentimental treble, "I would I were a boy again."

Jeff's voice was as unmusical as can be possibly imagined. No sooner had he begun to sing than Tolliver interrupted him.

"Say, Jeff; half a minute, please, before you go on. Have you got a house of your own?"

"Not that anybody knows of, so far as heerd from. Why?"

"Why, if I were you, I'd build one—a nice brick house in a nice big lot."

"Some burn of yours, Tolly? Well, my son, drive on about the house and lot."

"Well, Jeff, I'd work it this way. You just go to any vacant spot and begin to sing. Nobody will ever try to serve a warrant on you."

"You won't, Tolly. A man of your size! *You* won't try any such job on *me*—not while you're sober."

"And so, Jeff, you'd have your ground, all O K, don't you see? Now for the bricks. All you've got to do is just go on singing and there'll be enough bricks thrown at you to build a palace!"

Amid the chorus of laughter could be heard Jeff's voice, louder and more raucous than ever:

"I would I were a boy again."

Once more Tolliver interrupted:

"Oh, shucks! What's the use of wouldin' ye was a boy? *I* would *I* were a leetle, teenty-taunty gal-baby!"

Slowly and gropingly the regiments found their way in the dark to the now familiar ditch; lay down, or sat, or squatted, to wait for dawn and the order to advance.

Now, past the reserves, past brigade headquarters, past the brush houses, past the cooks' fires, past the ambulances and litter-bearers waiting for their sad work, past the intervening space of darkness, comes a little procession—four men carrying, on a litter, a fifth, an officer in uniform with sword and sash. The men stopped chatting and watched with curious eyes the advancing group. The recumbent form raises its head:

"Is this Company K, of the Sixth Illinois?"

It is Fargeon's voice, and a loud-answering "He-igh" is the response.

"Well, Mac, I'm glad to see you."

"Well, Captain, I'm sorry to see you—first time in my life, too."

"Oh, now, Mac, you mustn't be jealous about my commanding K once more. You'll have a chance before noon, like as not."

"I hope, Capt'n Fargeon, you'll command it as long as I'm in it—unless you get promoted and go higher."

"That's what I look for, Mac—a big promotion that'll take me out of your way for good."

They shook hands, and each could see, by the light of Mac's pipe, a loving twinkle about the eyelids of the other.

"Boys, can't you leave the litter here for me to lie on till we start? Yes? That's all right—there'll be work enough for it after I leave it. Now, Mac, let a couple of our men put in their time rubbing my feet and ankles and knees. That's right, Chip—you and Bob will do first-rate. There—hard—oh, ouch; no, don't stop; rub away like fury, no matter if I howl a little. Well, boys, Mark is getting on, all right. Wishes he were with us. Oh, Chip—that's right—oh Lordy, Lordy—but rub away. Looks as if it were going to be a fine day. There, there—you may skip the points of my ankles till some other day—after—to-morrow, week—after—next—oh, gee-whillikins! rub underneath my knee instead of on top."
And so on.

"Now, boys, I'm going to try my weight on them. Here are my sticks under me—now raise me and let me get them to the ground—there—I guess I can bear my weight. So; now I'm all right." His dangling sword wobbled about his legs and his sticks as he hobbled along the line, nodding to the men, whom he recognized partly from their place in the line and partly from the wintry gray that began to lighten the eastern sky.

"Say, Cap, this is an infantry regiment. We ain't used to marchin' alongside of quadrupeds. I'm afraid you'll beat us all on the charge bay-nets."

"No, Tolliver. But then I'll never run away on my four legs when I once get there." After a few steps more he added: "Perhaps I'd better start now, so we'll be even by and by." Which humorous suggestion was well received.

The gray grew lighter and the men began to peer into the unknown front, and, as usual, to make remarks.

"Now why in thunder don't the high mukkemuks start us out? We'd be half-way there before the rebs could get the drop on us."

"Oh, pshaw, John! I wouldn't care if they didn't start us for a month!"

Some of the men talk thus lightly and bandy jests; but the majority are pale, stern, sad, and silent. They are not the ideal soldiers; machines, indifferent to death; fatalists with their "kismet;" pious zealots mumbling prayers and glorying in any sacrifice "for God and Czar." They are common-sense, thrifty American citizens; fathers, brothers, sons, husbands; full of the hopes of peace and prosperity; regretfully though resolutely risking them all at the call of patriotic duty, with the inexplicable self-devotion of the man-at-arms.

Mac mounts the breast-work, field-glass in hand, and peers long and anxiously forward.

"Mac, come down!"

"Shortly, Captain, shortly."

"Lieutenant, I command this company for a while yet, and I order you to come down, and I mean what I say."

Mac slowly obeys, only to walk to another part of the mound and climb again on top of it, again peering into the increasing light, sweeping the field slowly from side to side with his glass.

Will gives it up.

"What do you see, Mac? If you will stick yourself up like a scarecrow to be shot at, you ought to find out something to pay us for the risk."

"I can make out the salient, and I know the flag-staff is just to the left—if the gum-boots haven't shot it away. There; now I've fixed it—the flag is flying."

"What did you expect—that they'd hauled it down?"

Mac's drawl becomes more drawling than ever as he goes on.

CHAPTER XVIII

WHAT MAC'S FIELD-GLASS SHOWED.

THE tall lieutenant in his long blue overcoat, both hands supporting his glass and both elbows level with his ears, stands perched on the highest point of the earthwork. His figure relieved against the gray sky in the dim light of misty dawn, seems of gigantic, supernatural height; but his voice has the same old strong, quiet, half-serious, half-playful drawl which his friends—his worshipers—have learned to associate with the flame and roar of battle; with trial and triumph and wounds and death.

"Well, Mac, out with it."

Through the dewy quiet the next words pierce like separate pistol-shots:

"Ye can't—'most always—tell—what—ye may least—expect—specially about—uncertain things—in this world—of chance—and change—the flag's—flying—and it's—a whi-te—fla-ag."

"SURRENDERED!" cries the captain.

"SURRENDERED! SURRENDERED!" shout the men who hear him.

The shout becomes a roar and the roar a yell of frantic joy, triumph, relief, congratulation, thankfulness.

Strong men, nerved to die to-day, laugh and cry and sob in each other's arms.

The roar spreads back to other commands, to the head-quarters of the stern, stolid commander, to hospitals where sick and wounded take new life at the sound. It flies on the wings of the lightning over the great awakening land—Chicago, Boston, New York, Philadelphia, Washington—cities, towns, and villages by the thousand take it up, and with it awaken the anxious mother and wife; the Wall street gold speculator; the money king; the hopeful, fearful, sadly smiling, burdened President. Fort Donelson, with all its strength and all its men, and all its armament and munitions of war, has fallen into the hands of the Union army!

Oh, what a Sabbath day!

Presently the nearest bands get together; and then, floating on the rays of sunrise, comes the grand, sweet air of "The Star Spangled Banner."

"Oh, say, can you see by the dawn's early light—"

And yet another ineradicable association is engraved on Will's memory.

The national hymn is followed by

"Hail Columbia, happy land!"

And that by a rattling quickstep—

"Yankee Doodle came to town."

The gun-boats catch the news, and over the water from each of them comes the same succession of well-known tunes; not very grand in themselves, but to their hearers always hereafter soul-thrilling with the meaning they express.

———

The troops who had stormed and taken the outwork before named had the distinguished honor of leading the triumphal march out from our lines, crowned with spectators, past the little village of Dover at the foot of the bluff, through the works that seamed the hill-side; through the tall grim fort itself, and into the enemy's camp beyond. But the Sixth came next, and excited much remark in the long, crowded line of friendly spectators that blackened the Union earth-works; not more by the proud figure of Lieut.-Col. Isaacs riding at its head than by a humble litter that accompanied its rear company.

"That feller was going to assault with his company, though he's got the 'flammatary rheumatism so he can't walk! Captain of Company K of the Sixth Illinois, is he? Well, he'll do."

The vanquished army presented a curious spectacle to the wide-open, excited eyes of the victors. Weful disaster as its most prominent characteristic. Even before our boys climbed the hill they passed houses which were used as hospitals; and in one court-yard particularly they could not help seeing many unburied dead, dragged out and left lying, with jaws dropped and sightless eyeballs uncovered to the morning sun, and to swarming flies seeking vainly for atoms of moisture in the dried-up founts of tears.

Thousands of muskets, a few in orderly stacks, but more in great, promiscuous, higgledy-piggledy heaps, "good enough for the dam' Yanks." Three thousand horses and mules and their hundreds upon hundreds of wagons. Forty-eight pieces of field artillery and eighteen siege-guns, including those mounted in batteries close to the river bank whence their level fire had been so terrible to the gun-boats.

"The saddest of all sights, next to a defeat, is a victory." The fearful evidences of loss by the storm of shot and shell were far more impressive and memorable than the sight of the captured property, which in its dirt and disorder looked absolutely worthless. Many dead were unburied; the stench was intolerable; in every hospital tired and sleepy surgeons were working over the wounded in a mechanical, perfunctory fashion; while laid outside —expelled to make room for others who might possibly be saved—were the usual pitiful collections of men past hope or help; not yet dead, but waiting for death as their only possible relief from suffering. Some were minus an arm or leg, but most had been abandoned without an operation. And always the swarming flies! After every battle, adjoining each hospital, lie these prostrate living forms; mostly silent, and merely gasping for last breaths, but sometimes neither silent nor motionless —writhing, moaning, hiccoughing—the most heart rending of all the distressing spectacles that meet the soldier's eyes.

At last the Sixth found a shelter (the first it had had since leaving Cairo) in the shape of a line of old-fashioned "Sibleys"—tall, round tents which taper in a drooping curve from ground to apex. These had once belonged to the United States, and had lately been in the possession of the confederacy; now they were part of the spoils of war and were allotted to the Sixth, both as a reward of merit and a necessity of existence.

Morphy soon started to hunt for Harry Planter, wounded and captured in the affair on the right. It seemed as if the poor boy would never be found; the conviction that he must have died becoming inevitable. Still Morphy kept on. Face after face, in scores and hundreds, did he peer into. The Union men in rebel hands were indeed few; yet more than once did a feeble voice meet his ear:

"Hello, lieutenant! Is it all true? Glory! Glory! Will our boys come and fetch me away pretty soon? Oh, thank God!" And grimy hands were raised to hide the tears that would spring forth.

Then again the familiar uniform would be half recognized by eyes that would never see flag, friends, or hope again. The sunlight of victory and joy for us, the blackness of night for them. To die with others, in defeat and disaster, is natural; to die alone amid victory and rejoicings is hard—hard. One young fellow, almost a boy, given over as mortally hurt, beckoned anxiously to Morphy to whisper to him:

"Oh, Lieutenant—my folks are—are very fine people— rich and all that—society and all that—they let me come though it broke mother's heart—they came down to Cairo with me—and if they knew—knew about—this— they would all come down and bring Dr. Brainard—he might know how to—to—to—to—save me, not let me die *now!*" And he sobbed as he gazed at Morphy with dry, pleading eyes that spoke a desperate longing for life.

"Well, my lad, I'm going to fetch an ambulance for a man belonging to my own company, and I'll see that you get carried over at the same time." So the boy's short march to the grave was at least illumined with the light of hope; soon to be superseded by the blinding glare of fever and delirium.

More faces—faces—faces. No, he doesn't know this man, nor this, nor this, nor this—

"Lieutenant! Lieutenant Morphy! Thank God I happened to open my eyes! I've been waiting for some of you ever since sun-up, when the firing didn't begin again as usual—and they didn't bring us nothin' to eat—and the man who brought round the water said they'd surrendered. And after all you was going to go by me!"

Sobs and tears choked his utterance, and he clasped Morphy's hand as if he was afraid to let it go. The lieutenant had failed to recognize the well-known features for which he was so earnestly seeking; pinched as they were with pain and privation, and grimy with dirt and powder-smoke.

Yes; Planter was glad of our success, but his wound hadn't been touched yet, and was already fly-blown. Ten thousand prisoners was a good many; but how about getting something to eat besides raw corn-meal mush? He didn't wonder the boys felt good—now how quick did the lieutenant s'pose he could be got over into our lines?

Morphy laid a wet cloth over his wound, gave him something from his haversack and canteen, and reassured him as to his future; and then sat down on the edge of the cot for a comforting chat. Company news was given and relished, of course. Harry forgot all his sufferings while he learned of the astounding arrest of Will and Mac; the brilliant outcome of the matter; the discomfiture of Col. Puller, and his final resignation under fire. To this last Harry could only say:

"Well, I *will* be blowed!"

"Mac," said the captain after dress-parade that evening, "Uncle Sam owes you a big debt. Suppose you had kept your mouth shut concerning our 'flank in the air,' what then?"

"Oh, the rebs would have got out, that's all. They couldn't have got their trains out, and what's an army without a train? We should have bagged them before they could reach any new base, I guess."

"An army isn't like a cannon-ball, that can roll around where it has a mind, is it?"

"No, not by a jug-full—more like a sword that you've got to hold in your hand."

The captain heaved a weary sigh.

"What a job we've got on hand, Mac!"

"Well, we don't have to do it all to-night. Let's have a pipe."

"Will it make me able to keep this leg still?" (He was lying on his cot with his knee bared.)

"Does it hurt all the time?"

"No; but just as soon as it gets into a position where it doesn't hurt, I've *got* to move it so it will."

"I notice you keep it going—budge it about six times a minute, right along."

"I study and try to make out why I can't let it lie still; but I can't, and I can't make out why, either."

With his hands he lifted the offending joint to an obtuse angle. "There—that's the easiest position; put something under it to support it; that Army Regulations will do; set it up on edge—so. Now just lay your hand on it, gently. Oh, that feels good!"

"It's burning hot. You wouldn't think it to look at it; only slightly swelled and red. Does it hurt now?"

"Not a bit. Now let's try the pipe. Thank you; that tastes good—pretty good."

"Of course it does. Didn't you ever hear the song of the soldier to his pipe?"

"Not that I remember. How does it go?"

> "Hunger and thirst. Hunger and thirst.
>   Give me my pipe; let 'em do their worst.
>
> "Cold and wet. Cold and wet.
>   Give me my pipe, I can soon forget.
>
> "Sickness and pain. Sickness and pain.
>   Give me my pipe, and I won't complain.

"Powder and ball. Powder and ball.
    Give me my pipe, I'll smoke till I fall.

"Battle and blood. Battle and blood.
    Give me my pipe, it'll still taste good.

"Wounds and death. Wounds and death.
    I'll draw my pipe with my dying breath."

"First-rate! Who made them?"

"Oh, some damfool soldier or other—on the march through the mud I judge by the sound." As he spoke he looked away, out under the tent flap; and Fargeon always suspected that the rude rhymes had originated with the rough campaigner, during some toilsome march.

After a few minutes of silent smoking, Fargeon leaned over and laid his pipe on the ground.

"How's the knee?"

"All right."

"Maybe you could get to sleep."

"Maybe."

Mac went out and lowered the tent flap, and Will dropped asleep. About five minutes later Mac heard his name called and reëntered the tent.

"Has it started to aching again?"

"N—o, but he's got to come down."

"Why not let him alone if he don't hurt you?"

"Don't ask foolish questions. Just put your hand underneath and lift him a little and take out the book. There—so—now lower gently--oh, Lord! that knee-cap feels like one great big boil! m-m-M-m-m!" He leaned up on his elbow and glared at the insensate torment; threatened it with his fist as if he would like to annihilate it.

"I told you you'd better let well enough alone."

"*Go* along about your business! Send me some deaf and dumb man that won't talk foolishness! m-m-M-m-m!"

Mac laughed, but did not go, and as soon as the acute paroxysm of pain had passed, Will apologized for his impatience.

"Oh, that's all right, Captain! If you'd just hinted you wanted me away I should have felt cut up—but a straight-out cuss like that don't hurt me."

"Did I swear?"

"Well—substantially. Now I'm going to have a surgeon here if it takes every hair off his head!"

"Mac, don't you do it! I'm calm and serious now, and I tell you that I shall be calmly and seriously angry if you allow any doctor to come near me. Think of it— a surgeon prescribing for my hot knee while such men as Harry Planter are waiting for the first dressing of their wounds! I won't have it, and that settles it. Promise to do as I say."

Mac promised, but he managed to get invited to dine at the mess of a surgeon whom he knew; and was comforted to know that the inflammatory kind of rheumatism, though the most painful, is usually the least serious type of the complaints that go by that name; that it has a regular number of days to run (if it receives no fresh aggravations by fresh exposure), and that in most cases the chief danger is that it may run into the chronic form.

Next morning a telegram came from Mr. Penrose, asking how Will was in health, and saying that a relief expedition was fitting out to help the hospital service. He offered to accompany the expedition, "bringing a member of my family along."

Will lay back with the yellow paper fluttering in his hand, and tried to fancy his sweet, pure, delicate, girlish Sally sitting by his side. Then he opened his eyes and looked at his shabby environments. The old tent was full of holes and rents, and smeared with dirt; floorless, almost seatless, quite cheerless. Soiled clothes here, crumpled newspapers there, sword and belt yonder, lying on dirty boots—worse than all, a certainty of in habitants in the old Sibley other than those entered on the army lists, either Union or rebel. He himself unshaven, unshorn, and wearing clothes that had not been even removed for more than a week.

His mind wandered out over the scene around. No cleanliness, no decency, no privacy, none of the conveniences of civilized humanity; no purity to the sense of seeing, of hearing, of smelling, or of tasting. Dead beasts polluting not only the land, but even the water of the river, along whose muddy banks their carcasses lay rotting.

Until now he had not at all realized the squalor of the place and time; but now he had to try to reconcile it with the state of things suggested by the telegram he held in his hand—with the presence of Sally Penrose! He could not do it. He wished—oh, how he wished!— that they would not come. He tried to frame a telegram which should not be rude and yet should prevent the visit.

"Confined to tent with inflammatory rheumatism. Not dangerous. Hardly fit to see you here. When I can I will ask leave and come as soon as possible."

Fargeon wrote this very plainly, and the telegrapher got the words all correctly; but by reason of one slight change in punctuation, it presented an entirely new aspect when it reached the parsonage.

CHAPTER XIX.

HE change in the telegram was simply the interpolation of a period after the word "ask," which made the closing part read thus:

"Hardly fit to see you here. When I can I will ask. Leave and come as soon as possible."

This was rather blind; but the closing sentence was unmistakable. Poor English, but plain in its meaning. They "left" at once.

It was not so bad after all. The "relief expedition" was united with a party consisting of the governor of the state and other high officials, and all were provided with a chartered steamer (the Athabasca) at Cairo; so that not only was there transportation to and from the battle-ground provided for, but also their shelter and support while they staid.

Sally and her sister Lydia were both of the party, together with others of their sex from Chicago and Springfield, where (as over the entire North) people were wild with joy and eager with thanks to Grant and his brave army, and offers of relief and aid.

What belles the young women found themselves to be on the Athabasca and in camp! Sally's alarm at the 'Come as soon as possible" message had been appeased by later advices, and she was moderately gay as well as conspicuously handsome. Solemn statesmen and politicians called her "Lady" and talked gravely to her on serious subjects, greatly to her delectation and eke to theirs; for she listened much and said little, gazing with great eyes that seemed to drink in their ponderous words as the embodiment of all wisdom.

Lydia, in all the rosy dawn of womanhood, took naive delight in the exercise of her newly acquired power over that strange creature, man. She made havoc among the hearts of the younger travelers—new-made officers, military secretaries, aides-de-camp and other fledglings, brimming with ambition and impatience to taste war's bitter cup that sparkles so alluringly. They awaited their turns to promenade the deck with her, and applied all arts to please her—quite unconscious that she was privately comparing each with McClintock, so strong, grave, quiet; her ideal of heroism.

"Sally, are you asleep?"

No answer comes, and a pretty face peers down over the edge of the upper berth, at a lovely face just visible in the lower, by the dim light of the state-room lamp.

"Oh, you needn't shut your eyes so tight! I can see, by your shutting them so *awfully* tight, that you are wide awake; so I am going to talk. Well, *another* man has said, when I told him that I had enlisted as a hospital nurse, that he was going to try to get wounded immediately, and then followed it by saying that he was wounded already and shot through the heart, and all that; and when I said that no man that was shot through the heart could be admitted to *my* hospital, he said they'd have to bury him, and would I come to his funeral; and I said I would with pleasure, and fire a salute over his grave; and he asked what kind of a salute, and said if it was the right kind of a salute he would come to life again just to be there and be struck by it! Oh, I wish you'd been there! You'd have just *died!*"

"Then I'm glad I wasn't. Now go to sleep."

"Oh, you old poke, you! You think nobody can be grown up but yourself. I really believe they all think I'm a great deal older than I am, and I just hope you won't go and tell them I am not. Now, will you?"

"Oh, no; I won't tell them you are not older than you are. How could you be?"

"Oh, you know what I mean. I think it's perfectly splendid, and I wish the old Athabasca could go on forever and ever, and we stay on board always, just sailing up one river and down another. Don't you?"

"How could the Athabasca get across after going up one river so as to come down another?"

"Oh, any way she liked. And I think the young officers are perfectly splendid; and you go and spend your time with those governors and things instead! Pretending to be so awfully impressed! *I* saw you shining your big eyes at that old fossil, Dubois, and making believe you hung on every word he uttered about Mason and Slidell, and all that! Talk about the attitude of England—I wish you could have seen *your* attitude! If you could only have stood where I did and seen yourself! You would have *died* sure enough."

"Died over again? I couldn't if I had died before when you say you wish I had."

"S-T-O-U-G-H, stuff! You know what I mean. And all the while you were thinking how you could get rid of him and write your letter to mother as you ought to have been doing, and you know it, Miss Pretense; so there now! But you're an old dear, and I love you of course—only your name ought to be Sapphira instead of Sara. How d'ye do, Sapphira?"

"Bunny!"

Instantly two pearly teeth, visible till then, were covered by a firmly compressed lip; and a small steamboat pillow came plunging down into the lower berth.

"Oh, how nice! I've been wanting another pillow. Now if I call you Bunny again, what will you throw down?"

"All the bed-clothes—and I'll freeze—and then you'll have no little sister!"

Silence reigned for a few moments, and then a fair white arm, half covered by a loose sleeve, thrust the pillow back into the upper berth.

"Sally, you are a blessing and an angel, no matter if you were to call me Bunny ten thousand times in succession; but I hope you will take some other time to do it, for it would keep me awake; and now I wish you wouldn't talk any more, because I want to go to sleep. 'Our Father Who art in Heaven—'" and she just managed to get through the Lord's prayer by slighting the last words into "freverneveramen," already nearly inaudible to her sister, and quite so to herself.

Next morning when the fair sisters greeted each other from berth to berth, Lydia asked:

"What can be the matter? Why are we so quiet, do you suppose?"

"I suppose that we are at Donelson."

"Oh, I hope not!" And then two slender arched pink soles, finished off with shining pink heels and toes, issued from the upper berth and hung down from limbs, round, shapely and—not slender.

"Oh, how sharp this board is! I feel as if I were a wounded soldier being amputated."

Down she came to the floor with a rustle and thump. Then a bright face, adorned with frowzy, curly hair and two ravishing teeth, peered out of the little window.

"Yes! We're here! I can see a tall, ugly, sloping, paved river-bank, and then a high, bare bluff with a real fort on top! And oh! such lots and lots of steamboats lying with their noses at the bank and their heels kicking out into the stream! And one steamboat, with sloping, black sides, is anchored in the middle of the river, and she has a flag flying, and a great big, *awful*-looking cannon on the deck, and another peeping out of a hole in her side, like a dog in a kennel.

"Come, dear; dress yourself, or else climb back into your berth and let me get up."

"And such crowds of men on the river-bank! And our fine gentlemen are standing in a row and are looking ashore—like your Sunday-school class waiting for the Christmas presents to be given out."

"Now will you dress?"

"Yes, yes; don't you see I am dressing?"

"No, I don't call anything dressing until you come away from that window and behave as a girl should who is old enough to have admirers. * * * Oh, yes, kissing and hugging are very well, but how about dressing?"

A great deal of hot water and soap had done their best for Will, and some boards and a chair by his bedside were striving to ameliorate the squalor of his miserable old gray tent. Yet, after all, who was it who greeted the parson and his fair, fresh daughters? It was a gaunt and grizzled elderly man, thin and pale with illness and pain; his hair too long uncut and his beard (which he had shaved off in Chicago) at its very worst—the ten-day stage. No linen about him—nothing but dingy, over-night-looking woolens.

Poor Sally struggled against the hateful, ungrateful, un-patriotic feeling, but it would intrude; a feeling as if she could respect this veteran as a heroic and honorable wreck—but not think of him as a lover. She bent down and kissed his forehead—just a duty-kiss, such as she might bestow on a sick but worthy uncle. And she sat by his side and held his feverish hand in hers, saying little, looking off through the tent opening, and feeling utterly foreign to everything about her, including Will. He on his part saw the incongruity of it all, and more than ever regretted the visit.

Will" (she spoke with an effort), "some of the ladies on the boat have formed themselves into a nursing corps to be known as the Burden-sharers."

"Oh, I hope, Sally, you won't go into any such scheme!"

"Well, they have none but married women." [She did not say that in a burst of patriotic fervor she had dreamed of having her father marry her to him so as to fit her for the "high and holy mission."]

"I'm glad of that, anyhow."

"We all thought, you know—

> " 'There was lack of woman's nursing,
>   There was dearth of woman's tears.' "

"Well, so there is and must be. It's part of war."

"We had a beautiful address from a Boston lady. She said it was woman's mission to bathe the brow of anguish."

"Well, but, my dear Sally, you know the brow is only a small part of a man. Who is going to wash the rest?"

Sally did not know.

"But couldn't I read aloud to them—write for them—pray with them!"

"Oh, yes, in a large northern hospital with separate rooms for different classes of patients—convalescents, and so forth. But there is no place in a field hospital for my pretty, delicate Sally."

"Are there absolutely no women in the hospitals?"

"Yes, they hire some black women to wash, and scrub, and—such things."

Mr. Penrose and Lydia (attended by some of her satellites) were making a tour of the fort and a few of the nearest defensive earth-works, under the guidance of McClintock and Morphy. Lydia and Mac extended their walk to the earth-work where the Sixth had stood ready for the assault, on the memorable Sunday morning, and saw the place where the captain's litter had been placed—they even found the footprints where Mac had stood when he saw the white flag through the morning mist.

"Mr. McClintock—Lieutenant, I suppose I ought to say, only I *never* can think of it—would you mind setting your feet in those very places again? Now look through your glass at the fort just as you did that morning! Oh, that is splendid! Can you remember how you felt and what you thought?"

"I guess the first thought I had, was that Captain Fargeon wouldn't have to hobble up the hill after all."

"What next?"

"Oh—how Colonel Puller would be wanting to kick himself black and blue in a few minutes."

"And then what?"

"Why, then the boys began shouting and yelling and laughing, so that I couldn't hear myself think—only to be glad they were all going to stay alive awhile instead of going dead that morning."

16

"Now come down and stand by me and tell me *truly* —cross your heart, as we school-girls used to say—didn't you think of yourself at all?—not the least little bit?"

"Well—come to think—after a while, when I saw all the boys shaking hands, and hugging each other, and sobbing for joy, it *did* strike me a little how curious it was that nobody on earth cared whether I was alive or dead."

He looked in her glowing face and met her shining eyes with a quiet smile, the look and smile lasting so long that she had to turn away, with a little laugh of embarrassment.

"Well—Lieutenant, if you'll promise not to laugh at me, I'll tell you what I thought just now as you stood there."

"Do tell me. You can't hurt my feelings—they're callous."

"Well, then—you'll try not to laugh at me, won't you? Because you know we ministers' daughters naturally remember our fathers' texts."

"I won't laugh. Was it Joshua tooting his horn before the walls of Jericho?"

"No, indeed! That's horrid of you! It was something very complimentary; and *rather* sentimental."

"Well, Miss Lydia, if you can stand it I can. *What* did you think?"

"I thought—'How beautiful upon the mountains are the feet of him that bringeth good tidings!' So *there* now!"

Mac looked away a moment in silence, while Lydia wondered how he would take it. When he turned to her again his face was flushed up to the very temples.

"That is the prettiest music I ever heard in my life."

They rejoined the minister, and the three walked up the scarred slope—a week ago so deadly, now so dull, commonplace, silent, and peaceful. A cow wandered about searching for spears of last year's grass. Birds were actively discussing the great nest question. Negro children were picking up fragments of shells, which they offered for sale, calling them (with unconscious accuracy) "Momentums." They bought some of these, and culled some other reminders of the place, moss and ferns, some dandelions, and even a few—very few—violets, until Lydia's hands and handkerchief were quite loaded.

"Mr.—— I mean Lieutenant—is this long mound of fresh soil another earth-work?"

Mac hesitated, then stammered: "Yes—yes, miss."

"Union, or rebel?"

"Well—a little of both."

"Nonsense! How could there be a joint earth-work? The men on each side would kill all the men on the other side! Then it would have nothing but dead corpses to protect."

Mac laughed. "Well, Miss Penrose, to tell you the truth, that's all it ever did protect. It's only a grave."

"Oh!" She shuddered and clung to his arm. Then, overcoming her repugnance, she went to the unsightly heap (Mac carefully guiding her to the windward side) and dropped the leaves and flowers here and there along its slope.

"How pitifully few they look!"

"Yes. Just about a leaf apiece for the boys lying below, piled side by side and over each other as close as they can be packed in."

They all returned to Fargeon's tent and prepared for a visit to the hospitals. Will insisted that Sally should accompany them; to which she readily assented—not that she would confess to being tired of that dreary old tent and Will's hot hand and irrepressible restlessness; but that she must make at least one effort to carry out some of the romantic resolutions she had fixed in her mind so firmly before coming from home, and during the journey; when she was thinking constantly of Florence Nightingale, and wondering if any dying soldier would ever kiss *her* shadow as she passed.

A memorable pilgrimage, that through the main hospitals, an experience that none of the civilians ever forgot. Here the bandaged stump of a lost arm, laid out on the blanket, or on a rude box beside the cot. There a leg, sorely injured, and yet to be saved if possible, supported by a cord let down from above. Again, a sufferer being nourished through a tube because his jaw was shot away. Worst of all, perhaps, the cases where only the pale, pinched face and fading eyes indicated that *that* bullet had found its way to some vital organ, and was necessarily a peremptory summons to "leave the warm precincts of the cheerful day."

One fine fellow, older than the average, specially attracted Mr. Penrose's attention. He seemed to be looking at the world with a kindly, hopeful, amused patience; as if he could contemplate life as a whole and easily put up with a simple episode like a sojourn in a field hospital with a wound received in the very first hour of his very first battle. After a few words which elicited this fact, the visitor said to the patient:

"My dear friend, I am a clergyman. Is there anything I can do to minister to your deepest needs?"

"Well—if you could give me a pipe and some tobacco, and permission to smoke here—"

This was not *exactly* what the good man had in view, but nevertheless he sought the attendant in charge to prefer the humble request. Being referred to the surgeon, the latter said:

"What—number thirty-eight? Oh, yes; let him have

whatever he craves. It won't make any difference. He can't possibly live."

And when he returned—pale, breathless, and sorely disturbed—the quiet man said:

"I see the doctor has told you it won't make any difference what *I* do."

After he recovered from the severe shock all this gave him, Mr. Penrose managed to secure the coveted solace; and at once he had his hands full of business, so many applied to him to do the same for them. He soon exhausted the spare supply of his own friends; then what there was to be found on the steamboat, and finally he was forced to spend in the sutlers' shops every cent he had with him. He wrote home to his wife that night:

"You would have been edified, my dear, could you have seen your reverend spouse spending a good part of the holy Sabbath flying about, purchasing very cheap tobacco at very dear rates from everybody who would sell it to him. I have always tried to be a humble servant of my Master. He said the Sabbath was made for man; and I must say, dear, that the looks some of these men gave me (though they said but little) seemed like those the painters depict on the face of the sick whom He healed.

"The 'Burden-sharers'—God bless their dear, kind hearts—set bravely to work in their mission. They visited all the hospitals, without exception, and repeated over and over again the offer to bathe the sufferers' brows, and the assurance that they would gladly have brought a bouquet to each patient if they had only had the needful flowers.

"They worked all the morning and up to dinner-time; some of them were even late for the one-o'clock dinner on board the boat! After dinner, being quite tired out, they thought best to husband their strength for the work, and not to climb up the hill again for the short time they would be able to serve before supper; so they decided to rest through the afternoon in order to be fresh for the labors of to-morrow.

"But between ourselves, my love, I begin to doubt the perfect success of the Burden-sharers' movement. Mrs. Simpler—Mother Simpler she is called in charity circles—seems more adapted to the kind of work needed, although the ladies, in forming the society, scarcely recognized her as one of them.

"Mother Simpler did not arrive in time for dinner, nor even for supper, I believe; for it was hours afterward—after dark in fact—I saw the steward setting a meal for her at one end of the long table, away down the cabin under the farthest lamp. I told her of the ladies' plans and asked for her report. I think I will set it down as nearly as possible in her own good-natured phrases, and her rude, untutored language:

"'Why, Lord bless ye, I haven't got nothing to *report.* I jest sot down between the first two beds I come to and 'tended to the boys as well as I could. I hustled 'round and got 'em some warm water an' soap an' a towel, an' they washed themselves *good.* Then a feller that had lost his arm asked me to help him out, an' of course I did, an' I washed his feet for him, an' I tell you they needed it *bad.* Then I asked the hospital steward if they didn't provide no fine-tooth combs; an', if you'll believe me, there wasn't such a thing to be had! The *idy* of a hospital without a fine-tooth comb! Well, I wasn't goin' to give it up so; an' I jest *made* 'em fix up a bottle of decoction of cocculus indicus and I spread it round *good* I tell ye! An' I'm a-goin' to stick to it, too. You may tell the folks up in Chicago that you left me down here fightin' varmin, an' they may call me old Mother

Cocculus Indicus if they've a mind to, but I ain't a-goin' to give up the fight till they're driven out of every hospital here—yes, an' out of every camp, too, that I can get at.'

"Dear old Martha! Before her I feel my littleness. The Lord will remember her in the last day of her much serving. * * * "

The next dawn heralded a brighter day for the young lovers. But that must wait for a new chapter.

CHAPTER XX.

HARD LINES IN PLEASANT PLACES.

SAY, Mac, I can't stand this."

"Worse this morning, Captain Fargeon?"

"No; I'm better. It's left my knees; though my ankles are catching it. It seems to be going off in that direction, and you see it's only got two feet further to go before I lose it altogether."

"Two feet? Oh, I see; that's a joke. Well, I guess you're getting better sure enough. What was it you couldn't stand?"

"Why, looking so like Time in the primer! Don't you suppose you can lassoo a barber off one of the boats to come up and shave me, and some one to brush my boots and clothes?"

"Better? I believe you! You are going to be our old elegant Cap Fargeon again. Hurrah for everything! The boys will just get up on their hind legs and whoop when I tell 'em you're all right once more!"

The day was bright and warm; the snow was gone and the ground almost dry.

"I suppose there are no boards to be had, Mac?"

"Not one, for love or money," said Mac, laughing. Then he whistled, and Chipstone appeared.

"Chip, the captain wants some floor-boards, and I tell him there are none to be had for love or money." He winked at the sergeant (just promoted), and Chip answered gravely:

"Not one, Lieutenant, for love or money!"

Then he disappeared, and within an incredibly short time a little group of K men appeared with enough boards for a good tent floor and an outside platform besides.

"I thought you said they couldn't be had for love or money."

"They can't, Captain; but we know of other ways of getting what *you* want—and we got 'em."

Will felt a little doubtful about the strict morality of this summary proceeding, but (not being so squeamish as of old) he did not inquire into it more particularly. The floor was laid; a "fly" of canvas was stretched overhead in front of the tent, a long chair was borrowed from the nearest hospital, Will, with some help, donned his cleanly brushed clothes, got his face shaved, and—looked like a new man. He could not quite stand it to put the boots on yet; but in their now resplendent appearance they were ranged in plain sight and really looked quite decorative—though the word is a later adaptation.

On the boat, Sally Penrose had had a rather bad night. *She*, a patriot and a Christian, a thoughtful, self-respectful woman, to find her foolish fancy shocked into repulsion by the personal appearance of her plighted spouse! His privations and sufferings—voluntary and heroic—which ought to add to her love, acting as an extinguisher to it!

Perhaps if all had been different—if Captain Fargeon had been wounded ever so dreadfully, and she had found him all gory, among the dead and dying, she would not have failed so utterly at the time of trial; but in his ill-smelling tent on that muddy hill, with his rheumatism—

In the morning she made a point of looking her best, and being ready for breakfast among the very first, and of getting herself, her father and her sister started up the long, hard climb at the very earliest possible moment. Firmness! No hanging back from the dreadful, horrid tent! And she *would* smile. She would laugh, and make dear Will laugh, with an account of the Burden-sharers' brow-bathings, done in her very most brilliant style! She would be a real "streak of sunshine" (as dear Will had often called her in happier days when she wasn't engaged to him) and not a cloud of gloom, as she felt she had been yesterday.

The effort, mental and bodily, made her feel better, and she arrived, flushed and panting, at the camp level. It scarcely took any force to institute the pre-determined smile as she tripped along, quite outstripping the rest.

What is this? An elegant awning-covered platform, in front of a floored tent; glittering sword and flame-red sash decorously hung up over a row of glistening black boots decoratively arranged below! And—her own lover sitting in soldierly state in the midst! his clean-shaven face thinned and paled by suffering, but handsomer than of old, because graver, and strengthened by the memory of battle and the late calm contemplation of impending death. Yesterday was all a horrid dream—it was some other woman who had shrunk from some other man.

She dared not kiss him in all that publicity; but when he clasped her hand she furtively pressed it to her lips and met his admiring gaze with a look of unmistakable reciprocity.

"You are a vision of beauty this morning," whispered he.

"You are my handsome hero and my love forever."

The boys of Company K cast many curious yet respectful glances at the fair sisters, and smiled sympathetically when sounds of hearty laughter (Fargeon's voice being audible among the rest) came from the group as it listened to Sally's story of the doings of the ladies in the hospitals, as reported by themselves. Word was passed down the line of tents that the visitors were coming down to see the men at home; whereupon they proceeded to make themselves decent. Those who were mending garments necessary for propriety hastened to put them on. Those who were washing their hairy chests and muscular shoulders, still black and blue from the recoil of the musket, got themselves into presentable shape as soon as possible.

When it came to the point Sally declared herself "tired," at the same time giving Will a hand-squeeze that translated her "tired" feeling into a reluctance to leave him. So the others set off without her. But almost the first group they stopped to talk with (much as they admired the budding beauty of Lydia) asked Mac:

"Ain't Cap Fargeon's young woman goin' to honor us with a call?" This was said in a tone of assumed indifference; but the lieutenant's quick ear detected an undertone of disappointment that made him interrupt Lydia and say:

"Oh, yes—she's coming of course. I'll go back and see what keeps her."

He went up and whispered a few words to Fargeon.

"Sally," said the captain, with gratified pride, "the lieutenant says the men will be hurt if you don't go and see them."

"Oh, indeed!" she cried, dimpling, blushing, and bridling. "I am awfully flattered, and I'll go at once."

"I don't wonder they love to look at you—you beauty!"

he murmured. "And give them your brightest, sweetest smile; for I love them like brothers."

"All right! I'll look at each one as if I were already his sister-in-law!"

Sally shook hands with them all (they were only about sixty now) and said a word to such as she had heard of personally. Happy they!

"Sarg'nt Chipstone, I heard of you after the corn-field battle." "Mr. Town, you're the one who got the first sight of the rebels over the corn-field." "Mr. Thrush, I've been waiting to see you to tell you that I went with Capt'n Fargeon to visit your mother, and am going again when I get back, so you must tell me what to say to her for you." "Mr. Sylvester, I remember you too, at Cairo. I'm sorry not to hear you singing as you used to. We all cried when we heard about Clinton Thrush. It almost makes me cry now to think of it." And so on, at tent after tent.

"Mr. McClintock has told me of your losing your blankets by no fault of your own, and about your being expected to pay for others. I think it is the most disgraceful, burning shame I ever heard of in my life! Gov. Yates is on the boat I am going back on, and I shall tell him the whole story."

"Thank you, Miss Penrose. It does seem a little rough to fine Company K a hundred dollars and more for going out and being shot from both front and rear."

"It shall not be so if I can help it."*

---

* The men had to have blankets at once, so Fargeon (against Mac's advice) receipted for them to the quartermaster, at the same time furnishing the proper affidavits to show how the men had lost them, and asking for a free issue. Col. Puller sent up the papers "disapproved." When the paymaster next visited the regiment each man found, in the appropriate column of the pay-roll, an extra blanket charged him and deducted from his pay. The captain made all these deductions good to the men, using up his entire monthly stipend and a little more. Then, by help of Lieut.-Col. Isaacs, he set the whole matter clearly before the War Department, only to learn (after a year's delay) that nothing short of a special act of Congress would afford him relief.

"My! Aint she peaches?"

After she had passed on one of the country boys (George Friend) was heard to say:

"My! ain't she peaches? I'll bet ye *she* kin play the pie-anner with her hands crossed an' her eyes shut *tight!* Yes, sir-ee!"

Mac's attentions were seemingly monopolized by Sally, but a close observer might perceive that his eyes followed Lydia wherever she went under Morphy's devoted escort. The gay party called at regimental headquarters and were flatteringly received by "field and staff." Dr. Ward pretended to be very much annoyed and hurt, both personally and professionally, that Captain Fargeon should presume to be getting well without his aid or sanction.

"However, Miss Penrose, I'll forgive him on one condition, and that is that he will let me prescribe for him just once and will take the prescription—as he will."

"Dear me, Doctor, under the circumstances, and considering your state of mind, I should be afraid your prescription would be fatal."

"I think it might. I don't think he will get over the remedy half so soon as he will over the disease."

"Then I shall object to his trying it."

"I don't believe you will; and I believe he will follow my directions to the letter."

"Well, what is the prescription?"

The doctor took out a prescription paper and wrote:

"Rx. Athabasca. Quant. suf. Quotidie. Ad infinitum."

Captain Fargeon "took his prescription like a little man," hired an intelligent black fellow to wait on him, and had himself transferred to the Athabasca, looking forward to a quiet, restful, luxurious time of perfect privacy and sweet enjoyment of the society of his lady-love. But things did not turn out exactly so. On the contrary, he found himself once more in danger of being spoiled by hero-worship. The Burden-sharers would have liked to stand in line, awaiting their turn to bathe his brow. He was publicly pointed at as the man who had prepared to follow the assault on a litter rather than be left behind. Governor Yates himself was flatteringly attentive, and talked with him with all the art and charm which nature had so bountifully bestowed on our grand, unfortunate War-Governor, and which lingers in the memory of thousands of Illinoisans to this day.

"Captain Fargeon, your State and nation honor such acts as that of yours, unimportant though you seem to think it. You are on this boat as the guest of Illinois. My only regret is that you did not come on board at once upon our arrival, instead of now, on the eve of our departure."

"What?" cried poor Sally, struggling against a return of her old foolish faintness. "I thought—we all thought—" Here tears came to her relief and she welcomed them as evidence that she should not faint.

"Do not distress yourself, dear lady. I am unexpectedly and unwillingly called back to Springfield; but why should not Captain Fargeon accompany us, at least as far as Cairo?"

"I have no leave of absence, Governor."

"I think I can arrange that for you, Captain," answered the Governor, and added, with one of his charming bows, "and in the service of beauty in distress" (a wave of the hand toward the still tearful Sally), "no effort of mine shall be spared to make your trip agreeable to all concerned."

The Athabasca started at midnight (convoyed by a gunboat), and Will was carried off a willing prisoner. After reaching Cairo no one remained on the boat except the

Penroses and their patient and Mrs. Simpler, who waited impatiently for the boat's return to Donelson, where she might continue her work—now armed with an official document that was to strengthen her hands and make her the savior of life to many men.

For some days the party on the Athabasca enjoyed a heavenly quiet; Lydia alone being at all cast down by the change. Then the boat prepared for a return trip and the lovers were parted; but it was not such anguish as before. Parting and meeting had now grown to seem more like natural and persistent occurrences, each following in orderly sequence.

CHAPTER XXI

FORWARD TO SHILOH.

ALL things come for him who can wait (only they often miss him, and inure to the benefit of some other fellow). This is true whether the waiting be voluntary or compulsory. The Sixth had to wait for its own camp and camp equipage; and they came. Also all things go from him who can wait—inflammatory rheumatism among the rest; so Fargeon got on his feet again, scarcely the worse for his affliction, which had been short and slight, and more than compensated by the visit from and with his friends.

"Tolly, show us yer card trick," said Chipstone, one day. "Ye 'llaow ye can tell the card a man picks out; naow we'd like t' see ye dew it. Put up or shut up."

"Well, boys, that's what. You're to shuffle the cards, I cut 'em and hold 'em backs up; four of ye draw cards, look at 'em and put 'em back, I don't look at 'em, shuffle again, and then, blindfold, show every man the identical card he picked out."

"Go ahead—talk's cheap; it takes stones to bring down persimmons."

"Wa-al—I don't see no money up, so fur."

"I'll bet a dollar, even, agin ye, if ye're playin' it square."

"Good enough, Chip.   Who next?"

"Count me in," sung out several voices.

"Hold on—four's enough. I can't afford to lose more'n four dollars.   Chip, 'n' Cy, 'n' Aleck, 'n' Ben—that'll do. Naow you shuffle—naow I cut, see?   Naow draw—thar, one at a time—so."   (Each draws, glances furtively at his card and replaces it quickly and warily.) "Thar naow, shuffle agin—see?   Are ye satisfied?   Any man that wants to can back out yet."

"Oh, go ahead!   Ye want to back aout yerself, I guess."

"Back aout?   Not by a jug-full!   But seein' I've got the dead wood on ye, I let ye know that the bet's off. I don't want yer money; thirteen dollars a month is millions fer me.   Naow blindfold me—so.   Don't draw the handkerchief too awful tight!   Quit yer foolin'!   I said blindfold, not blind!   Naow stand back while I jist lay out the cards in four rows, thirteen cards in a row— see?   Thar!   Naow, Chip, do ye see yer card?"

"Yes, she's thar."

"Cy, how about yours?"

"She's O K."

"So's mine," cried Aleck and Ben together.

"All right then," cried Tolliver, pulling off his blind-fold.   "Then I've showed each of ye the card he picked out.   "I've kept my promise.   How about the bets?"

Of course the delighted spectators took pleasure in de-ciding that Tolly, their unfailing entertainer, had fairly won the money; but he, as "straight" as he was gay, stood by his refusal and merely advised the boys to look out sharper next time who they bet with.   "Take the infant-class in a Sunday-school, my sonnies.   Ye might win suthin' from them—if ye have luck."

———

'Well, boys, we move to-morrow."

"Where to?"

"Oh, somewhere's down in Dixie, I s'pose."

"Go it, ye cripples!"

"No rest for the wicked."

"What's the matter with lettin' somebody else do some of the marchin' and fightin'?"

"Ya-as; that's so, friend Rice! Marched t' death, an' froze t' death, an' starved t' death, an' fought t' death, an' scairt t' death; an' now started out again jest as soon as we begin to git half-way comfortable!"

"You shut up! Where are we goin' to this time?"

"Oh, steamboatin' somewhere; I don't know where. Nobody knows."

"A free ride! Excursion tickets don't cost us a cent! Ain't we pampered autocrats? Reg'lar high mukkemuks!"

"Well, I didn't hear anything about any return tickets."

"Ah, yah! I'll bet ye! Lots of us won't need any."

Good-bye, Donelson. Good-bye, all the earth-works, the fields fought over, and the woods fought under; the horrible hospitals and the great graves; the scenes of agonizing effort, of devoted courage, of bright victory and black defeat. Even a small, second-rate struggle, such as this was (although with great results), included many, many acts of heroism which were unheralded and are forgotten; some because of the insignificant standing of the actor; some because of his dying in the doing of them—the torch of glory quenched with the blood of the hero; like poor Mark's matches in the fence-corner. [In any European army the victory would have been followed by the distribution of a thousand "orders" and "decorations."]

Bright, clever Sally Penrose took care that one little bit of compensation should fall where it was deserved. She secretly learned the mystery of brevets, and actually drew an application for one for Will Fargeon! She caused her father to sign it; then sent it to Governor Yates with a letter of her own; received it back with the governor's hearty indorsement, and sent it to General Grant, who at once approved it and forwarded it to the proper authorities. Not a word of all this reached the beneficiary, however, till long after the time we are now describing.

Once more we break camp. Once more the improvised seats, tables, chimneys, floors, couches, comfortable devices innumerable—"pulpits and piano-fortes"—are abandoned. The boys grumble, more for fun than anything else; for each and all were pleased and more than pleased with anything that looked like progress. "As though we were going to get to work and get through before judgment-day."

We steam away northwesterly, down the Cumberland to where it empties into the Tennessee; then turning southerly, we steam up the Tennessee past captured Fort Henry, with its gun-boats and military post, to the furthest point the Union army has yet penetrated. We are at Pittsburg Landing, where the Union lines include Shiloh Church, only a few miles from the northern boundary of the "Gulf States."

It is getting toward the beginning of April, and to northern senses the winds feel as warm and the woods look as green as they should at the end of May. There is something more repellant in untimely warmth than in untimely cold, and our boys are made languid and depressed by the unfamiliar, "unseasonable" mildness.

Our first permanent camp-ground is in pleasant woods within an hour's easy march of the landing-place, where we instantly begin once more the institution of "pulpits and piano-fortes." Brigade after brigade passes out and takes position; the various bodies occupying every good camping-ground that can be found, until there are more than one hundred regiments of infantry on the ground, besides artillery and cavalry.

"Well Mac, how do you like it?"

"What?"—removing his pipe—"tobacco? I like it very much."

"No; our place and our surroundings."

"Oh—food, forage and fuel plenty; water fairly good; paymaster comes regularly; and I'm not dead yet. Those are all the elements of happiness a soldier has any right to expect—a good deal more than all he gets, usually."

"Come now, Mac, you know what I mean. In a campaigning point of view, what do you think of our prospects?"

"Well, you might as well ask a number two mackerel in the Pacific Ocean to show you the road to Norwich."

"Oh, you can give some kind of a guess; what does it look like—attack or defense?"

"Certainly not defense. You see how we're placed; every regiment on its own front and nobody's else—just where it is handy to a road and to water. Where could we fire, this minute, without hitting our friends?"

"That means that we expect to march out and attack Corinth as soon as Buel joins us."

"Surely, if the rebels allow it."

"How can they hinder it?"

"Jump on us before Buel gets here."

"Ah! Now, Mac, that reminds me that I learned to-day that Beauregard had sent in a flag of truce, saying that if we did not evacuate the place in ten days he will attack it."

"What?"

"Just that. What does *that* mean?"

Mac laid down his pipe and began to check off his views on his fingers, a familiar indication of just the frame of mind to which Fargeon had been trying to lure him.

"It means either" (thumb) "that Bory wanted the flag-bearer to snoop some information, or" (forefinger) "that he thinks he can fool us into waiting here for an attack that'll never come; or" (middle finger) "that he *is* going to attack, and thinks that we'll think he isn't just because he says he is; or" (third finger) "that he doesn't know whether he's a-foot or a-horse-back."

"Well, that's four. Now take thumb—snooping information."

"I guess he gets lots of information better than any flag-bearer could fetch him; all these angry Southern-ers coming in com-plaining of depreda-tions on their planta-tions! They either come a-purpose to learn, or they go back

mighty ready to tell all they know. And you'll notice that they keep their eyes tight open, and always want to be taken right to the 'head general.'"

"Looks likely. Now how about forefinger?"

"Trying to fool us to gain time? Well, it lies between that and the next—trying to be taken by contraries. Albert Sidney Johnson is no fool, whatever Bory is."

"Looks more like the attack then—doesn't it?"

"It does squint that way. One thing is certain, if they

daren t venture to attack us before Buel joins, they can't either attack or defend *after* he joins."

"Humph! Now look here, Mac; you start by saying we are in no shape to stand an attack, and you end up by saying we're going to be attacked."

'What of that? Such things have happened."

"Well then, one of two things will come to pass:" (Will held up his hands and pulled back his thumb in mimicry of Mac) "either you're mistaken, or" (forefinger) "we'll get licked."

Mac never even noticed that he was being caricatured. He returned his pipe, and said between his teeth and between whiffs:

"Oh, I s'pose Grant knows what he's about."

"Perhaps so, perhaps not. What will become o. us if he doesn't?"

"We'll go dead, that's all."

"You know him. Go and tell him what you think."

"You *don't* know him, or that wouldn't ever even come into your head. Any general who would stand that from a line officer wouldn't be worth powder to blow him up."

After a time of silent puffing Mac went on:

"All I don't like about it is this: Smith is sick and Grant is not here; he's sixteen miles away down the river at Savannah, on the east bank, organizing the new arrivals."

"He's go. his mind set on attacking Corinth."

"That's what's the matter." [Puff, puff, puff.]

"Now, Mac, suppose you were Albert Sidney Johnson and P. G. T. Beauregard, and knew as much as you know now, what would you do?"

"Depends, Captain, on what else I knew, which I don't know now—the condition of my own forces. But if—*if*, I say—I had anything like a good fighting army—"

"Well, what then?"

"I'd attack this town-meeting-camp-meeting-country-fair so quick it would make your head swim."

"But suppose you were U. S. Grant, and knew we were going to be attacked—what would you do?"

"Oh, I'd fix on a line somewhere and throw up some little breast-works, and a few redoubts pierced for field-pieces here and there, so that the boys would at least know where they are *expected* to fight; whether they really do fight or half-fight there or not."

Will picked up his well-worn "Army Regulations" and read aloud:

"'Section 643. Unless the army be acting on the defensive, no post should be intrenched.'"

"Ya-as, I know old Section 643 by heart, and I'd make a special intrenchment expressly to bury Section 643 in."

"What do you suppose was the object of 643?"

"Oh, the cuss sitting in his office writing that thought we fellers out in the open would get fat and lazy if we weren't kept always on the anxious seat. *He* never served in the line, I'll bet a hat. Many's the fight *he* never fought in, and none at all that he did."

"No danger of the front line men getting pursy and plethoric to any great extent."

"Naw! Takes a bureau-officer for that. Fact is, everlasting watchfulness gets to mean no watchfulness at all; it's calling 'Wolf, wolf!' where there isn't any wolf. Sleep when you can, *I* say, so as to be able to keep awake when you must. If you want to be up bright and early in the morning you don't want to be called the night before."

"I suppose the book-writer thought the men would complain of the pick-and-shovel work."

"Ah, yah! Ask 'em! I'm not particularly timid, nor

do I love hard work overmuch; but I never worked so hard or so fast or so willing as I have when I was piling up a little dirt to stand behind when the enemy was in front. And it's so with every living man I ever set eyes on! Why, men will stand twice as long and twice as steady behind a lath fence that wouldn't stop a snow-ball, as they will in the open."

"I've heard our men laugh at McClellan for 'a dirt-shoveler,' as the newspapers called him."

"Capt'n Fargeon, that was before our men ever smelt powder, I guess. You mark a line on the ground and say, 'Boys, you'll fight *there;* now do as you've a mind to about building breast-works,' and what do you think will happen?"

Will laughed. "I think *I* should begin hunting picks and shovels myself; so I suppose others would too."

"Yes, *sir!* Or bayonets, musket-butts, rails, branches, tin-cups, dinner-plates, caps, shoes, feet, fists, fingers and finger-nails, if they couldn't find picks and shovels!"

"The breast-work would suit everybody but the enemy, I should think."

"If I were little Mac, I'd glory in the name of the dirt-shoveler. The newspaper fighters—back in their solid brick walls—may laugh and jeer, but you watch and see what the rank and file of the army in the field thinks of McClellan."

"I'd rather make a very big pile of dirt than a very little puddle of blood." [A long, smoky pause.] "But, Mac, what makes us talk and feel as if there were death in the air?"

"I don't know, Captain."

"Don't you suppose the outside service is being suffi-ciently attended to?"

"It *never* is that."

"Why not?"

"Oh, it's such hard work. You get out your regiment
and march five or ten miles along a blind road—see nothing, hear nothing, learn nothing—and get back tired out,
cussing the fool's errand, as it seems to have been."

"Yet it's just what you wanted to know—that there is
nobody there."

"Yes, of course. Then another time, perhaps, you
come to a clump of trees; bang, bang-bang-bang—bang; a
man killed and two wounded. You deploy and push
ahead, and never see or hear of another reb all day."

"Why not deploy first?"

"You can't make even five miles out and back in a day
deployed. It's work that ought to be done by cavalry."

"Well, why isn't it?"

"Oh—you know our *cavalry*." (The sneering tone of
the last word bespoke at once the veteran and the foot-
soldier.) "I saw a regiment come in last night—mud
hardly up to the horses' bellies, even with the roads as
they are—and they swore they'd been out ten miles on
the Corinth road and not seen a reb! Why, if they'd
been out *five* miles you couldn't have told 'em from a
herd of elephants for the mud they'd have picked up.
Now s'pose they sent Grant the same story, whether true
or not, and he believed them, that confirmed him in his
idea that we have nothing to do but get ready to march
on Corinth when Buel joins."

"Maybe that's the fact."

"Ya-as. Maybe. But I wish Grant were here. Hang
the cavalry! One infantry regiment is worth 'em all.
And one regiment in every ten of us ought to be out
reconnoitering every day. Then in ten days we should
all have been out, and the first ones would be ready to

go out again. But I haven't heard of anybody in our division going out."

"I heard Sherman started up some rebs and had a lively time."

"Yes? Well, Sherman is a good officer. I'm glad *somebody* is looking out for things."

CHAPTER XXII

THE SIXTH AT THE BATTLE OF SHILOH.

[*SCENE.—A group of men in K's company street, gathered about a smaller group seated on the ground, playing cards on a blanket spread over their knees. Many are munching the last of their breakfast as they stand.*]

Tolliver (aside to Chipstone and Cobb on his right)—"Now's our chance." (Aloud)—"Say, fellers, I'm tired of euchre. Tell ye what, I'll teach ye a new game. We call it 'Hog' where I come from. Who wants to learn hog?"

All—"We all do."

Tolliver—"Well, I deal the cards round (does so), and then each man passes one card to his left-hand neighbor. Each man picks out his suit, and when we've gone seven times round we show down and see who's got the best hand in any suit." [Passes a card to Cale Dugong on his left, and the game proceeds.]

Dugong (much excited)—"Golly, that runs good! Bet ye I'll lay over the crowd."

Tolliver (after a few moments)—"Thar, boys; that's seven. Now show down."

Dugong—"Hi! What'd I tell ye? Ace, king, jack, an' ten o' di'm'ns and four little ones! Who kin beat that?"

Tolliver—"That's so, Caleb. (Rising.) Boys, that settles it—Dugong is the biggest hog in Company K."

The loud chorus of guffaws at Dugong's expense is mingled with the distant sound of scattered shots. The captain and lieutenants have just finished their breakfast and are enjoying the usual peaceful smoke—at least they are all smoking, and two of them are enjoying it.

"Hello, Mac! What's all this? Somebody else is reconnoitering I guess." For the sharp, untimely musketry persists in making itself heard from the outposts. Mac looks glum and anxious. He hurries up all the morning operations with asperity and profanity not usual with him.

"Eat what you can, boys; dammit, eat a bite and shove the rest into your haversacks. One man from every tent run and loosen the tent-pegs. Get your blankets rolled up quicker'n chain-lightning; do you hear me? Captain, don't you think it would be a good plan to step up to regimental headquarters and get our orders? I'll have your orderly stow your things ready for breaking camp. I suppose we shall get everything into the wagons in short order—we ought to! Musketry as near as that, and we caught with our breeches down!"

Will, taking some food in one hand and a mug of coffee in the other, walks rapidly toward the colonel's tent.

"Only an affair of the outposts, Captain Fargeon," calls Colonel Isaacs as soon as he comes within hearing.

"Well, Colonel, if you'll allow me to say so, there are two whole brigades between us and that firing, so the enemy must be at close quarters already. My men are packing up, expecting the wagons. Lieutenant McClintock feels very uneasy."

"Mac thinks it serious, does he? Well, we'll be on the safe side". Then he orders the regimental quartermaster (much against his will) to have the wagons prepared for instant use; and sends his staff to each company street to hasten the preparations for a move. No orders have come from brigade headquarters, so he hesitates absolutely to strike the tents; short of that everything is put in complete readiness.

The rattle of musketry becomes more and more steady and continuous. Scattered men without muskets begin straggling down the road toward the rear.

"We belong to the —th. The rebs got onto us while we was eating. Our muskets was all stacked on the color line, and we didn't even git to the stacks at all— the Johnnies got thar fust. We just had to scoot. That's the second brigade that's doin' the firin'. We didn't git to fire a shot."

Even while the man talked the road is growing fuller and fuller of fugitives; here and there a wagon or ambulance, but chiefly infantry-men walking or running toward the river.

"Strike tents!" shouts Colonel Isaacs; and in little more time than it takes to pen these lines Company K's street ceases to be a street; it is nothing but a flood of wrinkling canvas and flying tent-poles; while in the uncovered homes may be descried pitiful remains of all the usual little devices for comfort and amusement—leafy beds, seats, checker-boards, extempore tables, and so forth. K's wagon is loaded almost as soon as the other streets have fairly fallen to the ground.

A few moments later an aide appears from brigade headquarters and in a consequential tone reports:

"General Blank's compliments, and would thank Colonel Isaacs to say by whose orders he has struck his tents."

"Be kind enough to say to General Blank," replied the quick-witted colonel, "that I am drilling my men in the rapid striking of camp and loading of wagons."

"Very well, sir!" rejoins the pompous aide, and he disappears, seemingly unconscious of the half-smothered laugh that follows him.

Many hundreds of unarmed men have now drifted past the Sixth, all telling the same story. Their officers are with them, but do not try to halt them, unarmed as they are. Now begins to come a different class: men carrying muskets, men who have done some fighting before they gave way; wounded men in ambulances and on foot, and unhurt men helping back the wounded—or, as Mac explains it, wounded men helping back the unhurt, by giving them an excuse (a bad one) for running away.

Still that rising and approaching rattle of musketry; still the utter absence of any orders from general head-quarters. The distant sound of cannon has been heard some time; now comes the welcome thunder of a battery which has opened fire from our own side, and a loud "Heigh!" runs along the brigade front.

The next new, noticeable feature is the appearance of stragglers direct from the firing line; not walking on the road, but straggling back through woods, fields, camps—anywhere where panic and cowardice can find a loop-hole of escape. The first one who comes within reach of Company K is seized and hauled away to the regimental guard-house, with the cheerful assurance from Mac that he shall be shot at sunset. But a threat to him does not deter others, and they begin to come back in droves.

"Sound the long roll!" calls Isaacs quietly. "Captain Fargeon, deploy your company as skirmishers a hundred paces to the front and halt all unwounded men; make them fall into your skirmish line, and let your reserve shoot down any man who refuses to stay and fight."

As the men gather on the color line in response to the long roll, they see the other regiments in the brigade hurriedly striking tents and scrambling them into wagons as best they can.

Company K "takes intervals on its left file," and spreading along before the face of the rest of the regiment, begins its advance. At every step some wounded man is allowed to pass, and some unwounded man is forced to stop and join the advance. As a general rule they make no objection, and the skirmish line soon becomes almost a solid rank.

One man refuses to obey Mac's order, saying:

"Git out of the way! You ain't no officer of mine!"

Mac whips out his sword. The mutineer lowers his musket (bayonet fixed) and cocks it. Why does Mac hesitate to rush in and kick the piece aside? It isn't like him! The reason is soon evident; he sees Chipstone approaching from behind. Chip clubs his musket and brings down the stock with a crash on the wretch's head and he goes down like a log. Mac calls to Morphy (commanding the reserve) to strap the fellow up to a tree, facing the front, and in that horrible position he recovers his senses; his curses, prayers, and groans fill the air and make the management of other fugitives an easy matter. They all take the hint and join the ranks of the fighters.

But what is the halting of a few score among the vast mass of retreating men who now fill the space? They pass in swarms to right and left of the steady rank of the skirmishers, in a seemingly endless and limitless throng. They all tell the same story.

"The hull rebel army came down on us. We was flanked both sides; an' we fit until they begun to fire onto us from right an' left an' behind."

By this time the road has become a pandemonium of flying forces. Wagons go galloping in the rear in a nearly continuous stream, while *twice* there comes a yet more harrowing sight—the flight of caissons, forge and battery wagon ; *but no limbers and no cannon!* The guns are lost —they may be turned on us already, and be swelling that advancing roar; be sending the very shells which we see bursting in the sky, making tiny white cloudlets that spring into sight, so beautiful and so appalling!

K soon finds itself supported on right and left by skirmish lines from the brother regiments of its brigade—an inexpressible comfort, especially as the fugitives now are fewer; they are coming on the run, and not after the manner of skulkers who have fled with scarcely an effort, all of which indicates that the next people they may expect will be the enemy. Already bullets have made themselves heard and even felt, for one of the fellows who had fallen back, thus far without a scratch, now has a serious wound to justify his going the rest of the way.

"Why, Mark, where's your sling?"

-"In me focket, Caftain. I can hould me fiece fretty fair, ye see, on me elbow."

"Oh, well, my boy—you needn't have come out to-day."

"I didn't intind to, Caftain, but when I sor ye start—" A nod, silent but expressive, fills out the speech with a thrilling eloquence.

The last Union men are coming in now, chiefly helping badly wounded officers and soldiers whom they have not the heart to leave to the tender mercies of the foe.

Fargeon has the right flank, Mac the left, and Morphy the reserve.

"Mac!" calls Will, "you'll feel 'em first. What will you do, and what do you want us to do? Give your orders—have 'em passed along, and we'll fall in with 'em."

"All right, Captain Fargeon," comes back in Mac's cheerful, sonorous, reassuring drawl. "We could take care of a whole regiment with this line of men, but we'll just fire one volley and then give the rest of the army a chance. We don't want to be hoggish!"

A laughing "Heigh!" greets this quip, and Mac goes on:

"Now, men, when you see 'em coming, fire one shot apiece, then run back. Don't stop again; get back to your place in our own line as fast as Goddlemity'll let ye. Recollect, the regiment can't fire till you get out of the way."

Suddenly firing begins in the Union line far to the left of K's position, and rapidly extends in its direction. Mac's place is the most ticklish; and high above the din can be heard that well-known drawl:

"Let the Forty-fifth boys shoot at nothing all they've a mind to! We'll show 'em that Company K can hold its water! No man fire till I give the word. You hear me?"

So the firing from our side extends up to where Mac stands and there stops for a considerable time, while dead silence reigns all along the front of Company K and its forced allies. Fargeon stands in miserable suspense waiting for a word from Mac, and peering into the impenetrable leafage before him. Ha! What is that? A swaying of the bushes? Why doesn't Mac open fire? Shall *he* do it without waiting? Where *is* Mac, anyway? Why, that is Mac out in front! He has been reconnoitering, and now is backing slowly and softly toward the kneeling line, which parts to let him through, and he resumes his place on the left.

"Hang you, Mac! We might have shot you to pieces!"

"Oh, the boys knew I was there.   I went out on purpose to hold them steady."

Now the wild yell of the enemy is audible, beginning far away on the left and spreading toward them.   Now it is directly in front, and Mac speaks—drawls out:

"FOR GOD'S SWEET SAKE DON'T LEAVE ME!"—Page 276.

"When I give the word, fire low—fire at their knees—you hear me?" (All he says is passed along the line.)

The yell becomes nearer and more plain; but the enemy is saving his powder. A movement in the underbrush is perceptible, a glimpse of butternut shows here and there, three or four scattering shots are heard, and the bullets go whizzing by.

"FIRE!"

More than a hundred muskets ring out their death-dealing cry (fully half of them being in the hands of the forced "recruits"), and the yell in their immediate front suddenly stops. The enemy has something else to think of, and probably imagines that this level, deliberate, destructive volley comes from a line of battle, not from a mere skirmish-line.

"Back, boys!" (No drawl now.) "Stoop down and run for your lives! But don't leave any wounded! Pick up every man that gets hit; you hear me?"

An irregular volley comes in response to theirs, mostly passing over their heads. One man (a stranger) goes down, but he is killed, and they leave him. The strapped-up mutineer falls to begging again for his life.

'Oh, Lieutenant—for God's sweet sake don't leave me here! I didn't mean nothing. My gun wasn't loaded—there it lays—you can see for yourself?"

"Will you behave yourself!"

"I'll fight for you as long as there's breath left in my body if you'll *only* take me along."

Mac, after glancing at the musket and seeing that it was not capped, loosens the belt that held the fellow and tells him to pick up his cap and gun and fall in with the rest. As soon as his hand is free he begins to rub the lump on his head—tries to put on his cap—gives it up and puts it in his haversack instead.

Bullets have been dropping among Morphy's men, and two have to be helped back. Soon all are in their places on the color line, Company K taking more room than it had ever filled before since it came out. Isaacs comes down the line and congratulates Will and the rest, and gleans what news they have to give. When they ask him about things in the rear, he only answers by an expressive shake of the head. Then they are once more alone.

One of the strangers leaves the line and runs toward the road. Mac draws his pistol and fires a snap shot after him—the fellow gives a yell of either pain or triumph, and runs faster than ever.

"I'll drop the next one!" said Mac, audibly but quietly; and no next one tried the experiment.

The interval of quiet is so long that the captain and first lieutenant, passing along the rear of their line, stop a moment together.

"Captain, what would you think of a little breast-work along about now?"

"Well, Mac, I was once worth a good deal over a hundred thousand dollars; and if I had it now, I would give every cent of it for a ditch two feet deep with a bank two feet high on the far side."

"A hundred dollars a foot is a good deal of money for a little thing we might just as well have had for nothing; but it would be worth it."

The ground is mostly clear of trees for a quarter mile or more in front of the color line, and across this space and into the woods beyond all eyes are anxiously looking.

Just now some movement is noticeable on the right rear of the Sixth. A battery of artillery swings grandly into position there and unlimbers for action—six fierce muzzles pointing terribly toward the foe. The horses are quickly unhitched and trotted clattering out of sight to the rear.

Will sees Mac look at the battery with unusual interest, finally using his field-glass to examine its guidons and other distinguishing features.

"What is it, Mac?"

"Captain Fargeon, those are regulars. That is a battery of the Fourth United States Artillery—and I feel as if I ought to raise my hat as I name the regiment."

Suddenly, from the woods in front, come puffs of smoke and a second later the reports of muskets, mingled with the shrill whistle of bullets.

"Now watch the guns!" cries Mac, regardless of the enemy's fire.

On the instant six terrific roars burst from the six field-pieces, each gun giving a frantic leap backward as the flame spouts from its throat.

Before the sound ceases the shells can be heard exploding in the opposite woods and the branches of trees be seen dropping to the ground, while the musketry stops utterly.

"Ha, ha! Johnny Reb! How does those pills suit your complaint?"

"But, Mac, it's only the musket that means business, you know."

"No—well—yes. But take a battery served like *that*, and—well, I'd full as lief have it on my side as against me." And Mac walks gayly back to his post on the left.

After a second round the battery ceases firing, the Confederate musketry in the immediate front having suddenly stopped and the distant woods grown as silent as a forest primeval. No sign of life in sight, except two buzzards circling lazily about high in air, floating with motionless wings—waiting, waiting. Their patience will be rewarded.

Meanwhile the distant battle rages to right and left, its horrid voice always advancing, and before long an aide is seen to gallop up from the rear, speak a few words to the battery officers and gallop back. Then the battery reopens, and Will says to himself:

"Thank God!   I wonder why they stopped."

How do men fall in battle?

Forward, as fall other slaughtered animals. Homer says, not once, or twice, but often, "Death unstrung his limbs." Again: "Then the hero stayed fallen upon his knees, and with stout hand leant upon the earth, and the darkness of night veiled his eyes."

As they fall, so they lie, so they die and so they stiffen; and all the contortions seen by burial details and depicted by Verestschagin and other realistic painters are the natural result of the removal of bodies which have fallen with faces and limbs to the earth, and grown rigid without the rearrangement of "decent burial."

To learn all these things, one needs only to watch Company K through this day, Sunday, April 6, 1862. Then one must pause to remind himself that war did not invent death; nor does even blessed peace prevent it.

> "War Is a game which, were their subjects wise,
> Kings would not play at."—*Cowper*.

CHAPTER XXIII.

THE battery was quickly enveloped in its own smoke, through which were dimly visible hurrying forms, wildly waving rammers and great spouts of flame at each discharge. Again the great roars burst out, and again, and again; and each explosion was sharp, ear-hurting, cruel. Not the grand, soul-stirring report and roll of a thunder-clap or a cannon afar off, but a *noise*, physically painful and abhorrent.

Will's mind sought relief from the dreadful tension of waiting for battle by straying off to untimely vagaries.

"That hideous sound is the sweetest music my ears ever listened to. No mother's lullaby to a frightened child was ever more comforting, consoling, soothing. How wretched must one be when *that* comforts him! Well, I am wretched! I am a miserable man—unhappy, low-spirited, *despairing*—in view of the things which this day has in store. This long, dreadful day! How hellishly they are fighting over there toward our left! Musketry and artillery—it certainly seems further back than we are! But so long as our immediate neighbors are on our line, we must stand fast and support our battery, as Mac says.

"That's right, gunners! Fire fast—make a wall of iron against them! Don't let your music stop an instant—shut out that rattle from the left! A man must be falling there with every tick of the clock. Oh, when will our turn come? Load and fire, gunners, load and fire—and God bless you for it!"

Mac approached again.

'Those battery-men are doing wrong, and they know it! I'll bet my life that some fool brigadier-general is at the bottom of it—shooting away all their ammunition at nothing under God's Heaven but gopher-holes and birds' nests.'

"Why, Mac, I was just wishing they would go on all day and prevent the rebels from coming across that open space at all."

"Oh, they can't do that. Amount of it will be that the rebs will bring up two or three batteries to silence them; then they can't help us when we need it. They ought to lie low now till the Johnnies show themselves again."

"Maybe they are told to keep firing for the sake of the moral effect on our men."

"Like enough. But I'd rather hold 'em for a physical effect on the other fellers."

They separated, much to Will's regret, for he loved to lean on Mac's cool strength and forgetfulness of danger. And then, too, the accurate instinct of the lieutenant made his captain now look with dread for an artillery attack directed against the laboring battery—and he did not have to look long before it came.

Several reports in rapid though irregular succession sounded from the far front, and missiles came plunging over, all evidently meant for the battery, but some of them straying far enough to make the neighborhood very uncomfortable for the Sixth Illinois.

"How under Heaven can the battery-men stand that dreadful storm? Oh, don't! Oh, *don't! Look* what you are doing!" he added aloud, apostrophizing the enemy.

A moment after uttering this childish supplication, Will saw the full absurdity of it, and could have laughed out at himself if he could have laughed at anything.

The sound of galloping came from the rear. Will looked back and saw a riderless horse, with artillery harness on, coming toward him at full speed. He tried to stop the crazy brute, but it only swerved, and rushed

on. As it passed he saw a rent in its side. A passed shell must have reached the place where the b a t t e r y horses were held.

"Look o u t ! Look out, men!" Too late. T h e b e a s t d a s h e d blindly through Company K. Three men went down; one got up and recovered his musket; one sat up and pressed his hand to his side; one lay still where he fell.

"Stand fast, men! *Stand* fast!" shouted Mac, restraining the overwhelming instinct of humanity to fly to the succor of a brother in distress.

"Sarg'nt Chipstone, take a file of men and bring those wounded here to me; then get back to your places." Then, turning to the rear, he called: "Litter-bearers, this way!"

One man, with ribs probably splintered, was helped back. But poor Harry Planter, just out of the hospital, was past help. His back was broken.   Twice hit, both times from the rear, and his task was done.

The horse, on getting into the open place, stopped and looked about him, showing no consciousness of his wound except by ceaselessly brushing that side with his tail.

"Tolliver," said Mac, 'see if you can fetch him." (Tolliver was a famous marksman.) While he was kneeling, waiting for the victim to present a favorable shot, the horse began to nibble at the herbage at his feet.

Will thought, "What a God's blessing it is to be without imagination!"

Tolliver's piece rang out.

"Missed him!"

"Missed him, did I?" cried Tolliver with sarcastic intonation while he reloaded his piece. At the same time the beast began to turn about as if on a pivot, and presently went down with a resounding thud. "Missed him right through the brain behind the eyes."

The battery, by irresistible impulse, had now turned its fire away from the point whence infantry was to be expected, and toward the artillery which was raining shell and schrapnel upon it. This left the opposite woods unmolested, and bullets began to come from there in deadly numbers. A good many of the Sixth's men had been carried back; and murmurs began to be heard.

"For God's sake, let us shoot, or lie down, or something!"

Lieut.-Colonel Isaacs, anxious for both the honor and safety of his regiment, came down to its left flank to hear what K's officers had to say. Mac spoke:

"Only one objection to lying down—that is that the men are almost sure to fire high. If you can stop that—"

"We'll do it. Lie down, boys, and mind what I'm going to tell you. Don't fire till I tell you, and then fire at the enemy's feet. Every man of you, try to put his bullet into the toe of a reb's boot! Tit for tat, and something to boot!"

Down went the company, officers and men, glad of the relief. Isaacs hurried along the line, repeating his orders, so that every man was sure to hear them. But the brave commander, now the most conspicuous mark, was soon laid low with a disabling wound; and then the group that gathered to help him off lost a man—killed stone dead. The major, stunned by the situation, seemed to have nothing to say, and the long line of gray coats now came into plain though distant view, advancing over the open space. Few of the men knew that the lieutenant-colonel was hurt, and all anxiously awaited his order to begin firing, as the regiments to right and left were doing.

At last Mac leaped to his feet and ran to where the major was squatting behind a slight rise of ground.

"Shall we open fire, sir?"

The major nodded dumbly, and Mac walked back along the line.

"Boys" (drawling), "if you're going to fire high, you can't fire at all; but if you'll aim low, why, then let 'em have it, and God have mercy on their damned souls."

The last words were inaudible in the volley that followed; probably one of the most destructive ever delivered by any six hundred men since the war began. The advancing enemy fairly withered away. Like ripe fruit when the gust first strikes the tree dropped the hurt, and like leaves before the wind fled the unhurt.

When the fugitives had melted into the woods again, the firing recommenced; evidently from a supporting line which would soon repeat the assault.   Mac did not lie down again, but came to where Will crouched, saying:

"Major Colemason is rattled, and there is practically nobody in command. You must take it if nobody else does."

"Get down, Mac! Get down! You won't? Then I'll have to get up, though I hate to. There! Now, where's Chafferty? Where are all the other captains who rank me?"

"Blessed if I know. But somebody's got to take charge of this regiment. We may have to advance or retreat; and when we do it ought to be by crders, and not by accident. God knows what's become of brigade headquarters."

"Well, Mac, look out for the company, and I'll go and see what can be done. If I take charge nominally, you've got to have it really. Don't, I beg of you, *don't* expose yourself needlessly!"

Mac disdained to reply, but walked slowly up to take the captain's place on the right flank, and stood there erect, watching the point where the enemy must be forming, under cover of their own smoke, for a determined advance.

Fargeon found the ranking captain, and together they visited the group surrounding the stunned major, including the adjutant and two of the staff, crouching together.

"Major Colemason, the enemy is massing for another charge. Have you any orders to give?"

The poor fellow (who had always done well in all subordinate capacities) had nothing to say. He was too dazed either to command or to abdicate, and the two captains returned to their companies, through a scattering drive (not a storm) of bullets. Fargeon had well-nigh forgotten them; and again his mind wandered off on trivial things. He wondered what time it was; and found that he could not guess—could not remember whether it was morning or afternoon, and whether his last meal, which seemed a month ago, had been breakfast, dinner, or supper. There were the enemy, visible and advancing. There stood Mac like a statue; there lay the dead and wounded who had been dragged back, and there lay Company K awaiting orders to open fire.

Lacking the restraining force of their commander, the Sixth began firing earlier than before, and, of course, less effectively. The brave enemy continued to come on, firing as they came. But the charging rank, partly through wounds and partly through defections, grew thinner and thinner; and its proportionate losses grew larger as there were fewer left to fire at.

Human nature could not stand it, and the foe at last wavered, halted, and turned back, leaving some of their fallen within what seemed only fifty paces of our front. Then, again, the absence of a restraining head worked ill for the Sixth. The men, unmindful of flank or rear, regardless of the absence of orders, jumped up with a hurrah and pursued the retreating line until it passed through and unmasked a solid brigade with loaded muskets, which met our force with a burst of fire that sent us reeling back in turn. We had a score or two of prisoners, wounded and unwounded; but almost a tenth of our brave fellows were laid low by that first volley or by the losses in the retreat. Most of our wounded—all who were not obviously past help—were lugged back by their comrades, some of whom were hit in the act of helping others. With difficulty were the flying men halted at their own color line; but Company K having set them the example (its officers calling "Halt, Company K! Steady, men! Steady!"), the others either stopped on the line or came back to it after drifting a few rods beyond.

As Fargeon recovered his breath and his pulse slowed down, thought resumed its mastery over feeling.

"Wholesale slaughter is less dreadful than retail killing. A dozen of my good friends—besides scores of men whom I know by sight—are dead or dying around me; and I am less affected than I should be by seeing any one of them lying there alone. Tolliver, the wit— he's gone. Those expressive brows will move nevermore while the world turns round. So is Aleck Thrush—that leaves the old mother with no son, those girls with no brother. Jeff Cobb is among the wounded. If Jeff goes under, what will the boys do for a laugh in their dreariest hours, without him to turn sufferings into drolleries? Oh, is there no God in Heaven?"

Now came cries from the right.

"Lie down, men! Lie flat down! The battery is going to fire over you!"

Down they went; lying closer from their friends' fire than they had from their enemies'. Even the gravest situations have their ludicrous side, and here was wounded Jeff Cobb's chance. He called from his lying place among the wounded:

"Say, fellers, I'll bet you can find this spot a year from now by the line of holes your noses are rooting in the ground."

A smothered laugh greeted the suggestion, and each man with a prominent or peculiar organ was congratulated with the promise of being able to identify his spot.

In sober earnest, it was a most trying experience. The shriek of the missiles which were passing over from behind them was indescribably appalling, and there was constant apprehension that a shell with imperfect fuse might ourst directly above our lines. Even short of this disaster there was the constant, vicious rain of fragments of the "sabots" or wooden sockets in which shells and schrapnel are encased; which give severe bruises, though not often dangerous wounds. All of the wounded whose hurts permitted it walked toward the rear; but the rest were left lying there, no stretchers having been available for a long, long time.

Company K, and indeed the whole left of the regiment, was comparatively out of the line of our artillery fire, which passed directly over the right flank; and McClintock continued to stand coolly erect. Presently he walked over to where Fargeon lay.

"The Johnnies are still coming, Captain."

"What!" cried Will, rising on his elbow. "Coming on through that hell-fire?"

"Ya-as. The shells are bursting mostly beyond them."

"Why don't we try grape and canister?"

"They aren't quite near enough for canister—couldn't fire it over our own men, anyhow—and we don't use grape-shot now except in the navy."

"Why, the newspapers always talk about 'grape and canister.'"

"That shows how much they know of what they're talking about.'

Fargeon got upon his feet.

"Mac, suppose we let K open fire. We seem safe here from our artillery."

"Just what I'm thinking of. K and I, and maybe H, might do some good. If K sets the example it'll spread. We're bound to support our artillery, orders or no orders. And I'm afraid (with an anxious look toward our left) that the battery ought to be getting back *now*, by the way the firing seems to be drifting past us over there.

"SEND 'EM YOUR CARDS, AND THEN GET DOWN AGAIN."—Page 290.

But good Lord! if the old Fourth gets no order to go, they'll stay there till the last man falls."

As he walked back to his place he said, in his own bantering tone:

"Boys, what's the matter with your raising up jest enough to see the rebs, and send 'em your cards and then git down again to load? But fire slow and fire low. You hear me?"

Permission was all the boys wanted, and a rattling volley burst from their front. Whether it killed or not, it had one valuable effect—that of diverting part of the enemy's fire from the battery (which had been catching it all) to the direction of Company K. Several hundred confederate muskets responded to the sixty or seventy pieces which were all the effectives K now possessed (even including its impressed men), and the concentration, together with the battery fire, was very severe; more so than any previous experience that Will had met with. Two men in Company K, after a startled shock and a cry, clambered up and made their way rearward; one gave the cry—but lay still, half turned on his side, his knees drawn up. Fargeon, stooping, started over to get from dear, splendid, glorious Mac, either relief or strength to bear the strain.

"Mac must have dropped his pipe; he is looking down for something. There, he is stooping for it—he is on his knees feeling for it—he is on his face! Oh, my God! Oh, GOD in HEAVEN!"

No one but Will had seen Mac fall. No one else saw the rent in the back of his collar where the bullet had came out; no one helped turn him over; then a shriek from the grief-stricken captain brought others to his aid.

Fruitless the care that dragged the fallen hero a little aside. When they laid flat his broad shoulders his fine head fell back and showed the deadly wound—sheer through the neck, a little to the right of the windpipe. The brave eyes were already sightless, though the jaw had not yet dropped and the breath was still feebly passing.

Will fell upon his knees and bowed his breast on the shoulder of his friend. His lips sought the cruel laceration, whence red blood was slowly oozing, warm, saltish, and sickening. He leaped to his feet, and his voice called the name of the Deity—the name and some of the merciful attributes. Certain men of the awe-struck group thought he uttered a prayer; others—those nearest him—thought that his words were a blasphemous denial of his God and abjuration of his cherished faith.

He faced the bullets, coming thick and fast, and made as if he would rush at the enemy for revenge and death. But in his path were crouched, loading and firing, the soldiers of Company K—the great lieutenant's fellow-soldiers—now reduced almost to a single rank.

Mac's voice seemed to reach his ears; to whisper to him, drawling through the uproar:

"Duty first; then death. You hear me?"

A sudden calm fell upon him. Mac's spirit entered his breast. He walked slowly along the line, saying in almost Mac's tone:

"Fire slow and fire low, boys. Fire slow and fire low."

He came to where Morphy was crouching, and heard him ask:

"Is it true, Captain?"

"Yes, Barney. Go over and take his place."

Scarcely had the second lieutenant got to the flank when he shouted back:

"Captain! Captain! The other regiment is gone from our left."

Fargeon hurried back. Not a man was to be seen on

that part of our line. He cried piteously, with tears in his tones:

"Oh, Mac! Mac! What shall I do?" But the beloved voice was silent.

A litter had come, and two litter-bearers, assisted by two of Company K's men, were placing Mac's body on it. When the litter started for the rear Will observed that his two soldiers were going with it.

"Come back! Come back here, you cowards! Take your places in the ranks."

One returned; the other, Dugong, pretended not to hear, but kept ahead of the litter, prepared to break into a run if followed.

"Dugong! Caleb Dugong!" He could have shot him through the heart without a pang.

"I will stop being myself. I will be Mac. Let me see —let me see—the last thing he said was 'we must support our battery.' No, after that he said 'the battery ought to be getting back.' That is my law."

He ran to the battery, now almost silenced by the deadly musketry, though one gun-squad seemed to be still working, sending its isolated missiles.

"Captain! Officer in command!"

"The captain and lieutenants are all killed or wounded. I am the sarg'nt in command. What do you want?"

"Get your battery back, for God's sake! We've got to go!"

"Very well, sir."

Then he saw the surviving artillery-men—splendid veteran soldiers—seize the prolonges and begin to pull the guns back by hand toward where the horses were held. He ran to where he had seen the major and adjutant, but failed to find them. He ran along the line of the Sixth, shouting:

"All our men are gone from the left of Company K. The battery is going. Let us get back in good order, boys, keeping between the enemy and the battery. It is all we can do." ["Was that like Mac? I hope so; I hope so."]

"Retreat! Retreat!"

The cry traveled along the regimental line faster than he did, and Company K had left its place before he got there. As he reached the line he observed that one man, Ed Ranney, lay still, as if he had not heard the order. He ran to him, touched him with his foot and screamed: "Retreat, Ed!"—to ears closed in death. Then he followed the rest, but not without a lingering look backward and a sob as he tore himself away from his dead friends.

"Steady, boys! Watch the colors and carry along our wounded, and don't go any faster than the flag goes." ["Was that like Mac?"]

"Load as you go, boys; and turn and fire when you can. Keep even with the colors." ["Was that like Mac?"]

They could easily get away from the enemies in their immediate front, but, alas! those on the left (now on their right hand) had passed them and were firing at them from that side. Friends fell faster and faster; it was in vain to try to care for them.

"Drop the wounded and close in toward the flag!" ["Was that like Mac? Oh, poor Jeff Cobb and the others! My God, my God!"]

As K crowded in toward the center, all order was soon lost, and the once glorious Sixth Illinois became a mere mob of running men and officers, protecting the flag more by the interposition of their bodies than by the use of their guns. Will was among the rearmost of the unwounded; while behind him came a pitiful, halting few of wounded, growing fewer as the strength gave out of one after another, though others were constantly dropping under the fire from front and flank.

The place of honor was with Will in the rear. Those who took no chances hurried forward, but the best and bravest would pause to fire back, while the rest outstripped and passed them. Will was gratified—and distressed—to observe that these were nearly all his blessed Company K men.

Suddenly the very nearest man to him dropped. It was George Friend. George climbed to his feet again—or, rather, to his foot—reversed his musket, gripped the butt, and began a frenzied effort to keep up by prodding the ground with the muzzle, and so helping himself along.

"Can you make it, George?"

"I could, Captain, if it wasn't for this cursed foot." Will looked down—the misshapen member was all awry and pointing inward. They were getting isolated—he must leave him.

"Oh, Cap! *Ca—an't* you take me alo—ong?"

Reverently be it said, there were tears furrowing the powder-grime on that brave face as Will saw it for the last time on earth.

Fargeon, running, gripped his own head with both hands, crying:

"Oh, God! I wish I were dead, dead, DEAD!"

The last word was a scream, but nobody heard it except himself.

Why can he no longer see plainly? What is this shadow they have run into?

Why—it is nightfall! He had forgotten there was any day or night—any flight of measured time. All seemed merged into an awful, hideous eternity.

CHAPTER XXIV.

THE fragments of the Sixth Illinois halted behind the first orderly body of troops they came to—a fine, large, new Michigan regiment, well posted, cool, brave, undismayed by the disasters in their neighborhood. When the Sixth got into line again it showed a little over three hundred rank and file; Company K only twenty-eight of its own men, all told. The line was only fourteen men long! It seemed as if Fargeon on the right and Morphy on the left could have touched swords! Will set his teeth hard to suppress a sob.

The pursuit died away with the light, and they heard no more of the foe that night. The Michigan men gave them some supper—it did not take much to go round now, and the boys would rather sleep than eat. Numb, dazed, silence and quietude was all they were good for. Their own lost and scattered wounded were almost forgotten. Many a battle-evening has seen a whole army in this state; to be hounded, later, by ferocious shrieks from the non-combatants (far in the rear) asking: "Why was not the battle renewed next morning?"

Nothing could be learned of the litter-bearers or of Dugong. (It afterward transpired that the latter was one of the many thousand "stragglers" who gathered on the shore and tried to board the transport steamers and gun-boats.)

The impulse to "ask Mac" kept recurring to Will at every turn, and he wandered back and forth like a lost soul, his nature struggling between pain and torpor.

"Caftain," whispered a low voice in the darkness, "I'm afreld—I smell smoak over thayre."

Will started as if he had been shot. Fire? Fire among those wounded? Is there no God in Heaven? Nothing but a devil? Why—his nostrils seem full of the smell of burning grass—or is it only his crazy fancy? He cannot tell.

"Doan't mind, Caftain, dayr. Mebbe it's nothin' at-all-at-all—nothin' but the ould fowder-smoak. Noah, it's not, flayze God; it's not. But he moight be a-lyin' somewheres about thayr yit."

"Mark! God bless you, Mark! Do you think so?"

"Well, sorr—there's nothin' loike thryin'—av ye'd gimme me lave, an' git me the countersign to come back wid, I'd snake along as far as I cud, annyhow. I wud; oah, I wud."

"Come back in a few minutes, Mark, and we will try."

Mark pleaded sore to be allowed to go alone, but this Will would not hear of; so, after the bivouac grew quiet, the two set forth past the outposts, into the shadowy golgotha beyond. Dead and wounded were scattered sparsely over the plain. A light rain was falling; thus the awful fear of fire was relieved, and the living were freed from the awful wound-thirst. As Will tramped along, grateful for the rain, he thought. "Yes, there is a God. Rains are apt to follow battles." But soon the hateful question obtruded itself: "Then did no wounded Mac ever die in the torments of fire and thirst? Aye, thousands!" So does war tamper with Faith.

"Do you think we're going right, Mark?"
"Divvle the fayr, Caftain. I remimber thim fallen

trees wid the underbroosh round 'em. We're all of half-way back."

A little later he added:

"Here's the shtraym we got wather fiam fer the camf."

They crossed it and pushed on.

"Nixt thing'll be our ground—the hornet's nest." (Mark gave the spot its name, which it goes by to this day.)

"Halt! Who goes there?"

They have run upon a Confederate outpost. Nothing for it but to go back; their errand of love has failed.

"Come back here, you corpse-robbers, or we'll fire on you!"

They start on a run for the fallen trees, and some random shots are fired at the sound of their retreating footsteps.

"Damn 'em! They're Yanks! Go for 'em, boys!' And they know that either a rebel prison or that brush-heap is their refuge. Fargeon's legs are not even yet what they were before his rheumatism; but he is making pretty good time in Mark's wake, when he stumbles and falls heavily, just in time to escape a bullet that hustles above him and strikes the ground in front. Mark has turned round to see what keeps his captain, and the spent ball, or a stone dislodged by it, strikes him fair in the mouth.

"Dom yer sowl—ye found me wayk sfot!" he mutters as he spits out the blood and stoops over Will, slowly rising from the ground.

"Lay low, sorr! It's our only chance!"

Low they lie, almost breathless with apprehension. The confederates either pass wide of them or give up the chase when they cease to hear footsteps to guide them; and after a quarter of an hour Mark ventures to get up and look about him.

"All's clayr, Caftain." He speaks with even more in-distinctness than usual, for his unlucky lips are hurt almost beyond speech. "Shall we tthry it wanst moar?"

"Well, Mark—there's something very queer about my ankle. It's broken or something. I can't seem to put my foot to the ground at all."

"Lemme sthrike a match an' tehk a luk at it, sorr. Howly Mother of God—ye're wownded, caftain!"

Will groaned. "When I fell I only thought I'd struck my foot, and that the pain was a touch of the old Don-elson soreness." Then, as the thought came over him how much this calamity meant, he groaned again, and again; each moan more heart-broken than the last.

"Well, sorr!" cried Mark, in the gayest possible tone, "as the bye said, the nixt thing is something else. Ye must let me carry ye!"

"You couldn't begin to do it, Mark!"

"Who, me, sorr? Savin' yer frisence I'll carry ye to the broosh-file or break me dom back! I will, sorr; oah, I will."

Mark kneels down by Will, and the latter slowly lifts himself to his knees; then both together rise erect; then the taller throws his long arms over the shoulders of the other. [The captain thought of the Donelson fence-corner—memory is so closely allied with the sense of smell!] Next, little Mark bends forward until he has all the weight well balanced, and then runs forward with in-credible strength and swiftness for fifty or more short steps before stopping for breath, and pauses while Will puts his unhurt foot to the ground for a few moments. These spurts of desperate effort become shorter and shorter, but they do pass the stream and reach the brush-heap at last, without coming in actual contact with any of the robbers who infest the field. With one last fearful struggle, Mark carries his burden into the midst of the shelter and sinks down under him, all spent and speechless with exhaustion.

Soon he bursts out again as gay as ever:

"Thank God, Caftain, it's warmer weather nor it wor whin you'n me laid out t'gither befoar!"

"Yes, indeed, Mark; but what next? What next?"

"Well, sorr—I wish't I had me gun."

"Do you think these hounds may try to trouble us here?"

"Well, sorr—we'll not be scairt befoar we're hurted. But, by yer lave, I'll jist skirmish round a bit till I see can I lay hand on a gun."

He departs, and is gone a considerable time, during which the helpless captain plainly hears the sound of voices near. At last he becomes aware of some one approaching, and lies in anguish of apprehension until he hears Mark's tones whispering "Caftain" through the deep darkness of the thicket.

"Well, Mark, did you get a musket?"

"I did, sor; oah I did. An' more be token a coufle av 'em, an' a cathridge-box, an' some cafs."

"Did I hear you speaking to some one?"

"I jist passed the toime o' day wid wan av 'em, sorr. I made out I was wan of thimselves—God forgive me! An' they axed me had I a good find in the broosh here. An' I tould 'em sorra the taste av a man, kilt or wounded, was here at-all-at-all. But we'll kafe our eyes ofen —we will, sorr; oah we will."

He proceeds to load the muskets. To be sure, within ten minutes they hear somebody pushing in by the way Mark had come. When the intruder comes near enough to be dangerous, Mark calls out:

"Git out o' this, ye thafe av the worrld!"

"Shut yer mouth, ye dam' sawed-off Paddy! Ye've got a good thing an' ye're tryin' to hawg it all, an' I know it, an' ye can't do it."

Mark takes one of the guns and creeps out, not directly toward the sounds, but a little to one side. Upon reflection Will perceives his object in this. The thoughtful fellow knows he may be fired at, and wants to free his captain from the danger of a passed shot. The other gun Will pulls to him, prepared for the worst. Mark, killed or wounded, will not be undefended or unavenged, as the case may be.

After a moment of stillness, broken only by the slowly advancing footsteps, Mark's musket rings out with a roar that seems, in the close stillness of the time and place, like the sound of a cannon. This is succeeded by a silence more profound by contrast; unbroken until, after what seemed a wonderfully long time, Mark himself creeps cautiously back.

"Did you go to him, Mark?"

"I did, sorr; oah, I did."

"Is he dead?"

"Dead as Julius Sayzer, sorr."

"Well—I suppose he deserved it."

"Divvle the doubt av that, sorr; noa, there's not, there's not."

"Now, Mark, I've been thinking what we'd better do. You must go back to camp."

"Oah, Caftain dayr—doan't sind me off! Ye'd not be safe here, not an hour! Ye'd be robbed an' murthered an' soald for a slave before ye knowed where ye war! Ye wud, sorr; oah, ye wud!"

"Well, but, my poor boy, what do you propose to do?"

"Stay wid ye, Caftain—alive or dead, poor old Mark'll stan' by ye! Ye know ye stood by me wanst—doan't ye be harrd on me—lemme me be wid ye, whether ye're tuk by the rebels or fwhativer haffens. Loike as not our army's fell back ag'in—mebbe miles or more aweh by this—an' the inimy comin' forr'd—an' av I lift ye I'd niver set eyes on ye ag'in in the wide worrld!" And the poor fellow boohoos till the tears run down over his misshapen mouth, now swelling out of all human semblance.

"Now, Mark, listen to reason. If our army has gone back I've got to fall into the rebels' hands anyhow. Your staying here won't save me; while you can easily follow up the Sixth, save yourself, and tell them what became of me. See?"

No answer.

"While if we haven't fallen back, you may get together a squad with a litter and carry me in before day. See?"

"But, Caftain dayr, if they haven't fallen back they'll be out huntin' us before daybreak annyhow."

"But they'll never find us unless you go and tell them where to look."

"Oah, Caftain—I'd sooner cut off me roight hand than lave ye here aloan. I wud, soa I wud."

"You may help me by going. You can't help me by staying."

The faithful friend prepared for departure, laying his canteen and the two muskets within Will's reach.

"And Mark—just take these things with you." He took out his watch. "Just hand that to the surgeon for Mr. Penrose." His pocket-book. "That's for yourself." Some letters from his pocket he kissed before passing over. "Those you must burn as soon as you find that you'll see me no more. Now go—and good-bye, old fellow! Have your wound attended to the first thing."

Mark fell on his knees and wept sore.

"Caftain, if they've goan I'll niver goa afther thim! Ye'll see me by dehlight, wid help or aloan, as God wills."

He went away, and as long as he was within hearing Will heard the name of the Virgin, the evangelists, and many a saint, poured out in fervent though broken, tearful and imperfect speech. Then begins patience—where impatience would be futile. The grass is wet; the foliage is wet; the night-breeze wails as it shakes down the heavy drops. Nature gives sighs and tears to her dead and dying, while the black hours drag their slow lengths along. A bird utters his note. The east grows gray with sweet summer dawn—silent, peaceful, strange; yet no litter and no Mark Looney. Will sits up and looks at his wounded ankle. The sight makes him sick with nausea, and he covers it hastily. He takes off his coat, and tearing off one shirt-sleeve, ties it around the shattered joint without looking at it.

This fills the time till it must be near sunrise. A log is behind him; he lifts himself backward until his back rests against it. His shirt-sleeveless arm is chilly.

The day is going to be clear and warm. Not a sound of battle is yet audible. Doubtless the enemy is forming for a grand advance to follow up their success. Where will they meet with anything like organized opposition? Probably not till they get miles beyond where he lies—not till they come to the limit of the gun-boats' fire.

Long before that he will be a prisoner in the hands of the enemy. What does that mean? That means privation, suffering, delay in attending to his wound until, perhaps, gangrene sets in; then an amputation, then another, then slow death far from home and friends—far from Sally; near, perhaps, to Mac—glorious Mac, gloriously dead in battle. Well, whether near him or far from him, the thought that he met his fate while trying to find Mac will be a comfort up to his last breath.

Still no Mark and no litter.

Aha! There is a cannon-shot—afar off, but surely from our side! The enemy could not have got so far forward as the place that sound comes from! Another, nearer, followed by five more—a full battery. He thinks he can recognize a Union ring in the tone. No response yet from behind him.

The rising sun, and the stern determined sound of Union guns, brings an unmistakable revul- sion of feeling. Even he, helpless, wounded volunteer as he is, feels some of the "joy of battle" as the night's gloom meets the mor- row's reanimation.

Still no sign of friends or fellow sol- diers.

The sound of can- non has become fre- quent. Hurrah for

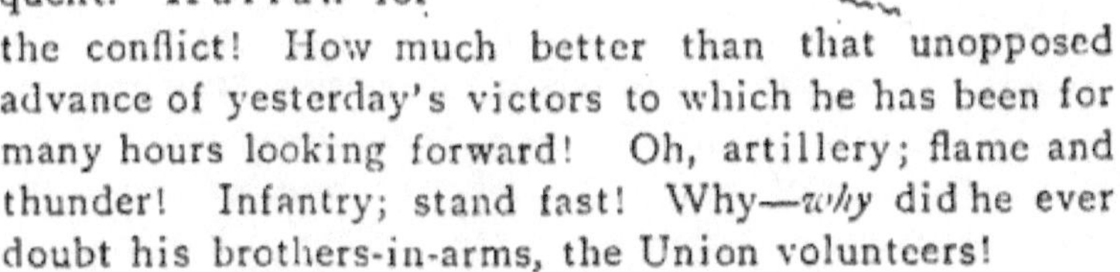

the conflict! How much better than that unopposed advance of yesterday's victors to which he has been for many hours looking forward! Oh, artillery; flame and thunder! Infantry; stand fast! Why—*why* did he ever doubt his brothers-in-arms, the Union volunteers!

Can he raise himself to a seat on the log? He can at least try. There, by doubling his well leg under him, and then getting his elbows against the rough bark, he gains an erect position. Now his hands on the log behind him raise him to its top. He lifts his leg with both hands; it does not hurt him much. The white shirt-sleeve is already soaked through with blood, and the wound is evidently too severe to be acutely painful.

What can he see?

Nearest him he can make out a reddish-gray object almost hidden in the grass and shrubs only a few rods away. It is, no doubt, Mark's victim of last night. A happy deliverance! Can any man on earth regret the sacrifice of a corpse-robber, violating the bodies of friend and foe; and making small distinction between the dead and the dying?

But perhaps the first Confederates who come will think that it was his (Fargeon's) hand that fired the fatal shot, and laid low one of their fellow-soldiers after the battle was done. If so, what fate may he expect? On this he ponders long. He does not wish to die, though Mac is no more.

What is visible beyond? Through openings in the thicket he can see the plain, studded here and there, though sparsely, with prostrate forms, stripped naked by the night-prowlers. Over toward where our lines ought to be he strains his eyes. No sign of the blessed Stars and Stripes. Not a man, nor a gun, nor even the smoke of a camp-fire. Now on the other side: With difficulty, hampered by his ruined foot, he turns his head around. There are the woods which border "the hornets' nest" where the Sixth Illinois yesterday offered itself on the Calvary of duty. No man, or gun, or flag to be seen there, either. But there seem to be pillars of light smoke, indicating camp-fires. No motion yet toward renewing their attack—their effort so desperate, so fiendish, so heroic. Other parts of the field are recommencing the struggle; but on this especial ground both athletes are thoroughly exhausted and disposed to "spar for wind."

Still no help for Will. Mark must have been killed, or wounded, or taken.

Ha! There opens a new battery from our own lines, on the right, and not far from this very point! He hears the flying missiles, and they come from our side. Six— twelve guns that seems to be. Another battery! On the left this time; yet nearer to the place where the Sixth and its Michigan friends were halted when he left them. Beaten? Why we have only just begun the fight! Who says the Union army is whipped or ever can be whipped? What difference does it make that Mac is dead and that Will himself is going to die? Hurrah for the Union!

"Oh, dear! Is this fever? Delirium? Well, it is not painful, so far. I can die so, if need be. Let me lie flat down on the log and think it over."

His "thinking" does not amount to much. Of course you can't sell dry goods when nobody wants any dry goods, nor pay debts when you've nothing to pay with. The idea is absurd. As poor Clinton Thrush said, give a man all the appellations in the world and take away his consignments, and what'll he offer next? Ha, ha, ha! Plain as the nose on a man's face. Extremely an- noying, though, this everlasting bringing up something, and turning away from it when it is just getting settled.

Sleep, or some kind of lethargy that takes the place of it, comes on and lasts—no one knows just how long.

"Front rank halt! Rear rank forwa-ard!" What is all this? Thirst, dizzy headache, and skirmish drill going on all at once!

Thirst is the most pressing consciousness. Instinct- ively he grasps Mark's canteen and drinks. as it seems,

20

for hours—or ages—at any rate all through the interval between unconsciousness and consciousness.

"Hello, Captain! How did you come here?"

Fargeon stares, bewildered, at the speaker—a spruce young lieutenant, a stranger to him and a Union soldier.

"Who are you sir, and where do you belong?"

"Pennsylvania, when I'm at home."

"Is this Pennsylvania?"

"No, Captain; but this is a Pennsylvania regiment."

"Why—I didn't know Grant had any."

"He didn't. We're fighting just now under Gen. D. C. Buel."

"Buel? Has Buel come up? Oh, thank God!" And Will burst into tears which clear his clouded brain enough to let him see that the battle was saved, and the army too, and he himself—all saved.

After the skirmishers have passed, the brigade goes by, fresh, steady, determined. And after the brigade, what? A squad of Company K, shouting and welcoming him, with friends to lift him and a litter to carry him. And Mark!—Mark, with a blood-stained cloth covering all his face below his streaming eyes, having only a hole cut for his mouth.

"Oh, Caftain dayr! I've eat me harrt out since daybreak, soa I have! The d— Michigan byes wouldn't let me in—ye niver gave me the countersign—an' then divvle the wan av me wud they let out for love nor money till they'd come out thimsilves, bad cess to 'em!"

They lift Will—now quite fever-stricken—gently to the litter.

"Now, Sarg'nt, give yer orders."

"Well, min; there's foive av yiz. Half of yiz go to the head and the other half to the fayt. I've a little business av me oan wid me butternut friend layin' there beyant, but I'll be wid ye shorrtly."

When he overtook them he laid on the litter beside Will a sword, two pocket-books, and a body belt doubtless containing money. He also had two Union jackets to put under Will's head, and a blue overcoat to throw over his feet to keep off sun and flies.

"The dom corpse-robber'll niver fay his way out av furgatory wid graynbacks. He'll not; nca, he'll not."

The things he laid on the litter were not quite all he found. Hidden in his pocket were a gold watch and a little, worn, crumbled thread-and-needle-case, with "When this you see, remember" dimly legible on the outside.

"Hello, Mac! Shake! Glad to see you, old boy! I'll tell you why—my arm is cold and my foot's asleep and—" he whispers mysteriously some unintelligible gibberish— "but they won't let me! But now you're here it's all right. You always make everything all right; don't you, Mac? Don't you? Of course you do. Ha, ha, ha!"

Who is it he is talking to and trying to embrace? Poor, bandaged, bloody, blindly blubbering Mark Looney.

"Ochone, ocho-one! Vad luck to the day I was vorn, and vlack was the light av it."

CHAPTER XXV

NOW FOR A CORK LEG.

"I LOOK for a relief from delirium some-time to-day; then all will be well if ever. And I can tell you, sir, we think ourselves very lucky to be able to save the knee for a stump. With a knee-stump you'll hardly know he has an artificial leg. Many will never know it at all."

That surely sounds like Doctor Strafford's voice.

"Thank God for all His infinite mercies!"

And that like Mr. Penrose's. What does it mean? What is this continuous rhythmical sound and motion? Why does every wave of that ceaseless fan seem to bring a breath of faint perfume that reminds Will of Sally Penrose? Has he been asleep? Can he open his eyes? Yes; he opens them. That looks like the skylight of a steamboat's cabin. Can he turn his head? Yes—but it must be all a dream; for it seems as if that angel-face with the fathomless eyes were the face of Sara—his love of long, long ago, in some former, half-forgotten life. The eyes meet his as if not expecting recognition, and he looks at them, contented and restful until explanation shall come of itself.

"Father! Oh, dear father!"

That is Sara's voice surely.

"The change has come; I can see it! I believe he knows me!"

"Why, Sally, how could I help knowing *you?*"

Who spoke? That surely is not *his* voice—so thin, so feeble and unsteady!

Yes, that is his love's face laid against his. It is her arm which encircles his neck, and her shoulder on which his hand rests, while her tones whisper words of love and gladness in his ear.

After a delicious minute his hand is taken in a clasp, strong, tender, and reassuring, and Will meets the smiling face of his dear old friend and companion, Doctor Strafford—meets it with an answering smile.

Again Mr. Penrose's voice is raised in a prayer of thanks to Heaven; and then follows a long, restful silence.

"Now tell me all the news."

"May we, Doctor?"

"Yes; if he'll promise not to ask questions."

Will nodded assent.

"Well, *Major* Fargeon!" (Sally pauses, while his eyes ask the question he had promised not to utter) "because you know you were brevetted for gallantry at Donelson. I'm sure you ought to be brevetted commander-in-chief for Shiloh! Now, *Major* Fargeon, you have been talking very foolishly for a good many days; so we had to bring you to the hospital boat St. Luke; and here we are, just started *for home*, Major, if you have no objection."

"Home," murmurs Will. "Home. Home. Home."

"Now, father, it is your turn," says Sally's sweet voice.

"*Major* Fargeon, Bue. s army came up and the battle was won, after the first day's disasters; and the rebels were driven back with immense loss."

Will closes his eyes and holds up his hand for silence while he lets this great thought fill his soul. Then with a sigh and a smile he opens them and waits for more.

"Now, Doctor Strafford," says Sally, "what have you to say?"

"Chicken-broth."

They laugh at this terse announcement of an important bit of intelligence; Will nodding assent to the suggestion it conveys. While Strafford is gone to order the broth, Sally resumes the thread of news.

"Father and Doctor Strafford and Lydia and I hurried down when we heard of your wound."

Here she grows uneasy and looks at her father, who in turn involuntarily glances toward the foot of the bed.

"Oh, I know my foot is gone," whispers Will with a smile.

"But," interposes Mr. Penrose, "by the mercy of Heaven, with a knee-stump you will hardly know you have an artificial leg—many never know it at all." [The minister had slightly misunderstood the doctor.]

Will nods indifferently, and Strafford returns, announcing that the broth will come directly. It is now his turn to speak. Will interrupts him to say:

"I know about my amputation and the knee-stump."

"Well, then, as Mark says, 'the nixt thing is somethin' else.' I have taken Mark's case in hand—the worst-looking lip you ever saw in your life."

Will nods.

"And I am going to make it a better lip than it ever was before since he was born—or before."

Will opens his eyes very wide.

"Yes, Major, I have taken advantage of that laceration to perform one of the loveliest operations of metaplastic art. That lip, when it heals up, will be a model from which a sculptor might sculp St. Cecelia playing on a Jew's-harp! Don't laugh! I mean it—and, besides, here comes the broth. Here, let me arrange you—there, Mark is to be the broth of a boy; and now you are to be a boy of the broth."

"Only one teaspoonful," whispers Will. But after one follows another, and then another, until the bowl is empty.

"Now some water," he says (not whispers). "Aha—that's *good!*" And as he lies back there is a tinge of color in lip and cheek.

"Now," says the doctor, and he says no more, but lays his finger significantly on his lip and looks in turn at each of the others; last at Fargeon, closing his eyes to intimate what he wished the patient to do. With child-like docility Will obeys, and is quickly in the land of dreams —and soon afterward even beyond that land, in the quieter region of space where the ether is too rarefied for dreams themselves to subsist on.

When Fargeon awoke again to the rhythmic motion and the ceaseless fan, Sara and her father were still beside him; Doctor Strafford away attending to other sufferers. They gave him hard-tack soaked in sugar-water, very refreshing to his fever-laden mouth, the dreadful breath whereof Sara had learned to know so well.

"Now some more news, please."

"Well, Major," said the minister, "through God's mercy Lieut.-Colonel Isaacs is rapidly recovering from his wound, and Major Colemason has resigned—or, rather, gone back to his captaincy, which he feels he never should have quitted."

Will smiled at these evidences of the mercy of Heaven, and Sally took up the thread of narrative.

"Poor Captain Chafferty was killed. Mark brought off a

sword and other things we took to be his, on the same litter with you."

"Poor Chaff!"

"And when Isaacs gets to be colonel, the other captain who ranks you will be lieutenant-colonel, and you will be a full-fledged major, instead of only one by brevet!   Am I not a wise woman on military matters?"

Will nodded, but gave her no answering smile.   He looked from one to the other with pleading eyes that seemed to say, "Is that all—*all?*"   Silence reigned. Then his bosom heaved with a great sob, and tears ran from both his eyes, down his cheeks and on to the pillow, before Sally's handkerchief could catch them.

"Don't cry, dear! *Don't!* It might be bad for you."

"I am crying for what you don't dare to tell me."

"We have nothing, dear—nothing positive. But we still have some hope—or at least *I* have."

"Tell me all—everything!"

"You know you promised not to ask questions," interposed Mr. Penrose.

"I am not asking questions; I am commanding you to give me full accounts concerning my—command."   The sick captain spoke with all the petulance of weakness —too feeble even to correct the absurd phraseology. Again silence, troubled silence, reigned.

"Forgive me, dear!" the quavering voice resumed. Then, when her face was laid by his, he whispered: "You may better do as I ask. I cannot live so—and I may if I know all."   She still hesitated, and still he pleaded with her, sobbing in a weak manner that alarmed them beyond words.

"If this request is denied—I feel a little as if I might —never make you another—another sane one."   Then they dared no longer refuse or delay. They told him that the latest accounts they had of Lieutenant McClintock were when the men accompanying the litter were assailed by a terrible flank fire from the left (their right as they retreated). They turned from it, but could not get clear of it. The wounded man was breathing when they started, but after that they did not all examine him. There were conflicting accounts as to who were with him last—two men asserting that the third had disappeared long before they were driven from their charge, and the third asserting that the others had left him alone with the litter. This made a preponderance of testimony in favor of the first-named story. But the third man was a member of Company K itself, which the others were not.

"Was the soldier a private named Dugong?"

"The very same! How did you know?" said Mr. Penrose with effusion. "Yes, it was Mr. Dugong. He seems an admirable man—faithful to the last in caring for his lieutenant, even when deserted by the others. I could not forbear giving him my personal assurance that you would not forget his services—alone, surrounded by foes, and cutting his way out only after all hope was gone of being of further use to poor Mr. McClintock. I ventured to hold out hopes of a sergeantcy, if not even a lieutenancy."

"Dugong! Curse his soul! The hound! I'll settle him yet!"

Sara sprang forward and placed her hand on Will's forehead.

"Father! Run for Doctor Strafford! Tell him to come at once—at *once!*"

"No, no, my beloved. No, Sally, dear, I am not going to the bad again. Mr. Penrose, don't call the doctor— I'm perfectly calm, and I'll tell you all about it."

"Not now, dear; please, to oblige me, not now! You frighten me so!"

"Oh, well," he laughed; "just as you like. Only—" She laid her dear hand on his lips, and he kissed the slender, pink finger-tips and was silent. After a little space he mumbled through the light obstruction:

"If I could speak, I should ask for more broth; but as I cannot, I will starve to death without a murmur."

"Oh, yes; you may speak to that extent. Father, please order some, if Doctor Strafford approves."

"With some boiled rice in it!" called Will.

So, for a few minutes the lovers are left alone together—minutes whereon even we, the unseen audience, will not intrude. We will walk, with Mr. Penrose, the length of the great steamer, between those interminable rows of beds, each holding a suffering hero's mangled form—Union or rebel, for all are treated alike. Over most of them hovers Hope; over some broods Despair. Around some are stretched screens that hide from view the final throes, or the pitiful, quiet form which has just passed through them, and is awaiting the night for removal to the open forward deck, where boxes are piled ready.

The St. Luke moves majestically down the broad river, her ponderous high-pressure engines breathing alternately; she, like a great whale, spouting vapor high in air, first through one blow-hole, then through the opposite— a planet, swinging through the realms of space, freighted with life and death, hope and fear, pain and pleasure, joy and sorrow, love and—but no; no hatred, unless it is thrown at her from the dark, unfriendly banks. The first blood that flows from a man seems to carry off all bitterness of heart, like a scum of bile on its surface.

Now we will thread our way back toward Fargeon's

bedside, with Mr. Penrose, Doctor Strafford, and the broth.

"You see, Doctor, what frightened us was his bursting out in violent—I may almost say profane—words against one of his own soldiers; a man who, if I am correctly informed (and I have it from his own lips) risked his life in a heroic effort to bring away Lieutenant McClintock—or his remains; for he says the lieutenant had died before he was forced to leave him."

"That violence is very strange—and very serious indeed, unless there is something back which we do not yet know."

"I presume you approve our course—checking the vagary at once?"

"Yes, yes—I dare say. Though I may decide to unwire the cork and let the gas effervesce, and so relieve the pressure. Tell you better when I feel his pulse and look at his eyes."

They arrive.

"Well, Major—here comes your commissary train with rations. How do you feel, old boy?"

"Just—delightfully! There's no other word for it!"

"Pulse—all right! Eyes—couldn't be better! Never mind your tongue; save that to hold, when you ought not to talk, and to eat broth and rice with."

"Oh, dear! Is that all you brought? What is that little dab, among *one?*"

"Oh, that's more than you think for. As my mother used to say when I took more than I could eat, your eyes are bigger than your stomach."

"Now let's see, said the blind man. Where did we drop the thread? But, Major, don't scare me as you did Mr. and Miss Penrose."

"Never fear, Doctor. You don't scare easily. They

were trying to tell me the last news—no, I'll not say that—the *latest* news from my own glorious Mac! my beloved Mac! my own brother-in-arms Mac—my more than brother!"

"Well, Major, let the dominie get clear through his tale; then you may fire off your mouth and free your mind."

"All right! Sally dear, lay your pretty hand close by, and clap it on my lips if I so much as open them to breathe."

"Well," began the dominie, "the two litter-bearers report that they were making good time to the rear—glad enough to have a stout soldier to help carry the heavy end. The first thing that disturbed them was that Union troops—not Sixth Illinois men—began to pass on their right in a steady stream, as fast as they could go—much faster than the litter could travel. After a while the stream grew less; the fugitives seemed to have all got by, and rebel bullets began to come from their right hand as well as behind them.

"So far their report agrees with that of Private Dugong, who was the soldier who had so kindly volunteered to help them."

"Oh!—" began Will; whereupon his remark was summarily extinguished, as a candle under a pair of snuffers, only the extinguisher was in the shape of four most kissable fingers.

"Now hear what Private Dugong reports, and with what seems to me the most absolute and soldierly good faith. He says that when the rebel bullets began to fly the other men incontinently set down the litter and fled, paying no heed to his urgent appeals to persevere. He even repeats the very words he made use of. Said he: 'Fellow-comrades' (that was his expression), 'Lieutenant

McClintock is acknowledged to be, by all odds, the best and bravest officer in our army. Consider what a loss he will be to our great cause! Why, my captain, Cap Fargeon, would rather give a hundred dollars out of his own pocket than have Lieutenant McClintock fall into the enemy's hands. Let us try once more. If at first you don't succeed, try, try again. As for me, fellow-comrades, you may do as you please, but I will never, never desert my superior officer.' Those were his very words, as far as I can remember them; though there were more to the same general purpose.

"But to resume. His appeal was unavailing. They did not even pause to listen to him, but fled in the most dastardly manner. Then the brave soldier went to the side of the lieutenant, resolved, as he had said, to die with him if it should be God's will. But alas, Lieutenant McClintock was no more! Bear up bravely, my dear Captain Fargeon, praying Heaven for aid—his heart had ceased to beat."

The good dominie put his hand to his eyes and was silent.

"Oh!—" began Will, fruitlessly as before.

"Now, Willie," said Sally, "I'll tell you what the two others say. They say that as soon as the bullets began to come from their right-hand side the volunteer dropped the litter handle and ran like a dog directly away from the firing. In vain they shouted; he only ducked his head and ran the harder. Well, they too swerved toward their left, and kept going—only stopping to change ends—kept going as long as they could stand it, and then gave up and ran toward our lines, but never caught sight of Dugong again until the next day."

Will took Sally's hand quietly in his own to intimate that it was now his turn.

"Caleb Dugong is a coward and a damnable liar.   If he says Mac is alive, he is dead.   If he says he is dead, he is alive."

Then he told them of the incident when he last saw Dugong; when the skulker made Mac's being carried off an excuse for leaving the field, refusing to return even when commanded by name to do so.

"Now, this is the third time the hell-hound has skulked, to my knowledge and under my very eyes!   If ever I get well and find him in Company K, I'll have him court-martialed; and if the court is afraid to have him shot, by all that's good and holy, I'll—"

Again the gentle hand checked the ungentle words, so strange from those humane, charitable, gentlemanly lips.

Contracted brow and sad, anxious eyes, and the absence of any demand for more news of the many things left untold, made the loving watchers uneasy, and Strafford cast about for something with which to effect a diversion.

"Major, a friend of yours is waiting impatiently to see you, though for reasons beyond his own control he will not have much to say for himself."

An inquiring look came over the major's face.

"Mark Looney is on board."

"Dear old Mark!   Bring him on, Doctor."

Mark arrived, the whole lower part of his face covered with one great bandage, only pierced at each corner of the mouth with apertures large enough to receive a tube.

"My only hesitancy about bringing Mark to see you is the fear that he may try to smile when he sees you so much better; for I have told him if he cracks a smile and disturbs those stitches, he is to be shot at sunrise!"

Mark's eyes smiled when he grasped Fargeon's hand, whether his concealed lips did or not.

"Now Mark has suffered a hundred times more pain than you have."

Mark shook his head, and Will could almost hear him say: "Sorra the taste of a fain I moinded at-all-at-all. No, sorr, I did not; oah, I did not."

"Well, he might well have done that. I haven't felt a pang to speak of, from first to last—bodily."

"Mark never whimpered when I put in the stitches—though I confess it hurt *me* to put them where they are! And I *know* that for two days and nights afterward he never slept!"

Mark tossed his head as if to say: "That's soa—but fwhat av it?"

"And since that he has refused to lie abed—insisted on acting as assistant about the boat, and the most valuable and efficient hospital hand I ever saw, speechless as he is."

Another deprecatory nod.

"Now, by the day after to-morrow I am going to let up on him—take off the plaster bands—and then, if all goes well, as I believe it will, he'll be well and able to look any man in the eye—or woman either."

Mark passed his hands across his eyes with a gesture that seemed to brush away a life-long trouble; and soon departed to go on with his manifold merciful avocations.

"Now, where's Lydia? You said she came with you."

"Yes; but she is not going back with us. I don't know that any one has told you, Willie, that a very sentimental feeling has grown out of the correspondence which has been going on between Lydia and Mr. McClintock."

"No! Do you mean so? That close-mouthed fellow never breathed a word of it. But Lydia is a mere child!"

"Not so much of a child. She had aged wonderfully since her visit to Donelson; and he has always been her hero since she first heard of him, before the regiment left Chicago. Every word you said or wrote about him she seized upon as if it had been the breath of life."

"And now she is waiting to learn his fate? Bless her dear heart! But who is with her?"

"Mr. and Mrs. Prouder."

"What? The old man himself?"

"Yes; they left their two little boys at our house and we all came down together, and between them all no effort will be spared to relieve our suspense."

"Yes, indeed! If old Zury is to the fore, money and shrewdness will never be lacking. I am very glad—*very* glad in the money matter, for as soon as I have time to think about things worldly, I shall begin to be anxious regarding the expenses your father must have incurred."

"Oh, Will, you need not worry about money."

"But I must, love; not at this moment, perhaps, but—"

"Never again."

"Oh, you dear, simple sweetheart! Are we now about to live forever upon your hundreds of dollars saved up?"

"Not on them, but on other hundreds—and thousands."

"Why, have you found a pot of money? I don't *remember* any rich uncle of yours on either side who can have died and left you a large fortune in silver and gold."

"Well, dear, don't let us talk any more about it now. Next week, when we are safe at home, if you go on getting well, I will set your mind quite at rest as to money."

A long, wholesome silence follows, during which there comes a stoppage of the boat's engines. They are making the landing at Savannah, to take on more wounded men and put ashore one who has already died under the surgeon's knife. The halt wearies the sufferers, for they reckoned their journey, not by its progress, but by its interruptions. At length all is ready, and the St. Luke once more rounds out into the stream. As she does so a band stationed on shore to speed the parting wayfarers, softly begins playing "Home, Sweet Home."

How many eyes fill with tears! Or, rather, how few of the listeners can restrain this evidence of weakness! On Will Fargeon's memory one more old melody is newly impressed in such tones that he can never afterward hear it without overpowering emotion.

"Will, dear?"

"Well, love."

"Achilles! It was in your heel after all!"

"Yes, Sally. Your fun was prophetic. Aren't you glad you didn't call me Hector?"

"Oh well—wait until I get you in my power! Perhaps both names will fit!"

And so they tried to forget their trials and their griefs in a comfortable present and serene future. But time and life were toning down both hopes and fears—happily.

21

THE FORTUNES OF WAR.

THE transfer from boat to cars at Cairo, and the long, hot ride thence to Chicago were very trying; and a tired, weak and docile invalid it was who at last sank to much-needed rest at the cool, heavenly-quiet parsonage. Strafford had remained behind; the medical staff declaring that he could not be spared, and insisting on his taking a surgeon's appointment, even if only temporarily. So Fargeon's "stump" was put in the care of Doctor Brainard; and Mark, with sixty day's furlough, was his able nurse and devoted slave. Poor Mark would have been glad to give an arm or a leg, or even life itself, for his beloved captain. Nay, he would almost have done more—foregone the benefit of Strafford's surgical operation on his old blemish! This, by the way, had provided him with a countenance reasonably like those of other men—if one be not too critical, and Mark was not. As he said:

"The docther putt a mug onto me noa man nay'd be ashamed av. He did; oah, he did."

"Thank you, Mark! Oh, this lounge is Heaven itself! You are as strong as a horse, Mark."

"Fehth, sorr —Mehjor; ye're not soa hefty as ye wor

fwhin I carr'd ye into the broosh-pile. Ye're not; noa, ye're not—worrse luck!"

"And, Mark, you will come back about dark and help me to bed again?"

"I will sorr—Mehjor; oah, I will." [Exit.]

"Now, Sally, dear, I must see Mr. Thorburn and arrange to have my pay account transferred up here and turned over to your father to help along. I wonder Uncle Colin hasn't called before now."

"He is—not in town, Willie. And as to money, I tell you we are all fully supplied, but I am not ready to tell you how, just yet."

"Oh, you mysterious financier! So deep and artful! Do you happen to know how Meyer Moss-Rosen gets on with my old debts?"

"Oh, everything has, as the newspapers say, 'gone kiting,' and the last time I saw Uncle Colin he told me the debts were all paid, but he added almost with tears in his eyes, that he had ruined you by making that arrangement we liked so much, turning over your store to Moss-Rosen on condition he should pay the debts."

"Dear old Thorburn! Well, I have known for some time that Meyer got the best of that bargain, as things have turned out—inflation and all."

"Yes; Mr. Thorburn said that you had lost, and Moss-Rosen was going to make $100,000 by the bargain, and that he, Uncle Colin, would never forgive himself until he had atoned to you for his blunder, as he called it.

"Oh, pshaw! He needn't trouble himself. He only helped me do what I had resolved to do if I could—tried to, and couldn't without his help."

Sally was silent.

"Now I must relieve his kind old heart. When will he return?"

"I—don't know."

"When did you see him last?"

"Just after Donelson. He brought the news of your glorious doings. He cried and laughed together—we all did; he walking the floor and talking constantly about you—his own 'braw lad'—loaded upon a litter to be carried to his death for his land's sake—the morning breaking—our boys saying good-bye—their guns loaded and their bayonets fixed—they looking out over their stony death-bed—the healthy cowards all left behind, and his own 'braw lameter' limping along so he mightn't be left alive when his brave lads should be dead and dying—and then the Heaven-sent white flag—when he came to that his spectacles fell off and we all laughed together but his tears blinded him so that he couldn't see his glasses till I picked them up and gave them to him—" Here the tears and sobs choked her utterance, while there seemed to be no laughter mixed with them.

"Don't cry so, dear! It's all over now—and how far away it all seems! That blessed old man! I *must* see him! Where is he, do you know?"

"No." (Faintly audible.)

"I'll write—no, by George, I'll telegraph! Somebody must know his address. Please get me pencil and paper, Sally my love."

"Oh, Will! Wait till to-morrow."

"But why, love? I want to write the message; then if it is going to cost too much—"

"Oh, it isn't that!"

"Well; whether we send it off or not, it will show our good will, and we'll give it to him when he returns. Just humor me, Sally. Give me pencil and paper, please."

She did as he asked, and Fargeon wrote:

"Best friend. Money all right. Army all right. Union all right. Leg all right. Heart all right."

"There! Seventeen words. Twenty will go by night-rate the same as ten by day. Can't we afford that?"

"Yes," answered the weeping girl.

"Well, let us make it twenty. Let's see; suppose we add 'wedding very soon.' How will that do?"

She only shook her head.

"Isn't it all true?"

"Yes, I hope so."

"Won't he be pleased to read it? Then why do you hang back so, dear? But here comes your father; I'll leave it to him. Now, Mr. Penrose, your daughter and I have fallen out, and you see she is crying, so I must be in the wrong—but how, I can't for the life of me make out. Here, read this proposed telegram and see if it is a matter for tears, not to say howls of anguish."

"Why, I see nothing out of the way in that. Money —army—Union—leg—heart—all right. So they are, to be sure! Wedding very soon; well, that's for you two to say. But to whom is the message to go?"

"Why, to Uncle Colin Thorburn, to be sure," cried Will, bursting into a gay laugh which died suddenly on his lips as he saw the minister stagger as if he had been struck. A full minute of oppressive silence followed; then Mr. Penrose said, with deep solemnity:

"The telegraph hence to Heaven is not of wire, but of prayer. Let us pray." Then, kneeling, he poured out fervent thanks for the blessings which the world had received in the life of a good man now gone to his reward, and for whose special goodness to those present, both in his life and in his death, their undying thanks should be given; first to God, then to Colin Thorburn, the instrument of God's mercy and His bounty. Will lay with face to the wall, his dry eyes covered with his hand. Men do not cry for the death of older men, however loved and honored.

Yes, the grand old Scot had died, most suddenly, during the time the Sixth was at Pittsburg Landing, before the dreadful days of Shiloh. His will, when opened, proved to be a curious document, the product of the kindly thoughts of a kind heart through many years. Though signed and witnessed very lately, some of the earlier legacies were erased, with the word "dead" written in the margin. Others were erased with other words to explain the change: "Society turned sectarian." "No charity school—only a land-speculation," and so on.

Finally came the residuary clause, added, evidently, just before the date and execution. "All the rest and residue of my estate, real and personal, of every name and nature, I shall now bestow in such manner as it seems to me will best undo part of the injustice which is to spring from this war, for I do perceive that it is to be the rich man's war, but the poor man's fight; that those will get rich who do not fight; and those who do fight will not get rich—no, never.

"I would give the said rest and residue direct to my brave and beloved young friend, William Fargeon, captain in the Union army and worthy to be its commander-in-chief, as I in my heart believe, since I have learned the manner of his behavior at Donelson and elsewhere. The reasons why I do not give it to him direct are:

"*Imprimis:* His valor may cost him his life, and I know not who his heirs may be:

"*Secundo:* For a certain cause I doubt his shrewdness and discretion in business matters, and the cause of my doubt is this; videlicet; that in a late crisis in his affairs he was unwise enough to follow the counsel of an old fool who thought a Yankee ell was to be measured by a Scotchman's thumb; whereby great loss accrued to him, the said William Fargeon; the old fool who gave the bad counsel being myself.

"Now, therefore, I do give, devise, and bequeath the said rest and residue of my estate, both real and personal, of every name and nature, not otherwise hereinbefore disposed of, unto Mistress Sara Penrose, spinster; whereby I fervently hope that it may inure to the benefit and behoof of the said Fargeon as her husband, and to their children, should God grant them that blessing which He hath denied unto me, for my own fault and short-coming, in that I married not. And should they have so many knave-bairns that they know not where to seek finer appellations for them all, I bid them mind that Colin Thorburn is a name that hath not, to my knowledge, belonged to any that hath been hanged for sheep-stealing."

Immanuel Penrose was named executor (with compensation and without bonds), and the said executor was advised to consult, as legal and business counsel, the testator's old, trusted, most valued and most invaluable friend, Mark Skinner.

When he came to read the will, Fargeon fell to thinking aloud.

"A rich man's war and a poor man's fight—a rich man's war and a poor man's fight. Yes; that's it—the soldiers are opening and shutting the gate, 'ike the man in the fable." Then to his lovely, tireless watcher:

"So you are a great heiress, Sara?"

"Yes, dear. Please be very humble to me, and always respect my slightest wish in every possible way, or dread the power of the mighty dollar."

"Heigh-ho! I remember your saying once that you were usually harmless, but terrible when roused. Be roused, please, Miss Penrose, and terrify me."

"But, dear Willie, you haven't thwarted my slightest wish yet. How can I be roused unless you rouse me? Make some unreasonable demand and see me flare up."

"Well—but first tell me how much your fortune is."

"Oh, don't ask me, dear, _re'._ In fact, we don't know yet, exactly."

"Is it six figures?"

"Six? Let me see." She turned and wrote something on paper. "One, two, three, four, five, six! You've hit it exactly! You are a wonderful guesser! That's what it is to have been a business man! Exactly six figures—not counting cents."

He turned his head languidly to the wall again and began tracing the pattern of the paper with his thin, white forefinger. A ring at the front door-bell was heard.

"Sara, I think that is Doctor Brainard. Will you please let me see him alone?"

"Surely, dear Willie," and she hurried out. After the usual routine belonging to surgical visits, Will asked:

"Now, Doctor, when can I rejoin my company?"

"Rejoin your company? Never, with my consent. No man will ever march on an artificial leg if I have anything to say about it. Your regiment, as a mounted officer, you might rejoin in, say, a month."

"Humph! Well, Isaacs ought to get his colonelcy and I my full majority by that time."

"Think so? Now let me tell you the latest doings of your precious Republican authorities at Washington." [The doctor was a stanch Douglas Democrat and opponent of the Lincoln administration.] "Will you believe me, Captain Fargeon, when I tell you that the order has gone forth that whenever a regiment falls below five hundred men no man shall be promoted to the colonelcy?"

"What? Oh, I don't—*can't* believe it!"

"That's the kind of a War Department you Republicans have given us!"

"Oh, I *can't* believe it. The regiments that save themselves get all the promotions, and those that sacrifice themselves go without? Oh, it can't be!"

"I know it can't be—long, but it is now; and it will be until we can put somebody in power of a different stripe from this stock-jobbing, office-seeking, money-grabbing crew! Give us a good War-Democrat like McClellan, and such disgraceful things will be impossible —and the Union will be saved!"*

When the doctor had gone, Sara returned in wild-eyed terror.

"Oh, Willie—the doctor says—you want to know— when you can—oh, I can't speak it!" and she burst into a storm of tears and sobs.

"There, there, there, my poor child! Don't, *don't* sob so! You'll break my heart." He stroked and patted her little hand in a vain attempt to soothe her almost hysterical distess. "What is it, Sara? I won't do anything you wish me not to do."

"Why do you want to go away? Why do you call me *Sara?* What have I done?" ·

"Nothing, my dear girl, except all that an angel could and would do for a poor old soldier, wounded and helpless."

She started up and stepped back.

"*Have* I done it for a poor soldier, wounded and helpless? Yes—but it was also for a friend—a man who professed to be my lover—promised to be my husband."

---

* The law stands to this day.

She tossed her head, compressed her lips, and glared at him with eyes that seemed fairly to snap, in their shining excitement.

He returned her look with one of admiring surprise. This was a new phase of her beauty and new development of her character. Still they waited, and still they looked. How was the scene to end?

In laughter, of course; albeit on her part a little wild, and verging on hysterics at first. Then she knelt by his side and hid her face, saying:

"Now you've seen me roused. Am I terrible or not?"

"Not merely terrible—irresistible! Such a blaze of beauty and spirit I never dreamed of."

"Oh, you base flatterer! You were rattled, as you call it, and now you are trying to disarm me! But I won't be cajoled. Promise me you'll never, *never* do so again."

"Tell me just how I offended you, so I shall know what not to do in the future."

"Why, call me by formal names, and try to escape from me, and pretend we are never to be—married! So there now! I've said it!"

"Why, my fine lady, beauty, heiress, woman whom all men must adore and of whom no man is worthy—who am I that I should presume to look at you? To hold you to a promise which I begged from you when you were poor and I was rich—a promise you never made, by the bye, after all!"

"Never promised!" she cried in dismay. "An unengaged girl treating you as I have done? That may comport with *your* idea of lady-like propriety—*your* experience of well-bred young women—but it doesn't with mine, I can tell you!"

"There, there, my darling; don't be roused again. Remember my feeble state—I really couldn't stand another vision of Diana offended. But think now, seriously. Every friend you have in the world will tell you that my duty is to leave you free to choose; and if I do not, I'm a mean fellow, unworthy to be your husband."

"As fast as friends told me so, I'd scratch them off my list of friends."

"Judge Skinner will tell you so—and he is in a kind of way your guardian, by virtue of Uncle Colin's having named him in the will."

"Judge Skinner? You don't know the splendid, perfect gentleman! He has let me know unmistakably that he thought my hero's love was more to me than all this money or a hundred times as much could be! Why, Will, don't you knew that his son has gone into the service?"

"Has Dick Skinner gone?"

"Yes, indeed! Richard, the judge's only son, the pride of his heart, is a Union soldier. So are lots of others, the flower of our young men—Will De Wolf, John Kinzie, Lucius Larrabee, and many, many more.* I can fancy Judge Skinner's fine scorn on hearing mere *money* set off against—things like that?"

After a pause, Sally added, as a clincher:

"Dear Uncle Colin said in his will that it was you he wished to help; and he gave me the money for that purpose."

"He placed no conditions on you—did not bind you in any way—and if he had, I should set you free, seeing how things have changed by my becoming a useless cripple."

"That's what I call *morbid!*"

"That's right—trample on me—call me proud, if you

---

* William De Wolf, killed at Williamsburg in 1862; John H. Kinzie, killed at Fort St. Charles in 1863; Lucius S. Larrabee, killed at Gettysburg in 1863; Richard Skinner, killed at Petersburg in 1864.

like; too proud to be inflicted upon a splendid woman who might come to just a sacrifice, devoting herself to a *worthy* man, a wreck who needed her help, as I did yours after Donelson, and since Shiloh."

Sally was dreadfully hurt at this unconscious reminder of the dirty tent at Donelson—of something she was always trying to forget. No heroics now; only tears, tears, tears, and sobs. She would not be comforted, though Will was doing his best to soothe and quiet her.

"You—only—see—my faults—and mistakes—and—fail ings—oh—oh—oh—I—can't—bear it!"

"There, there, there, sweet one! I only see my own— you have none! You are glorious; it is I who am nothing—nothing!"

The storm passed and sweet sunshine followed, the world being lovelier in its spangling of pearly drops.

"Now, my dear Will, don't let us talk any more about it. I knew you were so romantic—or rather so sordid and unromantic—that I was afraid of something of this kind, and had a dim notion that all this might be kept a secret until after we were—married. But you were always so *awfully* patient about *that* that I despaired, and let it 'out. Well—never mind. If you want to be let off your promise, I'll absolve you from it. Major Fargeon, we meet hereafter only as friends!" [Mock-heroic.]

But they did not part "only as friends."

All minor crises our wounded captain had safely passed; now was approaching a trial—perhaps the severest of all that had occurred since the knife did its sharp work. The Prouders and Lydia were coming home without a single additional bit of intelligence to indicate Mac's fate—or even to distinguish his grave among the un-marked thousands the confederates had made between our lines and Corinth.

Our army, splendid in size, equipment, and preparation, had advanced, with ponderous weakness, to Corinth, to find there only deserted breast-works, Quaker guns, beans burning aromatically in the ruins of confederate store-houses, two destroyed railroads, one hundred and twenty-five of the enemy's sick occupying the "Tishomingo Hotel," and lots of darkys occupying the rest of the town in great comfort and hilarity.

Let us not invidiously name the authority to which this example of the "mountain in labor" was chargeable. We will only say that Grant had been superseded, and that the whole absurd movement seemed to cry aloud once more, "An army of lions led by a sheep is less formidable than an army of sheep led by a lion."

Day after day did tireless old Prouder search those woods. Besides his own searching he hired all the trustworthy help he could secure, ranging from three to fifteen men. He could not use the negroes, because they were unable to decipher the pencil scrawls on the few head-posts which bore them. The very first day he hired them he was appalled to see them return loaded with these rude mementoes ruthlessly dug from the places where survivors had piously put them.

"Yes, baus—dis h'yer chunk wuz a-stickin' plum outen

a grabe dat look fer all de worl' lak it mought 'a' be'n 'Tenant Clenter's grabe. T'ought I'd fotch it 'long, so's ter jes' let ye see ef it wuz his'n er no."

Prouder was so shocked at the unintentional sacrilege that he did not tell his wife and Lydia of the circumstance, but paid the darkeys one more day's wages all round to take the sticks back to where they found them.

"Oh, yes, baus. We done foun' 'em all, 'n' stuck 'em plum back in de same holes dey kim outen. T'ankee, baus. Hope ye'll fin' 'im. 'Fore God I do! Fin' 'is head anyway, wever ye fin' de rest of 'm er not."

A pressing telegram from Governor Yates gave him all the help that could come from inquiries by flag of truce, and after all, his crowning effort was directed toward gaining admission to the enemy's lines for himself in person. This was one of the bitterest trials of his life; for the tears and clinging arms of his wife, whom he loved better than life itself, were used to prevent his going. [Even eloquently bitter words regarding herself and their children were added to her weapons of opposition.] Nevertheless, he tried—and failed. He might enter the confederate lines; but not to return, whether with Lieutenant McClintock or without him.

The Shiloh and Corinth camps (the unmilitary part) were very sorry to see Mr. Prouder depart, for an unfailing spring of greenbacks was then and there dried up. Sharp bargains he drove; but the cash was always ready to meet his part of each contract. One fellow, caught lounging about a sutler's tent when under engagement to search a certain part of the woods, felt the weight of the old man's hand and the hardness of his boot; but not without richly deserving it.

Telegrams have told of their leaving Pittsburgh Landing, of their passing Fort Henry and other points, of their leaving Cairo. Now the carriages approach the parsonage, where all the family are standing on the porch awaiting them. Mrs. Prouder's lovely face shines from the coach window—

"The mother-hunger glittering in her eye."

And she springs from the door almost before the wheels have stopped turning.

"He is getting well!" cries Sally, running down to meet her.

"He! Which? Have they been ill?" And the other flies past the younger woman, never stopping till she has her boys in her arms.

"I do believe she thinks more of those young cubs of hers than she does of Will!" says the mortified Sally to Lydia, as she greets her with kiss after kiss. But how much older you look! And how saddened—my poor darling! No wonder—all this suspense; but cheer up, dear! 'No news is good news,' you know."

"Yes," answers Lydia, doubtfully, despairingly. "No news that we get is ever good news."

As she weeps in her sister's arms, she already perceives, though dimly, that regarding the missing" in battle, "no news" is almost synonymous with "no hope."

Mr. Prouder had never encouraged them to look for tidings that Mac was still alive. He had secretly received from Mark (through Doctor Strafford, to whom Mark had confided them), Mac's watch and the little needle-case recovered from the marauding corpse-robber—mute witnesses of almost certain martyrdom. True, the ghoul might have stolen them from a helpless living man as well as from a dead body; but the chance of survival, always small, had now dwindled to the merest speck, as all must see.

CHAPTER XXVII.

ADVANCE, FRIEND, AND GIVE THE COUNTERSIGN.

FAR from winning any due reward for its heroic sacrifices, the Sixth was by them debarred from even routine promotion. It was not now large enough to call for a colonel. If it could be filled up again, then its offices would be filled; otherwise not.

"Well," cried the zealous and hopeful Mr. Penrose; "we must fill it up again, that's all!" And he sat down at once and spent a whole evening writing a glowing appeal, which he sent to the Fulcrum, in the columns of which paper he sought for it daily for weeks afterward. The fact is that the editor, as soon as he glanced at the signature, threw the paper, unread, into the waste-basket. "Drop Penrose," we remember.

New regiments were forming, filling up, and departing constantly. Why not divert part of the stream—already nearly 100,000 men from Illinois—to fill up the glorious Sixth? In season and out of season Mr. Penrose depicted the dreadful losses it had sustained. He had lists printed of the killed and wounded, and described their fearful wounds and their heroic deaths. He extolled their services, and prophesied that the Sixth would offer still more splendid opportunities for martyrdom and self-sacrifice in the future. Yet, strange to say, even these exhilarating and alluring pictures failed to draw in new men. The new men obstinately preferred to go into the new regiments, where new offices were to be had—regimental, company, and non-commissioned— even though the slaughter should never equal that in the older regiments.

When Will grew so strong that inaction became intolerable, he got an assignment to duty at Camp Douglas, high enough to use his brevet rank; thus becoming, at least in name, a mounted officer, with corresponding pay and allowances. Sorely was he tempted to get Mark Looney assigned to duty with him; but—"What would Mac say?" So Mark rejoined the regiment at Corinth in time to take part in the splendid defense of that post when it was fruitlessly attacked by the forces of Price and Van Dorn. Again the gallant few were made fewer, and promotion more distant than ever.

"My boys keep opening the gate," sighed Will.

He bought a quiet steed, contented to stand like a wooden horse while that awkward stiff leg could be thrown over the saddle, and that insensate toe be made to find its blind way into the stirrup; but just as he thought all was well, he saw some boys laughing at the "queer leg," that stuck out so! Will couldn't blame them —though Sara cried when he told her of it. So when real comfort and convenience were to be sought for, the quiet horse was harnessed to a buggy, and the quiet groom (or sometimes quiet Sara Penrose) accompanied him on his errands of business and pleasure.

"Morphy, my boy," he wrote to the lieutenant, "when you have a limb shot off, look out that it's an arm and not a leg. Nothing belittles a man, 'takes the tuck out of him,' and hampers every act of his life, so much as to be restricted in his locomotion. I'm the one winged goose in the flight—the one hobbled horse in the drove.

22

I'd rather lose one arm than two legs, Barney—I would, indeed." And Morphy, Irishman as he was, never saw the shadow of a joke in the letter.

The place where he felt happiest, happier than anywhere except, perhaps, at the parsonage, was in the hospitals. There, relieving physical pain, succoring the helpless, comforting the despairing, aiding the bereaved —there, and there alone, he forgot all his misfortunes, his maimed limb, his fallen friends, his halting and inglorious future—all, all fled and dissolved into nothingness at the sight of continually fresh batches of human suffering to be delightfully assuaged. In all this blessed and self-rewarding work, Sara Penrose was his faithful, willing helper; a burden-sharer of the right kind in the right place.

Filled with contrition, Will dwelt on at the parsonage during his helplessness, because he had no valid reason for going away; no reason which he dared to acknowledge. But when his assignment to duty came, he promptly took up his quarters at the post. Not all the officers did so; but he said to the questioning, loving folks at the parsonage that he *knew his duty*, whether others knew theirs or not. To himself he said:

"I know my duty to that lovely young princess—it is to leave her to her own devices, and try to hope that she can find a happier fate than marriage with a wreck of humanity."

Then he would "efface" himself, and be only one of the many—young, old, and middle-aged—who found themselves attracted to the minister's hospitable fireside, now more hospitable than ever since the executorship was yielding a handsome income outside the unlimited sums at command of the elder daughter. Fargeon even took care to bring up and present the most worthy

MARK ARRIVED.—Page 318.

339

youths, in the army and out of it, who came within his sphere. "Sara the fair" only looked at them smiling and polite, at him wistful and reproachful.

"I think I shall never marry," she said; and her words were repeated to Will. With jealous pain he would say to himself, "There's young Fortune again—a West Pointer, and a brigadier-general at thirty—she *ought* to fall in love with him!" Then the cold smile for the other, and the warm look for him, would raise him to the seventh heaven, and he would say, "I am doing her

an injustice—and myself a useless cruelty." For his veins were again filling with h e a l t h y blood, and his muscles, bodily and mentally, were h a r d e n i n g into vigorous manhood once more.

One e v e n i n g , after General Fortune had retired from the field, evidently disheartened, and Sara, as usual, had emerged suddenly from cold gravity into warm gayety, Will, exultant and indiscreet, broke forth:

"Loveliest—dearest—best of created beings—I believe I'm a born fool! When shall the wedding be?"

"*My* wedding, Major Fargeon? With General Fortune? Or if not, with whom?" (Bridling with a pretense of offended dignity).

If she had wanted to punish him for anything she would have taken delight in seeing his features fall into lines of utter dismay and confusion and the blood ebb from cheek and lip, leaving a look that reminded her of his most helpless time. But she did not. The dear girl scarcely waited a moment before, holding out both her hands to him, she cried:

"There, there! Don't look so—just come and kneel at my feet and beg my pardon for your heartless and frivolous behavior—throwing other men at my head as if you were a prince trying to get rid of a wearisome favorite!"

"My heart kneels to you, sweet one; but my kneeling days, bodily speaking, are past—unless you'll wait while I unstrap my cork leg."

"Never mind! If you can't kneel to me, I'll come and kneel to you.   There now; I can look right into your eyes and ask you how you *dared* behave so!"

"Well, it was audacious, I admit ; but you were so unutterably lovely—"

"So unutterably lovely that you let me alone?"

"No; asked you to marry me—to fix the wedding-day."

"Oh, I'm not finding fault with *th-at!*"

———

Could anything add to their unspeakable happiness? Yes, greatly; but some things might occur to detract from it. For instance, there was an untimely ring at the front door. Lydia (who had discreetly retired with the others and left them alone), came in, to find them calmly seated at an unexceptionable distance apart, but at the same time with tell-tale faces.

"I thought I'd come to see if you heard the bell. But I suppose it can't be a caller at this hour."

"A man to see Captain Fargeon," announced the "second-girl."

"Is he an orderly?"

"No, sir; he looks more like a tramp. He just rang the bell and then went back to the gate."

"Oh, Will—send out to find out what he wants! Perhaps he's—a copperhead—an assassin."

"Ha-ha, my love! Your father's own daughter;" and he disappeared. Step — clump, step — clump, step — clump, they heard the well-known and well-beloved halting tread through the hall, over the porch, down the door-step. Then they heard no more.

"Well, comrade, what can I do for you? Do I know you? Glad to see you, whoever you are."

"Captain Fargeon—"

Will's cry burst upon the still air:

"Oho-ho-ho-ho, my dear boy, my dear Mac, my dearest friend come back to me from the grave! Mac!—Mac!"

He began with a wild laugh and ended with a wilder sob as tears choked his speech, and he could only hobble forward, stretch out his arms and babble meaningless syllables, while the other retreated until he had closed the front gate between them.

"Hold on, Captain—hold on till I tell you—"

"Oh, Mac, Mac! what do you mean? You are Mac, aren't you? Not Mac's ghost?"

"Yes, I'm Mac, what there is left of me; but you can't come near me till I've had a chance to care for myself—had a bath and—so forth."

"Bath be hanged! You're coming right in, or I'll know the reason why! I'll get you your bath and your clean clothes—give you every clo' I've got in the world down to what I have on my back! Let me open this gate, I tell you!" And he tried to loosen the other's hold on the top bar.

"If you do I'll run down the street!"

"Why, Mac, what do you mean? If it were anybody else in the world I'd get angry."

"I'm just out of a rebel prison—and clear of a steamer-

WILL'S CRY BURST UPON THE STILL AIR.—Page 342.

load and a train-load of fellow-prisoners—and I haven't had a single cent in my hand since I saw you last—and I'm dirty, and starved, and I want you to lend me ten dollars."

"I've a great mind to say no, because you won't come in and take everything I've got in the world instead of your beggarly ten dollars!"

"Oh, I guess you won't refuse me."

"No; but why won't you come in, clean or dirty, you blessed old prodigal son you! I tell you there are some arms inside you'd find harder to fight shy of than mine!"

"Oh, yes—that's all very fine—but here, let me whisper to you."

He whispered.

"Oh, ho, ho! I see! No, you can't come in. I won't allow it; if you'd said only five hundred I might—but a thousand! Well, I must go inside for the money. Wait a minute till I get my eyes wiped dry and my face straightened out. If they find out you're here they'll all be out here in a jiffy."

"Then I should have to run away."

"Yes—you tearing down Wabash avenue with the Penrose family after you, would be an edifying spectacle— and I bringing up the rear on my one leg.

"Left one at Shiloh? Good God!"

"Yes, but this minute I don't care for it—not a hooter!"

He entered the room where the sisters were anxiously waiting.

"Another of them I suppose, Will?"

"Yes, my dear banker, another of them. How much money have you?"

"Oh" (pulling out her purse), "there; you'll find several dollars in it."

"Any more upstairs?"

"Yes.   How much do you want to give him?"

"How much have you, you blessed gold-mine?"

"Oh, I have fifty dollars, all but that in the purse, which I took out of the fifty."

"Well, bring that, please.   And do you suppose your father has any?"

"I'll ask him if you wish."

"Have you any, Lydia?"

"Why, yes, a few dollars."

"Well, I have a few myself.   Bring it all, please, and I'll tell you why, in less than five minutes."

The entire contribution-box made a bulky roll, which Will squeezed into Mac's hand and bade him good-night, and told him to come back at noon next day, "clothed and in his right mind."   Then he went back to the sitting-room and lay flat down on the rug, that he might laugh and cover his face and roll about at his ease.

The sisters looked at him and at each other.

"Lydia!")
"Sara!" }

"There's only one thing that could make him act so!"

"Is it true, Will?"

"YES! THAT WAS MAC!"

Lydia ran out of the room, and they heard the gate bang shut behind her flying footsteps. Presently she returned, almost crying.

"Why did you let him go?" she asked in hot, hurt tones.

"I just had to!   He was neither to 'haud nor to bind,' as dear old Colin used to say.   As soon as he heard *you* were here he fled wildly into the night—and it *may* be that he has sought relief in suicide.   If not, you'll see him here at high noon to-morrow."

When Lydia had left them again alone, the lovers had

their longest, sweetest talk all about themselves and "the others."

"They'll be the very church-mice of poverty, Sally."

"Oh—I guess dear Uncle Colin's pot will always yield enough broth for us all."

The war is long past and gone—dead and buried and forgotten except for political purposes. We are now devoted to business, and every thing is on a business basis. Greenbacks, worth forty per cent. before we won the fight, are now worth par, so *that* account is squared off. Eighty per cent. of the war debt is paid. Twenty per cent. of the war taxes are abolished; and if more are not done away with it is not because the United States Treasury needs the money, but because some favored citizens are not yet as rich as the United States Treasury, though they wish to become so. The nation is forty per cent. bigger than when the war closed, and a million per cent. more booming than any other nation ever was, ever dared to be, or ever will be. Fifty per cent. of the taxes collected are yearly paid out in pensions. Fifty per cent. of the dead are forgotten, and the other fifty per cent. are half forgotten; so that to the rest of the world (and to them) it is all the same, within twenty-five per cent. as if nobody had been killed at all. As to the wounded, each of those who still survive has come within from forty to sixty per cent. of becoming accustomed and reconciled to his disability; and this last-named percentage is further mitigated by the pensions paid—including one to Private Dugong, who is supposed to have strained his back carrying a wounded officer off the field at Shiloh; whereby he feels forced to walk quite bent over on four several days in the year—those on which he goes to draw his pension. He lately got an increase (including large arrears), on its being shown that he was once a corporal, though not so at the time he incurred his injury.

On the whole, the fighters, dead and alive, ought to be very thankful that things have turned out so well; and to feel entirely satisfied with the general result.

Mentioning the wounded brings us naturally to Captain and Brevet-Major William Fargeon. He is one who comes within sixty per cent. of being reconciled to his wound; and he does not enjoy the pension mitigation because he foolishly but persistently declines to apply for a pension. He irrationally says that for support he does not need the pension (though he does need the other leg), and as to taking the country's money as pay for his services—money cannot pay for such things; they bear no more relation to money than the Aurora Borealis does to a pig's eyebrow.

His wife and daughters do not agree with him in this view. They think that since papa's profession (surgery, which he studied during the war and has practiced since) seems to yield him so *very* little, there is no reason why he should not do as other men do, and make the country pay at least a small part of the debt it owes him. "But, then, poor dear papa is *so* peculiar."

Yes, alas! he is "peculiar." He will not apply for a pension, although so many are getting it who are really not as deserving of it as he is. He rarely talks of war, except with old soldiers. He cares nothing for politics, and never even *tries* to get into office. There are some tunes he cannot listen to, in general company. He eats what is put on his plate, no more and no less, and calls it a "ration." He loves his pipe more than he does— most other things; and then his funny regard for a sim- ple match! ("Marcloonies" as he calls them, or, for short "marcs.")

Mark, by the way, is orderly sergeant in Mac's company of the —th infantry, U. S. A. This is the height of Mark's ambition; and he, with his arm nearly covered with "Service stripes," and his purse overflowing with "fogy rations" (greatly to the delectation of the young McClintocks) is probably the most serenely contented of our three volunteers.

Will is sorry his profession yields so little—sorry and at first surprised. He studied thoroughly and has practiced successfully (from a professional point of view), both in military hospitals and outside. His rich old friends are most cordial, and often say to him:

"You know, Major, that we who did not go out—I *could* not, the way my business was situated—feel that we owe you fellows who did go a debt of gratitude that can never be repaid."

And so, naturally, they don't try to repay it; but they do recognize his position as an ex-soldier, a man, and a surgeon, for they throw into his hands a great deal of business of the charitable, non-paying kind. He is always fully supplied with it; in fact, could have more of it to do if he could possibly attend to it. When there is anything "with money in it" to be done, of course it goes elsewhere, but when a soldier's widow and orphans want anything Will is always appealed to, and never in vain.

Similar laws seem to govern his other experiences. His voluntary contributions to current publications are often accepted (unless there is about these a suspicion of "free advertising" of some object or other); but when he tried a magazine article—which his wife and daughters thought really quite good—it was returned to him with a printed blank assuring him that the editors did not presume to judge of the merit of his work; simply they did not find it adapted to their present purposes.

And, what was still more consoling, was an autograph note (unsigned) saying that the public was "tired of the war." So of course it was not its own quality which condemned his article, but an outside circumstance.

"Curious, too, to think how tired *I* was of it once when *they* were not; and now they are tired of it when I am not. Well, I'll go on tending gate."

Captain and Mrs. McClintock and their numerous flock are always at some out-of-the-way post on the frontier. Their Aunt Sara is sorry she cannot entertain them more—but dear  Bunny has such a perfect raft of children, you know; and then, of course, dear brother Mac has only his pay and cannot spare much for traveling expenses. But, then, there are only thirty-nine ranking captains between him and his majority; and that will help materially if his life is spared. We don't know why he never seems to get any of those pleasant eastern berths. Probably he is too valuable an officer to be brought away from the frontier. Every year a box of our dear girls' things, only a very little worn, goes to them, costing them nothing but the expressage.

In Washington a very Great Man taps a bell which calls his secretary into his office.

"Now, about those damned assignments. How far had we got?"

"To Captain McClintock."

"What about him?"

"First-rate officer; wounded in the war; fine, large young family; been out eleven years steady."

"Is he—?" [A nod of the head toward the Hudson River fills out the sentence.]

"No! Ranks."

"Any letters from anybody regarding him on file?"

"No. No letters nor personal calls."

"Well; pass him for the present. Who's next?"

Each gives a little sigh and forgets all about poor Mac.

Blessed old Parson Penrose, saint on earth, goes about serving God and doing good, under certain discourage-ments. When (not long since) he jocularly suggested to his congregation that he was getting too old to keep his pulpit, they surprised him by taking him seriously, and retiring him on a pension. All this he could forgive —has long since forgiven—but alas! the "indifferentism" that is undermining everything!

"To my arguments they make, and can make, no reply whatever, yet these same arguments are like cannon-balls fired into Lake Michigan!" [The dominie is fond of military similes.]

This coldness, this apathy, is the only thing he could ever complain of in his daughter's household. He strug-gled with it at first, blaming himself, of course, and ask-ing wherein he had failed of doing his full duty toward them. Time softened this regret, but later, when they took the occasion of his being retired from his old pastorate to desert the faith of their parents and take one of the best pews in St. James', then the iron entered his soul.

Nevertheless, he always shares their birthday dinners,

and dear mamma is careful (out of respect to his feelings) not to forget to ask him to say grace.

The Fulcrum and the Rostrum are both gathered to their fathers, and the place that knew them shall know them no more forever.

Fargeon is sorry he has no son. In the first place, there is in his heart an unsatisfied longing to send down to posterity the name of old Colin Thorburn, the source of all this prosperity and luxury. [A deep sigh.] In the second place, it would be pleasant to think that the uncommon name of Fargeon was not to die out, in his branch, with him. Half a dozen stalwart boys would keep alive for a few years the knowledge that their ancestor fought among the rest at Donelson and Shiloh. But as it is—[another sigh].

An old ragged shirt sleeve, once white and red, now yellow and black, is tucked away somewhere—unless it has been destroyed with other rubbish.

Well, after all is said and done, the major has more to be glad of than to be sorry for. When, every year or two, he says the question has again arisen whether he shall get a new leg fitted, or keep the old leg and get a new man fitted to it, he doesn't really mean it. "It is only one of Papa's jokes, you know." So he treads through the world the even tenor of his way; step——clump; step——clump; step——clump; step——

FINIS.